THE ARCHAEOLOGISTS

THE ARCHAEOLOGISTS

Hal Niedzviecki

ARP BOOKS WINNIPEG

ARP Books (Arbeiter Ring Publishing)
201E-121 Osborne Street
Winnipeg, Manitoba
Canada R3L 1Y4
arpbooks.org

Cover by Mike Carroll
Typeset by Relish New Brand Experience Inc.
Printed in Canada by Friesens on paper made from 100% recycled
post-consumer waste.

ARP Books acknowledges the generous support of the Manitoba Arts
Council and the Canada Council for the Arts for our publishing program.
We acknowledge the financial support of the Government of Canada
through the Canada Book Fund and the Province of Manitoba through the
Book Publishing Tax Credit and the Book Publisher Marketing Assistance
Program of Manitoba Culture, Heritage, and Tourism.

LIBRARY AND ARCHIVES CANADA CATALOGUING IN PUBLICATION

Niedzviecki, Hal, 1971-, author
    The archaeologists / Hal Niedzviecki.

Issued in print and electronic formats.
ISBN 978-1-894037-79-2 (paperback).--ISBN 978-1-894037-81-5 (pdf)

    1. Title.

PS8577.I3635A74 2016   c813'.54   C2016-903639-1
                                        C2016-903640-5

Woe! Woe!
Hearken ye!
We are diminished!
Woe! Woe!
The cleared land has become a thicket.
Woe! Woe!
The clear places are deserted.
Woe!
They are in their graves—
They who established it—
Woe!

PART ONE

TIM
Thursday, April 10

TIM STANDS LEGS APART, ARMS AKIMBO, on the steep muddy embankment. The grass beneath his boots is long and stringy. It sticks to the seeping earth. His neck cranes up and back as he reconsiders his decision to climb down the hill into the river valley. He can just see the battered car at rest in the clearing above. He shifts his gaze to the dark basin below him. This causes his body to tense, his muscles to realign. He feels the worn bottom of his right boot beginning to slip. His gangly legs slowly spread. Tim tries to adjust his stance, but instead he loses balance altogether. He falls backward and finds himself half scrabbling half sliding down the hill. He picks up speed, bouncing over all manner of sharp, foreign objects, detritus from the make-out spot above: crushed cans, burger boxes, wet toilet paper wads, a cell phone with its circuit board guts exposed. Tim's boot heels dig in. Mud furrows. He grabs at bush ends and wet branches. Finally, he arrives, not quite tumbling, at the soft bottom of the ravine.

He climbs to his feet. He brushes himself off. Wet mud cakes the rear of his pants. *Uncool. Who's gonna see me down here? Still...* Tim scans the crest of the hill. There's nobody around, but he feels like he's being watched. *Uncool.* Reflexively, Tim pats down his pockets. Lighter. Check. Car keys. Check. Wallet. Check. The letter—

Shit. Where's the letter? Carly says he's always losing things. She says he needs to be more organized. *Yeah*, he admits sheepishly, *I'm working on it.*

Tim rams his hand into his army jacket pocket. He feels it— folded paper gone soft and greasy. He thinks about pulling it out, scanning those words again, as if there might be something else in the barely legible pen scrawl, something he missed the first forty times he read it. The letter arrived more than a month ago. Tim hasn't shown it to Carly. He knows what she would say: that he should forgive him, go see him, hug him, help him. Carly's parents, almost but not quite retirees, live in a bungalow in the northern part of the city. They call and visit and ask questions. They hover over her. She's their only child. Their special little girl. It's easy for Carly to envision him forgiving, even forgetting. Tim sees it too—like a movie, actors filling in the cracks that real life just seems to widen. The letter uses words he could never imagine his father saying out loud: regret, forgive, sorry. *Sorry? Sure you are, Dad. But let's get to the heart of the thing.* Tim feels it, a sucking hunger in his chest. The soft, wet, oh so deep empty heart of the thing. Sorry about *what?*

Tim walks. The gully of the ravine isn't as impenetrable as it looked from the clearing above. It's the opposite, in fact: branches point to suggestive clearings and last summer's leaves carpet accidental footpaths. Tim plows through scraggly shrubs and bare-limbed trees. The ravine feels entombed, dead to the world. This is just a quick pit stop, Tim reminds himself, a quick look at his old hideout. He'll smoke a joint and calm the nerves. Then he'll go and see for himself if it's not too late, if he can put the past behind him. He hasn't seen his father in almost twelve years. He doesn't want anything from him. He's worked in bars for almost as long as he lived in what he once stupidly thought of as home. He's a high school dropout. He's a bit of a stoner. He has a girlfriend.

—Carly.

He'll call her after. He'll tell her the whole story: the way the letter arrived out of nowhere; the way he kept reading and re-reading it, words circling restlessly round and round his skull like old Evil Knievel getting ready, one more stunt, nothing left to lose. *I'm dying. Cancer. I'm sorry.* Tim's sorry too. Sorry he didn't call or text or at least leave a note. Instead, he carefully folded up the letter and stowed it in his back pocket, searched for her car keys and his wallet from the coffee table clutter, slowly pulled on his boots, and marched out of the apartment, a man with a plan. Tim stops walking. The river gurgles. He can't see it through the rustling underbrush. There are birds and squirrels. He notices, for the first time, how loud it is. He hears heavy breathing—his own—and the sound of sweat dropping off his nose and splashing onto moss, roots, dirt, whatever else is mouldering away underneath the trees, the names of which Tim doesn't know. It's better that way; knowing would just make the whole thing louder. All those elms, pines, alders, firs and maples demanding they be paid attention to.

He thought it would be quiet in the forest. His ears are still buzzed from the drive, from the rattle of Carly's twelve-year-old Pontiac, rusted orange hand-me-down from her mom lurching past the speed limit, past the outer suburbs, past the short ribbon of yellow farmlands squeezed between an ever-expanding grey zone of housing developments and accompanying mini-malls. Tim's dad always drove big black sedans, a new one every six months. Carly's car sports a tinny cassette radio. Tim had turned it up as loud as it would go, Bob Marley blasting...*don't worry*...Tim lit a joint, veered slightly to the left, responded to an indignant honk with an equally indignant middle finger. Then he toked. The interior of the Sunfire filled with smoke. Tim cranked down his window and highway air poured in. Carly did not like him lighting up in the car. The car rides he used to take with his father had been still, sepulchral, the air thick with cigar and cologne. His dad's Cadillacs moved smoothly ahead as if they were drifting just above the pavement; and no matter how fast the scenery outside sped by, his little boy self stayed lost, enveloped by a succession of slick, cavernous, black back seats.

He's a big boy now. A grown-up. Sort of. He urges himself forward. He feels his heart pumping against his ribs. When was the last Tim walked farther than the corner store? He's a cab man. Tim struggles on through the spring mush. He follows the river, keeps the river in sight. This much he knows for sure: the spot he's looking for—*his* spot—is near but not right on the bank of the river. Which he can see now, flowing slowly by like a giant contiguous wad of chewing tobacco effluvium. *Smells like it too*, he thinks.

Tim tilts his head, looks up. Through the branches he sees tiny patches of grey-smudged sky. The sky seems close and also far away. He can just make out the upper floors of the houses on the ridge. He's trapped down here. Tim breathes deep into his abdomen. It's cool. He's cool. Once upon a time, he lived in one of those houses. *Almost there*, he thinks. He's just going to find his old spot. No biggie. He's not trapped. He can leave anytime. *Just turn around and go.* Carly says he has problems finishing things. Carly says he has to finish what he starts. So: *Plan's a plan—right Carly?* That's the way his father used to talk: Plan's a Plan. Use It or Lose It. Smoke 'Em If Ya Got 'Em. Tim hears his father's voice, contemptuous and impatient: What plan ya idiot? You call *this* a goddam plan?

Tim closes his eyes. He's trying to visualize, to see how this is going to go. How it's all going to work out.

Relax. Close your eyes.

That's one of Carly's things. Inner peace. Or something.

Behind his eyelids, Tim sees naked trees, possible paths, scrubby bushes, everything the same brown-on-grey camouflage.

Tim opens his eyes. He feels calmer, not calm, exactly, but less like he's trying to breathe hot sticky molasses. His slack calves itch. His forehead pulses. The worst are his long skinny legs, knees wobbling from all that humping over fallen forest, thighs burning from the sheer effort of self-propulsion. Still, he wills himself forward. The sun comes out, late afternoon dappling of faint warmth through the interlocking overhang of branches, like hugging Carly in her thick winter sweater. Skin underneath. Tim's on the final bend of the river's S curve, feeling dizzy from the constancy of rounding motion.

He stumbles past and doesn't notice.

But he stops anyway.

He's ten feet from the riverbank. Between him and the escarpment sits a large rock, almost a boulder, jutting out of the earth. There's a cluster of weedy birch trees so tall and thin they actually manage to sway in the breeze. There's a hole in the ground, more like an indentation, the earth slightly darker, scarred—

The fire pit! How could he forget the fire pit?

It's all in the details: the fire pit, the birch grove. He forgot about those. It comes back to him now, not in one mad dash for the mimetic finish line but in starts and stutters. Synapses slowed by time or, perhaps, by a certain degree of overindulgence in what his dealer Clay always calls—with just a hint of proprietorial pride— *the product*. And then there's the tree, the giant oak that forms a triangle with the boulder and the birch grove, the fire pit sitting in the middle of Tim's boyhood territory. The tree. Not, as might be reasonable to assume, smaller than Tim remembers it, but actually much bigger. He staggers over, puts a hand on the tree's cool craggy exterior. Immediately he feels ridiculous.

Tim wipes his nose on the shoulder of his army jacket. He squats on his haunches and puts a finger in what remains of some crude hacks in the bark. He used to carve words into the tree, stream-of-conscious fragments from his addled teenage mind. His finger traces the outlines of a letter F. FUCKFACE, Tim says out loud. FUCKASS. FUCKWAD. Tim laughs. A heat in the pit of his stomach. Here it is. *Proof.* Proof of what? He'll bring Carly here one day. He'll show her the big rock and the even bigger tree, the scar in the forest floor where the fire pit used to be. They'll stand there and neither of them will have to say anything. She'll just get it.

He gazes up the long craggy spine of the tree. The steps are still there. Well, sort of. Some are rotting, some just barely dangling from ancient rusty nails. But at least half of the ten or so stairs leading up to the tree's lower branches appear sturdy enough, orange nail-heads still visible buried in the dry dead planks.

The view from up there. That's why he's here. To see that view just one more time.

Tim leans back and stares at the dizzying vision of the treetop breaking out of the wooded ravine like a god looming over puny worshippers. Tree must be *old.* He's never thought about it that way before—trees having an age. Tim can feel sweat cooling on his forehead. He shivers. It's suddenly cold. *Just get it over with*, he thinks to himself. Or forget about it. He could leave, hike back up the muddy hill, slide into the frayed bucket seat of the Sunfire, light up a spliff and close his eyes. He doesn't owe his father anything. He doesn't owe anyone anything. Well, okay, he owes Clay around two grand and Carly eight hundred or so. But that's a whole other issue. He pats down his pockets again. Car keys. Check. Pre-rolled joints. Yup. Che Guevara lighter. Present. And the letter. Tim fingers the ragged edge where the paper was ripped off a pad. *I know you blame me for what happened.*

HAL

Thursday, April 10

HAL DOODLES ON HIS REPORTER'S PAD.

Okay what else do we have for this week? the Boss asks.

A sewer being expanded. The mayor promising a new school and more funding to deal with the rapid expansion of housing developments in the West End. A local pet store joining forces with the Wississauga fire department to lead a campaign about cat and dog safety in the event of a home or apartment fire.

What else team? The Boss scans the three people in the shabby meeting room, the entirety of the Wississauga Cable TV Community News Channel 47 *team*.

Hal keeps his head down.

Hal? she finally says.

Hal's pen freezes over the shading in of some abstract collection of twisted triangles.

Hal, isn't it time to catch up with Wississauga's oldest citizen?

It's Hal's time of the month! cackles Trevor.

Sarah, sitting next to Hal, titters.

Let's send Sarah this time, Hal offers.

Sarah digs an elbow into his ribs. She does weather, lifestyle, and local sports. Hal does news, mostly, plus the occasional in-depth interview. Once a month, he's tasked with interviewing 104-year-old Rose McCallion, known not only for officially being Wississauga's oldest living resident, but also, unofficially, for being the closest the scattered edge city has to a bonafide, genuine homegrown celebrity. Hal's monthly sit-downs with Rose are one of Wississauga Cable's most popular features, much to the delight of Hal's co-workers.

Sarah, laughing again, puts an arm around Hal's neck. He can smell her perfume. You're the one she *wants*, Hal.

Hal groans.

You'll get it done, right Hal? the Boss asks.

Yeah. I'm on it. He crosses out his heap of shapes.

Okay, the Boss says, come on guys. Let's focus. What else do we have?

They go around the room again. New 7-11 opening up, will anchor the mini-mall at the corner of Hurontarion North and Elm. The store's handing out half-price cups of Super Fusion All Energy Organic Slushie infused with Ginseng and Jicama during the first week of operation. A local ten-year-old has created his own comic, "Amazing Fatso Man," selling over 200 copies and closing in on raising the $750 necessary to buy a water buffalo for a needy family in Pakistan. A 43-year-old hit by a car after parking illegally on the shoulder of the 472 and attempting to cross eight lanes of traffic to take advantage of Free "Arabian Roast" Coffee Wednesday at McDonald's new McCafé is going to make a full recovery. Police have decided not to press charges. McDonald's has sent over a get well card signed by the manager and staff, and issued a statement reminding customers to obey traffic laws.

And it's going to get cold again, Sarah says happily. Forget spring! Winter's back.

That's always a good story, the Boss says.

I've got some clips from Groundhog Day we can use, Mitch pitches in. We can do a whole thing on how much longer winter will go, compare it to previous decades, multi-year trends, get someone from the national weather service, work the climate change angle.

Good, good, you two get on that. What else?

Um. Hal clears his throat importantly. He starts off tentatively, like he hasn't been waiting the entire story meeting to bring it up. There's the community meeting at the school about the riverfront expressway.

Right, the Boss says. Right. She waits for Hal to say more.

It's likely to be very contentious. There are a lot of rumours swirling around, a lot of anger about the idea. Also there are accusations that the planning committee is pushing this through at the last minute and not really interested in public consultation.

One angle, Mitch jumps in, might be to interview an environmentalist at the university. I've got a lead on—

We've already got the climate change angle on that weather thing, Hal says, pretending he's thinking aloud.

Right, the Boss says, let's just stick to the government-consults-local-community angle. No need to do two environment stories. Hal, I want you on this all next week. Preview it, report it as it happens, and follow up. Community reaction, comment from government, local opposition, the whole bit.

I'm on it, Hal says, this time with more enthusiasm.

Great. Great. Keep me posted.

Will do, chief. Hal writes *Keep Me Posted* on a fresh blank page. He snaps his notebook closed. Meeting over. Everyone gets up. He's got the top story again. Mitch tried to horn in. Sarah's looking at him like he's a superstar. She keeps cornering him by the coffee maker, leaning in close and whispering little gossipy tidbits.

You wanted to see me, Boss?

Hal, come in. Sit down.

The head of Wississauga Cable TV Community News Channel 47 is Carla Fairlane. She's got pictures of her three grown up kids arrayed on her battered desk. She wears minimal makeup and is remarkably resilient, having survived decades of internal re-thinks, corporate reassessments, industry realignments, government regulations, and government deregulations. It's been a lengthy process of consolidation, cost-cutting, and malicious neglect, all of which have culminated in their present-day state of bare-bones, barely watched, repeated four times daily cable access local news bookended by several hours of inane amateur-hour talk shows. Behind the Boss hangs a series of cheaply framed plaques commemorating awards the television station earned in previous decades. Hal notes that the plaques stop some ten years before he was hired, around the same time their corporate taskmasters replaced local news coverage with a national news broadcast anchored by a greying dignitary whose singularly sonorous voice relegated their government-mandated community coverage to a semi-amateur skeleton staff of underpaid journeymen, has-beens, and young up-and-comers just passing through.

Which am I? Hal wonders.

The Boss, looking at him, smiles. Hal, she says warmly. How are you?

I'm good, Hal says carefully.

So…it's been a year since you joined us.

It has?

Yes it has. And I just wanted to sit down with you and just see how you were doing.

Oh. Okay.

So...how are you doing?

Good. Really good.

How are you finding our little community?

I...I like it. It's different, of course, from the city. But I like it.

He'd acted as if it was a major hardship to say goodbye to his apartment in the village, to his friends, to the clubs and restaurants and lounges none of them could even afford though they somehow seemed to keep ending up in. He'd pretended that moving to a place like Wississauga was an unbearable setback. But, really, he'd been relieved. In Wississauga, there are people everywhere but you don't see them, you don't feel their eyes tracking you as you walk down the street—Who's he with? What's he wearing? Where's he going with who he's with? In Wississauga, people avert their gaze, hide behind drawn shades and tinted windshields, move from interior to interior without making a big show of themselves. Hal feels freed by the nothingness, liberated by the generic mix of malls, parking lots, high rises, highways, and pre-planned neighbourhoods. Fences, walls, and locked doors mark the terrain, delineate spaces, make everything clear.

He's on TV every night, and no one even knows him.

I'm glad you've settled in, Hal. The Boss puts on a news casting face, blank and important.

Here it comes, Hal thinks.

You know, the Boss says, leaning in, you've got real talent. And you're hungry. I can see that you're hungry. And that's great. I've been in this business for a long time. I won't even tell you how long! And I can see that you have something, Hal.

Thanks, Boss.

But you know, Hal, it takes more than just drive and ambition and smarts. You've got that, I've seen it. You also need more.

Oh. Okay. Hal feels colour moving to his cheeks.

You need to soften up a bit, Hal. The Boss looks at him. Our viewers like a bit more of an…informal approach. They want to feel like they know who they're dealing with, like if they saw you on the sidewalk they could just come right up to you and shake your hand and give you an earful.

An earful, Hal says uncertainly.

You know, shoot the shit with you.

The Boss's phone rings. She waves it away with her long fingers. The voice mail will get it, she says. Voice mail! I remember when we used to have real people answering the phones around here.

Hal isn't sure what he's supposed to say. He doesn't say anything.

Are you getting me here, Hal?

Uh…sure.

I want you to lighten up. Try to be less stiff, less formal.

Sure. I can…be…

Just be yourself, Hal. I mean c'mon! It's not like you're reporting breaking news of earth-shattering consequence. We don't have much of that around here. The Boss laughs at her own joke. Relax. Let loose a little. Connect.

Relax. Let loose.

Exactly.

Connect.

That's right.

Hal fingers the fraying cuffs of his cheap, blue, no-wrinkle Oxford button down. He needs another one. $21.99 at Mens ClothingWarehouse.com. Scott buys his clothes at boutiques in the city.

Are you seeing someone, Hal?

What? The word comes out raspy, like there's something in his throat.

You know, dating, going out, whatever you kids call it these days.

Oh, uh, no. No. I just…I've just been…

I understand. You're focussed. I respect that. But live a little, Hal. Get out there. Have some fun. Play the field!

Fun.

Yeah, you know, lighten up. People want to see you out and about.

They do?

Sure they do. Sure they do. They want to see you putting on a little bit of a show. Preferably with a nice young lady on your arm.

Ah…

Get out there young man. Time's a wasting. Don't be so serious!

Get out there, Hal says.

You're going to go far in this business, Hal. I really do believe that. Now, do you have any questions for me?

Uh…I'm…Sure. I get it. Loosen up. I can do that. Hal lets out a stilted laugh.

Great, the Boss says. That's great, Hal. And thank *you*. Thank you for all your hard work.

Hal gets up. The Boss extends her hand and he shakes it, her cool dry palm against his moist hot one.

Hal stands in the hall. It's quiet. Everybody else has probably gone home. Hal is usually the last one to leave. Scott says he works too hard. Scott says he should take it easy. *Just like the Boss*, Hal thinks. How weird is that?

The door to the ladies room swings open and Sarah pushes out.

Hey! Hal! Sarah's smiling. It's the end of the day, but she smells fresh and soapy. She's perky and blonde and Trevor is always making comments about her "knockers." She could have any guy she wanted. Just about.

Sarah...hey...

You in a hurry?

I was just—

What did the Boss lady want?

Oh...nothing. Nothing really.

Really? Nothing?

She just wanted to...it was like a...one-year kind of review, kind of.

Really? What did she say?

Hal looks longingly at the dimly glowing red exit sign at the end of the hall.

Hey! Sarah says with pep. We should celebrate! It's your one-year anniversary! Let's go have a drink! Do you want to get a drink?

Scott calls her the weather girl. How's the weather girl? Whoo... nice blouse weather girl...

Oh, Sarah, I can't...I've got a...I want to but I've got a...thing.

In another minute he'll be in the car, on the way to the Save-A-Centre Grocery. Scott's coming over for dinner tonight. Actually, it's a celebration too. It's their three-month anniversary. Another anniversary. Hal's promised to cook something romantic.

A date? Sarah teases.

No, it's not a...it's just...Hal pretends to look at his watch. I'm...late, he announces. He can feel the heat on his cheeks. *Lobster*, he thinks suddenly. Hal saw them cook lobster on *Wississauga's Cooking with Wanda*! It looked pretty easy. You just toss them in the hot water and wait until they turn red.

CHARLIE
Thursday, April 10

HERE WE ARE, CHARLIE! They step off the elevator into the dingy hall. All the other kids are downstairs in the main floor recreation room. In the recreation room there are balloons, streamers, and plates of cookies. There's a banner that says *Welcome Columbus Secondary*. Up here it's dark and quiet. There's a nurses' desk but nobody's sitting behind it. The lady steers Charlie by the elbow of her red parka. She's not Charlie's teacher. Charlie's teacher stayed downstairs with the rest of the kids.

It's just at the end here, the lady says cheerfully. Are you sure you don't want to take your coat off? I can hang it up for you downstairs.

Charlie crosses her arms and hugs the puffy red jacket.

No thank you, she says in a small voice. I get cold.

It's true. She does get cold. But it's hot in the old people's home. The rest home, Charlie thinks, correcting herself. Their teacher told them to call it the rest home.

It's like the dog pound but for old people! Billy Zuckers called out. He was sent to the principal. He's always getting sent to the principal. All the other kids asked stupid questions like What do they eat? and Are they allowed to leave? On the school bus everyone talked about how lame it was—*Worst. Field trip. Ever*, Katie

Mills had pronounced before pulling out her cherry lip gloss and re-applying it for the fourth time.

Charlie knew it was the fourth time. She'd been watching her. Katie wears skirts with leggings. Her long brown hair shines and shimmers down the back of tight white sweaters that show off her already prominent boobs. Charlie wears jeans and sweatshirts. She wears her red parka.

When they first got to the home, all the other kids were introduced to their senior partners. Then the lady came over and explained that Charlie's senior partner, Rose, was still in her room. So the lady asked Charlie if she'd mind going up to her room to visit her instead of having the visit in the dayroom like everyone else. Charlie shrugged. There were supposed to be games later. And there were the cookies. Everybody else was already busy meeting their senior partners.

Here we go! the lady says, knocking loudly on the door. Rose is very special. You'll see. She's the oldest person in Wississauga, you know.

I know. Her teacher already told Charlie that her senior partner was named Rose McCallion and that Rose was the oldest person alive in Wississauga and she knew Charlie was the right person to be her partner because Charlie is so mature for her age.

The lady knocks again. Rose! Yoo-hoo! Hello! Rose! She doesn't always hear, the lady mock whispers to Charlie, smiling brightly. Rose! I've got your student from the school here! The lady pounds on the door a few more times. She needs a lot prompting, the lady whispers to Charlie.

Charlie blushes. The lady talks like Rose is stupid. But Charlie's dad always tells her that respect for elders is the most important thing. Until today, Charlie hadn't actually gotten a chance to meet any elders or seniors or anyone like that. Only one of her grandparents is still alive—her mom's mom—but she still lives in Mumbai. And the few friends her parents had over to the house weren't much older than her mom and dad. But Charlie's read lots of stories with old people in them, and not just grandpa and grandma, those kindly storybook figures Charlie's never met and probably never will. Charlie likes to read about other places, other times. Her favourite stories are about the Natives. Not the Indians like Charlie, but the other kind. In those stories, the old people are also called Elders and everyone is always listening to their stories. They tell important stories about the gods and hunting and who should marry who, which is way better than calling them seniors and putting them in a home to rest.

Rose! We're coming in! The lady pushes the door open and walks in. Charlie, embarrassed, head down, chin on the slick surface of the red parka, follows her.

The room is dimly lit by two shaded lamps. It smells dusty and stale. This makes sense to Charlie. Why wouldn't old people smell old? It's not a bad smell. It reminds her of the books she takes out of the library. A lot of the books are really old and they smell like no one has opened them for a long time.

Hi Rose! the lady says, her voice reverberating loudly in the enclosed space. Charlie looks around. She doesn't see her, Rose.

I'm old, not deaf. You don't have to yell. The voice is throaty and irritated. Charlie finally tracks down the source of that raspy voice—a small withered head sticking out of an easy chair, the body lost under a heap of knitted blankets. Charlie looks, then looks away. The lady takes Charlie's elbow and steers her in front of Rose.

Rose! This is Charlie!

It's like she's the one who's deaf, Rose mutters.

Charlie peeks up at Rose. Their eyes meet. Rose's eyes, sunken into a shrunken wrinkled face that looks like an apple peeled then forgotten, sparkle blue and silver.

Who's this? Who are you?

I'm…Charlie.

Well then! I'll leave you two to get acquainted!

The lady swishes out of the room. The door closes behind her.

Why are you wearing a coat? You're inside for goodness sakes. Take that off immediately.

Charlie shrugs, reluctantly shimmies out of her parka. She holds it awkwardly.

Didn't they show you where the coats go downstairs?

Charlie nods.

Never mind. Just put it on the chair.

Charlie diligently drapes the coat over the back of the empty chair.

Now, what did you say your name was?

Charlie.

Charlie? Come closer.

Charlie steps forward. She can see the plaster of yellow-white hair sticking to Rose's scalp.

You're a girl.

Charlie nods.

Charlie's a boy's name.

Charlie nods again.

Do you understand me? Do you speak English?

Charlie nods again. Why wouldn't she speak English?

What's a girl doing with a boy's name? Or don't they believe in that where you come from?

What does she mean? Charlie was born in Wississauga.

My real name's Charulekha.

Well never mind. Go make me my cup of tea.

Charlie follows Rose's gaze to the kitchenette. She finds tea bags and an old plug-in kettle. She boils the water and dunks the tea bag. She knows how to do it. She's made tea for her mother lots of times. She returns proffering a steaming mug.

Your tea's ready.

Thank you, Rose says pleasantly. Just put it on the table here.

Charlie carefully puts the mug of hot tea on the side table. Then she hovers near Rose, not sure if she should sit in the empty chair. The quiet in the room is occupied by the rasp of Rose's breathing and a farther away background sound, a kind of steady, empty thrum. It's cars, Charlie realizes, the sound of traffic nosing along Wississauga's busiest thoroughfare. Rose regards her with a bright-eyed stare. Charlie blushes again. Rose is supposed to tell her stuff. About how it used to be and everything. Charlie looks away, looks around the dark, crowded room. Silk-white roses greying in a vase, fraying quilts, the credenza heaped with yellowed cuttings from old newspapers.

See anything you like? Rose snaps suspiciously.

No...I...

It doesn't matter. I'll be gone soon either way. I don't even lock my door. Why bother?

Rose waves a dismissive, translucent hand. They're always barging in here, trying to get me to take this pill or that pill. I don't need it! Before they stuck me in here, I didn't see a doctor in...well, they had just built that new road leading from the highway. So that would have been...let's see now, 1992? That busybody daughter-in-law of mine insisted.

Charlie nods. She wasn't even born in 1992.

Doctors! Rose lowers her voice conspiratorially. They make a good living, don't they?

Charlie looks down at her sneakers. Both her parents are doctors.

Rose slowly raises her mug to her pursed grey mouth. Liquid sloshes.

Did you put in the sugar?

Charlie nods.

Put three in next time. I can't taste it.

Next time? Charlie thinks.

They sit in the silence of passing traffic. Rose takes a few more sips, shakily returns her mug. She closes her eyes. Charlie stares at her white running shoes, at her knees, the weave of her blue jeans. She concentrates on the distant hum of traffic and the steady rumbling sound of the old woman's breathing.

But then, suddenly, she can't hear it anymore.

Charlie holds her breath. She hears: car wheels treading asphalt, thousands of shoppers circling the Middle Mall.

Uh...Excuse me? Miss...Rose?

She tries again, louder: Miss? Rose?

Finally she wills herself to look up. Rose is a shapeless form tucked into a heap of fraying yellowed spreads. Charlie's never seen a dead person. She approaches gingerly. She inspects the old lady's pruney lips. In first aid they talked about the airway. Signs of breathing and movement.

Rose? Charlie leans in close. She puts her ear over that wrinkled gash of mouth.

I'm not dead yet, dear!

Ah! Charlie jumps back.

Ancient crone eyes sparkling.

Scared you, did I?

Charlie's heart pounding.

That'll teach you to sneak up.

I didn't—I wasn't—

Ha! You're just like the China-lady. Sneaking around! She stopped coming. I asked them where the China-lady went and they said cutbacks. Cutbacks! Well, they'd skimp on their own mother's gravestone. I remember when you could walk right into the office and see the mayor. Walletville had the same mayor for twenty years, you know. A very respectable man from a wonderful family. The Cartwrights. A very proper family. But things are different now, aren't they?

I...I don't know.

Never mind. Rose sighs. Well, I suppose you'll have to do. So let's just get to it. Rose looks at Charlie expectantly.

Uh—I—

Rose holds up her see-through hands, showing her long gnarled nails. Never had any use for them, Rose says, even when they were the fashion. They just get in the way of doing what needs to be done. Now you'll need to get the scissors. They're in the bottom drawer in the kitchen.

Charlie stands there. Rose looks at her expectantly.

In the kitchen, dear.

In the kitchen Charlie finds an ancient pair of steel scissors, a heavy ominous object nipped with rust. She returns to the living room, holding them in front of her like a gun about to go off.

These?

Of course. Now let's start with my toes. If you'd be a dear and just help me take off my slippers.

Your...feet?

Well where else would my toes be?

Rose wiggles her feet, soft lumps under the heaped blankets. Charlie digs around underneath. She finds pink slippers, the fuzz long since flattened and worn away. The smell is mothballs, talcum powder, wet wool, decay.

Take them off now, dear.

Charlie slips off the slippers. She starts pulling down a thin brown sock. Rose winces.

Gently now.

Sorry.

Fabric keeps catching on the nails. Charlie slowly reveals them, long yellow serpentine twists, some kind of relic holdover from past times, evolution's not yet completed task. Charlie gingerly grasps a big toe, wizened and turtled into itself. The flesh is cold and listless. The scissors are huge, not altogether inappropriate. Charlie fits the blade around the nail, a spiralling thick fossil.

Um, are you sure I should—?

Just cut them right off dear.

But I think it might—

It'll be fine.

Wouldn't it be better if I ask…the lady?

Just cut them. Go ahead, girl.

Charlie closes her eyes. She wishes she was in the woods by the river. She goes down there sometimes. She'll go after school. It's quiet down there. She lies in the leaves by the river and thinks about how it used to be a long time ago when the First People Indians lived down there.

Go on now, Rose says. Get it over with.

JUNE
Thursday, April 10

JUNE PARKS IN THE DRIVEWAY. As she gets out of the car it suddenly occurs to her that she didn't actually accomplish the one thing she left home to do. There are no groceries to haul into the kitchen. No reusable bags bulging with organics to virtuously heft over to their gleaming new stainless steel refrigerator with French doors and a digital thermostat. No cases of Lime Perrier, Coke Zero, and Diet Green Tea Ginger Ale to lug to the basement, no frozen shrimp and T-bone steaks to store in the freezer chest for spontaneous you-should-stay! quick defrost barbecues. *There's nothing for supper*, June thinks absently.

They've run out of everything from canned tomatoes to EZ-cook rice. Fresh produce is non-existent. There's no sandwich meat, forcing Norm to buy lunch everyday this week from the Portuguese bakery in the strip mall next to the medical complex where he has his office. Norm says buying lunch is a waste of money. It's just plain old dollars and *sense*, Norm says.

In the dark, cool foyer, June blinks, waiting for her eyes to adjust to the transition from the unfiltered light of day to the soft illumination of the front hall. It's not that the house is poorly lit like June's old apartment was. It's just the opposite: the house is big, spacious—five bedroom, three bath, den, dining room, living room with a fireplace, fully finished basement—sitting on a generous lot. Large and methodically lit, everything is noticeable, every speck of dust glowing under the relentless warmth of swivelled recessed dimmable LED pot lights. They've been living in the house for a year-and-a-half now, and June still hasn't gotten used to the large rooms, tall ceilings, wide-open spaces. They'd bought the place from a gruff senior clearly impatient to get the whole thing over with. His indifference, even rudeness, was made up for by the effusiveness of the real estate agent, all smiles and lipstick and commission. *Maybe*, June thinks, *I should go into real estate?* But, no, she can't imagine talking about property values and area schools and proximity to the Middle Mall in such enthusiastic terms. Sure to appreciate! Guaranteed value! Now's the time to buy!

In June's mind the house has depreciated. The solitude the agent promised—backyard facing the river gorge, high fences ensuring their privacy—seems to have slipped into the firmament of June's life. Several of the rooms still await furnishings. Others lack lamps, shelves, pictures on the walls—what Norm likes to refer to encouragingly as "the finishing touches." Norm calls it "the retreat." How's "the retreat?" he says when he phones home from work.

Cold, June thinks as she takes off her coat. She stands shakily, uncertainly, in the hall. The house makes her feel like a visitor—or an intruder.

June switches off the hallway lights. Outside the sky is darkening for early evening. *Rain tonight*, June thinks. She suddenly feels exhausted. She didn't sleep last night. *The last couple of nights*. Lying in bed next to snoring Norm, she kept trying to bear down on the problem, on her sense that there was some kind of problem, some thing following her through the immaculately appointed rooms of their new oversized house and out into the unfamiliar, unsurprising terrain of Wississauga. What was it? *Where* was it? All winter, June had lain in bed waiting for it to transform, to turn tangible and become not some *thing*, but something. *Well, winter's over now*, she tells herself. Her second winter here, long and cold and wet and lonely, all her friends and familiar haunts at least an hour's drive away. *It's no wonder*, she kept assuring herself as she tossed and turned in the big bed. *You're still adjusting. Get a* SAD *lamp, join a gym, find a book club—Jesus Christ girl, do something.* But every time it felt like something was about to reveal itself, June found herself descending into familiar drift, her body lying inert in the soft sticky bed, her mind pulled into the haze of inevitable half-sleep.

June moves through the front hall, through the kitchen, and into the living room. A year ago, everything seemed so sharp, crisp like the picture on the 65-inch flat screen that she sometimes catches Norm standing in the living room admiring, as if it was a painting slowly revealing its brush-stroked meaning. Two years ago she was newly married. She was buying a house. She was renovating that house from top to bottom. She was doing, doing, doing, moving from one thing to another in a constant swirl of motion. And then, things just sort of...stopped. Norm wakes up, goes to work. She doesn't go to work, maybe she doesn't even wake up. The more she tries to think about it, the more she feels as if she's wandering around in pointless circles, padding up and down the plush carpeted stairs, poking her head into rooms that, for now, sit empty and purposeless—*like me*, she thinks. It's this house. Of course it isn't. But somehow it is: a nothing emptiness expanding, blocking her out. Which doesn't even make sense. How does nothing expand? But it did. All winter, June's felt it, a nothingness turned corporeal, a nothing that through its sheen of voided emptiness seems determined to become that all-consuming something. Be careful what you wish for. She's stopped shopping.

She's stopped idly scanning the online classifieds looking for a job she might apply for. She's stopped cooking. She's stopped sleeping.

June drops herself on their leather sectional. The couch is huge. *Sits six without their legs touching*—June remembers that line from when they bought it. She stares through the big bay window into the empty square of their backyard. It's as if all this time she's been waiting. Waiting for something to happen. *And now*, June thinks, *it's happening*. What's happening? *Nothing*, June thinks. *Nothing's happening*. It's getting dark. She'll just sit a minute. Then she'll get up. She'll jump in the car again and go get a few groceries. She doesn't have to do a big shopping trip. Just pick up a few things to make dinner and Norm's lunch for tomorrow. June shivers, her slim arms in goosebumps. *What's wrong with me?* April chill. She draws an afghan around her, sinks further into the big leather couch.

Wakes up.

In a strange place. Déjà vu: on the couch, asleep. Rain lashing the big bay windows. The bare branches of the trees dancing in dark saccades.

Blinks. Blinks. Asleep, awake.

June is looking down at herself, this dumpy and pale woman in jeans and a sweatshirt. Plump in the cheeks with an emaciated puffiness, her face a white smear framed in lank brown hair that could use a trim, a wash, a hot oil condition.

So that's me, she thinks dully.

Where is she?

Floating above herself in a big room on the edge of an ancient gash in the ground. Sleeping.

June? June honey?

Drops from Norm's blunt nose splash her forehead.

June startles awake.

Norm's looking down at her.

June?

Norm?

June, are you okay?

I'm...awake?

Of course you are.

You're...wet?

I'm soaked, Norm says congenially.

Oh. June brings a hand to her mouth. Feels hot breath on her palm. Oh.

What is it sweetie?

I...fell asleep.

That's okay. No big deal. It happens.

No—I—

Norm kneels down in front of her on the carpet. He wraps his arms around her.

It's okay.

Hey! You're all wet. June twists away.

I couldn't get the car in the garage. You parked right in the middle of the driveway. I had to park on the street. Why didn't you park in the garage?

I...I...thought I did.

Norm is in front of her. His shirt is dark where the cold, fat drops hit. His clothes smell like the wet spring, like weather and fresh decay, but underneath that, there's his skin, which exudes the odours of his office—fluoride and antiseptic. It's not a bad smell.

You're soaked, June murmurs, now leaning into him, letting him hold her. You need a hot shower.

Yeah, I guess I do.

I fell asleep.

I know.

I'm...I was...tired.

Slowly June sits up. She's dizzy, distant. But her heart is racing. What's wrong with me? She left the house planning to pick up groceries. Instead she drove around aimlessly, in circles, in cul-de-sacs, plied her Volvo station wagon through neighbourhoods that looked so much like her own that in the end she couldn't find her way out of the maze and had to activate the built-in GPS. What city? it asked her. June pulled over, suddenly not sure.

June, Norm says, looking at her. Are you okay?

I'm fine. June stands and Norm stands too. She feels woozy and resists the urge to lean into him.

So, Norm finally says brightly. Anything for dinner?

June feels herself stiffen. She's not the maid. She doesn't have to make him dinner.

No, she says brusquely. She hears him exhale. She knows what he's thinking. What did she do all day that she can't even make dinner? But—then—what did she do today? Why can't she make him dinner?

I'm sorry, she says. I, uh, was going to go to the store. But I've just been so...tired.

Maybe you should see a doctor, honey.

No, no, I'm fine. It's no big deal. It must be the rain. June laughs uncertainly. You go take your shower.

But maybe you should just get it checked out.

She can tell he's annoyed.

Don't be mad at me. She nestles up against him. I just—fell asleep. We'll order in, she says definitively. From that place you like. With the noodles.

Okay. Fine. I'm going to get changed.

Norm pulls away. He loosens his tie as he heads upstairs.

June falls back onto the couch. The dream she had, like she was outside of her life, looking down on it, hovering just over the surface. She crosses her arms against her chest. She moves to the window and peers into the backyard. It's still raining. The water starts running upstairs. Norm is taking his shower. He's annoyed. His routine disrupted. Norm's older than her, 41 to her 32. He has a routine. He comes home hungry. He expects to have his dinner. He's a dentist in Wississauga Heights. That's what June married. That's what she chose, what she wanted.

In college, June went through an artsy phase, a slutty phase, a party phase. She graduated with a BA in English Lit and a boyfriend, tall and gangly John Baker—everyone called him Johnny. He was in a band and some kind of arts collective. They had a manifesto he was excited about; he read it to June, his voice loud and emphatic. Johnny was all chaos and excitement, his endless "gigs," his bands breaking up and reforming with ever more elaborate names, his lengthy random road trips with his buddy and bandmate Rich and Rich's weedy nasally girlfriend, singing backup vocals, stroking the tambourine and their egos. They were living together then, by default mostly, Johnny coming and going though it was June's tiny apartment, June's name on the lease and the phone bill. While Johnny played basement clubs and posted an endless stream of photos to his band-of-the-moment's Myspace page, June mimicked her friends, burnishing her resume and applying for internships. She interned at the public relations department of a pharmaceutical company, then got hired on for six-month contracts that kept getting extended. One day, June came home to find Johnny passed out drunk on her second-hand couch. She stood over him for a long time, studying the rise and fall of his scrawny chest. Then she shook her head as if to clear it and found herself stuffing everything that belonged to him into a garbage bag: scribbled scraps of song lyrics taped to the walls and lost in the carpet, muddy sounding burns of his band's attempts at recording marked with sharpie-scrawled dates and times, dirty socks, ripped T-shirts, a battered volume of Whitman's collected poems she never once saw him read.

Done with Johnny, June focussed on her work. She got hired on permanently for $42,000 a year, the kind of job an unexceptional English degree holder might expect. Three years later, she met Norm through her job, at a dentist trade show in Orlando. He took her out. Courted her. Asked her all kinds of questions. He wanted to know everything about her. He was older. He had his own practice.

The shower water stops.

She pictures him, hairy Norm dripping, towelling off.

Another image slips into June's mind—a woman splayed out on a couch, fingers twisting and twining messed hair.

Me?

She shivers. It's like someone's spying on her. It's like she's spying on herself. She pulls the curtains shut. Any minute now, Norm will yell down and ask in his perpetually cheery and courteous voice what she decided to order and when it's likely to show up. I'm hungry, Norm will call. Guilt will run through her like a snapped branch suddenly coursing sap. Norm likes to eat at 6:45. It's now 7:34.

June hurries into the kitchen. She grabs the menu for Thai Tastes. She barks random dishes into the phone. Can you, will you, we're in a hurry, she says.

Thirty-five minutes, says the ambivalent voice on the other side of the conversation.

June sighs. She hangs up the phone. She doesn't remember a single thing she ordered. Something with chicken. And maybe, she hopes, the pad Thai? She considers calling back.

Norm, honey, she yells in a pre-emptive gesture. Her voice careens up the empty stairs. I ordered Thai. It'll be here soon!

A muffled response she can't quite make out.

I got the noodles you like. You like that, right? Not too spicy? That's your favourite, right?

June figures if she didn't order it, she can just claim they forgot to pack it. She must have ordered it. *Who cares anyway? What am I so worried about?*

The kitchen is all sparkling metals and buffed woods. June recalls being excited about the counter tops once. Through the big glass doors leading out to the backyard, June sees rain splashing into the puddles forming on the lawn. She snaps the blinds closed. Nothing to see out there. Her hands are shaking. *Cold. I'm coming down with something.* She makes her way to the dining room liquor cabinet. June pours two scotch whiskeys in the matching crystal tumblers they got as a wedding present from one of Norm's dentist school buddies.

Thanks sweetheart. This is just what we need, right? Terrible weather…Well you know what they say?

April showers, June says sweetly.

Right, right, Norm agrees, absentmindedly flipping through the mail.

June takes a hit of scotch, doesn't feel the usual heat searing inside her belly. Instead, the nothing. Instead, the shifts and creaks of the house, beating raindrops hidden by the night, millions and millions of raindrops.

She sits in a chair with her back to the wall.

Norm is still working through the stack of mail they get every single day. On her own in her apartment, June rarely got more than two or three pieces of mail a week. Bills mostly. Here, they get at least ten items a day: catalogues, fliers, charity solicitations, dental magazines, community newsletters. Once a week, June gathers up the pile of previously perused solicitations and catalogues and dumps them in the recycling box for pick up. This doesn't alleviate her guilt. So much junk mail. She read in the newspaper—more fodder for the box—that the city only actually recycles something like ten percent of what gets put out on the curb.

So what did you get up to today? Norm is busy ripping open an official-looking letter.

What should I have done today? June thinks. The way her voice sounds in her head: petulant and angry.

Norm continues without looking up. Maybe tomorrow you can drop by the garden centre? Ask them about helping you put together a plan for the backyard?

A plan for our backyard. I'll get right on that. *God,* June thinks, *when did I get to be such a—*

The doorbell rings.

June jerks, startled.

Norm's face in some letter.

I'll get it, June sighs.

Outside air, cold and scummy. *What's so great,* June thinks, not for the first time, *about living above a goddamn swamp?* Two bags of Thai food, two proffered twenties, thank you and good night. She shuts the door and locks it.

Food's here, she calls.

She shivers again. She can't seem to warm up.

June opens containers. She gets out two plates. She could dump the stuff from the Styrofoam into nice bowls. But then she'll just have to rinse them and load them into the dishwasher, and who cares anyway, just wasting water. Bad enough all these containers and lids and everything are going in the garbage. She could light a candle. Open a bottle of wine. Make it nice for her Norm.

Food's here, she yells.

Finally Norm shows up, flailing the letter.

Look at this! he says. Will you look at this?

What is it?

It's a letter from the Walletville Regional Authority. They say they're going to turn the gorge into a road.

A road?

Can you believe it? I can't believe it.

June spoons eggplant curry, pad Thai—she remembered—and basil chicken onto Norm's plate.

This is crazy! Norm says. They want to run it all the way up to the 472.

They do?

I cannot fucking believe it!

Norm only uses the f-word when he's really mad.

Here. June passes him a plate. Norm starts shovelling food in his mouth.

Listen to this, he says, between mouthfuls. The consultation with the public will take place April 15 at the Hardwood Community Centre. April 15! That's in five days! Five days!

But June isn't listening. She's staring at his mouth moving, his strong white teeth masticating, his lips shiny with sauce.

Idiots! Do you know what this will do to our property values?

Norm rants on. Chews. June refills his plate. June pours him a glass of ice water. June doesn't eat. Her stomach is both bloated and empty.

Five days! They probably think we won't have the time to really put up a fight. Well they're wrong about that!

June can't shake the feeling of her dream. Like someone's watching her, only not watching her. Like she's watching herself watch herself.

I'm going to write a letter to my councilman. Courier it over tomorrow. Norm chugs his water and stomps out of the kitchen and into his study.

A road by the river, she thinks. *That's crazy. It'll never happen. It's too crazy.* June puts the leftovers in the fridge. She feels validated, re-using the containers and their lids even if it's only temporary. She sticks Norm's soiled plate in the dishwasher and stows hers back in the kitchen cabinet. June sits back down at the kitchen table. Now what? She looks around. Everything gleaming, polished, bright. Outside, it's just the opposite—dark sticking like wet mud. And inside, her mind is full of shadow. June closes her eyes. Something's going to happen. When? She takes a deep breath. Waits. Nothing happens.

They're in bed watching the blatantly low-budget ten o'clock local news on the community access channel. June's already dutifully praised Norm's letter to their councillor. She'd stood in his den and nodded as he droned on. Now Norm's hoping for signs of burgeoning dissent against the planned road. Nothing, Norm says. A smiling blonde sticks a microphone in the face of a high school football coach. Norm switches channels impatiently, finally lands on the national news. On the other side of the country there's a protest, something about missing Native women. *Horrible*, June thinks. They watch in silence for a few more minutes before Norm glances over at June.

Well, he says, ready to turn in?

June nods as she knows she's supposed to and Norm kills the TV. He fumbles on his night table for his eye mask.

After a bit, June slips out of bed. I'm gonna read a bit downstairs honey, she says. She pecks him on the cheek.

But honey, I thought you were tired?

I was, June says, I mean, I am, but after that nap I'm not quite ready to sleep yet.

Try not to stay up too late, Norm says, clearly trying to avoid allowing himself the hint of irritation he thinks he's probably entitled to.

June deposits her book on the kitchen counter and lets her feet take her aimlessly through the main floor of the house. She finds herself standing in the front hallway, her hands fidgeting through her ropey hair. Her head buzzes. She keeps having these glimpses of herself from odd angles, out of body, just plain out if it. This is new—this sense that someone is, that there's someone, somehow—

looking down at her.

Of course there's no one—

But still. She just wants to—make sure.

June searches the main floor. Front hallway closet, all the shoes lined up, coats hanging. *Someone could be*—

June flips through coats. Ridiculous. *This isn't working. I'm*—

She turns, suddenly, to catch an image of herself. She's in the backyard, twirling in a wet white T-shirt. Nipples sharp like a horror movie starlet's.

What the hell?

She should get Norm. *He's probably asleep by now. So what? Wake him up. Tell him—just say, hold me. Can you hold me?* Norm sleeps like it would take some kind of major disaster to stir him out of slumber.

I'm not going out there, June mutters to herself. Instead, she heads into the basement. She reaches shakily for the string light in the furnace room. The good thing about one-bedroom apartments is that they don't have basements. June peers gingerly into the dark gap behind the water heater. Nothing. She opens the storage closet. Vague shapes, an old bread machine, a parka, two pairs of cross country skies, their bindings stiff and cracked, stuff they don't want but can't seem to throw out. For some reason, she reaches into the black space behind a musty smelling tent. She feels her hand close around a cool weathered wood shaft. *A shovel*, she thinks.

Oh! Another sudden flash. Herself. Outside. In the backyard. Digging. She's—

digging.

She pulls the shovel out. It's an old thing, worn-down handle, rusted blade with flecks of red dirt from a previous decade's labour. Nothing that she can imagine ever belonging to Norm. Probably left here, forgotten. But still: an object with—

history.

June hefts it, feels underused muscles contracting.

Fine, she suddenly says. Who's she talking to? Fine then.

Outside the backyard light hazily illuminates the centre of the large lawn. The hairs on the back of June's neck stand up. She shivers. She's taken off her sweater. Why? She's preening. The thin T-shirt sticks to her chest. It's part of the show, the craziness. *Do you like it? You like what you see? Keep watching. There's more where that came from.*

Of course there's no one. Who could be watching her? But she talks to—whoever, him, it's a him, she thinks—whoever he is. She talks to him, keeps up a running muttered monologue, words and thoughts blurred together like the rain and sky. *Just keeping you informed, okay? How's this? Is this what you want?*

She pushes the shovel hard into the ground and leans on it. A chunk of grass turns over, roots and all. Empty earth underneath. June's hollow stomach churns. Rain runs cold down her neck.

Tomorrow, she promises herself, *I'll be done with this. I'll be a good wife,* she thinks in the direction of the dark forest canopy breaking out from the river gorge. *I'll go to the grocery store,* she promises the pressing grey-black blob of the sky. *I'll make a nice dinner,* she tells the strange emptiness of the sodden backyard. *I'll rub up against Norm. I'll let him…*She's defiant now, her face flush with guilt and exertion. *You see? You just get to…watch. I'll let him… in me. I'll tell him to. I will.*

But right now, June just wants to dig. She yanks the shovel out of the ground, fills it, tensing from the weight, the muscles in her arms now synchronized to this repetitive, instinctual motion. Time passes—an hour, two. She keeps going. Then, suddenly, she hears something, a pained cry, incoherently guttural. She whirls around, trying to surprise the gully emptiness of tree and wet sky. Who's there? No one. No one's there. Just—the nothing inside her, a fog settling in. Anyway, it's too dark. Too dark to really see.

TIM
Thursday, April 10

Climbing: a series of physical actions Tim's body has become completely unfamiliar with. His soft palms and willowy fingers scrape against the tree's trunk. He clings to the tree's skin, wrapping his long legs like a vine. His toes curl in prehensile imitation. Then he squirms, motion measured in inches, his face pressed against the tree, stubble dragging, clothes sticking. And so he propels himself upwards, shinnying his skinny, tired, muscle-devoid frame toward the partially visible and, once again, grey sky.

Tim makes it to the lower branches. Sweat runs into his eyes. He feels the sting but can't let go to wipe. He's only, maybe, fifteen feet up. *Still*, he thinks, *some serious damage if you fell*. And it feels higher. From here he can actually climb. Big branches spaced monkey-bar lengths apart. This is how he remembers it. The bottom of the world receding, the branches just the right height to grab on to.

He emerges into the sky. The sun is gone for sure now. It's getting late. It could be getting late. Either way the brackish monotony of spring is not exactly evoking a fresh brand new day. Tim's gotten himself twisted around. He can see the river now, a brown band below him. The river isn't as sluggish as it looks from the ground, white rapids discernable upstream, spring melt chafing against the bank. And beyond that, there's the thin strip of woods, considerably thinner on the east side, since the river has no cliff drop to protect it from the inevitabilities of development. On that side the river abuts sprawling lawns sporting elaborate decks with hot tubs. *Nice life sitting there and watching the river go by*, Tim thinks. The river on its way to the lake, carrying with it the unmistakable scents of growth and rot mixed in with upstream factory chemicals, bobbing bits of random garbage, dog shit, cat shit, car parts, more than a few streams of lite beer-infused urine. But it's pretty in its own weird way, from a distance, from up above, a giant waste disposal system spiralling into the great lake.

Tim turns away from the rotting river. He cautiously gropes his way to the cliff side of the tree.

He arrives on the other side. Struggling to catch his breath, he gingerly lowers his body into a horizontal Y-shaped crevice, a spot, he realizes, that his body is familiar with. *This was it*, he thinks, surveying the view in front of him: the lookout hideout of a boy named Timmy. Tim wills himself to let go of one of the branches he's holding on to. Awkwardly, he uses his new free hand to wipe the sweat off his forehead. Then he fumbles in his pockets. *C'mon*, he tells himself. *You've earned it*. The pre-rolled joint he finally pulls out is in surprisingly decent shape. Next, he searches for his lighter. *It's time*, he repeats in his head like a mantra. Where is it? *It's time*. Tim's fingers, scraped, dirtied, crawl urgently through his pockets. *Ah, there it is*.

On autopilot now, as if he's been smoking up in trees all his life, he dexterously pops the rollie in his mouth, uses his thumb to call up Che's flame, lights up, puffs, puffs, and inhales.

Tim closes his eyes. He swallows. He feels his lungs expanding. It's the opposite of the panic clawing at him, the ticking inevitability of some internal explosion. This is smothering implosion, inward relief repression.

He swallows spit and exhales large.

Oh yeah.

There it is.

Heat in his chest.

There it is.

Right in front of him.

Spreading then lingering.

His boyhood home.

Well what did he expect? That the sky would burst into tears? That the world would stop spinning, Carly would float down in front of him and hug him, give him head, tell him everything is finally alright? It's stupid, he knows. To think that something in your life will change because you've driven an hour west on the highway, rolled down a hill, and climbed a tree.

He shrugs. *Whatever.* He just wanted to see the old place again. He's not even sure why. This is where he lived. Where he grew up. He was happy here, once. Wasn't he? He'll get down now. He's done what he came here to do. He'll tell Carly: I went to see it. I went home. She won't say anything. She won't have to.

It's getting dark now, evening sliding into night.

It's time to go, Tim reminds himself. But his muscles have gone loose, his arms dangling at his sides. He's just getting comfortable. *Home,* he thinks. Emboldened, he takes it all in from his perch over-look. Tim lets his gaze travel up the large sloped lawn to the big house, freshly repainted, Tim notes, with red shutters and a nice white sheen. There's nothing special about the house, an early-eighties colonial, facsimile of some other era. From his bird's eye nested vantage point, the house doesn't even look real; more of an idea of a house, utterly lacking in past and present secrets. Still, this is it. This is where he grew up. If he ever did grow up.

Carly says—

Tim sighs. He digs into his pocket and pulls out the joint, half smoked. He re-lights it. He takes a drag. Then, without breathing out, he takes another. He plays the smoke over his tongue, tasting the burn, like a sweet summer field set on fire. He doesn't swallow or exhale. Not yet. He lets the cloud settle on the back of his throat. Reflexively, his body settles back into the crook of the branches. He squints at the house again. It's newer looking now, refreshed, but in its blank essence, it's the same. Only the trappings have changed. His dad sold it just a few years back. A cheque arrived from a lawyer. Tim froze when he saw the fancy envelope. He immediately thought the old man must be dead. But it was just a cheque. An allotment of the proceeds that Tim immediately began shredding and then, still unsatisfied, set on fire with his Guevara refillable.

Dumbass. I could have bought Carly a—

cooler car.

The tip of the joint burns down, near enough to his forefinger to sear, but Tim hardly feels it. It's the only callus he has on his body, a permanent blister of dead skin. He lets it smoke and smoulder a bit more, just to prove he can. Then all at once he breathes out a cloud of smoke and flicks the roach stub into the spread of foliage below.

So. Now.

Now he's really high.

The good stuff.

The China, Clay calls it, because he sources from the Triad. Tim doesn't care where he gets it from. He cares about the way the buds look and smell, the way they feel as he gently pinches them with pursed fingers. See this, he tells Carly, gently stroking the tightly packed tips with his index finger, this is premium. When Tim smokes, he likes to burn it slow, take his time, watch something on TV, The Simpsons or something, Homer's bovine eyes bulging bigger and bigger until Tim can't stand it anymore and he just starts giggling like a girl.

But this is a different kind of high. Tim stares intently at the house below and in front of him. Now his body has lost its slackness. His hands are in fists, clenched but ready to grab on. Again, he peers through the gathering gloom at what was once his childhood home. In the backyard of the house sit two empty plastic chairs. They stand side by side on the lawn about a foot off the patio. They are the only objects that seem to even remotely suggest that the house is occupied. The lawn is mowed, though not particularly taken care of. Tim dimly remembers his mom having a nice table and chairs out there, candles, flower pots. Now the patio is bare, empty. Tim studies the back of the house intently. Grey stacked stone facade. Sliding glass door to the kitchen. Upstairs, the big bedroom windows. The shades are pulled. Tim stares. He can't quite—what was that? He sees it again, a swirling hint of motion. He jerks back instinctively, almost hits his head against hard bark.

It was nothing of course. What could he be seeing? The house is dark, quiet, shut up. The curtains are closed. His dad never closed the curtains. Tim had binoculars back then, the Scout 200 or something like that, ordered from the back of a Daredevil comic—*naw, probably not*. He can't remember where he got them from, but he had them. He would hang them from his neck, feel them bounce against his scrawny chest as he climbed. He would stay up in the tree—*up here*—for hours and hours, just sitting, staring, waiting. Most of the time, the house was empty. Occasionally, there was his father to scrutinize through twin magnified scopes. His father: biting into a cold chicken leg; yelling into the phone; nodding in and out of sleep with a bottle between his legs and a ball game blaring. Tim squints harder at the house. Nothing. What he thought he saw, just in his head; hadn't it always been like that? Even back then? He'd never seen it, not really. The thought depresses him. Time to climb down. Time to put his pointless quest to rest. All these years, all those hours of watching his father from the distance of the tree. Watching and waiting. All those years suspecting in silence. He isn't a boy anymore. His father is dying. This is it. One last chance.

I know you blame me for—

It's not true. He doesn't. He blames himself. For never finding out. What did happen? How could it have happened? His mother wouldn't just have—

He blames himself. For spending the last six years of his life delivering pints with an affably crooked smile maintained by the joints he puffed in the alley out back on his break.

He should have done this a long time ago.

But he hadn't been—he wasn't—

There's always a price. That's the one thing Tim's learned about this world from his father. *Use it or lose it. Pay up or shut up. Time is money, kid, and don't you ever forget it.*

Now he says he's dying. Now he says he has regrets. Tim can't imagine it. He can only picture him as burly, angry, always angry. His face a perpetual smoulder. *He wants me to forgive him.*

And maybe Tim will. Hope smoulders in his lungs, an after burn. Forgive and forget, right Carly?

—Carly—

With effort, Tim tries to pull his gaze away from the house before him. The long backyard wavers, goes hazy. The grainy air merges with the clouds. Tim feels distance, emptiness, increments and measures. The space between things. At last, unable to resist, he closes his eyes.

He wakes up with a jerk. Rain falls hard and fast, big fat drops splattering off his forehead. Tim startles, grabs for balance, feels his legs dangling in the dark. He drops half a foot, his heart lurching to his throat before he finally makes tenuous contact with the branch below and manages to steady himself.

He stays like that, his eyes clamped shut, his muscles clenched, his breathing ragged.

Finally, Tim opens his eyes.

Despite the rain, it's quiet. Tim hears his exhalations, his lungs filling and emptying, the staccato of raindrops hitting the leaves above a kind of muted soundtrack. He hears it all, everything, his senses sharp and alert in a way he can't remember them being in years, in decades, since, maybe, before he started methodically emptying his father's liquor cabinet, since before he discovered the way the pungent honey mustiness of smoke could cloud over everything, since before he left home at sixteen, caught a bus to the city and never looked back.

This is it, Tim suddenly thinks. He leans recklessly, eagerly, into the hazy blackness. At first, there's nothing to see, just the night, a charcoal veil obscuring everything. Until, gradually, something else comes into focus: a dark outline, darker dark against the angled plane of the lawn. Tim stares hard, so hard it hurts. The form moves, becomes the outline of a person. The house, a black centre, frames its—*her*—movement. *This is it*, Tim thinks. This is what he came for. He shivers violently. It's freezing. Not like being cold up in a tree in the April rain. This is different, a liquid ice churning inside him. He's not crazy. He's not high. What he's seeing, it's—

Carly's told him about astral projection, leaving the body, flying through the night sky on nocturnal adventures.

But this isn't some projection. This is—

real.

Once, a long time ago, not so long ago, he was a boy. His parents screamed at each other. Something—a glass, a plate—shattering. Muffled shouts. The sound of a door slamming. Voices, his father's brusque baritone, silence, a car starting, then a scream. A scream.

For weeks after, Tim would come home from sixth grade and stand in the empty foyer and call out, as he always did, as every kid did: Mom? I'm home! Mom?

Then school ended. Then the summer's empty days spilled together like the endless glasses of Jack and Ginger his father drank, sitting in a kitchen chair he'd pulled into the backyard. Just sitting there and staring into space.

Tim remembers how quiet it was that summer. Neither of them did much more than grunt at each other. When the phone rang the sound cut through the house like a shriek.

The phone hardly ever rang.

That's when Timmy started spending his days in the tree, absorbing every movement, every shift of light as the sun crossed the sky. His father stopped going to work. He just sat out there in the backyard. At first he did nothing, but then he started watering. Watering the lawn. Not the whole lawn, Timmy realized. His father's interest was directed exclusively toward one particular bare area of earth hardly discernable in the patchy terrain of interlaced weeds and grass. Days and weeks went by. Long hot muggy July afternoons gave way to dry dusty August evenings that stretched on and out past forever. The brown patch turned a light shimmering green. Tim watched his father and his father watched that rectangle of twitching grass. Every day, every single freaking day, his dad watered the patch, fertilized it, got down on his knees and, scissors in hand, inspected it, gently evened out each individual blade.

Tim can still close his eyes and summon up the colour of that summer: a chartreuse sheen, a shimmering new growth madness.

Toward the end of that hazy muggy season—which Tim doesn't so much remember as feel imprinted in his memory (because, he, too, began developing a taste for Jack Daniels and ginger ale, knocking back several short glasses of the stuff before heading down to the river and climbing up to his special place)—Tim came to a conclusion. Call it an epiphany, a realization, an ordering of facts. The grass was beginning to darken and blend with the rest of the lawn. And still his father attended to the coffin-shaped plot. His father, who had never tenderly cared for anything, obsessively groomed this particular patch of Kentucky Bluegrass as if his life depended on it.

His mother wasn't coming back.

Tim hung onto his branch and threw up, sweet sour sticky boozy mess burning his throat. His father got up off his knees and scanned the horizon for the source of the sound.

At some point, Timmy turned twelve. He spent the next four years plotting and scheming and drinking and smoking and wondering: Was he, too, going to disappear?

Of course he was.

You were just a boy, Carly's told him, pulling him into her chest and stroking his hair.

A burst of rain, drops slapping against leaves, cold thin wet spray reaching Tim where he holds on, staring out.

Carly again.

The house, that centrifugal emptiness.

He wasn't. They took that from him. They stole it away before he even knew what was happening.

Fuck! Tim bellows, swaying in the tree.

That's when he smells it. A stench of rot laced with sweat on skin. Fear courses through him. What is it? The smell is animal. Putrefied. But rich and fusty, feminine, sexual, a lingering secret scent suddenly released.

Perfume.

It smells like his mother's perfume.

Then Tim feels the light brush of a soft finger tracing down his stubbled neck. Everything stops. The only sound: his beating heart.

He pulls away. What's happening? Someone—? It's no longer raining. The audio switched back on. The forest drips gently. Tim casts urgently into the deep night. He sees nothing. Shadow on shadow where the yard meets the cliff. Then—a light. *Light?* Tim squints, blinks. Quick blur going dark then bright. The patch of light remains. It gets, maybe, brighter. Now he can see her. In the middle of the night. In the middle of a rain storm. Tim hunches forward. He shifts his body farther out on the branch. He feels the wood swaying, unstable. There's a sound now, too, faintly audible. What is it? Tim thrusts his head into empty dark space. A shape slowly emerges. Long hair. A woman. She's moving methodically, her limbs, barely illuminated, swinging in and out of view—light, dark, light, dark, light, dark. And the sound, metal on dirt.

Digging, Tim thinks. Tim in the branches, wood bowing, his whole long body folded over, pressing in, holding on to the wet bark. Then he smells it again, a powerful miasma surrounding him, sticking to him, a cloying need, a syrupy thick rot, death discharged.

She's digging.

PART TWO

JUNE
Friday, April 11

GREAT BIG STREET GOING NORTH. Hurontarion, artery to the highway. Other roads are capillaries winding through the flesh of the edge city. Cars penetrate like blood, coating subdivisions, new developments, bare fields promising communities named after absent trees and elusive glimpses of the river.

Hurontarion is three lanes each way, traffic bumping and grinding in a striptease of progress. 18-wheelers, minivans, SUVs, even the occasional car trolls the congested laneway seeking access to the Save-A-Centre grocery store, the Next Future Shop, the Bed, Bath and Yonder, huge stores leading up to the biggest attraction of them all: the Middle Mall.

June sees a gap in traffic. She speeds up. She's alert to the ebb and flow, the way the cars surge and recede, the way life itself seems to stall, then shoot forward. She can feel it now. How everything can matter, how even a trip to the grocery store can be—real. She just needs to stop thinking so much. That's the problem, that's what it comes down to. She's spending too much time alone in an empty house. It's amazing how easy it is to get lost in your own head.

June signals her turn into the grocery store. She's out of it now. She's back. Last night—*it was like a dream*. But it wasn't a dream.

Whatever else it was, it really happened. She can still feel the rough grain of the heavy shovel against her palms. Her forearms ache, muscles pulsing. Maybe that's all she needed. Something physical. Something actual.

When she worked at Phfizon all the employees got a fitness rebate of up to $300 a year. She joined a gym for the first time in her life and came to enjoy it. StairMaster and treadmill, she stepped along, going nowhere fast, feeling the sweat drip down her inner arms, involuntarily picturing the crisp files stacked up on her desk, each one marked Confidential in red, important letters. *Sample size*, she would think with each panted stride, *co-morbidity, clinical trial, generalizability, patient response, efficacy, pregnancy*. But gradually, her head cleared of pharma jargon. Then, back at work, everything would flow: she would find herself clearly, even artfully, building the text for the brochure the reps needed to promote their new choles-terol-lowering drug to physicians. She and Norm were just starting to date. She was learning on the job, speaking up in meetings, join-ing her co-workers in company-sponsored picnics and bowling outings. Then, all of a sudden, it was gone. Despite a 1.3 billion-dollar annual profit, she was abruptly downsized, her position one of several thousand identified as more efficiently performed by out-sourced contractors, overseas freelancers, she later learned, doing the writing she did for pennies per word.

June makes the turn into the grocery store parking lot and pulls into an empty spot. She stretches her arms above her head, feeling her sore muscles. She bears no ill will toward whoever ended up get-ting the work. They have to eat too. Only—it had been a grim time. She'd had no inkling, no warning. Her performance review had been stellar. She'd bought a bike and started to cycle to work, ped-dling silently through side streets misted with early morning frost, soon to be dispelled by the sun's slow rise. *Ancient history*, June tells herself. She'll get a bike here, she decides. She'll join a gym. She'll get back to figuring it out. Whatever *it* is.

June releases her seatbelt, which snags on her bulky sweatshirt. She's in sweats and jeans; she didn't even take a shower. She just wanted to get out of the house, breathe the air, fresh and cold after the storm, move, keep moving. Now she feels clunky. She could have at least gotten properly dressed. Norm bought her a cute workout jacket from lululemon for her birthday. That was three months ago. *It still has the tags on it. I should have*—Why? So she can look good for the Save-A-Centre cashier? This time of the day she won't even get the pimpled high school version. *One of those used-up ladies, bad dye job, sour-faced.* Dump your change on the counter and make you pick up the coins one at a time so they don't have to touch your pretty palm. Sighing aggrievedly, June swings herself out of the car.

June pushes her cart down aisle nine looking for those crackers Norman likes. She's already rolled through snack foods. Not there. Why not there? They keep them somewhere else, in some other section—"organic" or "ethnic" or "party planning" or "gourmet." She scans the shelves.

June? Juney?!!

June turns, sweatshirt heavy on her shoulders.

Christine?

Christine looks sharp, looks like a woman, like a grown up. Her hair in a glistening brown bob, cream silk blouse offsetting a black skirt and jacket number that reveals long legs, always, June recalls, the girl's best asset.

What a surprise! June abruptly exclaims, forcing her face into an enthusiastic grimace.

I knooooow, Christine giggles. I haven't seen you in ages! How *are* you?

I'm fine, I'm great. June smoothes at the crown of greasy honey brown ringlets escaping her fraying ponytail. How are you?

Wow! Christine says. Look at you!

No! June says. Look at you!

June grips the handles of her cart, overloaded with bulk toilet paper, cases of Coke Zero and Canada Dry, ten-pack Save-A-Centre brand nutty nougat chocolate bars.

Christine puts down her mostly empty basket—mango, tub of lite yogurt—and plants her high heels in the middle of the aisle.

You live around here?

I—sure, we—live not far from here.

Wississauga Heights, Christine says.

That's right. June smiles, keeps smiling. And you? You don't—

I live downtown. Little Italy?

Sure. Yeah. Of course. It's great to see you, Christine. Christy. I go by Chris now.

Chris. Sure. June laughs nervously.

So, Christine says, her pupils narrowing in the bright track lighting. What are you up to these days?

I'm well, in between things…right now, I guess. I…got married. June holds up her ring finger and grins apologetically.

And it's hard, of course, says Christine. With kids and everything.

Oh, June says. We don't have kids. She follows Christine's gaze to the jug of chocolate milk sweating in her cart.

I'm working on Bay Street, Christine says quickly. At South and Copperman. You know I went into law, right?

Sure, I heard that. June's bunched cheeks are starting to hurt. Christine gazes at her expectantly.

So, uh, June says, what are you doing here in the 'burbs?

I was just on my way back to the city. I had to meet a client. Normally they come to my office, of course, but he's an elderly gentleman, and he's not doing so well, physically. Cancer, Christine faux whispers. Anyway, she resumes in her normal clipped tone, he's revising his will. So I met with him, and then driving by I thought, it's now or never. Who has the time to shop these days? I'm so busy—

As if on cue, Christine's cell bleats.

Ah, excuse me, I just have to—

Listen, June says, great to see you. She awkwardly negotiates her cart around Christine.

Yes, Christine says impatiently, I did receive the file. She waves at June, bye or wait a second. In her lacquered fingernails a business card that June snatches as she squeezes past, catching a whiff of Christine's tastefully elegant perfume. She hurries to the end of the aisle and steers the cart left toward the meats. Christine's probably a vegetarian.

June in her baby blue sweatshirt. She pushes her greasy hair off her face and picks out a roast.

Hurontarion narrows, framed by a series of gas stations and family restaurants—Appletree's, Taco Terrace—promising early bird family discounts. June hesitates at the turnoff, her foot wavering between gas and brake. Maybe she should just go home. Lie down. Have a nap.

But you cancelled last week—

And for the first time in months, June's not tired. She dug and it rained and she dug some more, filling her shovel with the heavy, wet, cold earth. But she felt weightless, the shovel floating in her arms; she could have dug forever, the depression slowly and inexorably turning into a bottomless pit, her anonymity in the dark night underscored by the unshakeable conviction that she was being observed—no, not observed: *watched*. Then came a slight shift in the texture of the air, an early onset reminder of a coming grey dawn. Suddenly everything hurt, as if she was being forced to lift a load well beyond her means. Gripping the shovel, she had stared into the hole she'd dug and saw it: her true burden—an astonishing discovery.

June accelerates. She's sticking to the plan. Make the rounds at the home, then head to *her* home and prepare dinner. She'll dine with Norm on salmon-stuffed pinwheels matched to a highly recommended unoaked South African chardonnay. The curtains will be kept closed. Nothing to see. Nothing to see out there.

And tomorrow, she'll go to the garden centre. She'll fill the dead space with a blooming jungle of—it doesn't matter. *Whatever grows. Whatever keeps Norm happy.*

Fill it in. Cover it up. If it didn't happen, it didn't happen.

The short road to the home is easy to miss, more of an extended driveway than a road, really. It's just off the main drag, but the low-slung building obscured by a thick row of hedges feels like somewhere else, somewhere far from anywhere. June arrives at the mostly empty parking lot adjoining the building and slows to a near idle. Weird pockets of emptiness are everywhere in Wississauga. They disturb her, these sudden moments of lapse, gaps in the sprawled city's coverage. Finally she parks, carefully fitting the station wagon between painted white lines.

Temporarily permanent, Cartwright is home to eighty or so seniors. June's assigned to the fourteen of them who live on the seventh floor. She brings cookies, offers tea, struggles with awkward minutes of conversation. She signed up in a fit of industriousness when she first moved to Wississauga. She told Norm she was considering going back to school, maybe social work, something to do with gerontology. Norm made appropriately encouraging noises.

June moves through the unstaffed, unadorned lobby and into a spacious elevator built for walkers and wheelchairs. The elevator dings and she steps out into the hall. The smell is of something spilled on the floor then haphazardly wiped up with a dirty mop dunked in vinegar. The nurses' station is empty. June hurries past and knocks on the first door to the left.

Anonymous senior opens up. He peers at her suspiciously. Hi! she says with enthusiasm. It's terrible, but June can't remember the old fellow's name. It doesn't matter. Room 714 grudgingly takes a cookie from June's proffered plastic plate. Mostly, they accept June's ministrations as part of their daily routine. Even so, they're as eager for her to arrive as they are for her to leave—their eyes half hooded, their TVs blaring, their days passing like the incessant sound of cruising cars one block over. They're lonely, but not so lonely as to forget that June is part of a fleet of able-bodied intruders whose peering eyes are ever fixing on further evidence that Grandpa has lost his mind, his hip, his sight, is no longer able to help himself, will never again work, drive a car, make love. Only one of June's charges seems to actually be eager for her arrival, seems to be able to separate her from the conspiracies of a quasi-confinement marked by intermittent calls to bingo and bland institutional meals served up three times a day with a regularity designed expressly to mock the unpredictable bowels of the confined diners. June hurries through the other residents, saves Rose for last.

Rose it's me! June finally gets to announce, opening the door without bothering to knock. Rose, unlike the other residents, doesn't bother to lock her door. Rose says she has nothing to steal, and nothing anybody would want either. *True enough*, June thinks. A constant stream of cars passing, but nobody notices the seniors, even enough to bother to rob them.

Hi Rose. Sorry I'm a bit late…

Not to worry dear. You just come on in.

…traffic was terrible.

Gets worse every year dear. They say these days everyone's got two cars. Two cars! Can you believe it? Rose's voice, throaty and authoritative, makes June think of a chain-smoking high school girl's softball coach.

Shall I make us some tea, Rose?

That would be delightful dear.

Alright then.

Feeling prim and vaguely nun-like, *dear,* June plugs in the kettle sitting on the counter of the kitchenette, really just a tiny space separated from the rest of the room by half a wall. It's dark in the little unit. June squints down at the teacups, checking their cleanliness. Rose keeps everything murky, shades drawn, lights off except for one small tabletop lamp. She's not quite blind, says she sees better with the lights off. June suspects she's economizing on an electricity bill she doesn't pay anymore, habitually saving money—for what? The future? Who knows? She could live another twenty years. June shudders. *Somebody walking over my grave.*

June bustles around making tea. Ritual. *Calms us down,* June thinks. She pictures Norman in the morning slurping his decaf coffee. Decaf, what's the point? Ritual. Something to do. He didn't notice that she was up all night, rummaging around the basement, waving a shovel around in the backyard in the rain. *What was I doing?* It was pouring out; and there was—

No—I just—

The back of her neck, cold—eyes on her.

Eyes.

No.

In the morning, she was there, beside him in the bed. She made him coffee. Toasted the last of a frozen bag of bagels. Nothing for lunch? he asked hopefully. I'm going shopping today, she told him. I promise.

Milk and four spoons of sugar. That's how Rose likes it. Brownish sludge, sweet and sour. June unplugs the hissing kettle. That's the extent of the cooking that happens in Rose's kitchen. There's no stove, not even a microwave or a toaster oven. At home they've gone state of the art, easy clean flattop electric that blooms a deep red with just the gentlest touch of a dial. *But it's better this way,* June thinks. She can just imagine Rose immolating herself trying to produce the sort of thing nobody makes anymore—apple pie, meatloaf, gingerbread cookies.

No. Rose won't be cooking any time soon. Her brittle fingers can barely hold the handle of a teacup. Can't cook. *Can't do anything,* June thinks. Except stay alive.

Which she's remarkably good at.

Rose's body, pruned and stunted, has atrophied further than the majority of June's antediluvian charges. But her mind is as sharp as her tongue. Charlatans, Rose announces. Liars and crooks. Rose's favourite story. How she faced down the municipal planners and their corporate cohorts. In the end, they kicked her out anyway, built over what Rose describes as her *lovely little cottage.* It was just around the corner, there, dear, Rose likes to explain, waving her hand at the permanently curtained and closed window. June pictures a small shaded house, a once white panelled exterior yellowed from decades of exhaust. A little house sandwiched between a condo development and a Reno Depot. Rose refused to sell, wanted to live out the rest of her days in the house she grew up in. But her daughter, in her sixties and living on the other side of the country, cut a deal with the city and sent her packing. By now June's heard the details at least five times: the moving truck carting away her furniture to god knows where, the ambulance they took her away in—I was healthier than they were dear! No matter how many times June's heard the tale, she still feels disquieted by it. How could someone do that to their own mother? And how could the City let it happen? After all, Rose is something of a celebrity, the oldest person in Wississauga. As Rose tells it, they threw her out of home and hearth just days after she was shown on TV amiably chastising the mayor before cutting the cake to celebrate her 101st birthday. But, June supposes, it was for her own good. How could she have stayed there, all alone? Rose dismisses this argument. They were bringing me that Meals on Wheels! she announces indignantly. She prefers to talk about revenge. They stole it from me, she says. Rose says she's not going to just wither away *in some home* while *certain people* live *high on the hog* at her expense.

June plunks tea bags into the chipped white pot adorned with— what else?—roses. Pot was pretty once, she's sure, as were the many rose-themed dishes, knickknacks, and decorations that fill the small space. Rose was pretty too. June's seen pictures.

Thank you, dear, Rose says as June puts a cup of hot tea on her the side table. Rose puckers her shrivelled lips and leans over a steaming cup to expel what air she's mustered. The liquid barely swirls. Rose digs around for a cookie, prepares to dunk the hard disc into the hot brew. She doesn't eat much anymore. A slice of bread, a cup of tea. She's toothless, doesn't bother with false teeth. At my age, she snaps, why be false? Rose tastes the cookie now. June can see the wet white dough stained dark brown slowly mashing between the old lady's beige gums. June won't let herself look away. The first time, feeling queasy as her stomach turned and Rose chewed, June got up to admire the corner display of dusty figurines, tiny pink-cheeked porcelain dolls, each one clutching a faded bouquet of roses.

Am I boring you dear? Rose had snapped. June flushed, spun back to attention. She's taught herself, since, to watch in dispassionate awe.

Rose dips, gums, dips, gums.

June sips her still too-hot tea primly.

So my dear, Rose eventually says, my bones are a horror today. Damp out there, isn't it?

Yes, June says. And it's cold. It's like it's never going to be spring!

Rose makes a tssking sound. Terrible, the night. The damp. I can feel it in my bones. It's all this rain we've been having.

It's supposed to rain again tonight, June says.

Is it now? Rose leans down. She purses her lips and gasps over her steaming tea. Ah well, she says jauntily, no rest for the wicked.

Come on Rose, June says. You're not wicked.

Then what am I doing in here? Rose emphatically gums a cookie. Dip and gum. Dip and gum. June hones in on brown crumbs sticking to the side of a face with the texture of a shrivelled prune.

Well, June finally says. It'll be hot soon enough.

The heat nowadays! The summers! Terrible.

It's hotter now?

Of course it is! My lord in heaven the heat these days! What do you people expect? They've done away with all the shade haven't they? When I was a girl living just around the corner—again, the wave of a tiny shrivelled hand, teacup teetering precariously—there were trees lining the road on both sides, big trees, and the shade was wonderful. Just wonderful!

There were trees along the road? You mean…Hurontarion?

Of course, dear. Didn't you hear me? Now it wasn't called that, mind you, plain old Main Street was good enough for us back then.

How long ago was that, Rose?

There wasn't much of a road, either. More of a track. Not like we have now. You risk your life just crossing now! Horses were more the thing back then. You barely ever saw a car come along.

Really? June sips her tea. She's never thought of Wississauga as a place with *horses*. It just seems so present—a perpetually expanding now, a done deal of new roads, cul-de-sac developments, and strip malls.

Yes indeed. They finally had to widen the road when the factory up river expanded. My husband, Morton, he worked there. The Great Lakes Starch Company. Oh starch was in great demand back then, it certainly was. You were either a farmer or you were up at the starch plant. You could smell it for miles! But good for the town, you know, men have to make a living. Of course back then we were just good old Walletville. You couldn't imagine what it would become. Dear me! I must be boring you right out of the room.

No, not at all, Rose!

The old woman scowls down at her tray. She considers the remaining cookie as if momentarily perplexed.

Sugar, June announces helpfully.

Eh? What's that?

Sugar, Rose. It's a sugar cookie.

Of course it is. Rose grabs the cookie in her claw and shakily lowers its exposed flank into her dun-coloured tea. Then she looks up at June: You're a queer one, aren't you?

June blushes. What does she mean?

Rose lifts mushy dripping sugar cookie to her toothless mouth. Her hand shakes as her lips purse in anticipation. Slowly, the mush becomes more mush as Rose gums triumphantly. Another day, another hour, another cookie squashed like a stray squirrel foolish enough to try to cross Hurontarion during rush hour.

Rose swallows. Closes her eyes.

Rose—?

Uh, Rose?

Rose lifts her sagging head, opens her eyes.

I'm still here!

I know, Rose. June laughs nervously. It feels damp in the building, despite the dry heated air seeping restlessly out of a centrally programmed furnace. June feels it in her bones. The damp. And the quiet, too. An all-encompassing silence if you transcribe the constant sound of cars hurtling past into a sort of muted wind.

Rose sips at her tea and makes a face.

My tea's gone a bit cold, she says. Could you…

Back in the closet kitchen, June consults her watch. She'll head home soon. Put a nice dinner together for Norm. He's home at 6, everyday, on the dot. When you make your own hours, he always says, you never have to get stuck at the office.

Here's your tea, Rose.

Lovely.

Rose lowers her mouth to her cup. June can see the moustache of greyish hairs on her upper lip. Draped in a faded nondescript nightdress and an unravelling cardigan, Rose's body is formless. June imagines that nude Rose is nothing more than a head propped up by thin strips of gnarled joint dried out and ready to snap at any moment.

But Rose's eyes pulse relentlessly. Milky blue, they see every-thing, seem capable of excursions into June's yielding soul. The way the old lady looks at her, it's as if, June thinks, Rose knows some-thing, something about this place and June's place in this place, something everybody else suspects, maybe even feels, but only Rose really and truly *knows*.

Now then, what were we saying dear?

I was wondering, Rose, if you remembered when they changed the name to Wississauga?

Dear me, that was some time ago. They opened that big mall around the same time. Biggest mall in the country, they said. I was at the opening, you know. Must have been…oh…let's see now…1972? I would have been your age then.

No, June thinks. Older. Much older. Rose was already an old lady then. It's incredible, how long she's lived.

Of course I'd already lost my Morton.

They'd been through that on past visits. Tireless worker Morton who died in his 60s in the Sixties. It was the cancer, Rose told her. A cancer he surely got from his lifelong exposure to the chemicals that stewed in the bowels of Rose's beloved Great Lakes Starch Factory. Amazingly, Rose still seems to miss him. Did he hold her at night? Dance her around their small living room like they were a couple at the ball? Did he make her feel like she was the only thing that mattered?

Now as I recall there was politics involved. Politicians! Terrible. You see several towns were being put together. Mashed into one big city. That's what happened. And they said Walletville was a name from the past. They couldn't name the new city after any of the old towns. Politics. A name from the past! Can you imagine? I guess I'm from the past too.

No Rose, June says feebly.

Rose waves a dismissive hand. Paper-thin, it barely swirls the dusted air.

Of course I am. There's no need to lie to an old lady. It used to be just farms around here. Even the Indians used to farm up where that Country Club is now. Moved them off to god knows where. We used to walk to church, to school, the winters were terribly cold, the snow blowing up from the lake. We used to walk everywhere. There weren't all these cars like there are now. All this driving around. Everyone's from somewhere else, speaking who knows what language. The other day, some people knocked on my door, gave me quite a fright as you can imagine. A group of Chinamen going around talking about Jesus. I could barely understand them! Imagine, *them* telling *me* about Jesus! Now, dear, this must sound very old fashioned to you. But in my day, there wasn't all this...mixing. You know, there was nothing wrong with good old Walletville. Rose lowers her face. Her shaking claw elevates her teacup two inches off the table. She pinches her lips and sucks.

I...June says. I'm not from here.

Of course you aren't dear. Nobody is, anymore.

June isn't sure what they're talking about. She feels disappointed by this Rose. What is she saying? *Is she...? No! Things were different back then, everyone was probably from...England or something.* Rose doesn't mean any harm. She's just...stuck in another time, in the way it used to be. *She's leading up to something,* June tells herself. Something that really matters. June can't shake the sense that if she hangs around long enough, they'll get to the present, to June, to the problems of a thirty-one-year-old suburban house wife, a *queer* one, sure, why not? The truth peeling away under Rose's paint-thinner gaze. June looks down, looks at her watch surreptitiously. It's getting late. But she doesn't move. *Tell her,* she thinks suddenly. *Just tell her.*

Uh Rose? Her voice cracks as it comes out.

What is it dear?

I—uh—wanted to ask you something.

Yes dear?

I...

On the wall, a clown with a bouquet of pink roses, the garish oil still glistening under a layer of dust. When she dies they'll sell it. Five dollars at a garage sale. Who gets the money? Who gets what Rose is going to leave behind?

Go on now, dear.

June exhales. Remember, Rose, you were talking about...the Indians?

The Indians, yes.

How they used to live around here?

Yes, of course they did. Didn't I tell you that already? When I was a girl they had farms up where the Country Club is now. Then the government moved them off.

Where else did they live, Rose? I mean, before. Before they were at the golf course. Were they living other places...?

What do you mean dear? They lived on their reservation, of course.

But *before* that Rose.

Before that? Well before that they just lived...everywhere.

But, do you know *where* Rose? I mean, did they have...villages?

Some things are even before my time, dear. I'm not *that* old.

Of course not, Rose.

And it's not good to talk about it. The Indians.

Rose! Please!

Rose purses her lips, moistens them on the dark surface of the still steaming tea. Well, she finally intones, when I was girl we used to find old arrowheads and little bits of pottery down by the river.

The river?

Can't you hear me dear? The Indians used to catch salmon there. That's what they ate. My father told me that when he was a boy there were so many you could just reach in and grab one with your bare hands.

You mean…the Indians?

No dear! The salmon, of course.

In the river?

Well where else would the fish be?

How long ago was that, Rose?

Rose crinkles her furled face. She takes another teetering guzzle of tea.

Oh that was a long time ago now. We'd find all kinds of things down by the river. But we weren't allowed to keep them. Oh no. They were cursed.

But that's where they lived? By the river?

Well the Indians were moved off by the time the starch factory opened. And anyway that was the end of the fish in the river. But men have to make a living, now don't they?

Yes Rose.

Now that's enough of all this kind of talk. A bad business. What is it you were going to tell me?

I—

June takes a deep breath. A finger in her hair, twining a lustreless brown lock.

Rose I—

Now out with it! I don't have all day you know! Rose laughs, pale pink gums and a withered stub of tongue.

Rose, I…keep feeling like…like there's someone…in my house. Watching me.

What do you mean, dear?

I don't know, Rose. I don't mean someone. I mean, like, someone who—I know this sounds—but I keep getting this feeling…

Are you talking about a ghost, dear? The old lady looks her straight in the eye.

Do you believe in…ghosts, Rose?

Well I'm practically one myself, aren't I?

Rose! Don't say that!

Now then, there are all kinds of unfortunate spirits that walk the earth. May the good Lord Jesus claim their souls, dear.

Rose! You're making fun of me!

Certainly not. I haven't seen one myself, but when my great aunt Penny drowned after falling in the river, uncle Hamish used to see her once a year on her birthday. Because she went before her time, she did. Now then, did you get a look at it?

It?

The ghost, dear. The *en-tee-tee*. Did you see the ghost of a dead Indian?

Rose! I don't know if it's—I mean, I didn't, it wasn't a…

Now just calm down, dear. I don't mean to upset you.

You're not upsetting me Rose! It's just, I'm not even sure that—

It's bad luck talking about it. The Indians are cursed. Doomed. And their bones are…

What Rose?

Angry, dear.

June gulps lukewarm tea. Liquid going cool. How long has she been sitting here? In Rose's room, time seems to stop. Days pass, but no one notices. *Nutty old lady with her Indians and her Chinamen. Jesus Christ Rose, it's the twenty-first century.* Now, at last, June feels exhausted. Last night. Digging. She couldn't stop. She tore into the earth, threw huge clots of grass and dirt over her shoulder. She couldn't control herself. Her muscles sit heavy on her as if thick blankets have been wrapped around her arms and legs. But the weird thing is, she likes it, likes the feeling, the weight in her submerged flesh. She wants to go deeper and deeper into the ground until she's sunk under the firmament and disappeared into the truth, into what's been there all along.

June finds herself on her feet. Her legs feel thickly substantial. Outside, the steady reverb of traffic heading to and from that giant mall next door. Rose is right. About what she saw. The hole in her backyard. That man, watching her. How could it be good? It's—he's—

Life, June thinks, inadvertently catching Rose's pulsing blue eyes before quickly looking away. *Life. Then death.*

Since you're up dear, could you make me another cup of tea?

Alright, Rose.

TIM AND CHARLIE
Friday, April 11

HOT BUBBLE GUM BREATH tickles his wide forehead. Tim groans and rolls over. He sniffs the air and smells spring: unfurled leaves drying in a new breeze.

Mister?

Tim opens his eyes. A round brown face over him, coarse black braids straddling his cheeks.

Mister? Hey mister? Are you alright?

It's a girl.

Tim feels the cool forest floor pressing against his back. Behind the girl's concerned, frank stare, the tree—his tree—fills the void of the sky, stretches out of the gorge toward the sun. Suddenly remembering, Tim jerks into a sitting position. He almost butts heads with her. She jumps back just in time. Tim examines his arms and legs, his joints creaking. Nothing broken. He's fine. How can he be *fine*?

He doesn't know. He must have climbed down out of the tree somehow. Otherwise, he'd be—

Tim looks around him. What does he expect to see? Piles of spotted bones? Some weird totem warning in the form of branches bundled together to conceal a wet, warm heart? Carly says he spends too much time getting high and watching movies.

—Carly—

He was supposed to drive home last night. She wasn't even going to notice he'd been gone. Guilt surges through him. He was in the tree. His tree. He saw—and smelled—and most importantly, *he felt*. He felt her. Something. *Someone*. Not *someone*. *It was my*—Tim shakes his head slowly. He can't think that. Jump up, run back to the car, put the key in the engine. He'll apologize, explain as much as he can. He'll tell her what happened. He doesn't know, of course. Something happened. *Carly*, he thinks. *Carly will know*. He'll tell her: a sweet hot smell; a touch ever so gently curling down the arc of his chin; then a light; that woman—

That woman. She was digging. It was the middle of the night and she was digging. What was she digging, out there in the dark and the rain?

The girl, her eyes wide, the whites highlighting dark brown pupils, is backing away. She looks at him warily, preparing to flee.

Hey, he calls. You got the time?

Charlie stops, a startled doe caught in the headlights. There are deer in the gorge, she knows, she's seen them. Lots of them.

Tim inspects the girl now. Pudgy and shapeless in a red parka meant for the dead of winter. She wears cheap gold-wire glasses, small for her face, ridiculous braids accentuating her bulgy brown-red cheeks.

It's cool, he says as she resumes her slow retreat, her back edging out of the clearing into the underbrush. I just wanna know the time.

The girl pulls out a cell phone. She looks at the little screen.

4:22, she says shyly in a voice just hinting at a lilting accent. After school, she adds.

Tim nods. After school. Okay, it's coming back to him. He climbed down the tree. Must have. He doesn't remember that part.

But he remembers it being morning, late morning, probably. He remembers reading the letter. He paced around the clearing. He refolded the letter, put it in his pocket, then unfolded it and read it again. He smoked up. He lay down on his back to watch the branches and the sky and the clouds. *I must have—closed my eyes, for a bit, there.*

You go to school around here?

The girl nods. Christopher Columbus.

Yeah, huh? I went there.

The girl takes a step closer. You did? she says in a small voice.

Yeah. Like. A long time ago.

Oh.

It sucked.

The girl stares fiercely.

The breeze pushes through. The late afternoon sun dapples down, forms patterns of light and dark. Two chipmunks chase each other through the dead leaves, kicking up a dust of decay. Tim feels the urgency of last night seeping out of him, ache becoming lassitude.

Hey, he says casually. Aren't you a little young to be down here?

I'm allowed. Charlie blushes.

That's cool, Tim says. No problem.

The girl's glare softens.

I used to live around here you know. He points to the top of the gully. Up there. You live around here too?

Charlie blinks, plays with her hands.

Whatever. It's cool. I'm Tim, by the way.

I'm…she hesitates. But there's something about him, this guy, Tim, his broad open face and pale blue eyes. He doesn't look dangerous. Not even a little. I'm Charlie.

Cool. Cool name. Charlie.

That's not my real name.

What's your real name?

The girl—Charlie—shrugs.

Doesn't matter, right?

She nods.

So, uh, Charlie. You, uh, got anything to eat?

Charlie looks at him doubtfully.

I, uh, forgot to bring food and I'm on, like, a camping trip here. I'm just trying to, clear my head, you know?

And you're not eating?

Uh…yeah…kinda, I guess.

Like the Natives! I read a book all about it! They would go out into the woods and pray and stuff. They wouldn't eat for a whole month! Not until they had a vision.

Like…Indians?

It's called a vision quest.

So…what were they trying to see?

Charlie takes a step closer. Their animal totem! Their spirit animal!

Huh. Tim considers the girl, framed by the giant tree above them both. Her pudgy face, her eyes in coke-bottle blurs. A vision. Is that what he had? Some kind of—

But uh, like, you know, of what exactly?

Charlie shrugs.

So…Tim tries. You're…Indian?

No…

But, you're, uh—

We're from *In-di-a*. It's totally different.

Oh. Right. Cool. That's cool.

Charlie looks down at her knock-off sneakers. She's embarrassed now.

Hey, Tim says. Don't worry about it.

The girl sneaks a hand into her coat pocket.

I've got these. She proffers a roll of Lifesaver candies.

What flavour?

Wild berry blast.

Nice.

You want one?

Tim nods.

Charlie walks to where Tim sits, his knobby knees pulled into his chest. She crouches, extends the roll.

Can I have two?

She stares balefully. Alright.

Tim rolls the candies around in his mouth. Their sticky sweet coats his tongue. That other taste—the sour lingering of fear—recedes. What's there to be scared of? It's all starting to make sense. He gets it now. He'll tell it all to Carly. This is what he's come for. It's like the girl says: a quest, a vision. He clicks candies against his teeth.

You're not supposed to bite them, Charlie protests.

I'm not.

Like this. Charlie sucks slowly.

Tim copies, pulling in his cheeks.

Charlie giggles. I'm not really allowed to have candy, she announces.

At all?

She shrugs. I still get it, though.

But, I mean, at all?

She shrugs again.

Your parents are crazy strict, dude.

I guess. Charlie inspects the colourful striped wrapper.

Hey, Tim says quickly, these, uh, Indians. They ever see anything like…really weird?

What do you mean?

Like, uh, you know, I dunno, like…ghosts or stuff?

Charlie jumps up.

Sure! All the time! Sometimes they wouldn't see animals at all! They'd see the water spirit, the fire spirit, all kinds of stuff. I bet they even saw stuff right here.

Here?

Sure! There were lots and lots of Natives who lived right here.

This is where they lived? The Indians?

Sure! I've read all about it. Only you're not supposed to say Indians. *I'm* Indian. You're supposed to say *Naaa-tives*.

Okay, but, I mean, they lived *right* here?

Sure, they had their villages all along the river. I read about it in the library.

And they saw ghosts and stuff?

All the time!

Like, what kinds though? What kinds exactly?

I told you! Spirits! Fire spirit, water spirit, wind spirit. Sometimes they saw the spirits of their ancestors.

Their mom and dad and stuff?

No! Like way older than that! Like their great great great grandfather who would come in the form of an eagle, but they would know right away that it wasn't an eagle; it was their ancestor who was a great and powerful medicine man!

Not their parents?

No! You go on a spirit quest when you're *my* age.

Yeah, but, I mean, what if, like, their dad was like a great warrior or something and he, yeah know, got killed in a big battle. Then maybe they'd see him? What if they were, like, dead, your parents?

You're weird.

Tim crunches the last bit of thin crystalline candy between his teeth. I'm just asking, he says. You're the one who's going on about Indians.

I told you. You're supposed to say *Naaa-tives.*

Natives. Alright. Whatever.

The Natives lived down here for hundreds and thousands of years. And anyway, I know where—Charlie stops. She puts a hand over her mouth.

What? You know where what?

Nothing! Forget it!

Okay. Chill out. Don't have a shit fit.

A what? Charlie giggles.

A *shit* fit.

Ha ha.

Say it.

I'm not saying that!

Why not? There's no one else here.

Wind rushes through the upper branches of the giant maple.

I gotta go, Charlie announces.

Hey!

The girl disappears into the woods.

Tim flops back on his back. He stares up at the tree. Its branches are dotted with leaves emerging from their bud cocoons. Winter is over. The sun in patches on his face. He's exhausted. He closes his eyes. He has to get going. Call Carly. Go see his father. Then leave this place. Leave it forever. But he doesn't move. His bones want to stay here. *A change of plan,* he thinks. The girl—Charlie. Nerd type. Making up a bunch of stuff. Indians. Trying to impress him. What's she doing down here anyway? Indians. She doesn't know what she's talking about. *Indians didn't live here. I never heard anything about that. I mean, wouldn't there be a museum or something?* But something about what she said rings true. Visions. A quest. Last night. Something was revealed to him. A great big shimmering piece to the puzzle of his life. Whatever happened—to him, to his mother—finally within his grasp.

Tim sits up. He opens his eyes. His legs are stretched out in front of him. His body seems wrong, an occupying presence, an anomaly. He should be dead. Or at least broken.

I climbed down. Somehow.

His clothes are still damp, almost wet. It rained last night. A lot. At least it's warm. I was high. I was really fucking high.

He's remembering now: he was up in the tree. The rain was coming down hard. His entire body was shaking. Different kinds of cold. Varieties of cold. He never thought there were so many ways to be cold. That's what he remembers most. How cold it was. Then it got colder.

Late. It was really late. I feel asleep. I woke up. It was—

The rest of it comes back to him, spill-over ferment filling him like some internal upchuck. A cold in his chest, in his heart, a slow cold spreading up his veins. It was so cold he couldn't breathe. Then there was that smell. It's still with him, familiar the way absence becomes familiar. Something touched him, his face. *Yeah. Sure. A leaf or something.* Something touched his chin, his cheek, his throat. Gently.

His heart pounding.

It wasn't a leaf.

Tim feels his throat. He swallows his bobbing Adam's apple. Stubble demarcation of a nascent beard.

Dead Indians. Why not? Maybe they did live here. Maybe they're still here, drifting around, waiting, waiting for someone to give a shit. Sorry. Too late. Nobody cares around here. You're in the wrong suburb. Try downtown, try Queen and Cowan, where Tim and Carly live—it's so sad, Carly always says, referring to the bums out there on the street begging for change. Yeah, Tim agrees, shrugging. But there's nothing particularly special about them. They're just another bunch of addicts—white, red, brown, yellow. This has nothing to do with—

Indians.

Tim touches his throat, grazes skin with the tips of his fingers. Last night, what he saw. It wasn't a ghost. It was more like—*what that girl said—*

A vision.

Carly believes in visions. She believes you can see things that aren't there. The forest floor, all soft putrefaction. Leaves and pinecones and ants and beetles and branches slowly slumping into clay. That shovel flaring in the storm, reflecting lightning, reflecting a face lost in backlit glare. Someone digging in his old backyard. Digging into the perfect patch of grass his father laboured over all that hazy, humid, endless summer. So now what? Now what are you going to do? Of course it was just his imagination playing tricks. Some kind of weird wishful thinking burbling up from his subconscious. Carly's got half a degree in psychology. Tim's going to help her. He's going to pay her tuition so she can go back to school and make something of herself.

But right now he needs to clear his head. And he should call Carly, tell her where he is, tell her he's okay.

But first he just needs to…take the edge off. A relief to have such an obvious relief. He pulls out his stash.

SUSAN
Friday, April 11

SUSAN PROUDFEATHER watches through a dirty window as the bus crawls up Hurontarion toward the Middle Mall. Outside is overcast and distant, a crowded rush-hour scene framed by bumper-to-bumper traffic and adorned with a low grey sky. Inside, there are the inescapable confines of the bus slowly pressing in on her: the wheeze of air vents, the sickly surges forward, the pulling whine of brakes. A baby cries over the faint murmur of her mother. Somewhere behind her, a man snores loudly. Susan's fingers twine around the off-white cord of her headphones, no longer attached to the iPod that lost power somewhere around Thunder Bay. *Keep still*, she tells herself, trying to repress the surges of anxiety jolting through her heavy limbs. Abruptly, Susan draws a deep breath and exhales. *It's okay*, she tells herself. *You're almost there.*

This image—of the end to the endlessness—doesn't help. She imagines disgorging into the bowels of the sprawling Middle Mall, still trailed by pale flickering light the colour of exhaust and over-whelmed antiseptic, colours seeping into smells, her senses dulled and rendered pointless. The whole scene fraught with the same sapping melancholy she's been struggling to leave behind since departing the far coast five days ago. *Five days on a bus,* Susan thinks. That will do things to you.

But that's not it. Not all of it. Shane came to see her off. He'd wanted her to stay. Suggested that they set up together in a squat he knew of, Downtown Eastside, of course, rough but roomy, he joked—and rent-free! He smiled his I'm-broke-but-who-cares broken grin, and Susan couldn't help but smile back. She'd told him all along that she wouldn't be staying, that she wasn't looking for a long-term thing. Of course he hadn't believed her. She'd seen it enough times to know how it was going to play out. What she said wasn't taken at face value, was seen as some kind of protective mechanism, a default masking of her inner vulnerability. Eventually, thought whichever man she was bedding at the moment, she'd let down her guard, let him scale the perfectly understandable wall and saunter into the inner sanctum where he'd find the girl who really did need a man, even if she didn't want to admit it.

Only, this time, maybe Shane really had known what she needed. Like the song goes, Susan thinks bitterly: *You don't know what you've got till it's gone.* Shane, inexhaustible optimist despite being a refugee from the flat apathetic middle of a big apathetic country. Shane, whose Cree mother still lived on a reservation "back home," as he put it, and whose white father had long since absented himself. In the months out West attending the endless series of protests, meetings, hearings, and—hardest of all—depositions of the families of the dead and missing women, Shane had been her solace. She could still feel his lean chest against hers, his rough palms—hardened by years of tree planting and casual construction work—running over her body. Not to mention his quick wit, his refusal to believe that things couldn't be helped, his encyclopedic knowledge of the people's struggles all over the world. And of course his smile, so big and bright—too big and bright.

So she missed him and she didn't want to miss him. *But that's not it either*, she impatiently tells herself. She'd been out West for almost a year. The government had finally caved, a commission announced, her group's depositions and files submitted to the courts and entered into the permanent record. She'd racked her brains and talked endlessly with Shane and the rest of the ad hoc collective— what else could they do? They couldn't find them. No one can find the dead. Sitting in meetings, twirling her finger in a paper cup of weak lukewarm coffee, she'd begun to feel that familiar swirling restlessness: knock back your drink, read the grounds, what's left at the bottom, auger up the future, keep moving toward whatever's coming next. You're a restless soul. She'd heard that more than once. Most recently, May, a woman she'd met—the cousin of one of the disappeared—took her to meet her aunt, a shriveled Elder living alone in a tiny house several long bus rides away and out of the glittering emerald Pacific city. May's aunt gave them tomato soup and, eventually, took Susan's hand, looked into her face at length, and said kindly through gummy lips, Where's your place girl? May—face pockmarked by hard living, lover of heavy metal and loud powwows—had burst out laughing. She doesn't have a *place* auntie! Susan's cheeks had burned, from shame and revelation.

The bus jolts to a stop for a red light. Left lane, one last turn, and she's back. *This is your place.* She knows how it looks. Like she's failed. Like she's coming crawling back. The strange doppelganger irony of it—her journey ending the same way so many of the girls and women started and ended theirs. Debbie, 19, last seen boarding the Greyhound bus to Lethbridge to stay with her best friend. No record of arrival. Eden, 26, boarded a bus to Surrey to visit her second cousin. No record of arrival. Dakota, 16, boarded a bus to Prince Rupert, was asked to leave the bus due to erratic, possibly drug-induced, behaviour. Last seen hitchhiking the Yellowhead Highway on a grainy afternoon gone prematurely dark. No record of arrival.

Of course, she's not like them. She's not running away. She's not setting out into the night hoping against reason for a new chance, a new life magically free of centuries of genocide, institutional racism, and a legacy of poverty and addiction. She isn't ruled by fear. She has, as a point of principle, always refused to be. Look at all the people in the world who live without jobs, without knowing where their next meal will come from, whose pension is a couple of crumpled bills and a handful of rattling coins dropped in a jar. But even with every-thing we have, she thinks, we are afraid. It's an addiction, the desire to control our surroundings, to know where we're going before we even get there. Where is she going? She never could get used to the misty wet weather of the Northwest Pacific winter; a feeling in her bones—time to go. Over the last few months of meetings and report writing culminating in that final Pyrrhic victory, snapshot images kept flashing in her mind: her old school—Columbus High; the ravine where they gathered on a Saturday night to pass around a bottle and a joint; the sprawling suburban colonial with its wall-papered walls and wall-to-wall carpeting, the '80s haven she grew up in. There was nothing particularly notable about the images, the fleeting flashes of memory, except they repeated themselves with exponential intensity, seeped into her dreams and filled her with a sense of dread and foreboding. Eventually she accepted it—some-thing was pulling at her, pulling her east, pulling her home, of all places. *Home*. Or, at least, the place where she grew up. It was here where she came of age, where she fought and railed against her par-ents, her school and its stupid teachers, where she eventually drove away her few friends with her insistence on endlessly chronicling the evils of the Western world in general and the Wississaugan way of life in particular.

The bus lurches into that final left turn and moves down the ramp into its underground arrival point. Susan feels her stomach sink as they descend. *This*, she thinks, *this is it.*

Susan twists and untwists the tangled headphone cord around her fingers. She's here, she tells herself, so that's where she's meant to be. Goodbye Shane. Goodbye vistas of mountains and towering cedars and tall buildings glittering in the mist. Goodbye parks blighted by needles, goodbye homeless addicts panhandling outside the EL, goodbye Eden and Debbie and Dakota, missing, lost, presumed dead—women written off almost before they were born. The bus ticket cost about a tenth of the total sitting in her credit union account. When the time finally came, she hadn't hesitated. She never did. She'd bought the ticket, promised Shane she'd keep in touch, and climbed on board.

Her father picks her up at the station. He's fashionably dressed, as always, in a sleek-fitting tan sports jacket and brown slacks. He's greyer than when she last saw him—more than a year ago—but still trim and vital. He hugs her, his handsome face crinkling into a smile and she leans into him, her head on his shoulder. She feels herself relax for the first time since she clambered on board the first bus.

Susie, his father breathes in her ear.

They separate after a moment and she follows him through the underground parking lot to his car, a ruby red, leather-embossed Honda she hasn't seen before and doesn't remark on.

Thanks for coming to get me, Dad, Susan says as they coast smoothly out of the parking lot and onto the main drag. She fingers the automatic window opener and, unable to resist, rolls the window all the way down, letting the cold air wash over her face.

Of course, her father says. It's great to see you.

You too, Dad.

They drive in silence for a few stoplights before her dad asks, Are you hungry? Should we stop for something?

Susan, who had eaten the last of her trail mix twelve hours back and had been unable to bring herself to buy any of the items they passed off as food at the suffusion of smoke break rest stop donut and burger joints that marked the final stage of the journey, nods. Let's do that, Dad, she says softly. She sees his hand on the gearshift. It looks smaller than she remembers. She covers his hand with her own palm.

Over their meal—a large kale, strawberry, and pecan salad for Susan, curried butternut squash soup of the day for her dad—her father tells her about the educational cruise he's about to take with his girlfriend. The boat, apparently, comes equipped with experts on everything from marine life to the local tribal culture. He chatters on, delicately avoiding the series of questions her parents inevitably and eventually put to her. The same questions over and over again ever since she'd dropped out of university a decade ago in the middle of her junior year. She'd helped organize her campus's contribution to a massive rally, a protest against world leaders gathering to ratify yet another secretive agreement meant, Susan had come to realize, to further codify the systematic denial of the vast majority of people on the planet the basics needed for human dignity and liberty. She hadn't actually meant to drop out. She'd woken up in a sleeping bag on the floor of someone's flat in Quebec City, her eyes still oozing stinging tear gas ether and her mind reeling with images from the protest the police had seemed determined to turn violent.

Her friends and accomplices had been clubbed, gassed, hauled off. Susan had been stunned. She was due back at school the next day. School! Her joint degree in Women's and Native Studies overseen by a gaggle of fussy professors with a collective fetish for social justice and historical grievances—talking talking talking while the world quite literally burned to the ground.

Her father had taken the departure from school in stride. Susan, at the time, had the feeling that he even supported her. But as the days turned into years, her dad fell silent in the face of her mother's ardent disapproval—all this activism and caring is great, honey, but what about a career? What about settling down? Have you met anyone special, honey? How are you for money, dear? *Taking care of number one*, Susan thinks. *That's the way it's supposed to be.* Hobby liberalism, token concern.

Are you still hungry? her father asks as Susan stabs the flecks of green at the bottom of her bowl. She's avoiding looking at him, doesn't want to give him an opening, doesn't want to have to see the worry in his face. She's skinny and her clothes are faded and rumpled and hanging off her, and she smells like stale sweat and bus bathroom and itinerant cigarette exhale. She looks older, she knows. She's felt herself age this last year, her face etched beyond its thirty-three years, her pale orange hair starting to grey. So what can she tell him? Is she still hungry? Is she?

Finally, she wills herself to look up. Dad, she says, thanks for—all this. I hope I'm not—I didn't mean to barge in and—

It's no problem, he says. It's been way too long.

She nods, smiling shyly at him.

So…her father says, delicately returning his coffee cup to its saucer. How were things out West? I read about some of it…in the papers.

He speaks, now, with a halting tone. Does he really want to know? Before he retired, her father supported causes, lent his graphic design firm's talents to developing posters for Greenpeace and ads for anti-bullying campaigns. He isn't bad, Susan tells herself. He asked. So he wants to know.

Dad, it was…it's hard to…The plunge she felt in the pit of her stomach as the bus entered the underground parking lot beneath the Middle Mall abruptly returns. Oh! Susan gasps. Feeling the room start to spin, she drops her face in her hands.

Hey, she hears her father say lamely. Are you okay?

Susan isn't a crier. All that time out West, meeting with the families of the murdered and the disappeared, looking at their fresh-faced pictures, their happy smiles and beaded dresses and glossy pigtails, she didn't cry, not once. They cried. Susan could not—would not—cry. She didn't deserve that. Not even in the end. They had cheered the announcement and some had cried. It was what the families wanted—I know she's not coming back, a pale, grizzled dad had told her during one of the depositions. Clutching a picture of his daughter to his scrawny chest he addressed Susan with righteous intensity. I know that. I just…I don't want this to happen to anyone else. The man had been crying, tears dripping on the snapshot of his little girl. Susan had felt like crying then and several other times, but had been able to push it away. What had they done? What victory had they earned?

I'm…Susan wipes her face with a napkin.

It's okay, her dad says.

No, Susan says fiercely. It's not okay.

In the car she apologizes to him. She feels embarrassed now amidst new leather bucket seats and a voice-activated Bluetooth-enabled satellite radio system. Their family has never been expressive. None of them are criers. When her parents split up seven or so years ago, they came to see her. They told her the news, and she'd nodded and murmured bloodlessly: If that's what you think is best. Susan closes her eyes, leans back against the perfectly firm seat. She's just so tired.

She barely remembers it happening—her dad leading her into the house she mostly grew up in. Showering in the spare bathroom, then wrapping herself in a plush towel and padding over to her childhood bedroom. Sliding into sheets tinged with a vaguely recognizable scent. Falling instantly asleep.

TIM
Friday, April 11

NIGHTTIME. Tim feels like he's the only one on foot in all of Wississauga. He pulls up the zipper of his thin jacket. Army surplus, its drab green lends him a menacing don't-screw-with-me vibe, helpful for dealing with the rich kids, the hockey and football types who think they can intimidate him into discount dime bags. He bought it after Clay pressed him into service. Welcome to the team, Clay said unctuously, slapping him on the back. He hasn't told Carly he's been promoted to dealing pot in the alley behind the bar during breaks and after work. She'll be pissed. *She's right. It's a bad idea.* But he said yes anyway. What else was he going to do? He already owed Clay a few grand by then. The situation, Clay said, speaking in that slow careful way of his, is becoming untenable. Tim hadn't actually known what the word meant at the time. But he'd gotten the idea.

Part of him likes it. He likes the way his customers tiptoe around him—as if a wrong word or look will send him into a deadly rage. People watch too much TV. Anyway, he bought the jacket figuring he might as well look the part. He was even gonna shave his head. Buzz-cut. Travis Bickle badass. Yeah he's a real tough-guy, hoofing it down the suburban sidewalk. *You talking to me? You talking to me?* Tim blinks, blinded by passing headlights. Cars cruise by in exhaust wakes, their taillights glowing as they slow to get a look at him once he's safely in the rear. He suppresses the urge to flip them off. He sticks out. They want to know who he is. Just a guy going for a walk, he thinks. Is that such a crime? You should try it sometime. It's how we used to do it. Anyway, he's on a quest. Who drives around in an assembly-line pseudo-sporty aging Pontiac reeking of stale smoke and sweaty patchouli when they're on a god-damned honest-to-god quest?

The car wouldn't start. So he's on foot.

It shouldn't be too far, from what he remembers. The street in question was just a tree-lined conduit in his day, a shortcut between the main drag and the less opulent working class neigh-bourhoods that were slowly spreading south from the 472. A street called Victory Drive, a long dark speedway framed by thick forest. This is where his father lives now. In some place called the Victory Colonnades. What the hell is a colonnade? Carly would laugh. She'd say, smiling, How am I supposed to know? But she'd know.

Tim turns up the collar of his jacket. He puts on an angry face, glaring at oncoming headlights. He left his cell at home. When he gets to his dad's place, he'll call Carly. First thing, Tim tells himself. *I shouldn't have just—*

He hoofs on past a sprawling new high school, concrete complex complete with multiple parking lots and sports fields. Used to be all woods here. Across the street, a housing development squashed together in semi-detached efficiency, each domicile adorned with a two-car garage in lieu of lawn. Tim keeps moving. Further on, three or four condo high-rises sticking into the night sky. *Victory Colonnades*, Tim thinks.

He looks up to find himself lapped by two women in spandex and name brand running shoes. They huff silently as they move past him, weights in belts entrapping their ankles and wrists. The women each carry a plastic bottle of designer water. Tim feels their stares. *Who, me? I'm nothing to worry about ladies. Just little old Timmy. From the neighbourhood.*

What neighbourhood?

Nothing looks quite right. But it all seems familiar. None of it was here the last time he was on this street. What does he expect? That was more than ten years ago. Everything's changed, only as he walks, Tim feels a familiar constriction in his chest. Regret, remembrance, revenge—the noose tightening around his heart reminding him. He doesn't want to forgive him. He doesn't want to see him. Whatever he has to say, it doesn't matter anymore. Not after—

last night.

Tim can still smell it—*her*—time unearthed moment by moment, a truth in feeling. He knows. He *knows*. Whatever happened, Tim's got his answer. Maybe he's not ready to say it. Or even think it. But he knows, he knows what he has to do: dig into the dirt; hold what he can with his bare hands and do his best to cover up what's sunk in too deep and too decayed to ever pull out. The clouds shift and a sheen of hazy moonlight lights up the long empty sidewalk in front of him. He puts his head down and picks up the pace.

Tim pulls on the handle of the building's front door and feels glass rattle against a lock. You have to buzz up, he realizes. *Sure. No problem. Hey Dad. I'm baaack! Yeah, it's been a while. Like, uh, twelve years. So I got your letter. I heard you were on your way out. Figured I'd drop by to give you one last chance to tell me—*

He didn't look for her, Tim thinks. He never looked for her. He didn't look for Tim either. *You had a wife and son, you fuck. Once*

upon a time. And then you didn't. That doesn't bother you? You ever
kinda wonder where they went?

Last night.

It's true, he'll tell Carly. A vision like that girl said.

I know, you fuck. So just say it. Admit it.

Then I'll—

Shove that letter up his—

Here's your letter ya fuck. Choke on it.

You're so angry. Why are you always so angry?

—Carly—

Tim ducks behind a potted bush so green and luminous he
thinks it must be fake. He rips a leaf. Huh. It's real. The plant looks
nothing like the scraggly, denuded plants in the river gully. A vertical glistening emerald, it smells different too, chemical and soapy,
weirdly clean. A lady and her stroller-entombed baby push out of
the entrance. Tim waits and then steps quickly to the closing door.
He silently sticks a hand in the diminishing crack.

The door crunches on his fingers. *Aww. Fuck.* Anyway, he's in.
He wiggles his swelling fingers and looks around. It's a dimly lit
lobby adorned with thrift store chairs and several more aggressively shiny plants. The trapped odour of cooked food and wrinkled
feet sticks in Tim's nostrils. This is it? He imagined his father in
something swank: uniformed doormen, walls of upholstered velvet,
mirrors on the ceilings, marble floors polished too slippery. Not
some cheap building full up with old stink.

He takes the elevator up to the tenth floor. The fingers of Tim's
hurt hand pulse in a tight fist. He should have smoked on the way.
Now it's too late. He could go back down. Roll a fatty. Why not?
What's the hurry? He wishes Carly were here. She'd understand. She'd

tell him to take his time. She'd tell him that he needs to be patient, that he needs to give himself space and *evolve* toward the moment.

Whatever that means.

—*Carly*—

Ding, short ride, he arrives too soon. He slinks down the corridor. What if he isn't evolving? What if there isn't a moment? He knocks, the sound ringing hollow.

Knocks.

Knocks.

Not home? Where else would he be? Out on a hot date? He's supposed to be sick. Dying. Tim hits the door. The thud feels loud on the palm of his hand, but disappears into an echo absorbed by the musty carpeted halls.

Hello? he tries. His voice comes out tinny.

Nothing. Nobody.

Tim pounds the door. He rattles the knob. The door, unlocked, swings open.

Tim stands in the entryway hearing his own breath pushing hot blood into his throbbing clenched fingers. The apartment is dark. He waits for his eyes to adjust. *Dad!* he thinks. *I'm home!* Home. He isn't home. Anyway, there's nobody here. He's too late, he thinks. The tightness, sweat beading his forehead, it's hard for him to breath. *Too goddamn late. The old man's*—

Even the smell, like something left behind: sweat and canned soup and Band-Aids. A death smell, hospitals, old age homes, places where they drape a sheet over what's left and wheel it away.

Tim creeps down the hall into the living room. The sharp edge of a coffee table digs into his shin and he stumbles.

A lamp flicks on. Tim blinks. He sees the couch first. Forest green leather he recognizes from the sold homestead. Then: almost lost in the couch's cavernous corner, a withered, slumped creature. Tim thinks of victims on the History Channel—prisoners or survivors.

They stare at each other.

Dad?

The wan slumped figure raises his head and Tim freezes. Bulging, yellowed eyes shimmering with anger, disgust, and triumph. It's him. Tim stares back, trapped and wild and barely able to breathe. Suddenly, the man—his father—doubles over and retches into the plastic bucket on the floor at his feet.

Throat. Cancer. Tim, perched on the opposite edge of the couch as far away as possible from the skeletal imposter father, feels his own throat constrict. They. His father speaks in one word guttural gasps. Can't. Do. Nuh. Thing. He gags and coughs, his neck bulging and swollen, strangled from the inside.

So, Tim says, how, uh, long…

His dad shrugs.

Shouldn't you be—is anyone—?

Nurse. Left.

She left?

Quit.

His father reaches for his smokes. He pulls one out with a shaking hand and drops it. Tim doesn't help him. The errant cigarette rolls along the coffee table. Both men trail its path with their eyes. On the kitchen counter, a stack of tins: Ensure High Protein Drink.

You supposed to be drinking those?

Tim's dad shrugs. Points to the bucket.

Jesus, Dad.

Son, Tim's dad whispers.

Son? The word tastes bad, bile floods Tim's dry-dust mouth.

You. Got. The. Let. Ter?

Yeah, I got it.

In the lamplight, Tim sees invisible movement, micro-abscesses, migrations of disease. Tim's dad leans over the bucket again. His face darkens with effort and finally a wad of blackish slime drips out.

Uh...Dad?

His father collapses back against the couch, gasping for breath.

Dad?

Tim looks down at the cluttered table, looks away. *Say it*, he thinks. *Why don't you just fucking say it?* His dad is doing something now, with his hands. Tugging at a finger. Tim pulls the letter out of his pocket. He holds it in a fist, slowly crumpling the thin piece of paper. *Say it. You have to say it. He's dying. So what? So fucking what?*

Take it, his father mutters, extending his thin quivering hand. Tim remembers a different set of hands. Strong and thick and swollen. Fingers like juicy sausages. Bursting fists.

The man, a stranger, proffering a shaking palm.

A gold ring. His wedding band.

Take. It. Their eyes lock and Tim, again, sees him—the man he remembers, good old Dad, bloodshot black moon pupils as arrogant and hungry as ever. *He knew*, Tim thinks. *He knew I'd show up.* His father stares into him, eyes blazing, hand outstretched. The dulled ring dances in his quivering hand.

Don't take it. Don't even touch it.

Tim snatches the ring off his father's white palm. He weighs it in his own hand. It's heavy, heavier than Tim thought it would be. *Now what? Put it on? No. Throw it in his face, shove it down his throat.* His father looks on and, for the first time, Tim sees something else, something he doesn't recognize, in the man's expression. Tim's fingers curl around, the ring forming the centre of a fist. His dad, just some old dying man, closes his eyes and drops his chin to his pajama-chest.

Tim's dad is slumped, semi-conscious, his chest heaving air against an almost closed throat. Tim sits in the easy chair across from him, ring in one hand, long thin unlit joint in the other. Time in moments. In seconds. In gasps. *Wake up*, Tim thinks over and over. *Wake up wake up wake up.*

Finally, the old man stirs. He wheezes, coughs.

Hey, Tim says. Are you—how do you feel?

His father regards him balefully. Tim hears what he's thinking, what the old man would be saying if he could get the words out: Like a big bag of shit, asshole. How the fuck do you think I feel?

Or something to that effect. Carly says Tim talks like he's in a bad movie. You should hear my freaking dad talk, Tim says. Another reason to hate his father, who inculcated him in the many glories of the catch phrase: *Use it or lose it. No point flogging a dead horse. Early bird catches the worm. Old enough to bleed, old enough to breed—*

Ugh, gross! He *said* that to you?

Tim doesn't remember now. Did he say that to him? Did he say any of it? He remembers a burly man with a loud barking voice used to issuing commands and orders. An excessive man who smacked his lips, ate takeout Chinese with grotesque gusto, grease smearing on his chin. Tim should have known that he would never admit to—*to what?*—to *it*. To anything.

Dad, Tim says quickly. We're going to—I want you to smoke this. It'll help. Okay?

It's true. Clay sold to cancer patients. He charges them extra, Tim remembers him saying.

He makes room for himself on the couch. The smell is strong next to his father: stale sweat and fresh vomit. Tim lights the joint. He holds it to the old man's lips.

Here, he says.

His dad sucks in. He closes his eyes.

Tim does the same.

His dad exhales, doesn't cough.

Tim cracks open a can of protein drink. They sit smoking the rest of the joint in a condo silence extenuated by the barely perceptible sound of the TV news from next door. After a few more hits, the old guy chokes down a few sips. Then, cheeks flush, his dad looks around, suddenly more animated. Tim watches, feeling that ever-present tightening in his chest—desperation, last chance hope. *Do it*, he thinks. *Say it*. He stares at his father, now nothing more than a wasted heap. Tim wants his dad to glare back, wants him to let loose from his full, fleshy lips with one of his patented streams of all too familiar aphorisms: *Be careful what you wish for. The apple doesn't fall far from the tree. Don't kick the messenger. Don't knock it till you've tried it!* And then a couple of stinging slaps on the back for good measure. *Fuck you.* Tim feels that familiar rage coursing through him, his muscles cordoned, his fists tight. *Fuck you, you dying old fuck.*

You killed her, he finally says, staring down at the thin, frayed carpet. His ears buzz. He can't tell if he's whispering or shouting. You killed her and you buried her in the backyard and you planted grass over her. Fucking *grass*.

No, the old man says. He shakes his head frantically, pants laboured breaths.

Tim had always believed that he'd find her, one day, that she was out there, maybe even looking for him too. But now he knows the truth. What he's always known.

She wouldn't have left me, he says. She wouldn't have done that.

No! Tim's dad groans. No!

Last night. He saw—

She's gone; he knows that now. Whatever happened, she's gone.

No, his father says again, muttering now, sounding unsure. No...grass...

Tim's father closes his eyes and leans back. He breathes easy.

Dad? For fuck's sake, Dad. Are you fucking *high*?

Tim stands up. He digs a hand into his pocket and pulls out a thick zip-lock. Part of his stash. Most of his stash. He looks, one last time, at this old man, this wasted stranger. He drops the bulging bag on the coffee table next to the open can of protein drink and his dad's pack of Pall Malls.

HAL AND SCOTT
Saturday, April 12

THE CAR LOT is separated from the Pacific Lucky Dragon Mall by a groomed park filled with unfamiliar oriental flora: mini-trees with emerging red leaves, compact bushes cut into the shapes of bugs and animals, bright pink peonies and delicate white chrysanthemums reaching for the not-quite arrived spring. Ponds gently gurgle, seemingly awaiting the time when a fresh crop of oversized, bulgy-eyed goldfish once again swirl complacently in their murky depths. Hal can see that there are several such parks surrounding the Mall, their benches occupied by Chinese grandmothers bundled in cloth coats and quietly chatting in the shade of paper lamps. It's like they've stepped into another country. But no one bothers them, gangly giants—especially Scott—amidst all this intricate foreign perfection.

So they keep going, following a tiled path to the main square. The Pacific Lucky Dragon Mall is a huge building built to look like a series of interlocking pagodas. From a distance, it seems quaint. But up close, the building looms, a succession of engulfing boxes, the main one decorated with ubiquitous Chinese characters and a gigantic mural relief: two impassive snakes entangled with each other, their serpentine forms curling off the walls.

Hal glances over at Scott, wanting to catch his eye. So what do you think? It was Hal's idea, a rare outing for them that didn't involve going directly from Scott's suv into Hal's apartment. Sarah did a story on the Chinese mall, how it was a hub for the local community and was also becoming a popular regional attraction, people coming all the way from the city for the shopping, the food court, the stacks of illegally copied Hollywood movies still in theatres. Hal suggested they go check it out. He promised Scott lunch, Scott loves Chinese—moo shu pork, egg rolls, Kung Pao chicken, all regular items on their delivery itinerary. I dunno, Scott said noncommittally. C'mon, Hal said. It's something to do.

It's more than just *something to do*. It's something to do *in public*. Scott looks nervous. Hal wants to grab one of his meaty hands and assure him that everything is going to be just fine.

Somehow, they've managed to never directly talk about it. But Hal knows why they never go out. It's that word. *Out*. Scott's a personal trainer. He spends his days encouraging everyone from housewives to executives to make the most of their 45-minute sojourn with their own sweat. His body is their motivation, an unattainable trophy just out of reach. Scott's not just peddling his knowledge of fitness, but the proximity of his perfect physique. The guys want to become him. The girls want to attract him. It's all part of the package. Scott plays it up. He flirts with his lady clients, trades racy jokes with the middle manager men. Maybe Scott wouldn't deny it if you asked him point blank, but who's going to ask him? Hal didn't have to ask. He met him in the gym. Scott showed him how to use the elliptical machine, off duty; it wasn't a work thing, just one guy doing another guy a favour.

The truth is, Hal's not exactly flaunting his stuff either. Would he deny it? If anyone asked? He thought about his meeting with the Boss. *Less stiff. Pretty young lady.* In a way, Hal figures, they're in the same business. It's all about the hair and the teeth and the image. It doesn't matter what you say, but how you look when you say it—how people think you look when you say it. You have to be in love with yourself, with the way you look when words come out of your mouth. All newscasters are kinda gay, he's ranted at Scott over drinks at their occasional hangout, a nearby Mexican broasted chicken restaurant complete with dark back booths and free fountain soda refills. But you can't *really* be gay, because if people think you love yourself *that much*, then they won't love you.

Huh, Scott said, showing his big teeth. He stabbed a French fry, chewed thoughtfully.

Well, anyway, here we are. Together. At the Chinese mall. So what? It's not like you would look at them and think: couple. Hal leans closer to Scott, brushes a hand innocently, suggestively, against Scott's hip.

What? Scott asks, feigning, or perhaps even actually being completely oblivious to the way he's doing his best to seem not completely terrified.

Nothing, Hal says brightly, smiling up at him reassuringly.

Inside, there are more stores—an endless number of stalls, stands, booths, and small shops announcing mysterious wares via a veritable visual cacophony of indecipherable Chinese symbols. They make their way down the main artery. It's bright, loud, and crowded. Hal hasn't been packed into a space with this many people since, he thinks, gay pride back in the city. Tiny old ladies emit frantic bursts of greeting to each other; mothers scream admonishments and pull their toddlers along; packs of teenagers bark loudly into cell phones. Generally speaking, the all-Chinese weekend shopping crowd happily ignores them as they saunter past. But Hal finds *them* harder to shut out. It's all that chatter in another language. It's not so much loud as it is persistent and surrounding. On TV, the cacophony was dialled down to an authentically ethnic background, the beat for a sinewy column of bright-eyed seven-year-olds undulating through the mall in their imitation of an attention deficit disorder dragon—all jerky shimmers of metallic red and green. It was some kind of holiday. In person, the noise is encompassing; it's not the background, it's the thing itself.

Today the youngsters sport runny noses and formless blue sweat suits. *Made in China*, Hal thinks meanly. Deeper in, the mall gets darker and quieter. They wander through a maze-like dried food area, catching whiffs of ginger and earthy mushroom and pausing, briefly, to consider a bin of oddly shaped dried fish sporting bulging, agonized cheeks. Then there's a store that sells nothing but comics featuring similarly wide-eyed, round-faced girls in skimpy tunics. Hal glances over at Scott and is surprised to see him looking around with interest. He feels the muscles loosen in his shoulders. *See, this isn't so bad.* Something new. They drive by it every day. Why not check it out?

The centre of the mall is the massive food court. All paths lead to the sprawling room festooned with outlets adorned by brightly-lit cardboard signs listing prices next to Chinese characters and the occasional semi-explanatory English word pairing—cod bamboo, mussel black bean, bok choy xo sauce. A heavy atmosphere of deep fried steam traps scents of seaweed and garlic. Downtown, in the city, Hal's seen pigs and ducks hanging by their feet in restaurant windows, their glazed burnished skins dripping. But this is beyond anything. He watches Scott contemplating bright tongues spewing tentacles, orange discs of organ dangling like skewered aliens. Scott looks mortified. Hal scans a steam table's vast array of burbling stews. A grinning old woman shows what's left of her yellow teeth and proffers a heaping ladle full of what looks like offal boiling in grey oatmeal. Hal shakes his head, smiling ruefully. Uh, no thanks. He tugs Scott's arm and motions to a brightly lit beverage stand promising freshly squeezed watermelon juice. Better to stick with liquids, Hal thinks. They move gingerly through the throng, but jerk to a stop when a very perky Asian woman sporting a tight pink workout outfit steps suddenly into their path.

Scott!! Hal hears the woman say in tones of cheery surprise.

Hey, Tina, Scott says, sounding considerably less enthusiastic.

Scott! Tina says, and she throws her arms around him in a big hug. So good to see you!

Oh, uh, yeah. Good to see you too.

Is it? Hal thinks. He inspects Tina, a lithe girl with an impressive (fake) rack and fashionable blonde streaks in her long hair.

Oh my god, *how* are you? Tina enthuses.

Good, yeah, really good, Scott says. Hal watches him grin lamely.

I've been meaning to call you!

Have you? Hal wonders, cooling his heels and waiting to be introduced.

Oh my God I miss you! Tina widens her gaze, then, to take in Hal, lingering off Scott's elbow.

Oh, Scott says, following her glance and still smiling blankly. This is Hal.

Hi, Hal says, extending his hand. He shakes hands with Tina, who looks at him curiously.

Hi Hal.

Tina, Scott explains, used to work at the club.

I left a few months ago, she says.

Oh, Hal says lamely.

So how are you? Tina says, turning her full attention back to Scott.

I'm good, Scott says. I'm really good.

That's great. God. I can't believe I'm running into you here.

I know.

It's the first time we've been here, Hal offers.

Scott gives him a quick look.

Oh, really? Tina's attention is back on Hal, or, maybe, back to the notion of Hal and Scott as an entity, a "we."

I come here all the time! I'm meeting my grandmother and aunt for lunch. Hey, aren't you…that guy on TV?

Yes, Hal says. I do the cable community news.

Right. Right! I thought you looked familiar. You're the guy who's always interviewing that old lady. What's her name again? Tina giggles. She's hilarious! You should put that stuff up on YouTube!

She'd hate you, Hal thinks.

Hal's one of my clients, Scott says quickly.

Oh, Tina says. That's awesome. Scott's the best trainer in Wississauga.

He just started, Scott says definitively, as if that singular fact explained everything—

Hal's appalling lack of muscle mass, how they ended up together in the middle of the Chinese mall food court.

Everyone stands there awkwardly. Scott seems to be staring at a point just over Tina's shoulder. Hal wants to keep the conversation going, wants to be more than just some guy who pays for Scott's attention and randomly happens to be with him for some inexplicable reason. He tries, and fails, to think of something to say.

Well, Tina finally says. I should go catch up with Grandma.

Yeah, Scott says.

It was so good to see you! I can't believe it! Scotty-Scott! Tina gives Scott another hug. Nice to meet you, she says cheerily to Hal. Then she twirls away.

Back in Scott's truck, Hal keep his mouth flatly shut. The scent of deep fry and incense lingers. Scott fires the engine. He gears into reverse but keeps his foot on the brake. Staring intently into the rear-view mirror, he says, quickly and quietly, Sorry about that.

Hal looks out the passenger side window. It's clouding over. Like it might rain again. He blows hot air through pursed lips. Yeah, okay. Hal's sorry too. Sorry for being such a sorry creature. That girl—Tina—she summed it all up, the entirety of his pathetic existence. He's the guy who interviews the old lady. He's the guy whose boyfriend strongly prefers not being seen with him. He's the guy who's going nowhere because he's so fucking uptight.

They pick their way through the heavy afternoon traffic. Hal looks out the window. Cars jostle past the anonymous nothingness, shoppers on their way back to their subdivisions. Scott turns off Hurontarion and they're about five or so minutes from home. *Home sweet home*, Hal stops himself from saying out loud with an ironic cadence. But after thinking it he finds himself actually looking forward to it. Being alone with Scott, watching TV, ordering in, stumbling into the bedroom. Maybe that's what he wants after all. Maybe he doesn't have to *come out*, make a big show of it, tell the boss, tell Sarah, tell Scott's busty body-building pal in the Chinese food court. Isn't that why he left the city? Gayness defined him there. It was like that was all he was and all he was ever going to be. Hal has other ambitions. He wants to tell stories. He wants to report the issues. Rose is just the beginning. *A stepping stone,* he thinks. Unexpectedly, he feels the anger simmering out of him. *Scott didn't do anything wrong,* Hal thinks. It's what they both want. Wississauga's special kind of freedom. Being free from the job of having to be *gay.*

Hey Scott, Hal says suddenly. Do you believe in fate?

Scott grins cautiously. He's relieved. Hal's not mad at him.

Like, he says, coincidence and stuff?

Yeah, you know, kismet, coincidence, destiny, everything happens for a reason...

Ah...Scott takes a quick look at Hal, searching his face for the right answer. No. I mean, not really. I guess.

Me neither.

They slow to a stop in front of Hal's building.

So...Hal says. You coming up, *Scotty-Scott?*

JUNE
Saturday, April 12

JUNE STICKS HER HEAD IN THE REFRIGERATOR, lets the cold light wash over her. She thinks of that other cold, the river gorge veiled in night rain—the feeling she had, the shiver of being watched, of liking it, of *wanting* to be watched. She contemplates the fridge's suddenly overflowing shelves. Mustards, jams, salad dressings, mayonnaise, chutney, marmalade. June's not hungry. June checks the time on the stove. It's just past one. It's the second Saturday of the month, which means Norm is working until four. That's the way Norm does things, makes a schedule and sticks to it. You can set your clock by Norm, June thinks, finding the thought oddly reassuring. Not that she needs to set the stovetop clock. Accurate, the salesman said, to one thousandth of a second. *Sure. Sure it is.* They'll say anything to get you to buy. The stove blinks 1:12. Norm and the oven: always on time.

The phone rings, its peal jolting June. One thousandth of a second, she says out loud. Her voice mixes with the phone's bleat and lingers for a moment, then disperses into the creaky silence of the empty house. June feels shaky, lightheaded. She sits down at the kitchen table. She hasn't eaten. Today. Or yesterday. The back of her neck is tingling. She keeps having to stop herself from spinning around to see what's behind her. Nothing's behind her.

Only: *something* led her into the basement. Something told her to find the shovel, pushed her out into the backyard, into the rain. And Rose said, though June isn't sure whether or not to believe her, that the Native people used to live all around here, right by the river. *For thousands and thousands of years.* So, okay, June reasons. Not a ghost, nothing as horror movie as a ghost. *But maybe a...presence.*

Rose is an old lady with a bunch of crazy old lady ideas. *Norm would laugh at me.* Norm would be like: Now honey, let's be reasonable here, okay? June's tired. Tired of being reasonable. When she's in the—backyard—she feels alive, unreasonably alive.

A noise upstairs. June tenses. She has that feeling again, someone else in the house, skulking around, watching her. Just a floorboard shifting, a wall settling. Big houses make all kinds of noises. Only it's more than that. More than just—

It's like the house or whatever—whoever—is trying to get her to—

June risks a glance out the window. Murky afternoon settling over the empty backyard. And the day is passing, she thinks. She feels her rigid muscles, tense and tensing. The house wants her to go out there. The house wants her to—

dig.

No—that's—

And what does June want? She wants Norm to come home so she can ignore him, not cook his dinner, not rub his shoulders while he watches TV, not offer encouraging words regarding his latest offended missive to their city councillor. But Norm's at work, he's still at work, it's the second Saturday of the month and Norm's at work. Why isn't *he* her? Why doesn't *he* have to—

It's his house too. But she's the one who spends her days pacing back and forth, moving through the tastefully furnished rooms wondering why she isn't doing something productive—getting a job, watching over a brood of offspring, crocheting a couch cover, *planning the garden.*

June jumps up, the chair shoved back, teetering, almost falling. She can feel the blood pulsing in her veins. *Am I going...?* Only there is—something—someone—

Not hubbie Norm. He doesn't watch me. He just goes about his business, makes inane suggestions about how he imagines his wife could spend her time. While he's off burrowing into smiles and saving the world from tooth decay and gum disease, she should be at home trying to decide where to put the rose bushes. All of a sudden, everyone wants me to dig. So why not? What else do I have to do? Nothing, June thinks. Her skin crawls in the empty kitchen. The bright pot lights follow her like eyes trolling over her neck, her back, her ass, her calves. Okay, she says to herself. You win. I'll dig.

She's never felt comfortable in the fenced-in backyard. The flat-sloped plane of grass, the sudden drop of the gorge. And below that, the river—an occupying, ever-present presence. It's totally empty, she complained to Norm. Not even a tree. So, he said cheerily, you'll plant stuff. But for all its space, it gets very little sun. The backyard is dwarfed by the house in front and the tall fence on the sides. And most of all by the trees stretching out of the river gully, angry giants whose black bare limbs remind her of something elemental—insistent in a way more foreboding than comforting. They were here first. That's what Rose said.

June steps into the curvature of displaced earth she started two nights ago. The overcast day presses low on her and the small descent into what she refuses to think of as a hole confirms the aura of emptiness that seems to be a permanent presence in the backyard. June's in just below her knees, but she can feel the depth change the temperature, a cold seeping up her. Working against the permeating cold, June energetically stabs at the packed clay at the bottom, loosening the dirt then scooping it into the shovel and throwing it up over her shoulder. Her palms sting where the worn wood of the shovel handle presses against drawn skin. She just digs, losing herself in repetition and pattern, establishing a rhythm that she discovers she is loath to break. She works steadily, loosening, emptying, digging. She doesn't stop to catch her breath and survey her progress. She digs, not even registering her slow descent.

Finally, after an hour, maybe more, her shovel hits a rock. Jarred out of rhythmic motion, June plants her shovel in the earth. Dazed, she turns her hands up and contemplates the red sores on the undersides of her hands and fingers. She rubs them together, feeling the heat rising from her palms. Dimly, she registers that she's thirsty. She needs a drink. She needs a pair of gloves. Far above, a bird circles then passes with a single caw. June feels eyes on her. A chipmunk scampers then screeches a warning. She has this feeling of descent, of being in the process of slowly descending. The crevice into the core. The sores on her hands sting and burn. Dig, keep digging. It's almost a trance, automatic motion, a feeling of belonging in your body, the certainty that comes from giving oneself over to the doing of—*whatever I'm doing.*

She grabs her shovel.

Then she's in to her thighs. Exhausted, she slumps down, her knees sinking into the seeping clay. She pants, unable to catch her breath. She leans forward, putting her hot hands on the dirt at the bottom of the hole. Cool and wet, the top layer of mud soothes her blistered palms. Her arms hold her up, the muscles taut, pulsing. The pit looms over her, its walls sloping. And it's dark. She can barely make out her white hands in the muck. She can hear her own panting breaths, she can't breathe, can't get enough air, can't keep up with her body's sudden need for oxygen, her lungs burning and bursting, she can't—no—you're—okay, you're okay—

just—

breathe.

Still on her hands and knees at the bottom of the hole, she feels her breath slowing. She contemplates the pink knuckles of her half-buried fists. *I'm underground,* she thinks. The thought quiets her. She considers the enclosure of space she's carved out of the earth. It's tomb-like, with grey hard-packed clay walls seeping. But she doesn't feel enclosed, trapped. Her muscles throb languidly. Her eyes track every permutation, every mark of the shovel. Her nostrils flare and she takes a deep inhalation of sediment, compost, renewal—*life,* she thinks. Her brain is alert, a conduit to sharpened senses. An unconscious gesture, buried conviction abruptly released. Her wrists shake from the weight of supporting her body. She should get up but she doesn't move. The hole is hers, now; she feels it. This is where she's meant to be.

When June was downsized from her job, she felt humiliated. She hadn't experienced that yet, hadn't yet felt the way the world turned regardless, its rotations carrying on no matter what random mishap might befall one of the creatures on its surface. She'd been fired, for no reason and with no warning. It was the randomness that rocked her. She'd been called into her supervisor's office and told, kindly but firmly, that through no fault of her own, she was being let go. She would get an excellent letter of recommendation, an extra two weeks of severance pay in addition to the severance specified in her contract, and access to the human resources career counselling services. But right now she'd need to go clean out her area. White-faced and nauseated, June had allowed her boss to escort her back to her cubicle where together they packed up her things. The box was handed to a nondescript security guard and the whole procession then paraded through the office past fellow workers who, their heads down, surreptitiously followed her progress as their fingers furiously typed nonsense. Past reception, out into the lobby, and then ushered into a waiting cab and handed a taxi chit. June, finally alone, dug her nails into her forearm to keep from bursting into tears.

She'd been good at her job. *Really* good at it. Finding out through the grapevine of office gossip that despite a record profit the company was outsourcing her role—and up to 1,000 other jobs in Canada and Europe—to achieve maximum efficiency did little to comfort her. She felt culpable in a failure that nonetheless had nothing to do with her. She could have stayed late every day, finished months-long projects in a week, received every commendation and recommendation in her department—and nothing would have changed the outcome. The realization produced a feeling of torpor in her, a sense of isolation and ineffectuality slowly settling into the flesh of her mind like some slow-acting poison.

It isn't fair! she thought over and over again. But when Norm came over—they'd been dating more seriously by then—she'd barely managed to utter a word. He had come over as soon as he'd heard, talking calmly about the potential illegality of replacing her with offshore workers and offering to help her sue for wrongful dismissal before finally shepherding her on to a plane to a Dominican resort for a week of R&R. It was when they got back that June first took him to meet her parents.

June's head dangles. Sweat slides off her brow and the sound of her own ragged breathing fills the hole. Did she marry Norm and move to Wississauga because she'd been fired? No. She gives her head a good shake as if to drive out the thought. Norm had been there for her. She'd always love him for that. His complete and utter devotion. The earth presses up on her palms, solid yet divisible. Her body slumps. Her palms slip and she falls against the bottom of the hole. She's so tired. She feels the warmth being pulled out of her, sucked into the earth, into what's below that. She breathes deeply, trying to calm herself. The *en-tee-tee*, she thinks, remembering the way Rose relished the word, drawing out the vowels. Rose believes her. *Because it's true.* Even the taste of the air seems to confirm what she's sure she now knows—tinged rotting rancid expectation, the scent of old mixed with the carnivorous demands of the new. She raises herself up again and carefully inspects the surfaces she's uncovered. Squinting, she presses her hands against the dirt, investigating by touch her new underworld of ridges and protrusions.

And then, underneath the chafed bruised skin of a pressed palm, she feels something rough and porous. Another rock? She knows it's not. Using her hands, she shovels around the hard object, forcing her fingers against the tough clay. It hurts. She digs harder, clawing at the thick soil and wet muddy earth. Bone, she thinks calmly as the shape emerges, all curved edges and grey-yellow jags. Thick brackish ground water seeps around her fingers. Certainty fills her. This is what she was brought here to find.

June? June honey?

Shit.

June?

Shit. It's Norm.

Inside, their big kitchen gleams. June blinks. Norm stands there watching her, seems to be waiting for something to happen, waiting in the kitchen in his blue buttoned-down shirt and red striped tie. She imagines him in his white coat, officiously peering into someone's open mouth. What does he see? Just teeth and gums and drool? But there's something else there too. There must be.

Hi honey! You're home? She speaks quickly, breathlessly; she can feel her face going red. She's unnerved by the illumination, the bright kitchen, the Norman-ness of it all. What does he see?

I'm home, Norm agrees. He says it like he's not sure.

Good. June smiles. Good! She keeps smiling. I'm glad. That you're home.

Good. Yes.

Norm looks uncomfortable. Like his tie is too tight. He swallows. June watches the bulge in his throat bob.

Uh, June? Are you…? You're all…dirty—

Oh! Well! I was just…digging.

Digging?

Of course! What do you think I've been doing? Look at me! I'm covered in it! June laughs, the sound swirling around the bright kitchen. She puts her hands to her sides. Lets them dangle. They feel like prostheses, filthy trowel tools. They must look…horrible. Scary even. Dirt jammed under nails cracked and ragged.

You're…planting?

Oh! Not yet! I've been…digging. I read an article about…the soil. Helping the soil. You can't just stick things in the ground you know. Our soil is very—it's practically dead. So first I need to…fertilize.

Norm peers doubtfully through the glass doors. Fertilize?

What? June squints as the kitchen sways and swirls. She's having trouble breathing. Everything is so bright and empty.

June?

What? Oh! You, first you dig a big hole. Then you fill it. With special…fertilizer. It's a new technique.

Huh. How's that supposed to work? It seems pretty…elaborate. Can I see the magazine?

The magazine?

With the article?

No silly. I saw it on TV! You know, that…local channel?

Huh. Norm's looking at her. He moves around her to lock the sliding doors. Are you feeling okay June?

Sure! June laughs abruptly, wills herself to stop blinking like a lunatic. She feels great. Never better. In possession of herself, or something else. Her body is heat, tingling humid weather. First spring. Then summer.

C'mon Norm, she says. I need—let's take—a nice hot shower. She strokes his cheek, leaves a smudge.

In the shower she turns away from him. Wash my back, she teases. She gently scrubs her fingers. Her nails are ruined. Her fingertips are raw. Norm soap-glides his palms against the notches of her spine and down to the soft shake of her ass.

Mmmm. She rubs against him. She reaches behind her. He's hard now. She turns to face him, has a sudden vision of them, from above, like the love scene in a scary movie, something watching, lurking. She buries her face in his chest. Pushes against him. Their bodies, slick.

Hot under hot water. Steam. June trails her breasts down. Nipples sharp. She slides to her sore knees.

June…Norm hisses.

Then, in the bed, still wet, she straddles him. He arches into her.

June, I'm going to—

Do it, she pants. Do it in me.

June—really? Are you—? I'm going to—are you—

Do it!

—sure?

He does it. Hot splash inside her. Sudden life. Spring. Summer.

PART THREE

HAL AND ROSE
Monday, April 14

THE REST HOME SITS MAROONED in a sea of shopping and traffic. Actually Hal finds it weirdly peaceful. No overly enthusiastic colleagues. No danger of running into some frisky former gym rat best pal of Scott's. Plus, let's face it, Rose doesn't even know there's such a thing as gay. Hal contemplates the elderly island sedately anchored amidst frantic currents of traffic and shoppers swirling around the 73 stores of the Middle Mall—"Where fun goes shopping!" *Fun is relative*, Hal thinks. Rose has fun. She rarely leaves her room, but she has her fun. Her fun is Hal. He's her entertainment. She's always ready and waiting for him with makeup applied and hair neatly combed. I don't know how she does it, Scott says sarcastically. Makes herself look like the million-year-old buzzard lady! Half dino-bird, half zombie! Yeah, well, imagine what you're gonna look like at 100, Hal snaps. He compulsively defends Rose. He's not entirely sure why. Scott's right. She barely looks human. Rose's attempts to beautify only seem to make things worse: limp grey hair thinly spread across her scalp, red blush thickly smeared against waxy yellow cheeks, orange gash of lipstick coating her shrivelled lips. After the weather as breathlessly revealed by the bodacious Sarah, Rose is their most popular segment. She's old, she's ugly, she's cranky as hell, but there's something about her. It's the way she leans into the camera, Hal thinks, the way she licks her receding lips and unequivocally announces that things *have gone to heck in a handbasket.* In Rose's world, rural Walletville will always be far superior to the quarter-million commuters now busily buzzing their cars through Wississauga, a hive of rapidly growing partially built barely connected nodes. People love to hear how crap their lives are. And maybe, just maybe, it gives them some idea of how things could be better. Yeah right, Scott says, rolling his eyes. Scott doesn't care about Wississauga.

Hello, Hal calls, pushing in without waiting for an invitation. Anybody home?

You're late, young man, Rose announces.

Hal smiles jovially and starts to bustle around the tiny room unpacking the equipment.

I don't have all day you know, Rose snaps.

That's what they love about her, Hal thinks. *Her grace and charm.* Never mind. Rose is the closest thing cable community news has to a star. Hal adjusts the tripod, fixes the lights. He peeks into the camera's viewfinder. Rose's flat head sticks out of a gnarled blue cardigan.

Okay Rose, we're just about ready. Hal draws a deep breath, reminds himself to smile and takes his seat next to the old woman.

Hello, I'm Hal Talbot and this is Wississauga Cable Community News!

Rose scowls expectantly into the camera's lens.

Once again we're here with Wississauga's oldest resident, living legend and dispenser of the wisest wisdom you'll find anywhere, Rose McCallion. Rose, it's great to be here again, how are you today?

Oh, well, she says, I'm alive, which is accomplishment enough at my age.

Hal smiles. Ha ha. You're not only still with us, he says, but you look great.

Well that's very nice of you to say young man, Rose drawls in a tone that makes it clear they both know how, as Rose would say, full of baloney Hal is. Anyway, I'm still here, thank the lord Jesus. She raps brittle knuckles against her chair's armrest. And I'll still be here tomorrow, too.

Of course you will, Rose!

With his grin on auto pilot, Hal guides Rose through a ser-ies of predictable and popular dialogues: Rose on the weather (too cold, too hot, too wet, too dry), Rose on politicians and bankers (liars and thieves), Rose on people these days (so rude, where are they going in such a big hurry?), Rose on her childhood (we didn't have so much as three wooden pennies to rub together). Hal steers away from other subjects Rose tends to veer into, topics that make Rose look less like a cranky seer and more like an attack dog gone senile. These include the rest home staff, anything to do with what the cable community news team officially calls multiculturalism, and, of course, Rose's daughter. Get onto any of those themes and Rose goes bitter and rancid. The rest of the time, Hal thinks, she's acting, playing a role, hamming for the camera, sure, why not? But when she gets really angry, she forgets herself, forgets the camera, and the results are not particularly pretty. People want the cliché, Hal's tried to explain to Scott. Not the real person. When things go bad, Hal ends up back at the office in front of his computer, labor-iously editing together Rose's sporadic congenial moments. Plus, Hal thinks, it can't be healthy for the old bird to get so worked up.

All the same, he can't resist throwing something unpredictable into the mix. He waits until the end so he can easily edit out her response when things inevitably turn sour. It's become tradition to show some of Rose's more, uh, contentious pronouncements to Sarah. They sit in one of the small conference rooms and ohh and ahh and *I-can't-believe-she-just-said-that* as Rose blames the China people, the homosexuals (as she calls them), her daughter, and the lazy rest home staff on any number of her misfortunes. Hal always feels sullied after these sessions with Sarah. He'd rather just press delete, consign Rose's misanthropic ravings to the netherworld of erased data. But Sarah's so eager, so excited. She gets the room all set up and practically drags him in.

So, Rose, he says, after patiently nodding his way through a discussion of how, in Rose's day, an orange was an annual spherical marvel carefully peeled and sectioned out to the entire family over the course of the Yuletide season. So Rose, this week the City's unveiling their plans to build a new road down by the river.

Another road? Rose barks. When I was a kid the Cartwrights were the only family in Walletville that even had a car. It kept getting stuck in the mud! Not much good, that's what we thought of cars!

Then you're against the road?

I didn't say that, now did I? After all, men have to work, don't they?

Yes they do Rose.

But I'd be careful, if I was them. I'd be very careful.

What do you mean Rose?

It's an old graveyard down there, isn't it? Everybody knows that! Some things, young man, are best left alone.

Hal takes a sip from his tea. Actually it's just water, but the tea cup makes the whole thing look more homey. Where's she going with this? Is she acting or serious? The problem is that when Rose is at her best, it's usually a bit of both.

So you're saying...

They're cursed you know. Those Indian bones! Men have to make a living, but it's a foolish thing if you think you can just pave over all of *that*. Damned if you do and damned if you don't, I'd suppose.

What do you mean Indians bones, Rose? There's no way he'll be putting any of this on the air, but he might as well find out exactly what she's getting at.

These days people don't put much stock in things like that. But it still happens, believe you me. Even just the other day the girl who comes to see me—nice girl, a little bit queer—she told me that she's got, may Jesus help her, an Indian ghost right there in her backyard just above the river. She lives on that old Grove Street, the one with the big houses. It's the second oldest street in Wississauga after Main, and I bet you didn't know that Mr. Reporter.

Hal puts on a sheepish face. No Rose, I certainly didn't. You got me again. Now Rose, do you really think she's being haunted by…uh…Native spirits?

Of course she is dear. She came to ask me what she should do about it, didn't she? That's what happens! Those bones are cursed! Oh all those doctors and science folks they have today, they think they've got an answer for everything. So how do you explain it then? People still get the evil eye, don't they? People still get the curse, Jesus help them. I told her, you move out of that house. You get out of there right this minute.

On the way back to the cable community access van, Hal stops at the nurses' station. Two women in pink look up from a lackadaisical game of cards.

Look at that, one of them says dryly, it's that reporter.

Hal flashes them his best broadcaster smile.

Good afternoon ladies.

They nod crustily.

I was just wondering if you could help me out for a story I'm working on.

More on that dried out frog! one of them exclaims. The other nudges her sharply with an elbow.

Oh, ha ha, no, Hal laughs. No, it's something different. I'm doing a piece on volunteers in Wississauga, like, for instance, how you hardworking ladies mentor volunteers in fine institutions such as this one. And I heard that one of the volunteers right here on this floor was telling our Rose over there just how much she's learned from her work here. I didn't catch her name, but I'd sure like to get in touch with her for the story.

Volunteers...one of them says, puzzled.

Let me see, the other says, flipping through a binder.

That would be fantastic!

Ah, let's see now...the volunteer on this floor...that would be... June Littlewell.

Never heard of her, the other lady says.

Sure you have. She's the quiet one, pretty girl, with the ponytail.

Oh yeah, her.

June Littlewell, Hal says, scratching the name in his reporter's pad. What's she like then?

She's fine.

Nice enough girl.

You should ask our manger.

Of course, Hal says. I'll do that. Thanks so much for your help.

They pick up their cards.

Anybody home? Scott yells. He's got his own key. He likes to just walk on in and plop himself down on the couch. *Home*, Hal thinks. That word keeps coming up. Grubby bachelor apartment on the ninth floor of the Victory Colonnades. Hal's in the dark tiny kitchen, his face illuminated by the glow of the open refrigerator. He's holding a carton of milk in his hand. He quickly licks froth from his upper lip. His tie hangs loose around his neck. Moores-for-Men knock off. *Just temporary,* he thinks. *Everything is just… temporary.* Hal wipes his face with the tie. Stupid. It'll stain. He's only got three. He pulls the tie over and off as he takes the four steps from the kitchen to the living room.

The living room is the biggest room in the apartment with just enough space for a second-hand couch, a scratched coffee table, and a pathetically oversized tube TV. With Scott standing in the middle, the room gets even smaller. Scott's six-foot-four, muscled like a jungle cat—lithe and perfectly proportioned. Add to that a tousled shock of brown hair and a perpetually boyish grin and you get what Hal thinks of as The Scott Factor: an irrepressible, larger-than-life care-free buoyancy that instantly fills up a room—infects it, Hal thinks. Today Scott's wearing an Adidas tracksuit. He should be the one drinking from the carton, Hal thinks. Like in one of those milk ads.

Hey, Hal says. He sighs and throws himself on the couch.

Scott nimbly lowers down beside him. The couch's springs creak. Hal cringes, half expecting the whole thing to collapse. Scott offered to buy him a new one. Leather. And a flat-screen TV too. Hal said no. Thanks but no thanks. Scott earns $75 an hour. Hal's making $27,000 a year.

Hard day? Scott puts a big hand on Hal's neck, squeezes gently. Hal just exhales.

I had Mrs. Crabapple today, Scott offers. She told me the exercises are making her arthritis worse. She told me her doctor says I'm a fraud.

What'd you say?

I said she was in remarkable shape and that with a little more effort she would look like a woman half her age.

You said that?

She booked another appointment for Friday. Scott giggles. His hand tightens on the corded muscles in Hal's neck.

Hey! Take it easy!

You're really tense.

Yeah. Well. We can't all be…Hal doesn't finish. Be what? Nothing bothers Scott. His life just happens. He pushes Scott's hand away and stands up. He surveys the apartment again. The building is only ten years old but already has a distinct air of decay. Scott lives in a spacious, brightly lit penthouse condo. In the city it would be right downtown, minutes from the party district, fancy lounges, pricey restaurants. Hal imagines Scott's place full of gorgeous girls with long blonde hair and impressive bosoms, a post-millennial Three's Company knock-off from the people who bring you the Wississauga Cable Community News.

So whadya wanna do tonight? Scott says uncertainly.

Next door is playing dance music. The guy upstairs rattles his throat again, can never seem to get it clear. Somewhere a TV's on, the news broadcast. Not mine, Hal thinks. Network news from the city.

We can go out, Scott says, sounding worried. If you want.

Hal looks at Scott. He doesn't have a clue, generally speaking.

What do you think? Scott says, putting on an encouraging grin.

Hal's suddenly filled with tenderness towards him.

Let's stay in, he says, as if that's some big shakeup of their routine.

Okay. Scott smiles, relieved. So what's up with you? Bad day? Boss yell at you?

It's true. Hal doesn't feel like himself. He's restless, edgy. Normally he's fine with it. Their routine: take a shower, order in, wait for the 10 o'clock broadcast to come on. Hal watches himself intently while Scott fidgets and tries to get a hand down Hal's pants. Quit it, Scott, I'm watching this!

But eventually Scott succeeds. By 10:30 they're going at it, Sarah's weather forecast a familiar soundtrack to the main feature.

I'm just...Hal pauses. I don't know. He shrugs. I've got a lot on my mind.

Oh, okay. That's cool.

The boss thinks I'm too serious or something.

Like when you're on TV?

Yeah. And in general.

Oh, well, we've just go to...loosen you up. Scott looks up at him expectantly.

Hal catches himself almost grinning. Scott's enthusiasm makes it seem true. He just needs to...relax. But he finds himself thinking about something else entirely. That thing with Rose, and her volunteer. Indian graveyards, curses, ghosts, the new road. It all fits together somehow. He can close his eyes and practically see it. Hal's going to be the one to make a picture out of the pieces. *Relax*, he thinks contemptuously.

You know what we should do? Scott demands, bouncing up and down on the couch in excitement. We should do a weekend in the city! That would be so fun!

He's like a puppy, Hal thinks. One of those little dogs with big feet that you bring home without even realizing how huge they're going to grow up to be. In the city they can go *out*. Dancing. Clubbing. *Gay stuff.* Hal doesn't want—doesn't need—to go back to the city. He was supposed to hate Wississauga, a sprawl of nothing where nothing ever happens. *But,* he thinks, *things* are *happening here.* It's hard to explain, exactly. That's the challenge. To show what's actually going on. New buildings and stores and subdivisions and condominiums spring up practically every day. Immigrants pour in from all over, not just from other cities, but from all over the world. Anything could happen, the place is a blank slate, tabula rasa, land of opportunity. Everybody at the station says it won't be long before head office realizes their mistake, sees how fast this area is growing and starts a real network affiliate. They'll be looking for someone young, someone pretty but smart, someone who knows the local issues. With real resources Hal could do real stories. Cameramen, editors, cutting-edge equipment. Not to mention a six-figure salary, move out of this shithole. What does Scott want? To go to *the city?* Sure, why not? Party central: clubs, restaurants, bigger gyms, more clients. He could market to the gay village; they've got lots of money, especially the older guys. Just imagine, Hal thinks, how much those sixty-something yuppie queers would pay to work out with a strapping young buck breathing encouragement all over them. *He'd make a fortune.* And there's that other thing: being *out*. Hal's done that already. The lifestyle. Clubs and hook-ups and summer parades. It's just another kind of hiding, he wants to explain to Scott.

So what do you think? Scott says again.

Yeah…maybe.

C'mon! It'll be totally fun.

Let's order a pizza. I'm hungry. You want to order a pizza? Hal's legs are hot under his polyester blend. Spring is coming. Things are warming up. He's got to focus. The new road they want to put in, that's going to be a big story. And…Indian bones. He's going to look into that. That could be huge. If there's some kind of burial ground near the river, that could scuttle the whole deal. *Bones.* Hal's onto something. He's onto the kind of story he's been looking for, the kind of story that changes things, that actually matters.

Hal? Earth to Hal?

Scott is still sitting there looking up at him with those big brown boy eyes. Hal tugs at the button of his pants.

You order the pizza. I'm gonna—get out of these clothes.

JUNE
Monday, April 14

THE WISSISSAUGA CAMPUS is the satellite branch of the downtown university June attended not all that long ago. It's a seventies-style jumble of long, low concrete buildings. June wanders the paved paths that connect them, occasionally stopping to consult the map of the campus she printed before driving over. Students bustle past hurriedly in purposeful groups. *Exams soon,* June thinks. She suddenly feels nostalgic for something as simple and straightforward as a final exam. The students, bright-eyed, thrive on manufactured, self-perpetuated urgency. June moves slowly, her muscles pulsing under her skin. She's wearing a windbreaker over a sweatshirt. Her jeans are streaked with mud and dirt and her hair is pulled back into a ponytail. Unintentionally, she fits in. Just another clueless student in dirty jeans heading aimlessly into the future with all the vigour she can muster. June checks her map.

She's looking for The Cartwright Centre for the Arts and Sciences. Cartwright. She's heard the name before. He was the mayor, right? One of the founding fathers of Wississauga. Or Walletville. Or whatever you call it. Also has a wing named after him at the hospital. *Probably owned that starch plant too,* June thinks. The one Rose's husband slaved away in for practically his entire life.

The Cartwrights were a rich family from England, but the students swirling in and out of the centre seem anything but. June pushes open the door of the building and stops just inside to get her bearings. Robes, veils, turbans, and hijabs mix and match with ubiquitous t-shirts, jeans, and varsity sweats. What would Rose say about this? June's own inner city campus had been so much more— *white*, she thinks. Not that there's anything wrong with it. It's just that she'd always thought of Wississauga as a Cartwright sort of place. And the city was where all the...mixing went on.

Not that there's anything wrong with it.

A giggling group of girls flow around June in a wave.

C'mon, one of them says, her voice ringing in June's ear. We'll be late!

June checks her watch. The class she's looking for will be over in five minutes. Anthropology 303Y: History and Settlement in the Lower Wallet River Valley. Professor Nordstrom. Classroom #201. June finds the stairs, takes them two at a time. She likes the feeling of moving so deliberately. She walks into the class just as the Professor is wrapping up. Next week, he says loudly, we're reviewing the major themes for the final. The students, thirty or so, pack up their notebooks, murmur to each other. June stands pressed against the back of a lecture hall that could easily seat eighty. Tell your classmates, the Professor yells. Perhaps some of them will be good enough to join us for a change. The students file out, talking loudly, eyeballing June, obviously not chastened on behalf of their truant fellow scholars. Professor Nordstrom packs his notes in an absentminded, semi-agitated way. He looks young to June, a slightly pudgy fellow with pink Nordic skin, thin blond hair, and wire-rimmed glasses.

June approaches, stands near the lectern.

Professor Nordstrom looks up, startled.

Ah, oh. I thought you were all—he considers June. Are you one of my students?

No, Professor, I'm—

Good. Good then. Because I've never seen you before. And I usually like it if my students attend at least one of my lectures per semester. The Professor laughs sardonically, exposing small white teeth.

Nordstrom speaks with a Nordic lilt and formal British construction.

No, I'm not a student I'm…

June thought he'd be from here. Someone teaching local history.

Professor Nordstrom hefts his briefcase. Well then. Come along to my office and we will get you sorted out.

Professor Nordstrom's office is an unimpressive cubbyhole lined with books. A small window lets in a rectangle of greying afternoon. The Professor has to suck in his gut to squeeze behind his desk. June wants to turn away from the sight. Nordstrom lands heavily in his chair, sighs, and jovially pats the pot of his soft protruding belly.

Now then, Miss…

June. June Littlewell.

Miss Littlewell, then.

June nods.

What can I do for you today?

June fidgets with her fingers. Well I, I used to go to—I graduated from the downtown campus…

Nordstrom winces visibly at the mention of the downtown campus.

Not that, June says quickly, there's anything wrong with—I mean, I live in Wississauga now and I'm sure if I had...I mean, it's so much more...diverse, here, than I—

Er yes, Nordstrom brightens. *They* are the only ones who take anything seriously at all. Hard workers. Fascinating, really, when you consider that *they* would be the last people you would expect to have an interest in local history. Nordstrom laughs, as if he's made some kind of joke. June reddens.

It's quite something, Nordstrom says reassuringly. It really is quite something.

Yes, well, I was—I mean, I graduated eight years ago, from downtown, so things were—

Eight years ago! You look so young, my dear. Now let me guess. You are thinking of, perhaps, graduate work in the field? You do not have your heart set on it, I hope. Because it is, well, I would not want to discourage you, but you would have to be exceptionally dedicated and talented because, you see, opportunities are limited. Everybody wants adventure, everybody wants to search for, er, buried treasure. So it is a bit of a crowded field, right now, and for the, er, foreseeable future.

No, Professor, I'm not here to find out about graduate school.

Then, er, Miss Littlewell, why *are* you here today?

You see...I recently moved into a house just above the...river. And I feel like, I've been wondering about the...history.

So you want to take the course next year? We would be delighted to have you, naturally. Campus policy is very clear on the issue of, er, community relations. Continuing education students from the area are *always* welcome. You'll have to enrol with the Mature Students office if you can forgive the bother. And of course,

Professor Nordstrom continues, looking at June in a greedy way that leaves her suddenly uncomfortable, you must also put out of your mind the inappropriate, er, nomenclature, after all, you're hardly what we think of, that is, er, it's just that word: *mature*.

Professor, June says, conspicuously placing her wedding ring hand on top of a closed file folder. I, yes, thank you, I would like to take the course. It sounds very interesting…but what I'm wondering, Professor, what I really need to know is…

What is it? What does she really need to know? The clock ticks. Someone is talking on the phone in the next office over. Professor Nordstrom looks on curiously, his eyes beady, his lips shiny, his cheeks rosy, his thinning hair plastered to his pink forehead.

Who were the first? June blurts. Who were the first people to live in…She's blushing again. Not, she pushes on, like the first… white people. I mean…the really first people…here.

Nordstrom looks at her with bewildered alarm. He's not used to dealing with the public, he's done a few interviews with that young reporter on community television regarding the occasional find of a spear tip. Happy to do it. Good for the university, public profile and what not, increases his overall exposure. Of course he's not one of those who craves the attention, isn't about to get caught up in junk science and outrageous speculation just so he can make the newspapers. Slow and steady, that's his motto. His latest paper is sure to get published in the prestigious Stockholm Journal of Anthropology, which will lead to further advancement in his career, funding, postings, so on and so forth. The more he gets what he deserves the less he'll find himself having to deal with this kind of…he doesn't even really know what to call it…

Professor?

Nordstrom does a little quiver, emerges from his flustered reverie. But that is…er…that is an interesting question!

It is?

Of course it is. I mean, do you realize…well, obviously you do *not* realize, but let us just say that if I knew the answer to that, well, I would not exactly be sitting…er, I would be, that is…well, Nordstrom giggles awkwardly.

But you must know something.

Nordstrom sighs. Surprisingly little, Miss Littlewell. Surprisingly little.

June resists the sudden urge to reach over, grab the man by the collar protruding from his argyle sweater and shake him.

Please, Professor, she says through clenched teeth.

Well…er…I…really…er…He stops and rescans her, as if a bulb had been suddenly turned on, revealing her in a totally different light. Well then, Miss Littlewell, as you might have observed, office hour continues and much to my surprise no paying customers seem to be lining up at my door. Ah ha ha. So why, as they say, the hell not? I will endeavour to—what do they call it? Give you the, er, "cheat sheet" version? How will that be? The Professor's gaze roves over her, lingers on the folds of her sweatshirt. Now, you want to know who the first were? The very first people to occupy the Lower Wallet River Region?

Yes, I—

Well at least your inquiries are ambitious. You see, what you are really asking is, perhaps, the most contentious debate in archaeology today. Who were the first people to enter into the Americas? How did they get here? Do you understand what I am saying, Miss Littlewell?

Yes. Of course.

Good. Good. Some believe that the Americas were populated by Asian nomads who followed herds of, oh, er, woolly mammoth or beefalo—ah ha, a joke, Miss Littlewell—but, er, some such type mammaloid, across the frozen landmass that is now the Bering Strait waterway separating, er, Siberia from the continental North America, from, er, Alaska. That, at least, is the accepted theory. This, of course, all would have had to take place during the ice age around, oh, 12,000 years ago.

12,000 years, June repeats, without exactly meaning to.

Yes, well, it is quite a number, nothing, of course, as impressive as the finds in Africa, homo erectus and all that, half-a-million years old, those are. At any rate, okay then, it freezes over, makes for a convenient passage, and a bunch of chaps wander over from Siberia and the next thing you know you have some fifteen hundred different tribes from the Arctic to, er, Brazil.

So, June says uncertainly, the first—I mean, the first people who ever, who lived in…Wississauga…came from…Russia?

Ha, very humorous, an interesting way of putting it. But they were not sporting fur hats and leaving a trail of vodka bottles for us to follow, I am afraid. You see, it is—well, er, where to start?—first of all Miss Littlewell, there was no Russia. There were no countries at all. We're talking about a pre-modern era. Before the dawn, so to speak, of civilization. They were primitives, for lack of a more appropriate word, though of course these days we have to be, er, aware of the, er, cultural sensitivities and of course do what we can to express ourselves, er, appropriately. So these people that we are talking about, they had no countries. No writing. No towns or cities. A rudimentary language at best, the bare beginnings of culture.

But—

And if the first visitors to our, er, little suburb were, indeed, descendants of the nomads who wandered over across the Bering Strait, then we can safely assume that it would have taken them many, many generations for that migration to take place. After all, it's a long way to walk, from the Alaskan hinterlands to Wississauga. Professor Nordstrom chortles clumsily as if he'd just told a dirty joke.

June stares at him. He's like some kind of awkward boy. She thought he'd be serious. Tell her something real.

As if sensing her annoyance, Nordstrom shifts tone: Have you ever been to the Arctic?

June shakes her head.

Of course not. But I did not want to assume. I have been several times. The quiet is so intense it feels like the loudest sound imaginable. A vast, wide-open space that defies imagination. Pre-history is like that, as well. It is, you see, er, the study of a time before time as we know it, er, existed. It is a topic so vast and imponderable it is like—here, give me your hand.

Professor Nordstrom eagerly grabs June's right hand in both of his. A soft digit probes her palm.

You see, Miss Littlewell, the lines of the palm intersecting. Contradictory. Intricate. Who put them there? What do they mean? They have found, my colleagues, sites in New Mexico and South America, that clearly predate the earlier sites discovered in the North. Sites that seem to even predate the ice age. So where did those people come from? Well it's really quite impossible to know. Did they boat over from Africa? From Australia? Maybe your Russians are really Laplanders from Greenland? You see Miss Littlewell, we are dealing with an, er, extremely complicated question. It is a maze. We have been following the lines of a palm.

His finger, tracing delicately, perversely.

Your hand is so rough, he says.

I've been dig—working—in the backyard. Gardening.

You have been *digging* Miss Littlewell? What *have* you been digging? Did you find something that might be of interest to—us—here? Is that why you have come to see me? Because I'd be happy to, er, work with you, to include you in my…research.

Professor Nordstrom's eyes acquire a different glint.

You know, he continues, there have been, er, several significant sites found, here, in the Wallet River valley. In construction sites, mostly, but that doesn't preclude a significant find in, say, a backyard. Sadly we haven't been able to study the findings closely. They are carted away by my colleagues in Natives Studies two buildings over, Miss Littlewell. Two buildings and a whole world apart. Yes, they are the ones who make the decisions around here, and I am afraid that these days the findings—precious, very precious evidence, Miss Littlewell—are quickly covered up again. Well, it is all done for the right, er, reasons, of course. In fact it's really, er, quite something to see, all kinds of ceremonies and whatnots performed, of course, yes, they still have their customs. But, still, Miss Littlewell, such a shame to have to…well…sometimes, it is possible to do just a quick survey, of the, er, findings, before—So! Nordstrom gives her hand an encouraging squeeze. You say you live over by the river?

No—I mean, yes, but I—

Because the native peoples of the area date back some 8,000 years. Of course there are very few, er, findings from that time. Most of the materials we have of the pre-contact life of the native peoples come from the last, oh, 600 years.

8,000 years?

You *did* find something, didn't you, Miss Littlewell?

She pulls her hand out of his grip.

June wanders aimlessly through the campus. The sun peers out from behind distant clouds. Yellow grass borders pavement paths. It's late afternoon. She should head home and cook dinner. She's hot under the windbreaker. The low long concrete buildings sit awkwardly in the sun. They're built for winter, squat forts meant to keep out cold dark days, not let in the spring light. She's not going back to school. She might be dressed like them. But that's about it. To that Nordstrom it's just numbers and facts and statistics. He doesn't get it. He doesn't know that it's—real. A gaggle of co-eds scamper past. The late afternoon early spring sun warms her pale face. Nordstrom made it sound like they were animals. Savages. Wandering around in the ice and snow thousands and thousands of years ago. But June knows something else, something else about—

he—

he was—

A building juts over her. June stops walking and looks up. The footpath dead-ends at a larger square of a building, the only structure that seems to have more than three floors. *The library,* June thinks. Why didn't she just go to the library? She feels like an idiot. *There's no curse, Rose.* No ghosts, no scary spirits. It's all just science, what can be explained, what can't be explained…yet. She's gotten out of the habit of reading. Norm's not much of a reader. He likes books about famous inventors and rags-to-riches entrepreneurs. Even then he prefers the TV version. Sum it up, he says, when the telemarketers get him on the phone. He calls his little office the library, but it's more like a museum—*a mausoleum,* June thinks. A repository for objects fixed in time; the way things were, the way her husband likes to think they are. A wall of framed diplomas hangs over an imposing cherry wood desk. The desk, vast plane of glazed wood, sits almost empty except for a few strategically placed gold fountain pens, journals of dental science, a blank pristine yellow legal pad, and, finally, a sealed box of Cuban cigars, probably a gift from a grateful patient—Norm doesn't smoke, bad for the lungs, not to mention the dent it would put in what he likes to call *the old pocketbook.*

June ponders the dark entrance to the library. Students bustle by, hurrying to get things done before the end of the day. Her muscles are stiff, each movement of her arms and legs a conscious effort. It seems dark. The sun dropping. Already? Is it that late? Wind gusts down the path. It's suddenly colder. Cold out here. June wishes it was summer, feels a hunger for heat, in the summer she'll travel, have Norm take her somewhere, somewhere tropical, balmy. No. What she really wants are the summers of her childhood: fire flies and the waft of freshly cut grass, the buzz of mosquitoes, the sun gentle on her face, her mother calling her in for dinner. Suddenly she aches for it. Her body bruised with longing.

June wills herself up the steps.

And on into the stacks, tight pressed walls of books dwarfing thin aisles just big enough for one person to move through them. June walks aimlessly, scanning spines. She finds herself in Physics, then Chemistry, rows of over-sized texts with equations in the titles. She keeps moving. History, she thinks. Or Anthropology. Maybe there's a whole Native section. But she stops at Biology. A row of seriously thick books with names like *Complete Human Anatomy.* Complete. She likes the sound of that. Here are answers. Facts. Cold hard truths. What was she thinking? Rose, that horrible Professor Nordstrom, they don't have any answers.

June pulls out the book. She needs both hands, rough palms against a thick, grainy cover. Her muscles are taut, and under them, the bones, flexible yet rigid. Bones.

She takes the book over to one of the little study tables jammed in here and there against the walls of the library. She puts the book on the desk. She opens it to the contents. *Description and Detail of the Human Skeleton.* June finds the section. There it is. Figure 2.1. She traces the bones with a red, ragged finger. She's thinking about him now, imagining him. He's squat and powerful. Legs, June thinks. Strong, short legs. Tibia, she reads. Fibula, patella, femur. June says the words out loud, whispers them, hears them fade out and disappear in the dusty empty library. *They were here first,* Rose hisses with a note of disgust. Crazy old lady with her ghosts and curses. *It's not like that,* June thinks. So what's it like? June peers back down at the diagram. Bones. She has to start somewhere. She'll figure out the parts, put them in order. Then she'll see. What they are. What they want to be.

TIM AND CHARLIE
Monday, April 14

WHEN TIM WAKES UP he's back on his back. The ground underneath is cold and hard. He rubs his eyes against the soft, filtered light. It's late afternoon, he guesses. He remembers leaving his father's place. He remembers moving automatically, inexorably, back to the woods, back to *his* woods. He climbed the tree. He smoked another joint. And then another. The black night going bleary. Flattened cut-outs of the house, the backyard, the hole in the ground...all of it swirling around him like a cheesy dream sequence in one of those old black and white movies Carly likes to watch, special effects made with glue and scissors, orbiting mobiles, the scenes so long Tim wants to shout at the screen, yeah, yeah, we get it already.

Get what?

Tim screws up his eyes, locking out the daylight. Ah Jesus fuck, his head. After visiting his father, he'd taken a pill. Passing by the Sunfire still parked on the edge of the embankment, he'd suddenly, conveniently, remembered the pills Clay had given him, little white pills in a small plastic vial. Here, he'd said. You look stressed out man. Try these. And Clay had laughed his sardonic, expressionless little laugh.

I took—

maybe two, Tim thinks, now sitting awkwardly on the moist dirt and leaf rot under the tree. And he'd climbed. And he'd smoked. And then. *And then?* Tim jerks himself to attention. And then—it happened. Again. The woman. The hole. A shift in the wind, a parting of clouds. The backyard loomed under him. He could see that the hole was bigger now, deeper and broader. What else? Tim pushes through his fragmented memories of the night before. He puts his hands on his head and presses down against the pulsing pain.

Carly—there was—in the—

He'd stared hard at the hole dominating what had once been that perfect square of turf carpeting his dreams. His father looking at him, his eyes bulging with disbelief, saying what his closed throat couldn't—*Grass? Why the fuck are you asking me about fucking grass?*

Because there is a woman digging a whole in the backyard. Because my mother came to me in a cloud of rotting perfume and gently traced the arc of my face. Because he saw, in the hole, a glimmer, a glow, a hint of—maybe movement, maybe just the protrusion of something slightly exposed—

something.

Tim strains his skull against his hands. Something, and he saw it and—

And he smoked and watched and waited, watched and smoked and waited. And without a schedule, without anything to demarcate one moment from another, the high just seemed to linger, a state of perpetual inwardness, a dream turning day-real, an oblong patch grown just for him to lie down in and disappear. He remembers looking at his hands. Touching his face. Fingers edging around his throat. Whose fingers?

Tim stretches his arms above him. His knuckles brush old leaves. He looks up at the vast canopy of the giant tree, patches of blue sky just visible through the reach of suddenly green boughs. He grimaces at the light through leaves stuck in the perpetual motion of unfurling. He needs a plan. He can't just keep—

lying here.

He should have been back by now. He had a shift last night; they'll fire him. And Clay will—

—Carly—

He'll tell her everything. His dad, his mom, digging ghost lady, Clay's unctuous assurances *it's all good there Timmy boy.*

Not all good. Not all good at all. He can't leave. Not yet. Last night—what he saw—things are happening, signs and symbols, it's like what that kid said. What did she call it? *Vision quest.* Fuck that old fuck. Let him choke and die.

Last night—he saw—

He's close. He's closer than he ever imagined he could be.

He tries to sit up. His limbs are weightless and weak. His head throbs with the effort. Nevertheless, he forces himself.

There, he thinks. *Now I just need—just a little—*

He shouldn't. But he needs *something.* To clear his mind. To help him think. He needs to—take the edge off.

Jesus Carly, give me a friggin' break here. I just need to—

He fumbles around in his coat pocket. He feels the ring, cold metal. He lets it slip away back down into the bottom of his filthy pocket.

Fuck him. Fuck him and his ring.

He tries again. This time his hand closes around the vial of pills. He opens the small bottle and peers in. There are ten or so pills left.

Hands shaking, he tips the bottle to his parched mouth. Then he lies back down on the cold ground and closes his eyes.

Hey mister?

Uh?

Charlie stands over him.

Are you okay mister?

Huh?

Mister?

Uh…

Mister? Can you hear me mister?

Charlie's looking down at him.

Are you okay?

Wooo. Dizzy. He jerks into a crouch, puts his palms on the ground seeking balance.

Don't try to get up.

It's that girl, Tim thinks. He can feel her hot hand on his shoulder.

She crouches down next to him. You fainted, I think. We learned about this in first aid.

No…I…

You don't look very good mister. Do you want something to eat?

I…

You better eat.

Charlie produces a small package wrapped in tin foil. She puts the bundle in his hand. Tim feels the metal paper prickly on his fingers.

Go ahead, the girl says. Eat it.

Tim's fingers, trembling.

It's good, she says. You'll like it.

He peels clumsily at the foil. Some kind of pastry, doughy skin flaking in his hands.

Eat it. Go ahead. It's good.

Huh?

Eat it. Charlie makes an eating motion, chews elaborately, her plump cheeks bulging. Tim takes a dutiful bite. The outer crust is soft, a tiny bit greasy. The middle is spicy, soft—potato, chickpea.

It's a paratha, Charlie says. My mother makes them.

Para-wha?

It's Indian food.

Tim nods, swallows.

Here. Drink this. Charlie pops the cap off a jar of amber fluid. Tea.

Tim feels the lukewarm liquid through glass. He feels the distance between him and the jar of tea. Increasing. Expanding. He's alone. He's a shadow. He wants to lie down. He wants to lean into the girl and disappear. He wants to hold on so he doesn't—

disappear.

He drinks. The bitter-sweet warmth fills his throat, his stomach. It spills out of his mouth, over his chin.

He gasps for air. Belches.

Charlie giggles. Tim shivers suddenly, violently.

Are you okay?

Cold. I'm...

Charlie looks at him, her eyes big with concern.

Let's...Tim's teeth clicking...build...a fire.

A fire? Here?

I...used to...all...the...time.

Won't we get in trouble?

Naw...who'll?...You get...wood.

Tim watches the girl scamper around the clearing, collecting twigs and brush. A bulky girl, but surprisingly agile. She works quickly, forms a large pile of dead branches.

She stops in front of Tim, limply gazing in the direction of the river.

You used to build fires here? she asks him.

Arms wrapped around himself. He's slowly warming. Sure I did. All the time. When I was your age.

Didn't anyone notice?

Naw. Who's going to notice?

I guess. Charlie giggles. She jumps up and quickly returns, dragging a thick branch.

I think we've got enough, Tim says.

How will we light it? We don't have any paper.

Tim picks up a small log, points at the white mottled peeling skin covering it.

What is it? Charlie asks.

Birch bark.

The Natives used to make birch canoes!

Yeah? Well it burns real good. The bark. It's better than paper.

Tim peels it off, his shaking fingers settling. Here. Put it under those twigs there. Good. You wanna light it? Tim extends his Che Guevera lighter.

Okay. Charlie giggles nervously. She crouches low and flicks the lighter. Metal grates her thumb. She tries again. She keeps trying. Finally, a thin blue flame. Fire flickers and creeps.

There, you see? Tim warms his hands. He closes his eyes then opens them. Hey, thanks. For before. That…ah….snack thing. I really needed that.

You fainted.

Yeah. Naw. I musta...I just...

Are you still on your vision quest?

Uh...Yeah.

What are you trying to see?

Oh. Uh. Nothing...really.

Charlie frowns. But that's not the way you're supposed to do it! You're already supposed to know what you're trying to see!

Weird kid. Tim's head hurts. He wishes she would leave so he could—

No you aren't.

You are too! Charlie spits a little in her excitement. Like you have to decide if you want to see like an animal or...or...an ancient ancestor... or a spirit that can make it rain or something. You don't just—

Hey kid, you know what? I did see something, okay?

You did? What did you see?

Tim pokes the fire with a stick. Red sparks flame out. It was... it's...hard to explain.

Was it an animal spirit?

Uh...kinda.

It was?

Not...really.

It wasn't?

Tim closes his eyes again. He can feel the pressure building again, in his temples. He has to—Hey kid. I can't really talk about it.

Oh, she says, frowning.

Listen kid. Giving in, Tim pulls the works from his jacket pocket. Starts rolling a joint. When I know, you'll be the first to know, okay?

Charlie has big brown irises, dark, almost black, like pools of night. Tim feels them tracking him as the girl watches in fascination.

Hey, how old are you anyway?

Thirteen, Charlie says defensively.

Thirteen, huh? Tim's fingers, working on their own volition, finish tapering the joint. He taps it into his mouth and raises Che's flame to his lips. Want some? he asks out of the side of his mouth.

They move through the woods. Charlie leads, clambering her way into the bush surefooted. She's not graceful, more like stoutly capable.

The light changes. The timbre of the gully. Green refraction turning brackish, as if they're descending.

Charlie stumbles, giggles. She's high. *Weird girl,* Tim thinks. He shouldn't have gotten her—

Why not though? He's sold to high school; he's sold to junior high, trios of nervous kohl-eyed anorexic mini-skirt fourteen-year-olds waiting for him in the alley behind the pub. I could get in big trouble for this, he lies to them, as if anyone cares. He charges them extra. Danger fee, he says. For his worst crap, of course.

Charlie smoked the good stuff with him. So it's not exactly a shock that she couldn't sit still. Coughing, fidgeting, giggling. She kept asking him about his quest, what he saw, when he would tell her. Finally she jumped to her feet and said she had to show him something.

What?

Something.

What?

You'll see.

Tim follows her through the woods. He's high too, mellow and limp, relieved to be just doing something, going somewhere, not particularly worrying about what will happen next. So Tim jerks along, trying to keep up with Charlie, who moves swiftly, her strong legs pumping, muscles bulging against a pair of too-tight camouflage-pattern denims—*not a good look*, Tim thinks lazily. Something her mother brought home from the mall under the clueless impression that it'll help her daughter fit in.

They move further and deeper, the trees getting closer together, their sharp branches and quills more abrasive. Brambly bushes open to Charlie's insistent gait then close as Tim stumbles through.

Ouch. *Fuck.*

Charlie giggles. Come on!

They're moving upstream, away from the stores and the church and the car. Away from the thin part of the woods Tim likes to think he knows. Here the cliff is higher, the space between the escarpment and the river wider and denser.

Tim's breathing hard, sweating. Hey kid. Can we—

C'mon!

She disappears into a grove of tall firs. *Angry fuckers*, Tim thinks. The trees are thin and angular, their short branches cramped and mean, pressing against each other. He scrapes through, too. They're in the wide bit of gully now, where the river thins and runs down in a white foamy rapid of protruding rock. Here the forest takes over, is thicker, emboldened. And it's steep. *We're going up*, Tim thinks. Climbing. Tim feels his calves stretch as his feet search for footing. The girl artlessly crests rocky outcroppings. *Like some kind of hyperactive hobbit*, Tim thinks.

Charlie stops in a bit of a clearing, a stunted knoll dwarfed by the sheer cliff side, the mean prickly trees, the river loud and irresistible, near and absent.

Hey, Tim gasps. Where are we going?

Behind them is the descent back to the flatter part of the gully. In front, the climb continues, the ground rocky now, the trees ferocious and crowded. Tim stumbles onto the cramped plateau rise. The girl next to him.

Is this where we're—?

Look, Charlie says. That's my house. She giggles like it's hilarious. Her house looms at the edge of the cliff, a sprawling white domicile with pillars and huge bay windows.

Wow. Tim says stupidly. It's pretty big.

Yeah, it's big, Charlie says matter-of-factly. I have my own bathroom.

Your parents must be loaded.

My parents are doctors.

Really? Both of them?

Charlie nods, smiling dreamily, her pupils huge.

Like…your mom too?

Uh-huh.

Wow.

They stare up. House on the ridge. Vast and empty looking.

How do you get up there?

I made a path, Charlie says proudly. It's really steep.

What about your parents?

They don't know. I go out my window and climb down that tree there.

Wow.

Most of the time they're not home anyway.

They're not?

They're always working.

My dad, Tim says haltingly, when I was a kid…he was like that…

Charlie looks past Tim into the thicker part of the woods.

Are you ready? she asks. Without waiting for an answer, she's off again. Blue-white camouflage pattern thighs merging with the disappeared sky. Tim plunges after her, sharp boughs slapping his face.

They hike. Tim looks down, sees his legs, long stretchy gummy things. The high is springy, bouncy. He feels not so much energetic as weightless. He bounds through the woods, finally catching up to Charlie. She's stopped, is waiting for him. They stand close to each other in an awkward space between bitter twisted trees.

We're almost there, she says.

He gulps, too winded to reply. She's breathing hard under a puffed out red jacket. Tim thinks she looks like a refugee sporting randomly donated western fashions. She smiles at him.

Are you okay?

I'm…fine…Tim gasping for breath. Just…a…little…

We're almost there!

She steps between two large squarish rocks. A dark gap forms a chasm. Charlie squirms in and disappears. Tim quickly follows to keep up. He doesn't want to be left behind. It's a cool damp descent. They're going down now. Tim's confused. Where's the river? You can hear it, a distant rumble muted by the fissure between gigantic boulders that is now their path.

These are from the ice age, Charlie yells back at him.

Tim traces a hand along lichen-covered grey stone. He expects it to be cold or something.

C'mon!

Charlie pumps her legs, she's practically running now.

They spill out into a clearing. Trees surround the depressed area. Inside the clearing it's all rocks and bare soil, stunted vegetation, moss, and creeper bushes hugging the fringes. Tim stands there, his chest heaving, sweat oozing off him. He feels alien from himself, alert and impassive, unencumbered by his pounding heart, his gasping gangly body. A few large boulders jut out of the ground, otherwise, not much to look at. Charlie marches to the far end of the depression. She stops in front of a bulge in the ground, like the protruding sloping ceiling of a sunken igloo.

C'mon! she calls, looking back at him.

But Tim doesn't move. He doesn't like this place. That aloof feeling of impartial detached observation has gone up in a puff of smoke, replaced by a more familiar sense of paranoia—Why did he waste it on the girl? She's a kid, she'll tell somebody; he'll get busted. Where the hell are we? He shouldn't be here. He needs to—

C'mon! This is it!

What? This? Pointing to the bulge in the ground, the sloped hill of dark menacing dirt.

The Natives built it.

Who? Tim looks around suspiciously.

Not now! It's old! Like a long time ago.

Huh.

C'mon! I'll show you!!

Naw, Charlie, I'm just gonna—

She drops to her hands and knees and squirms through.

Charlie?

He's alone now. He'll turn around and go back. Get in his car and drive to the city, to Carly, to—

Which way is the way back? The emptiness of this small clearing reminds him of something abandoned, something left behind that nobody else was ever supposed to find. The wind through the scraggly branches. He won't go in. He doesn't have to go in. But he kneels, inspects the tunnel hole. Charlie? he calls feebly. There's a crazed calm about her. Something solid. *She reminds him of—Naw she's nothing like—*

But she is. It's like she knows something, something he doesn't.

What if she's not coming back? Trap door secret passageway to—where? The tunnel hole. Portent darkness. Tim contemplates the exterior of it. Some earthy bunker. Indians built it. *So what? What makes her think I'm so freakin' interested in Indians?* Tim peers suspiciously into the tunnel. Last night, the deepening hole—a still limpid darkness.

Charlie?

Muffled yell. Come ooooon!

Tim sniffs. It smells musty, smoky, familiar. *Like our apartment*, he thinks. Carly snuggling up to him, joint burning, incense, candles, dusty air settling. Tim falls to his hands and knees. He flattens himself into the tunnel and begins to inch along. *This is it*, he thinks. *After this I'm done.* He'll go back. He'll go back and hug Carly for dear life and tell her he's sorry; he's so sorry. It's true, what she says: he can't be trusted. He stole her car. He stole her car and just—without even—

Daylight recedes behind him. His knees and elbows sink into the loose powdery earth as he crawls, his fingers digging. The ground feels strange: dusty, soft. Ash or fine sand.

And it's weirdly warm, getting warmer. Swollen drops of sweat swell on his chin, splattering onto the soft soot beneath him. Tim crawls. He blinks feverishly, trying to see what's up ahead.

Charlie?

Over here, she whispers.

Where?

Over here, Charlie giggles quietly. I'm over here.

He creeps toward her voice, bumps his head on her.

Hey, she laughs. He feels the slick of her parka against his cheek. Watch where you're going!

Tim feels something soft shifting. Sorry, he murmurs.

Give me your lighter, Charlie says. Tim stretches an arm back. He pats his pocket. On all fours, his stomach so low it's grazing ground, he twists around.

Here, he says. Charlie fumbles for it, her fingers against his palm. He can smell her, an earthen sweaty kid smell. He lies there, his belly and pelvis against the strange warm surface. The ground emanates a gentle heat.

The lighter clicks. Ouch, Charlie mutters. She tries again, producing a jittering flame in a tiny dance. Charlie lights candles arranged in points all around the enclosure. The dim light reveals a sloped ceiling made of some kind of clay. The ceiling is higher than Tim thought. He can sit. Half stand, even. They're crowded near the back of the dugout. The smell is old smoke, dried up sweat. Tim hoists himself into a sitting position. The rounded hard walls are dark with soot. Tim drags a hand down the wall; it's gritty, bits flaking off, but still smoother than he thought, and less impermanent. He pulls his palm off; it's smeared black.

Charlie is cross-legged in front of a makeshift mantle. Around variously sized candles sit a semi-circle of objects, their details shrouded in flickering flame. And behind the shrine, a kind of hearth, the stone walls of a fireplace and chimney. Tim whiffs fire, dust, ash—

bone, he thinks.

He shifts closer to Charlie.

So, she whispers. What do you think? She's smiling, her face beatific, glowing. I found it. I come here sometimes. I think it used to be a sweat lodge.

Huh. So…they…uh…

It's where they did their ceremonies.

So, he says cruelly, annoyed, now, by her know-it-all tone, you bring your *friends* here?

Charlie doesn't answer. She looks down at her hands in her lap.

Hey, Tim says gently. It's cool. I get it…sweat lodge, right?

Yeah, like a sauna, Charlie says excitedly. The men would come in here. They'd be all…naked…and the fire would make it really really hot. They'd smoke their pipes and chant and pray and stuff.

Huh.

Charlie is next to him, all coiled energy. *She's never brought anyone else here,* Tim thinks. *I'm the first.*

And what's all this stuff? Tim indicates the semi-circle of objects around her makeshift stuck-in-the-ash candelabra.

Oh, that's…Tim can tell Charlie's embarrassed now. It's… nothing.

Tim leans in, his pale cheeks sparsely bearded in wispy wheat stubble gone golden in the candlelight. He picks up a stone bit, knocking over an empty Hello Kitty Pez container in the process. The stone is a grooved rough-hewn triangle, sharp at one end, stubby at the other.

Arrowhead, Charlie says matter-of-factly. I found it in the forest.

Huh. Yeah? Tim fingers the object. He imagines using it. To hunt. Deer. Birds. Enemies. Who are Tim's enemies? *Stab or be stabbed,* Tim thinks. Kill or be killed.

Next Tim picks up what looks like an old comic book. He squints at the title. *Alpha Flight?*

It's—Charlie starts off excitedly. But then she stops herself. It's a comic book, she says flatly.

Tim brings the comic up close to his face. A price of 65 cents marks it as a relic from a bygone era. But the circles of water damage on the faded cover make it clear that this isn't going to be one of those finds some loser's going to shell out a thousand bucks for or anything. On the cover, the clearly identifiable evil villain is threatening a muscle-bound man and woman who, from their long black hair and beaded headbands, Tim gathers are supposed to be Indian or Native or whatever Charlie calls it. The choice is yours, Shaman, he reads out loud from the bad guy's bubbled dialogue. If you save Snowbird, your daughter dies. *Snowbird? Shaman?* Tim giggles.

Charlie plays with the bulgy cuffs of her ski jacket.

So it's like a team? X-Men-Avengers kind of thing?

I haven't read it in a while, Charlie says desperately.

Tim peers suspiciously at the comic again, before finally, mercifully, dropping it back onto the shrine of objects. Immediately, Charlie leans forward and repositions the comic to its original spot next to the now righted Pez dispenser. Tim is already inspecting a dirty stuffed animal, its purple fur ragged and matted. What do we have here? Tim says, pointing at the misshapen creature, a hippo or elephant or something.

Nothing, Charlie mutters. Just something from when I was a kid.

Tim picks up the hippo and holding it gently to his chest, tenderly sniffs the top of its frayed head. When I was a kid, he says, I had a kangaroo. I loved that thing. I took it everywhere with me. What did I call it? Kangy Kangoo or something. He grimaces in pretend embarrassment. Man, if my parents couldn't find that thing at bedtime, I would just lose my shit. Just go mental…

Charlie listens to him gravely, her eyes focussed on the stuffed animal. Tim makes to put it back, and she quickly reaches for it, plucking it out of his hands and hugging it to her jacketed chest.

This looks cool, says Tim, already in the process of grabbing the cylindrical piece of stone sitting in the centre of the semi-circle display of dusty objects. He's sweating, but he shivers.

Careful! Charlie says. I think that's like, really really old.

The coldness of the object spreads through his palm, up his arm and into his chest.

Tim shivers again, more violently this time. He wants to put the stone down, but instead finds himself inspecting it. He brings it to the candlelight and sees a face: gouged-out sunken eyes and protruding forehead. The carving is longer and more complex than he first thought, adorned with serpentine curves twisting and encircling a stretched body leading to a haunting, empty face that seems to be in mid-scream.

I found it right in here.

Tim's shivering freely now, his breathing ragged. The torso is twisted, a woman's arms tightly bound, wrapped above her belly, her hands skeletal imprints in the rock flesh over the bulge of her breasts. But Tim is pulled back to the woman's face, the way her concave cheeks seem to have been drained of air—*like she's buried alive*. Tim turns the object around and around in his hands, mesmerized by the way the rough porous rock eats the flickering light. Trembling now, he feels the walls of the cave pressing toward him, the pipe cold, so incredibly cold, the kind of cold that burns. *Hold on to it*, he tells himself, *don't fucking let go*. His ragged breathing is horribly audible, each pull of air like a death rattle. Hands madly shaking, he slowly brings the woman's twisted tapered feet to his mouth.

What are you doing? Charlie whines. Be careful! That's like, really really old!

Tim pulls in through the pipe.

What are you *doing?*

He tastes dirt, dust, ash, bone, smoke, ancient buried truth—life, then death. He coughs, trying too late to reverse the process, but now it's stuck in his throat, and, pipe loose in one fist, he flaps his arms around frantically.

What are you doing? Charlie is yelling. What's wrong with you?

Charlie, he gasps through the pressing particulate air. I…can't—

You're okay, she says evenly, eyes moving from his bulging cheeks to the jerky dance of the carving in his fist. You'll be okay. She puts her hand around his fist, stilling the jerky tremors. You're okay. Just…breathe.

Finally, Tim manages to swallow. He drinks down ashy spit. Then, still panting at the musty air, he gasps: Charlie. The other night. I saw—

He wants to tell her. Tell someone.

You saw something?

I saw—my mother.

Your mother? She doesn't understand. He lowers his head to her ear. Breathes in the smell of her.

She's dead, he whispers. She died a long time ago.

Oh…

What should I do, Charlie? He knows he can't ask her. Let's—hey, Charlie, we should—He puts the ancient carved pipe down in front of them. He fumbles for the last of his stash.

SUSAN
Tuesday, April 15

SUSAN WAKES IN THE QUIET ROOM and knows instantly where she is. It's the way the light pushes through the drapes and spreads softly against the yellow walls. She swings herself out of the small bed and pulls open the curtains. The window is open. Cool air flutters in, fresh but also somehow damp and musty. She stands looking out of her childhood bedroom at the familiar view: the front lawn with its lumpy spread of grass and single large misshapen maple tree; the empty street flanked by rows of parked cars; the rows of houses with more or less similar front lawns, plus or minus a tree or shrub or two. Behind the houses across the street, hidden from view, is the ravine, is the river. The river. That's what she's smelling, what she's tasting. She breathes deep, inhales the mineral sheen of water and under-growth and low-lying land recently drenched. The smell reminds her, more than anything, more than sleeping in her old room in her old little bed, of growing up here, of being a kid. A goofy kid with buck-teeth who liked to go down to the ravine and sit alone by the edge of the water and idly wile away a weekend afternoon tossing sticks and stones and long strands of yellowing grass into the cur-rent. Sticks and stones, pulled under, disappearing. Growing up, she didn't care for the other kids, didn't particularly want or need friends. They weren't mean to her like they were to some of the others. Sticks and stones. Break my bones. She ignored them, and they ignored her. Susan stretches her arms overhead, takes another deep breath. Growing up. Do we ever really? The smell: rocks and moss and sun on skin. The river, still flowing. Still there. Why is she here? What's coming next?

She finds her dad in the bright kitchen. He's bustling around, checking off a list.

Hey! Susie! You're up.

She kisses him on a soft cheek. Sorry, Dad, I guess I haven't exactly been much of a…guest.

It's fine, it's fine. I've never seen anyone sleep so much. I checked in on you a few times…just to…make sure you were still…okay.

That was nice of you, Daddy.

Yup. That's what dads are for!

They stand looking at each other, grinning.

You must be starving. Sit down, I'll make you something.

He makes her a tofu scramble. Susan watches him bustle around the kitchen, his movements precise and economical. When was the last time someone cooked for her? Out West, they survived on cheap diner meals, on dumpster-dived day olds, on the weak coffee and suspiciously rubbery grocery store muffins provided by government officials at public hearings. Her dad drops rye bread in the toaster and Susan's mouth waters.

When it's all ready, he joins her at the kitchen table. Susan makes no excuses, eats hungrily, washing down mouthfuls with gulps of extra pulp Tropicana.

I'm sorry, Suze, her dad eventually says, I have to get back to packing. The cab is picking me up at 12.

You're leaving! Susan suddenly remembers. Her dad is going on a trip with his girlfriend Laura. Chile and Peru, Machu Pichu and Lima, Susan vaguely remembers something about a jungle resort and mountain climbing. How long is he going for? Two weeks? Three? Daddy, I totally forgot. I slept all day yesterday and now you're...

No, no, you didn't know I'd be—

It's such bad timing, Susan says.

Her dad shakes his coiffed head ruefully. It is, he says.

But you'll have a great time!

Susan picks up her quarter-filled glass of juice and puts it down again. Her sweet father, he's always tried his best for her. He's shrunken a bit, his short hair gone grey, his face tighter, the lines around his eyes more pronounced. All in all, he seems smaller, more compact, a happier version of himself. He seems good, contented— *settled*, she thinks. Her dad clears the dishes and Susan finds herself drifting down familiar, dangerous territory. Is that what happens? We get older, more comfortable, more *settled*? What does he do all day? What does he think about? *Vacations?* Why shouldn't he go on his trip? That's what people do. They do things that make them happy. He worked hard, didn't he? He deserves it, doesn't he?

So, her dad says, are you feeling better? Maybe you want to go and see my doctor? Get a checkup? Just in case?

No, Dad, I'm fine. I was just—exhausted.

Okay. Good. Good. Her dad's got a dishtowel, is nervously polishing a gleaming white plate. And, do you think you're—are you—?

He can't quite bring himself to say it, but Susan knows what he's asking: What's she planning? How long is she staying? Where will she go next?

It's his house. He deserves, at least, to—

Dad, is it—is it okay if I...stay here a while?

Of course. You know that. Mi casa es su casa.

But the Spanish sounds forced and his grin curls awkwardly at the edges. He doesn't trust her. He doesn't want her to stay at his place all alone. What does he think she'll do? Anger rises in her, but she pushes it back. That's not why she's here.

Dad, she says, I'll take care of the house. Keep an eye on things. If you like, I'll stay here until you're back. Then I'm due back in Vancouver. A lie, slipping out of her. Or maybe it's the truth. Either way, she wants him to know: There are people out there who value her, who care about her, who are waiting for her. Don't worry Dad, she says, I'm not moving in.

Sure, of course, stay, stay as long as you need. That's fine. Can you—he says this uncertainly, as if the terms of their contract have changed—the plant, in my study?

I'll water it Dad. For sure.

And…if the lawn gets a bit…?

Mower still in the shed?

Yup.

They grin at each other again. That was always one of her jobs. Mowing the lawn.

Dad, she hears herself saying. I'm really sorry that you aren't going to be around. I was hoping we could—she pauses here, not sure what she was hoping. Anyway, she goes on hurriedly, I'm going to do some writing. I want to try and get down everything that's… happened. This friend of mine, from out West. Shane. He said…

She trails off, noting how alarmed her dad looks, alarmed at the prospect of one of her scruffy boyfriend radicals making an appearance.

Abruptly, her dad turns and starts putting the breakfast dishes, now clean and dry, back in the cabinet.

Shane read some of my essays. He thinks I should try and maybe get a book together.

A book! her dad says.

He sounds surprised, Susan thinks. But not in a bad way. Well, she says. I mean, I don't have nearly enough material and I'm really just at the very beginning of—

Her dad's cell rings. He hurriedly digs it out of his pocket. It's Laura, he says, giving her an apologetic look.

No problem, Susan says, but he's already walking out of the room.

Susan sits on the porch step. It's just after one, the street characteristically quiet and empty. *High noon in the suburbs*, Susan thinks. So now what? She thinks of Shane, who would make a great character in a western, her Indian cowboy in work boots. She's horny, she realizes. Maybe she'll draw a bath. Do—things. When was the last time she'd been alone? When was the last time she'd had a *bath?* Squatting, sleeping on couches, sleeping at Shane's tiny shared apartment. The space she now has seems gratuitous, almost inconceivable. A whole house to herself. The sun is high above, warming yellow-green lawns, expansive squares delineating perfect swatches of defined property—*mine, yours,* Susan thinks, the whole world diced and sliced into bits and pieces. So what? It's not like it was any different out West. If she's got a problem with the way things are— and she does, oh yes she does—she might just as well have stayed there as come back here. *But,* she tells herself, *here you are.* You got on the bus and rode across the country to be in this exact place. She takes a deep breath. Again, she smells the river rot of the ravine as it stirs to life. The smell fills her with sudden loneliness. She used to spend hours down there. It was her playground, her library, her friend. Her father whisked away in a taxi. Shane and his crooked knowing smile left far behind. Her briefly happy childhood, much of it spent down by the river—a time when her parents still loved each other, still loved her without conditions and judgment. Now she's here, alone. *C'mon Susan. Get a grip.* Susan exhales. The wind blows and here she is. The river, across the street, hidden, buried, inaccessible—a reminder. She tilts her head back and lets the sun's weak rays play over her face.

Miss, excuse me? Miss? She opens her eyes to a young man, skinny college kid, standing over her. He has on a green vest emblazoned with a logo—the words CEN in a leaf. Hi, he says perkily, now that he's got her attention. My name is Jared and I'm from the Credit Environmental Network? I'm here today because we're raising funds for the protection of…Susan fixes a crooked smile to her face and half listens to his pitch. She'd done her stint in organizations like CEN, gentle suburban affairs that spent half their time fundraising and the rest fostering corporate partnerships, win-win for everyone, a feel-good banner hanging over Hurontarion proclaiming Wississauga a green city sponsored by the local gas utility. *Well,* she thinks, regarding the scruffy young man's bright green eyes and taut cheekbones, *at least it gives cute college kids something to do.* A breeze cuts across and she shivers as the sun disappears behind amassing grey clouds. Now it looks like it's going to rain. She thinks of Shane again, his body wet in the mist, a white T-shirt splattered against his chest. He never seemed to feel the cold. God he was—

And with the road going in down by the river it's more urgent than ever that we—

Wait? What did you say?

He stops speaking, both of them jolted out of their separate orbits.

Uh, about the road you mean?

Yes, Susan says, about the road.

Well, uh…he's off script now. They're going to…planning to…put a road in, an expressway, along the river on this side of the valley.

But that's old growth forest down there, Susan says.

The young man, sensing his opportunity, tries to move back into his spiel. That's why we're out here connecting with people like—

Susan stands up. She feels the familiar heat spreading through her. Shane, her dad, her fucking mother who she doesn't speak to if she can help it, the river, hidden purpose momentarily revealed in a flash like lightning through night. The boy watches her rising, looking confused, awestruck.

Miss—?

And your organization? Susan says. Are they organizing protests against this *expressway*?

Uh…we…we're…CEN is, we're raising money in order to—

Susan waves away his words. You better come inside, she tells him.

JUNE
Tuesday, April 15

MORNING AGAIN. June bustles herself around the kitchen, feeling
the resistance of her heavy limbs. She'd been awake all night picturing it, picturing herself doing it. In the morning, she knew, she'd be
going out there. In the meantime, she had lain next to her snoring
husband. Hearing Norm step out of the shower, June drops two
pieces of multigrain into the toaster with impatient efficiency. She
is, she knows, moving farther and farther off the map. This isn't who
poor old Norm married. Norm wants something else for her, she
knows. A job, a gym membership, the cocooned heat of possibility deep in her belly. She wants those things, had them before, felt
them in inevitable predictable orbit around her. But somehow they
drifted off course, her orbit listing past ever-more uncertain constel-
lations. *Maybe that's the problem*, she thinks. There's something else
now. Some other thing pulling her off course. She's in uncharted
territory now, her only guide a nonagenarian who believes in spirits and curses.

Rose hadn't even blinked when June had told her. She'd taken
the idea of some kind of—*haunting*—as perfectly plausible, even
likely. What had she said? *Cursed, you know.* No, June hadn't known.
Now June is starting to know. She's starting to know that working in

the backyard is similar to the feeling she gets being with Rose. Being. That's a word for it. Only it's hard to get into words. There's a sense of…floating. Like she doesn't have to do anything. She can just—be. But it's not being like a surfing the web at your desk job being. Or stopping at the Pizza Pies Mamma Mia Express Takeout for a spelt crust Mediterranean special and a large garden salad kind of being. It's not killing time waiting for the day to end and Norm to come home being. It's like she's… connected, to something, something outside her, something—

deeper.

Finally, Norm ambles down the polished mahogany stairs. She watches, her fingers twisting her hair as he eats his toast and flips through the paper, occasionally issuing forth a harrumph of disapproval. June glances at the front page, an article about a provincial commission established to explore what the headline says is *the epidemic of missing Native women*. Another related headline describes a body found on the weekend: a 25-year-old Native woman in Winnipeg stabbed in the back and thrown into the Assiniboine river, which runs right through the centre of the city. Her body, apparently, was later found bobbing on the banks of what that the paper describes as *frigid waters*. Norm's on sports, he's an NBA fan for some reason. Several of his favourite teams are in the playoff bubble. He checks the scores of last night's games and shakes his head sorrowfully. They're not going to make it, he mutters, stuffing the last bite of toast into his mouth and chewing laboriously. June snatches his plate from him and jams it in the dishwasher. Duly prompted, Norm grumbles to the front foyer and puts on his coat. June follows him and receives her peck on the cheek redolent of shaving cream and aftershave. He notices her then, as if for the first time, and asks how she's feeling, how she slept. She adjusts the collar of his shirt and warns him not to be late to work.

It is nice of him. To ask after her.

Bye honey, Norm says almost quizzically, giving her a second peck at her cheek as if trying to chip off a bit of paint and reveal the true colour lingering underneath. June, in her robe, smiling passively, fire smouldering in her chest, locks the door behind him.

Now he's gone.

June moves decisively to the sliding door to the backyard. Warm, ripe air drifts into the living room. *Warm day*, June thinks, *first of the season*. She lets the breeze play on her face and expand into her lungs. Last night she'd imagined it differently, pictured throwing off her robe and plunging out into the dirt like some kind of super archaeology woman. Under the robe, she's in an old pair of sweats and a long sleeve flannel shirt. Under that, her body: breasts slightly slumping, stomach pouching, thighs just thickening. She's never been beautiful. But boys—men—always paid attention to her. Not gorgeous or glamorous, but pretty enough. That creepy professor. She's getting older. Is that why she let Norm?—she let him and then he fell asleep. He slept like a baby. She doesn't feel older. She's the same person she's always been. Isn't she? Norm drives off, the automatic garage door closing with a groan of chains. June drops her robe, leaves it lying on the floor in a slump.

And finally, she strides into the backyard. She's covered the hole—the site, she thinks importantly—with a large blue tarp she found in the garage. She yanks the tarp off, liking the sound of snapping plastic. She negotiates the steep slide down into the pit with confident ease. The cold at the bottom embraces her. It's not that she's getting used to it. It's that she's getting used to anticipating the way the cold will be dispelled, driven off by the heat of her body as she works her way deeper into its crevices. June crouches down and digs her fingers into a suspiciously lumpy protrusion of clay. The earth is loamy and resistant after the cold night. June winces as the dirt presses against ragged fingertips and jams under her nails. But she keeps going. She pushes in deeper, her fingers probing for gradations, fringes, boundaries that delineate the bones—*his* bones—recalcitrant and unwilling, but somehow insistent, as if they've been waiting all these hundreds of years to be unearthed. The bones of a betrayed warrior, she imagines. Or a medicine man, a tribal healer beset by enemies—devils in friendly disguise. He was murdered, she theorizes. Must have been. Why else would the bones be pulling at her, insisting that they be noticed, dug up, assigned truth and meaning? And yet, the bones are stubborn, elusive, part of a man too proud to admit what he has been reduced to.

It happened right here, June thinks, not for the first time. Maybe five or maybe even ten thousand years ago. *Murdered*, bashed in the head with a boulder or cut down from behind by some rudimentary early-version hatchet.

Norm would just make fun of her. He'd say, *It isn't a movie, honey. You can't just dig them up and bury them again with the right prayers or whatever mumbo jumbo.* She can hear him saying that phrase: *mumbo jumbo*. Anyway, she already knows that. She feels it. She's not planning on—well, okay, she doesn't exactly know what she's planning on. *It'll come.* It's like a puzzle. One piece at a time.

But how *will* she explain it to Norm? Come the weekend, he'll likely want to wander out back and take a peek at what she's been so industriously doing in the backyard. What will she tell him? What will he see? Somehow, she has to make him understand. This isn't—it's not some kind of ghost story. This isn't made up. This is—

real.

After she was fired, let go, downsized, whatever they wanted to call it, this old Billy Bragg song from a CD her sister used to play wouldn't get out of her head. To be honest, at the time neither she nor her sister had a clue what the song was about or ever made any effort to find out. It wasn't even the kind of music they usually listened to. Her sister, soon to graduate high school, had been going through a moody phase and had fallen in with a different crowd. A boy had lent her the disc. For June it was just background, but in the cab after being summarily dismissed, one line kept rewinding over and over again in her mind. *They stitched her back together, but left her heart in pieces on the floor.* The morning after the firing, the song still firmly in place in her cortex, June had downloaded the track from iTunes and started playing it, over and over again, permanent repeat. Norm found the song perplexing and kind of funny. He Googled the lyrics. He held his nose and pretended to sing in an English accent—*Wone dawkk Niggght*—June ignored him. She moped around her apartment with that single song looping in her head while she took half-hour showers, surfed the web for cookie recipes she would never bake and scrolled through season after season of *Hawaii Five-O*, the remake. God was it really as dramatic as all that? People lost their jobs all the time. Or couldn't get a job in the first place. She'd stopped answering the phone, reading her texts. Her parents were harassing her with offers to bring over supper, their worry overwhelming, overflowing. Her friends issued compulsory assurances then disappeared back to partners and careers, aggressively pursuing predetermined goals that she'd always been covetous of even when she'd seemed to be more or less on the same path. Even when things were going exactly as expected, June could never quite shake the feeling she was just pretending. But her friends, they all seemed so sure of themselves. So *into* it.

Never mind that. She has a new life now, a new job. *Yeah, I'm on the clock right now. Rebounded nicely, haven't I? Back on my feet, at the bottom of the pit, gravedigger, you see, noble occupation, well, grave robber to be more precise, perhaps a bit less noble, but still an occupation with a hallowed tradition.*

By then, Norm was coming over after work almost every day. He'd take her for walks. They'd go to the park or to the lake to watch the sunset. They didn't necessarily talk all that much. They held hands. After a while they started going back to her place to make love. In the end, it was Norm who saved her, who brought her back to the land of the living, convinced her to stop listening to what he called in his worst British accent *the depressing song by the English bloke*. It was Norm, only Norm, who sat with her, held her hand, cracked his cheesy jokes, waited patiently for her to re-emerge.

She'll tell him. Try and explain it to him.

What can she tell him? The truth is a feeling, a cold buried fossil come to life. The bones want something. June doesn't know what they want.

She scrapes, the soil clinging to the webbing between her fingers. She breaks up clay clumps, feels the ground loosen and give. As she works she imagines *him*: alone, walking, the first to ever plant his feet in this lush soil. The cliff protecting the river, a slice of sheltered forest teeming with game, with berries and wild mushrooms, how perfect it must have seemed. It wasn't like that squirmy Nordstrom said. He wasn't some kind of savage. *He was a leader,* June thinks. Leading a group of tired, hungry, desperate wanderers away from frigid northlands of giant glacier slabs. Through luck, through divine intervention, through the same kind of sheer persistent stubborn will that has June at the bottom of a hole in her backyard, he leads his tribe to this fertile land. At least it was, then, she thinks. Thousands of years ago. He pauses, smells the air. Stops, his journey over—he's found it: a home.

It's crazy. A fantasy. *Christ, June, you're really starting to—*

But Nordstrom—and Rose—

They saw it too. She can't hide it, it shimmers over her, a glow. She's found something…something amazing.

C'mon June. Get a job. Get a life. She has a life. *I let Norm—in me—I could be—*

He's come to her. He's chosen her. He wants her to—

dig.

Morning, then afternoon. The sun shifts, rolls over, the big house casting a stranger's shadow. June brushes with her knuckles, mines the damp cool earth with bare hands. She feels at home in the pit she dug. She feels safe.

It's a beautiful house. Everything redone just the way she wanted it.

But *he* got here first. He stood in Norm's prized backyard and saw the forest gully and heard the river raging.

Once, June went with Norm to see the river. They went by car, a fifteen-minute drive northwest, wide flat curve, the picnic grass dotted with goose shit and squawking gulls. The river was a disappointment. It smelled funny. There were signs everywhere warning people not to swim, not to feed the birds, not to fish. They stood and watched a Chinese man in hip wader boots stepping out into the middle with a rod. They'll eat anything, June remembers thinking. Then admonishing herself: racist. She remembers pitying the old guy and wanting Norm to take her away, to take her to the mall for lunch at the Cheesecake Club.

There. June has tunnelled under. She can feel it loosening now. With a final gentle tug, she pulls it out of the ground. A round, grey-ish object, hard to the touch. She gently brushes at it. Soft slopes, smooth yet striated. Bone. A thrill like a chill runs through her. Hard to imagine that one day she'll just be—*this*. She traces her hand down a worn yellowed curve. Hipbone, she thinks. She feels her own hip pressing out against the swell of her flesh, confined in dirty sweats that are just a bit too tight.

She thinks back to the anatomy books she examined. Diagrams and closeups. Photocopies she made at the library. And the books in Norm's study, placeholder leftovers from his dental school days. Diagrams. Illustrations. Illustrated diagrams. Bones. The foundation. What everything is built on, wrapped around. *Norm's bones would be white*, June thinks. They would gleam like his teeth in the light of the bathroom, mouth open to floss. In the pit, the air is still and deep, true like well water or the taste of fresh picked fruit. She puts the hipbone carefully on the ground and kneels over the next lump just barely protruding, already trying to picture it, trying to imagine how they might all fit together. How many bones in the body? She forgets. She'll check the books. She feels ridiculous consulting Norm's dentistry school texts. This isn't some anonymous car accident cadaver donated to a bunch of geeky grad students, a young Norm and his classmates playing show and tell. *You'll figure it out*, she assures herself, plunging her hands back into the cold hard dirt and grimacing as the hard granules of earth grate her fingertips.

Her back and legs ache. She has to be careful where she squats now. *It's getting crowded down here*, she thinks. All those lumps and pro-trusions. If she wants to assemble—him—she'll need more space. And to do that, she'll have to tell Norm. *No, he'd*—she needs to keep him out of this. How can she? She has to tell him something. What? *Lies.*

More lies. Yesterday she told him she was keeping the tarp over the hole to prevent the fertilizer from being exposed to the open air, to the wind and the rain. He looked out into the backyard dubiously, but didn't question her further.

Norm would want to call the police, the museum, the university. Nordstrom and his cronies. She won't let that happen. So she's telling bigger and bigger lies. How could he not notice? June's a bad wife. She can't even make him a decent dinner. She should make more of an effort. *I should—*

She let him shoot in her. Jesus Christ. *What if I'm—?*

She's hot now. She pulls her sweatshirt away from her body, fans the thick cotton, feels the cool, sunken, earthy air on her stomach. Morning has given way to day and June is sweating, damp under her clothes. June straightens to a stand. She stretches. This is the part of the day when the light manages to grace even her pit of forsaken sloping swamp. June leans her face back to catch the sun. Her limbs feel cold and long and ancient. Afternoon warmth on her cheeks. She closes her eyes.

Hello! Anybody home?

Someone coming in, fumbling with the backyard gate.

June freezes.

Hello! Hello? Anybody home?

June clambers out of the dig. She runs to the piled tarp. Hurriedly, she drags the plastic sheet over the hole. Earth slips in, spattering to the bottom.

Hello? Miss?

June makes the gate just in time to block a young man letting himself into the backyard. He wears khakis and a blue oxford button-down. He carries a reporter's pad. He sports a nondescript head of sandy hair and is smiling profusely.

Hello there Miss! Are you June Littlewell?

She wants to say no.

Mrs., yes.

Great. Great. *Mrs.* Excuse me. Do you mind if I ask you—I'm Hal Talbot. From Wississauga Cable Community News? I just wanted to ask you—

His sharp eyes on the tarp.

Why don't we—let's talk inside, June says.

In the living room June slams the sliding door closed and stands in front of it. Now, she says. You're from…Who did you say you were? Not waiting for an answer, she ushers her visitor into the kitchen.

Hal Talbot from the Wississauga Cable Community News.

One of the bulbs illuminating the gleaming marble countertop island buzzes loudly.

Oh! June startles.

The light suddenly flickers to dark.

Just a burnt out bulb, Hal Talbot says.

June stares at the smooth gleaming chin of the stranger in her kitchen. What?

Your bulb. It burnt out.

Oh. Right. June glances up at the now grey-glassed bulb.

You should consider going long life. CFL. They're more expensive but they last longer and use less energy. Better for the environment. My colleague did a story on them.

What?

Ma'am?

You did a…story?

Yes ma'am. I'm a reporter? For the cable community news.

Right. Yes. Of course. We…get that.

Everyone gets it ma'am. It's on basic cable.

Yes. Of course.

June looks at her hands. They're stained with dirt. She turns to the sink and begins washing her hands. I'm making coffee, she blurts, would you like some? Why would she offer him coffee? What does he want? Hal Talbot, reporter. The spacious kitchen feels crowded. She's being watched. The back of her neck. The grooves of her spine. Lumbar, thoracic, cervical, sacral. She knows the words. *You see, I know the words.* Finally, she turns off the water and faces her visitor.

Uh, ma'am?

—

Are you alright ma'am?

I'm fine. Just a bit…

Tired?

Yes. I'm…I'm just a bit…So, that's why, June laughs nervously, I'm making coffee. Please Mr.…

Talbot.

…sit down.

Thank you ma'am.

Call me June. June feels a fake grin stretching her cheeks. Who calls anyone ma'am anymore?

Coffee drips, streams, sputters.

Live Town, June says. That's the show that's always on. She has dim memories of passing it as she climbed up and down the programming ladder. Seems like so long ago. When she spent her nights watching TV while Norm flipped through the paper. Some hokey local talk show always on that channel, fake smiling volunteers pretending that they're real hosts and their guests are real celebrities, not just a bunch of wannabes mugging for the camera while whipping up a bunch of their purportedly famous Wississauga buckwheat pancakes, all you can eat Mondays at Dora's, the home of the buckwheat.

That's our flagship talk show, ma'am. I'm in the news department myself.

Oh. There's news?

We do a daily community news show at 7 am. It repeats at 12, 2, 5, and 11.

Oh.

We go off the air at 12 am.

Oh.

June brings coffee. Milk? Sugar?

Yes please.

Stirring. Spoon against ceramic. It reminds her of a by-now familiar sound. Tea. Tea with—

This is about Rose, isn't it? You're that reporter!

Hal Talbot smiles. She's quite something, our Rose.

Our Rose? June thinks.

She's a treasure, Talbot continues.

Is she?

The oldest woman in Wississauga, Talbot proclaims.

She's old alright. June reddens. The kitchen smells of lemon fresh cleaner. Rose's room, dark and cramped, crammed with dust-ridden mementoes, under siege by the malls and roads. Why would Rose send him here? She doesn't want to be on TV. Hal Talbot looking at her. Watching her.

Rose, you see, ma'am, she—

Will you stop with the ma'am? June tosses her hair. Tries to smile. I'm not that old am I?

Right. Sorry.

Call me June.

Will do...June.

How's your coffee?

Hal Talbot takes a gulp and swallows. His lips seem very pale, unnaturally pinched. Very good, thank you.

So...June thrums her fingers on the table.

Hal Talbot smiles broadly, speaks with predatory politeness. Have you been gardening, there, Mrs....June?

June follows his gaze to her red, ravaged fingers.

Oh. well. She curls them into fists. I've just been, doing some—I'm getting ready to...fertilize.

Wow! Great!

They sip their coffee. June's fingers curve around the cup handle, grated nails pressing into the soft part of her palm.

The reporter grins pinkly.

Mr. Talbot, I'm sorry, but if you could tell me how I can help you...I don't mean to be...but you see...I have to be—going out—soon—

When did she get to be such a terrible liar?

Well, June. Sorry to delay you. I just dropped by to follow up on something. You see, Rose was telling us about the river and how it used to be when she was growing up. And she mentioned something...interesting.

Oh. What would that be? She feels her spine crawling. Eyes on her, eyes moving through her.

Well, June, she was telling us about what a help you've been to her.

No. No. I just…

She was talking about, as I mentioned, the river and how it used to be. And she happened to mention that the area your neighbourhood is in was once a real hub for Native activity.

Was it? June's murmuring now. She's fascinated by the bloodless red of Talbot's lips, the white flashes of his teeth, very clean, perfect even. *Has he been to see Norm?*

And, in fact, Rose mentioned that you, yourself, had encountered, recently, some evidence of Native presence?

What? June wills herself to laugh. To look confused, incredulous. In the form of…

What? Me? No. Ha! Rose! She must have been—

June stops talking. He saw the tarp. My hands. What does he want?

Did you find something in your backyard ma'am?

—

June?

Something? No! I—

Are you aware, June, of the riverfront parkway development? That road they want to build?

The road they're planning on building, yes.

Jesus. Does he ever stop smiling? June wants to shut her eyes. Crawl back into her hole. The site. The bones. Her skin crawling.

You see, June, a finding in the vicinity of the development. That would be particularly significant, June. Very significant. To the community.

The community?

The people of Wississauga. They have a right to know, June. Before it all gets paved over.

Oh. June goes for her coffee. Calming ritual. Rose drinks tea. The sweat on her body is cold now, a trapped chill under her bulky dirty clothing.

June?

—

What's under the tarp, June?

What?

That tarp in the backyard. What's it covering, June?

It's a fertilizer…ditch. A new technique.

Really?

Rose gets, confused. She tells stories and sometimes she gets… confused.

She's concerned about you June.

Why should she be worried about me?

That's a good question.

Stirring her coffee. Spoon dinging the side.

Do you really think she's confused, June? She seems very lucid. Surprisingly lucid. Our viewers always enjoy her recollections because of their vividness.

She is very old, Mr. Talbot.

Yes she is, June.

—

June?

How can I help you, Mr. Talbot?

Our viewers are avid gardeners. Always interested in new techniques. Perhaps I could take a look. You could give us some pointers.

I don't think so. I have an—appointment.

Getting your hair done?

I think you should go now.

Some other time, then?

I'm not really…much for…being on TV.

Ah. More of a private person?

She gets up. Her legs feel surprisingly strong under her. She could kick him, hurt him. Thank you for coming, Mr. Talbot. Her voice goes loud in the kitchen, fills the achingly empty house. I wish I could have helped you. Boldly, not caring anymore, June extends her hand. It hangs in the gleaming emptiness of the kitchen, rough foreign stained paw from some lost era. Not the hand of a Wississauga housewife: white, prim, *soft*.

Talbot shakes gingerly. Thanks for the coffee, ma'am.

I'll show you out the front.

ROSE
Tuesday, April 15

THE TIME FOR THE GIRL TO COME has passed and the girl hasn't come. Not the queer pretty one with all her questions or the quiet plump brown one with the boy's name who only came once. It's quiet, they've taken away her dinner tray, evening settling over her small apartment like a veil. Rose resists the urge to close her eyes and drift off underneath that ever-present scrim. She twists in her chair, feels her bones creak and grind—spring is coming, the changing seasons getting in her joints—but that's not it, that's not what's bothering her. It's what the girl told her, and what she told the boy reporter. Bones. Indians. Curses. Bad business. She should have kept quiet. Stayed mum. All these years, 104 years, and she still can't keep her mouth shut. She never could. Of course these days it's less and less of a problem. She's alone most of the time. She's alone now. Is she? *Of course you are*, she snaps at herself. *Don't be stupid.* So what is it that she's feeling then? Something's happening. Something's going to happen. Rose sighs. She can't shake the sense that something horrible has been put in motion. *Right here*, she thinks, *right here in Wississauga.*

The phone rings. Rose startles. She forgets she even has the damn thing. It was her daughter who insisted she install it. And it's her daughter who's calling. Who else? After the girl comes and then goes, after the dinner tray comes and goes, that's when her daughter calls. Today the girl didn't come. But her daughter is still calling. Frankly Rose would've been happier if it'd been the other way around. Beggars can't be choosers. Not that she'd ever been a beggar. Her daughter said she'd pay for the phone line. I'll take care of myself, Rose snapped, thank you very much. She has money. She gets her old age every month, and the money they gave her when they threw her out of her own house like a dusty chesterfield no one wanted anymore. So, yes, she has money. Once a month she carefully writes out a cheque for the phone bill. Everything else they take right out of her government cheque before she even has a chance to say so much as a how-do-you-do.

The phone keeps bleating. She should just unplug the infernal contraption. But then her daughter would ring up the nurse. She's done that before, all in a foolish panic. They'd come barging in without knocking, asking their questions—How are you doing there, Rose? Why don't you answer the phone, Rose? Do you need to go to the lady's room, Rose? Some of them she can't even understand: the Black one, the China one. Speak English, she wants to tell them.

It's no good. She might as well get it over with.

She reaches a shaky hand out and grabs the heavy plastic receiver.

Mom?

Well who else would it be? Rose snaps.

Jesus Mom, happy to hear from me much?

Don't you take the Lord's name in vain with me, missy.

Sorry Mom. Her daughter sighs on the other end.

I'm still your mother and don't you forget it.

How are you, Mom?

I'm fine dear, Rose says, her tone softening. I'm just fine. She isn't fine. Even the air in her room feels different: alert and alive, like a night animal. The evening traffic sluicing by in the distance.

Are you sure, Mom? You sound…

How would she know how I sound? Rose hasn't seen her daughter since she came back to help her move into the home seven years ago. And even then she was barely there, rushing to and fro, constantly staring at some kind of gidget-gadget, tapping at it with her fingers. I'm over here, dear, Rose has had to announce more than once.

How are your knees, Mom?

My knees, dear? Well, you know, I'm not as young as I used to be.

Have you seen the doctor lately?

Doctors!

More sighing. Are you at least using that cream I sent you? And wearing the necklace? It's excellent for arthritis.

Yes dear.

Her daughter sends her things. A strange smelling tube of green paste. An aquamarine necklace dotted with *magnets* and blessed by some man, some Sri something-or-other. She went all the way to the other side of the country to be near this man, this stranger more interesting to her than her own mother.

And are they helping?

Well, dear, I'm still having a bit of trouble getting around.

She'd given the necklace to one of the nurses.

Rose's daughter is her youngest. And there are the two boys. Grown up now, of course, they both live in the city. They come to visit once a month or so. They bring their wives, sometimes their children; they aren't children anymore, all of them staring at their gadget-gidgets, tap-tap-tapping. Rose wonders what will become of them. She knows where she's going. She isn't worried about that. But the rest of them, she really can't say. They aren't young anymore. Her youngest, her daughter, she's over sixty already. She isn't married. All that way to be near Sri something or other and she doesn't even get married. It's not like that, Mom, her daughter says whenever Rose brings it up. Well what's it like? Rose wants to know.

Mom? Are you still there?

Yes, of course, where else would I be?

I'm worried about your knees, Mom.

I'm fine, dear.

Rose is getting tired. Even a phone call tires her out these days. She just wants to close her eyes and forget all about it. The queer girl, the Indian ghost, the reporter Hal Talbot. All of them swirling around her, some kind of unholy trinity, something terrible coming. Rose can feel it.

The devil's work, Rose mutters.

What's that Mom?

Of course she wouldn't believe in that. The devil.

Are you okay, Mom?

I think, dear, I'll just have a rest now.

Oh, okay Mom. I'll talk to you soon. Okay? I'll talk to you soon?

Rose lets the receiver slip from her shaking fingers and is relieved to hear it click into place. Now she's alone again, alone in the buzzing static silence.

Not alone. Not quite.

She's so tired. Rose digs her fingers into her scrawny thigh. She needs to wake up, rouse herself. She can't just sit here and wait for it to happen. She's tired of waiting. The girl comes, or she doesn't come. Her daughter phones, her sons visit—or they don't. Death hovers over her. Everyone waits for her to die.

They can keep waiting. But Rose is tired of it. Waiting.

It's teatime. The 7pm news is on, Hal Talbot talking about a meeting happening, a meeting about that new road down by the river. They're calling it an "expressway." They call every road an "expressway." Where's everyone going in such a hurry?

It's teatime, but nobody's come to make Rose her cup of tea.

Do they think she's just going to sit here, waiting, forever? The June girl, that Hal Talbot on TV, her daughter with those special necklaces and magic potions. Everybody thinks there's an easy way out. Well, there isn't. There's no such thing as magic. That's the devil's work, oh yes. You open the door a crack, just a crack, and it all comes flooding in.

Rose sniffs the air, catches the scent of burning toast. That scrawny beanpole Bernie down the hall is always burning toast.

He'll start a fire one day.

Hal Talbot interviews the man on the street.

Rose stares at the street on the screen. When was the last time she walked the "expressways" of the town she was born and bred in?

She just wants a cup of tea. They can't expect her to sit here all night without her cup of tea.

Rose fumbles for her walker. She leans forward and grabs its handles. Then, in a Herculean feat, she pulls herself up and over. Her knees creak like old stairs. The pain shoots up her thighs and down her calves. She stands, her swollen feet bobbling in her slippers. It doesn't matter. She's still here, she's still alive, and she isn't going anywhere—unless she wants to.

Hal Talbot is off now. The girl with the tight blouses and the makeup is doing the weather. Rose shakily advances her walker, ignoring the fact that she can't really walk. She gets the handle of the door turned. She presses into the door. It swings open. She inches out into the hall. Slowly but surely, she'll get there. She'll walk the streets of her town. She'll buy a car, a bottle, a shiny gidget-gadget that tells her where to go and what to do. She'll dance, alone at night, the devil pressed tight to her withered breast. Why not? What else is left for her? There are nights when Rose wakes up gasping for air, thinking: Don't you dare, don't you even dare.

Rose shuffles down the long hall. Midway to the elevator sits the empty nurses' station. Rose glances over. There are pictures taped above it, snapshots of children, scrawled crayon drawings. Rose feels her knees, tightening, buckling. She wills them to bend, drags herself forward. The pain is nothing. Rose knows pain. She buried her husband in the rain. Since then she's been alone. She's been vigilant. Not ever opening that door. Not even a crack.

Rose stops in front of the elevator. She stabs the button. She feels her strength ebb, her body slacken. *No*, she thinks. She'll get there. She tightens her grip on the handles of her walker. Where's there? The elevator dings. Rose prepares to haul her body across the threshold. She looks down and sees her bony knuckles, grey-white protruding as if she's already died, her flesh withered away.

The elevator door groans open slowly. Rose hears laughing. The devil's wet snaked tongue undulating. She lifts her head off her chest, her neck cracking.

Two nurses, giggling. They stare open-mouthed at Rose, the oldest person in Wississauga, hunched over her walker, just barely holding on.

Then the black nurse says, in the loud sing-song dialect Rose prefers to pretend she doesn't understand: Rose! Whierr ya goin' girl? Ya takin' youself down to the beauty parlour, now?

And they start laughing again.

PART FOUR

JUNE
Thursday, April 17

IN THE SCHOOL ASSEMBLY HALL Norm takes June's arm, directs her to the second row middle—right in front like it's a concert or something. The room is overflowing with concerned citizens turned out for the community meeting. Norm nods and waves, a big smile on his face. June feels her arm under Norm's gentle grip. Her bicep is hard, ready. She's wasting time. She needs to finish what she started.

Behind the lectern a banner hangs, proudly emblazoned with the Wississauga slogan: *Faith in Our Future. Pride in Our Past.*

What does that even mean?

Rose would—

That crazy old lady, June thinks savagely. The lights dim. June looks up from her lap as a sports-coat man too tanned for Wississauga's weak spring takes the stage. He taps the microphone, speaks earnestly through a broad, generic smile.

Hello everyone! Great to see you all here!

When this fails to get the crowd's attention, the man's smile seems to widen, as if trying to entrance, hypnotize, with his rows of glinting white pearls.

Hi everyone! We're ready to begin now, if you could all please—

June realizes that the crowd's buzzing is belligerent, a swarm of angry wasps, not the complacent worker bees she imagines her neighbours, her community, to be comprised of. They aren't here to shut up. They're here to be heard.

So, thank you, we're ready to—yes, hello everyone, it's great that you're all here, and we just need to, yes, *thank you*. If I could have your full attention now, we'll get started.

The crowd hushes reluctantly. In the silence, June feels exposed. She shrinks down into her seat.

So thanks everyone for coming tonight to this town hall meeting on the topic of the proposed parkway project. Now I'd like to start by introducing your own Councillor Lanny McLennan who's going to introduce the project and make some opening remarks.

Heavyset, balding councillor McLennan takes the stage with a cursory handshake and a spattering of applause. He clears his throat, ready to launch into his spiel.

TRAITOR! someone in the back yells.

I've been called worse, the jowly councillor jokes. A few people laugh nervously.

June notices that off to one side, that same reporter, that Hal Talbot who came to her house, is unobtrusively taking notes on the proceedings. June colours, quickly looks away.

I know there's a lot of passion around this issue, the councillor says, and I want to assure you that everyone is going to get a chance to speak about their concerns. But I do hope that we can keep things—

LIAR!

A murmur rustles its way among those assembled.

Please people, the tanned facilitator calls out in mock umbrage.

As I was saying, Councillor McLennan continues, name-calling and insults are not going to help solve anything. So let's just try and—

June feels eyes on her. She burrows further into her seat. *No—nobody's—this has nothing to do with me*, she keeps telling herself. Her breathing is shallow, self-conscious. She shouldn't be here. She doesn't want to be here.

And now, Councillor McLennan is saying, I'd like to introduce Paula Watson from Wallet Valley Integrated Regional Planning, who will provide us with an overview of the proposed parkway project.

Paula is trim, compartmentalized. She reminds June of lawyer Chris with her executive skirt suit and low-fat yogurt. Paula begins an aggressive PowerPoint presentation that moves along at a pace offering no opportunity for contemplation or interjection. Population flow charts, traffic density graphs, growth projections in spikes and valleys.

In the darkened room the malevolent crowd settles. June risks a peek behind her: blue graph forehead reflections, faces lost in data light. June feels the grainy earth in her fingernails, fights the urge to claw out of the dim room. The final slide is displayed, an artist's rendering of a four-lane "parkway" bordered by full-grown oak trees, bike lanes, cheery pedestrians, and a blue sliver of gently flowing ribbon river replete with jumping fish.

Wississauga, the planning factotum crisply concludes, needs this road in order to ensure its ongoing growth and central role as an important business conduit in the greater urban region. At the same time, this road will be a model of conscientious development with every possible environmental and community concern addressed. Wississauga, she says with no apparent irony or change in inflection. Faith in our future. Pride in our past. Thank you for your time ladies and gentlemen.

There is sparse applause.

Now, the mediator says, casting his brightening smile over the crowd. Are there any questions?

A pause. The audience has been momentarily lulled, pacified by statistics, dim lighting, and the professional even tenor of the imported host. On stage the councilman, the planning woman, and the moderator sit comfortably at a table staring out and over. June squirms, feels like a bug pierced for collection. *It's not real*, she thinks. Nothing seems quite real anymore. The hole, the hole she dug with her bare, blistered hands, that's where reality lies. *Facts on the ground*, June thinks. The truth, waiting to be found.

BULLSHIT! someone shouts from the back of the room. The bubble of passive silence is burst. The crowd rumbles to life, some calling out, some muttering. Hands gesticulate in the air. June feels lost, bewildered. Who are these people and why do they—*how* do they—care? Words swirl as citizens yell their questions: property values, air quality, taxes, pollution, traffic, and what about our goddamn property values?

What's the value of their property? June stares at her fingers. She needs to go home. Her work is there. *He's* there. Waiting. He's waiting for her. She's been at it all day, digging and loosening, gently pulling yellowed bones out of the ground. Parts of a man, slowly cleaved from the dirt. And the rest, still down below, waiting. Waiting for her.

Five more minutes, June thinks. Then she'll tell Norm she has to go. She's feeling sick.

One at a time, please! the moderator says. I know we're all excited about having our opinions heard and recognized. But that can only happen if we all—

The moderator points to a baby boomer in a white dress shirt and bright Looney Tunes Bugs Bunny vs. Martians tie.

Yes, you there, sir, please go ahead.

Looney Tunes has the Ben and Jerry's vibe, big money off a granola image masking upscale predatory business sense.

I can't tell you how important this issue is to me and my wife and our three wonderful children. We live right next to the river and that's part of the reason that I—that we—bought here. To lose the river would be a significant quality of life calamity. It would make me seriously consider relocating to a community that better reflects my family's values.

There are murmurs of agreement in the crowd. Planning lady quiets them with a long complicated answer about how a new riverside path and park will not only benefit the community, it will create more useable community space than had previously been available.

But, Looney Tunes points out, there will be a road. We'll be cut off. We're losing the river!

No one's talking about losing the river, the councillor pronounces congenially.

Oh get real, the man retorts.

June glances at Norm. He has his hand up in the air. He's looking straight ahead, eyes glittering with insistent conviction. *God,* June thinks. *He's one of them.* What's he got to say? Who are these people? These are her neighbours? Her community? She doesn't recognize anyone. Why would she? Her legs burn, muscles urging a return to the squat and crouch of the narrow pit.

Looney Tunes is replaced by an older guy in a tan blazer, face ruddy red. He says he's a practical man; he's losing too much money paying staff to just sit around twiddling their thumbs in traffic. This used to be a great place to do business, he says. But now he doesn't know. We need the road, he tells the crowd. How do you think we keep your stores so full of—

USELESS CRAP! comes an angry cry from the back.

Norm doesn't even twitch. Arm stiff in the air, pink slightly stubby fingers stretched skin tight.

People, please, it's great that you are so responsive and passionate about this issue. But, people, please, if we could try not to call out of turn so that we can all have a chance to be recognized. The moderator grins over a crescendo of chorus complaints. Please! The councillor looks on with benevolent concern. Watson makes a notation in her laptop. People! I know that you all want to contribute to the discussion! But we have to—

A woman pushes her way through, marches to the front of the stage. *Oh my god*, June thinks. She has to resist covering her eyes with her hands and peering at the sight through her fingers. Beaded buckskin vest, dark feathers in her curly red hair, some kind of animal tooth necklace lying feral yellow against lily-white skin. June feels personally offended, like the real thing being confronted by its Halloween dress-up fake.

I'm very disturbed! the woman repeats over and over again, her voice a methodical monotone cutting through the hubbub. I'm very disturbed. I'm very disturbed. She keeps saying it, over and over again, her words getting louder as the crowd's buzzing slowly starts to focus on her repetitive mantra: I'm-very-disturbed. I'm-very-disturbed.

Please, the moderator shouts, making quiet-down motions. Please!

The crowd finally quiets.

The woman fills the momentary lull, speaking loudly and earnestly: Hello, she all but bellows. My name is Susan. Susan

Proudfeather. I grew up here in Wississauga. And I'm very disturbed by what I'm hearing tonight! I'm VERY disturbed. These are precious sacred lands! Before us settlers came, these riverbanks were home to the Wississaugan people! Their ancestors are buried here! To build a road over them would be a sin! There are ancient remains everywhere in these neighbourhoods! In your backyards! Is that what we want, remains to be dug up like a bunch of old garbage for the sake of some *road?* The Wississaugan people have a saying: *That which you do always returns to you.* Is that what we want? To one day have our own bones just dug up and dumped to make room for *some road?* I'm very disturbed! I'm very disturbed!

June presses sore fingernails into the metal edges of the chair's frame. She looks over at the reporter. He's scribbling furiously.

All this digging up the sacred dead is wrong! We should be turning the riverbank into an *international memorial to the first peoples!* Has there been any discussion with the Wississaugan people? This is a matter of *federal law.* We can't just forget about whatever part of the past is no longer convenient for us. We have to teach our children to remember!

The government? Jesus. Jesus Christ.

Resisting the urge to bury her face in her hands, June sees that Norm hasn't moved, eyes headlight ahead, arm ramrod ready to defend his home from bone diggers and road warriors alike. Not in my goddam swampy, ugly, cold, extremely expensive backyard.

She can't get any lower in her seat.

The audience reserves its applause. They don't know what to make of this woman who is clearly not one of them. What is she saying? Whose side is she on?

June notices that she seems to have acolytes—several scruffy-looking college kids handing out some kind of flier. Amidst all this activity there's a deepening silence, the crowd watching I'm-Very-Disturbed and her helpers move through the room.

June's sweating. She's barely breathing. Her fingers methodically claw at the metal frame of her seat. Her rib cage presses in on her.

The moderator glances at the planning lady who seems bewildered, confronted for the first time that evening with a question that hadn't even been considered. The councillor smiles at everyone congenially, dismissively. The moderator half shrugs and quickly searches the audience for a normal counterpoint to the crazy red-haired lady. He points at Norm. Yes, you there, sir. Please, stand up, yes, you, go ahead, sir. Please.

Norm lumbers to his feet. June stares into the dark gap between the chair and the floor, her burning legs disappearing.

I live on Lower Grove Street, Norm begins, and I don't know anything about ancient burial grounds or anything like that.

Oh god—

But I will say that the community is clearly distraught about this plan. Now, I'm a dentist who just set up his practice a year ago, and I moved specifically to Wississauga for its quality of life and its ability to provide lovely secluded neighbourhoods and all the comforts of a growing modern city. And I have to say that what the council is planning is really very misguided. It makes me feel like we aren't really being consulted at all. I only got the letter a few days ago, which hardly gives me the time to respond in a meaningful way. I'd like to ask that the City consider delaying the decision until we've all had more time to study the needs of the community and come up with a compromise that works for everyone.

Norm sits down. The moderator looks at the councillor, an expectant grin on his face. Compromise is his favourite word.

Councillor McLennan smiles too. Yes, thank you, he says smoothly, I think we all agree that no one wants to find themselves in a situation that seems to have been unnecessarily expedited. And I'm sure that we can arrange to—

LIAR!

Let me finish please, McLennan says, his voice still amiable but his cheeks showing a tinge of red.

Moderator: Now people! Please do show Councillor McLennan the courtesy your community is known for. I'm sure that you wouldn't want to—

ASSHOLE!

Let the councillor speak, someone else yells.

Let *me* speak, another voice blurts.

Shut up!—a reply directed at no one that everyone takes personally.

I'd really like to respond to the gentleman's question, McLennan says loudly. For the first time he seems genuinely annoyed.

Don't you tell me to shut up, one man yells at another above the general murmur. In the middle of the auditorium, a fight breaks out, a shoving match, really. The throng gapes and necks are craned for a better look.

McLennan says something to the others on the stage. Planning lady closes her laptop. The moderator speaks quickly over the crowd's angry buzz. His smile sweats. We think it's best if—given the circumstances—thank you for coming everyone please do take the time to fill out the questionnaires we've made available on the way out. And please drive home safely! On behalf of the Wississauga Wallet Valley Department of Regional Development I want to thank you each and everyone of you for your—

McLennan exits stage left followed by a tight-lipped Watson. Main lights are switched on. The Faith in Our Future banner dims. June shoots up, scans for a view of the reporter, but he's disappeared into the throng. Norm is talking loudly to her about the meeting. It's crazy. They aren't listening to a single thing we're saying.

Norm, I'm—I'm not—feeling—

June, are you okay?

She's gone white.

I'm—very—disturbed.

The air is thick with the scent of bodies and lies.

Norm. Get me…out of here.

The garage door slides open. Norm drives in, puts the car in park. He looks over at his wife.

June? He gently pats her knee. June? We're here.

She stares out the side window. She doesn't want to get out of the car.

Are you okay, June?

I'm—I—she puts her hand on her belly. It's a…woman thing.

Oh. Okay.

I'll just, maybe…go and…get some fresh air.

June? He takes her arm. A woman's—like you mean your getting your—?

Norm—

Because I just thought, I was hoping you—I thought you might be—

She pulls away, jumps out of the car and slams the door shut. June marches through the house into the backyard.

SUSAN
Thursday, April 17

WASN'T THAT AMAZING? Jared is saying. Wasn't that just…so freakin' cool? The four others in the room—also college kids from Jared's local branch plant university—all nod and agree and talk among each other about how cool and awesome and freakin' it was. Susan considers Jared, sitting erect in her father's favourite armchair. He has not-quite shoulder length straight black hair. He's wearing scuffed leather boots and a jean jacket. His eyes are hazel, bright with the thrill of having been out in the world, having actually *done* something. He reminds her of young Susan, fifteen years ago.

She was a believer then, an acolyte even. Protests, lectures, info sessions, unconferences. By sophomore year she had joined every club on campus remotely related to *social justice*: Agents of Change, Equity and Accessibility, Feminist Action, Global Alliance, Students for Divestment, Students for Peace, Students for Justice, Students for a Free Tibet. She made coffee, put up posters, sent out the monthly newsletter. She met people who, like her, seemed to actually and genuinely care. It was the first time since she started sprouting breasts that Susan had felt like she could take off her armour of cynicism. There were people like her in the world. And that meant that maybe, just maybe, she could allow herself to consider the possibility that things could get better.

It wasn't long before she found herself in the inner circle, eagerly accepting invitations to join the planning committee for post-event Chinatown dinners feting guest speakers on water privatization, on the plight of the Palestinians, on sex workers' rights, on Indigenous struggle. After dinner it was over to lattés at Café Baldwin, the President of Free Nepal in a heated back-and-forth with the Treasurer of Students for a Sustainable Campus, free-ranging debate covering everything from clowns at protests to the possibility of real revolution in their era. And as things wound down, the inevitable pulled-aside hushed invite to come back to some senior leader's room or apartment for a tête-à-tête, green tea in chipped mugs, cheap rye whiskey spilled into smudged tumblers. After the act, Susan would smooth over the awkwardness by asking the endless list of questions constantly formulating in her mind, queries that would be answered grandiloquently and at length. No one was ever too naked or too tired to elucidate some finer point of strategy or philosophy—Trotsky, Bakunin, Goldman, the Shining Path, the FLQ, all new to her. It was fascinating and thrilling to be introduced to so much so fast so intimately.

Abruptly, Susan gets up from her cross-legged spot on her dad's Oriental rug and moves into the kitchen. She grabs a beer from the refrigerator, then pauses in the cold light of the fridge, opener in hand. She won't sleep with Jared. She doesn't regret how it was, then, but she sees it differently now. Sees the way she was taken advantage of, the way she took what advantage she could. He has a crush on her, of course. And he *is* cute, a gangly puppy dog, sipping one of the Coronas Susan found in her dad's basement and waiting for her to tell him what to do next.

What to do next? Follow the leader. What path could she take them down? She had surprised herself at the town hall meeting. The way she'd spoken, the way she'd moved and gesticulated. She wasn't usually one for the spotlight. She had always laboured behind the scenes, an organizer, a worker bee. What surprised her was how free she'd felt marching down the aisle of the community centre, shrugging off her self-consciousness, voice rising as she approached centre stage. She thrilled to the feeling of forcing them to face her, or not so much her, but the revelation of her existence: a party with no stake in the tug-of-war, present only to remind them that they were not who they claimed they were. Who were they? Who was she? Robbers, liars, thieves. She felt their eyes on her, felt their confusion, recognized their fear. Awesome! Jared had said. Really awesome!

She shakes her head and pries the cap off her beer. It lands on the tiled floor with a clink. What's next? She isn't sure. But she knows she needs to get them ready. Ready for what's coming. Because in all the late-night sessions she's had with various would-be world-changers, budding union leaders and burgeoning citizen-philosophers, there was one thing they never told her. Susan tips her head back and lets the cold liquid sluice through her. When you dredge up their deepest fears, they don't just slink away. After fear, Susan's discovered, comes rage.

Back in her dad's living room, she calls the group to order.

I don't want to replicate hierarchies, she says to the five kids sprawled over the furniture and floor. I'm not your teacher and I'm not your boss and I'm definitely not your mother. It's important to remember that this isn't about me, or any one of us. We're not here to go on an ego trip. We have to do things together, as a group, as a collective.

The others murmur their assent, then wait for her to tell them what to do next. They're just kids, Susan thinks, trying not to feel like the predatory leader of some nascent cult. Let's go around the room, she says. I want to hear from everyone, what you think we should do next. Lila, Susan says, addressing a pale girl with long brown hair and an unformed face, let's start with you.

They go around the room. The ideas are typical, forgettable: a Facebook group; an online petition; an education table at the university student centre. Maybe, Jared says tentatively, his cheeks adding colour as Susan turns to him, some kind of...rally?

A rally, Susan says. Yes. I like that. Or...not a rally, exactly. More of an...encampment.

By the river? one of the kids suggests.

Susan shakes her head. There's no one down there. A rally has to be public. It has to be seen.

Maybe, says an alt-type with a nose ring and greasy green hair, in front of city hall?

Maybe...Susan says slowly. She knows that's not quite right either. They need somewhere emblematic, somewhere that creates a focal point, a pressure point. Somewhere that embarrasses and reminds them. It has to start out theirs, she says out loud. But then we make it ours.

They all nod, though they have no idea what's she taking about.

Well, Susan says, clapping her hands loudly as though they are kindergartners being signalled to move on to their next activity, something will come up. She knows it will. She can feel it. Isn't that why she's here?

Uh...Susan blinks and there is Jared, looking at her with his big concerned eyes. Maybe, he's saying, like, in the meantime, we could set up a website, register a domain, give it a cool name? We could put a bunch of posts around, try to recruit some more people?

Yes, that's a good idea. That's what we'll do. Susan claps again and starts organizing them, assigning them tasks, relishing in the way they immediately move to pull out their array of laptops, iPhones, and tablets. Only Lila seems indecisive. Susan fixes her with a stare. It's late, the girl half complains. She has a class in the morning.

I promise, Susan tells her loudly. This will be worth it. It'll be like taking five classes. Like taking ten classes.

It's after two when they finally leave. Susan, still amped up, decides to treat herself to a sandwich.

Jared had lingered on the doorstep, of course, while the others negotiated piling into an old idling station wagon. Susan looked at him expectantly, magnanimously, aware that she had put this young man in motion, and that she had some small control over where he would end up. I'm really, he said, then stopped, leaning in as close to her as he dared. I'm just…it's amazing that we—met. This is just so much more…What we're doing. It's so…real.

Susan had nodded, kept her face impassive. But it was true, wasn't it? What they were doing *was* real. She could feel it, feel them staking their claim the way the roots of the trees in the valley just across the street dug deep underneath the river's banks and held on, held on no matter what. Out West it had been different. Everything coated in inexpressible grief, everything uprooted, there just didn't seem to be anything left to hold on to. Apologies, acknowledgments, promised reforms, all of them unable to shine a light down into the phantom pass leading to the nowhere land of the disappeared. It was a place of total darkness, a place she struggled to imagine—*the unreal.* She sees that now. They did their best, worked desperately to shine a light. But in the end, it hadn't really mattered. What could you see, in such a place?

But here…Susan thinks. She'd hugged Jared, just a quick hug from the top of her body, before pushing him off. Good night, she'd said. And he'd smiled at her as he squeezed his way into the beat-up wagon and drove off.

And so, midnight snack, she thinks manically, piling on the layers she finds in her dad's kitchen: lettuce, arugula, the innards of a perfectly ripe avocado, some Kalamata olive paste squeezed out of a tube. Then, guiltily and quickly, as if someone might discover her transgression, she adds a juggling knife blade of mayonnaise, Hellman's, the go-to spread of her 14-year-old self.

Her mouth watering, she puts the sandwich on a plate and cuts it slowly in half, revelling in the process, revelling in all of it. Resisting the urge to search for toothpicks, Susan pushes through the front door into the cold clear spring and its stretching night sky. She settles on the creaky old bench on the porch. After two, the street is dead in exactly the way Susan remembered it from her adolescence: a feeling, particular to the affluent suburbs, that everyone had been put under some kind of benevolent lockdown for the night. *For your own good, here there be conformity,* Susan's thoughts go, rambling unconstrained through the exhausted passageways of her mind. *Up early, in the office by 8, home at 7, in bed by 11. Sweep it under the carpet. Keep your secrets in the basement, where they belong.*

Finally, she lets herself bite, chews slowly as the segments of the sandwich become one unified delicious whole. When was the last time she made a sandwich? She is, she believes, seeing things much more clearly now. It's not about escape, running away or forward or anywhere else. It's not about baths and plush towels and afternoon naps and a kitchen with every appliance you can imagine. It's not about late-night snacks, though, god, this sandwich is so fucking good. *Thanks Dad*, she thinks, just letting her mind go where it will. Mental note: replace the beer and the food and vacuum the living room. Her dad likes things neat and tidy. *Not that there's anything wrong with that*, Susan thinks. The kitchen is well appointed, but it's not like everything is brand new top-of-the-line decadent. Her dad's never been exactly a gourmet, but after her mother left, he developed a decent foodie sensibility, avoided becoming one of those guys who, left to his own devices, lives on frozen pizzas and Hungry Man frozen dinners, if he remembers to eat at all.

Shane, she thinks then, slowing her exuberant chewing. *He doesn't eat much*. And when he does eat, he eats crap. She wishes he was here with her. Why isn't he? Why isn't he with her? She hadn't asked him. The idea, she realizes sorrowfully, never crossed her mind. With Shane beside her, she imagines the bus trip would have felt less like an exhausted retreat that would follow her wherever she tried to go, and more like the beginning of something, something new and—like college kid Jared said—*real*.

Only, hadn't she always known she couldn't stay with him? What they'd had, it was—*too real*, Susan thinks bitterly. She misses him. Misses him in a way she's never missed anyone before. She misses him tangibly, misses his breath on her ear as he whispers some sarcastic remark about a yellow smear on a lawyer's tie. She misses the way his broad smooth chest covers her when they fuck, their bodies fitting together. Finishing, his head would turn to one side, revealing the scar running ragged down his cheek and under his chin. He'd shrugged when she'd trailed it, dismissing her unasked question. He doesn't like to talk about himself. From the other side of the country, Susan sees, now, how much he tried to keep hidden, how much he's like so many others she met out West: desperately trying to keep those portals to the darkness sealed and shut. But the darkness seeps out anyway, doesn't it? She sees that now. When she was with him, he was so…*alive*. When he walked into a room, everyone noticed. It was the way he swaggered, the way his steps conveyed an excess of inner assurance. He was always moving. Only—he wasn't going anywhere. Not *moving*, Susan thinks. More like—forcing himself in place, holding his muscles at bay, holding the door closed. You can't live like that, hiding who you really are. But what's the alternative? Throw the door open, flood the world with your murky, blood-black soul. It's a relief, isn't it? Giving yourself up to that nowhere place of loss and darkness. That's why she couldn't stay. Shane's silence, whispering to her: *Come with me. Don't worry. It's easy. In the end, it's easy. You just…let go.*

She feels sick now, the rich middle of the sandwich pressing against her abdomen.

What would he say if she confronted him? It's all just a show, isn't it? You're not even here. He'd shrug and pronounce something oblique yet sharply true: If the cancer doesn't get you, then you better bet on the cure.

Shane is quiet, sits in the back of the room, rarely voices an opinion. But when he speaks, people listen.

He's one of *them*. Has been all along.

Susan swallows back the urge to throw up.

Goddamn him. And how much she misses him.

He's—

And she isn't. She can't be.

Susan slams the plate with the half-eaten sandwich down on the bench beside her. She jerks up, puts her hands on the wood railing and gazes out across the front lawn. She takes deep lung-fulls. *It's okay. You're okay.* Her long lean fingers reflexively tighten over the old worn rail. Susan's hands are glow-worm white on the peeling wood. Not everything is permeable, shapeless, endless expanse. She can't save him. What if she could have saved him? Sometimes things are solid, put in place, built to last. A road can last decades, centuries. It can turn one way, or another.

Susan squints down empty, straight, good old Lower Grove Street. The streetlights produce only the barest circles of illumination, obscuring more than they reveal. But for Susan everything is clear now. If you live in shadow, that's what you become. She doesn't want to live like that. What can't be seen. The river valley, long shrouded in darkness. To save it, it needs to be revealed. That's what she's going to do. Clear the brush from the thicket. Usher light into the dark.

TIM AND CHARLIE
Thursday, April 17

CHARLIE! HEY. CHARLIE.

He's getting good at climbing trees. Tim perches on a branch, one foot on the ledge of the girl's second floor bedroom window. He taps with his knuckles. The glass gently vibrates in its frame.

His breath is rotten. He can taste his own hissed whisper.

Charleeee…

Charleee…

Charlie!

Charlie moves groggily, long green nightshirt over her knees. She peers out, then opens the window. Tim smells girl, spices, cleanser.

Charlie. It's me.

Charlie stands there, looking out at him blearily.

You uh…wanna get high?

She lets him in.

Tim sits on the floor with his back against the bed. He crosses and uncrosses his long bony legs. He doesn't entirely know what he's doing here. He followed and this is where his legs took him. He shouldn't be here—he's not stupid, he knows that. But the last few days—it's like he's been in a labyrinth. Every time he tried to leave, he found himself further in. The river gulley. Criss-crossing accidental paths. His father, dying. His mother, a ghost, a fleeting presence. That woman—in the backyard—digging. He's been watching her. Day and night, he's been watching her. Tim shakes his head, trying to get it all clear in his mind. Who's watching who? What day is it? He needs to—

He puts his hands on the carpet, palms down. The soft give under him makes him feel like he's about to fall right through.

Charlie is kneeling across from him, her long nightshirt stretched across her bare legs. She watches wide-eyed as he slowly rolls a massive joint, methodically crumbling dry leaf into a wide funnel.

We'll smoke it by the window, Tim half whispers. So your parents don't smell it.

Charlie nods. She hadn't thought of that. She's never had a boy in her room. Her room is purple-plush, ridiculous. Charlie wants black paint reflecting glow-in-the-dark stars stickered to the ceiling. She wants pictures of movie stars cut out from magazines to form a messy collage that doesn't just cover over the purplish sheen, but repudiates it. She hasn't seen the movies the kids talk about at school. She's not allowed to watch movies at home, and when she goes with her parents, it's usually something rated G about nature. But Charlie's watched the trailers. She's studied the plots and reviews. Actually, most of them sound kinda stupid. But still, Charlie wants to see them. It's not about being like the other kids. It's not about that at all. It's about that feeling she has when she's with Tim; she just feels so much less like herself.

Tim holds the bulging cone up to the moonlight. His stained dirty hand in the foreground, and in the background the fringes and frills of Charlie's room: lavender pillows and billowy taffeta hanging over a white four-poster bed. He has to push himself up, the carpet clinging to him like thick wet mud. Behind Charlie is a girl-sized white varnished desk holding what looks like a brand new iPad. Tim absorbs the details of soothing suburban luxury as Charlie sits there, big brown eyes staring at him.

C'mon, he says.

She springs up. Tim steps towards the open, screenless window, sticks his head out the black rectangle and breathes deeply. Charlie moves in place beside him, their silhouetted faces darkened by overhanging moonlight. Tim lights the giant spliff and takes a gulping inhalation. He holds the smoke in while he passes the joint to Charlie, who grabs it awkwardly with trembling fingers. Tim watches her as his chest flares and the burn slowly recedes to an ember in his shrunken empty belly.

Charlie claps a hand over her mouth, her face going red with the effort of suppressing her need to cough out the smoke settling into her lungs.

Pass it over, Tim says, finally breathing out. You're wasting it.

He plucks the joint out of Charlie's baby fat fingers and takes another heavy drag. He's getting high. He should be—What? What should he be doing? That woman is—digging. His mother is gone, drifted away, dissipated. Now it's just a tension in his long spindly legs. Substance without matter, a yearning for something he can feel but never have. He needs to go. But he's—

Carly, I'm—I can't—

Smoke drifts between them as they silently burn the joint down. Tim lets Charlie suck at the last bit, watches her cheeks pull in as she tries to drag taffy air through the thick burning stub.

Nothing left, he says, taking the smouldering end from her. He throws it out the window. They both watch the small red spark arc down out of view.

Charlie giggles uncertainly, leans against him. Tim keeps his head out the window, breathing the marshy air.

Let's go for a walk, he says. Let's go down.

No...Charlie manages. She grabs his arm. Her room gyrates. No...

Yeah.

No...her face flushed, her eyes bright. I'll get in trouble.

Naw. Just for an hour.

It's too dark.

Naw. Look at that moon.

I—Charlie giggles uncertainly. Are you still on your quest and stuff?

Yeah, Tim says. He pulls in from the window. Put some pants on or something, he says. Let's get out of here.

Charlie feels her cheeks burning. Don't look, she says. She yanks her camouflage jeans out of a large wardrobe painted white with pink trim. With her back to Tim, she wriggles a leg in, falls back on her butt. She laughs, waving her legs around. Holy moly, she says. She lies on her back, flapping her hands in front of her face.

Quiet, Tim hisses. Then more appreciatively: You're fucked up.

Charlie finally manages to drag her pants on. Tim paces in front of the window. He wants out. He's suffocating in her hot house with its walls trapping rich scents of soap and cooking and appliances. Why did he come here? He needs to move, keep moving. The parts of his body are all disconnected as if floating away of their own accord. Just relax, Carly always tells him. Relax and feel. Feel what?

The girl pulls her zipper closed, smiles at him proudly. He should just tell her: he's not on a quest; he never was.

C'mon, he says between clenched teeth. Let's go.

Okay, Charlie says. In a second. She plops herself in her desk chair. Whoo…I'm…she giggles. Charlie spins the chair around, her arms waving in front of her. Whoo!

Quiet! Tim says. They'll hear you.

He should just leave. He doesn't need her.

It's sooo cool what you're doing, Charlie says. I was looking it up on the internet, like, reading about it? And it's sooo intense.

Yeah? Tim says.

Hey you know what I found? This really cool test that tells you about your spirit animal. Hey, you should take it! Charlie stabs the power button on her tablet. Her face suddenly framed in blue glow. I found it on this site that has all this stuff about, like, Natives and stuff.

Carly does that, Tim thinks. She shows him stuff sometimes, different funny movies and photos her friends send her from their backpacking trips in Thailand or wherever.

This will be so cool! Charlie's fingers dance and a site comes up. Tim leans over her. He can smell her hair. Okay, are you ready? So, first off, you have to pick a word that you really relate to, okay?

The blue light turns Charlie's round face unnatural, compelling. Love, Empathy, Reverence, Wisdom, Growth, Intelligence, Creativity, Passion, Beauty, or Stamina, Charlie reads.

Huh?

Pick a word!

Uh…The room is all fuzzy indigo glow. Tim absently scratches at an itch buried under his tangled, greasy hair. Passion, he whispers.

Oh-*kay*, Charlie says. Now. Which colour most describes you? Pearl, Coral, Ultramarine, Azure, Claret, Amethyst, or Vermillion.

Grey, he mutters.

That's not even a choice! Charlie yells deliriously.

Tim doesn't answer. He breathes. Feels the feeling of breathing.

So I guess…Pearl? That's like grey, she announces authoritatively. Now, what month were you born in?

Uh…May…

It's almost your birthday!

Yeah…

What would you say is your biggest flaw? Pick one, please: Vanity, Hot temper, Keeping your distance, Day dreaming, Forgetting, Control freak, Being too anxious to please.

Uh…

Mine's "anxious to please," Charlie says. Or sometimes, like, "control freak."

Day dreaming? Tim says.

Good. Charlie stabs the pad with gusto.

Your friends describe you as…pick one please: Devoted, Caring, Leader, Stable, Successful, Smart, Strong, Driven, Well liked.

The blue glow of the tablet makes his face hot. The smell of Charlie's shampoo. His legs feel wet, sinewy, about to give out.

Let's go, he says. We gotta…He puts his hands on Charlie's shoulders to steady himself.

Well I say…Leader.

Charlie, c'mon, let's…

Last question! Your ideal lover would be—Charlie giggles, blushes—would be: Nurturing, Sensible, Smart, Sexy, Strong or…Active.

Carly, Tim thinks. Or says.

What? Charlie asks.

I gotta, I'm…He stumbles to the window, heaves his head out.

It's the last question, Charlie insists. Her voice is ardent now. You have to answer.

Tim fills his lungs. He can feel his empty stomach churning.

Let's say…Strong. Charlie giggles again. She clicks. Okay it's figuring it out now. Here it comes. It's says you're a—Raven!

Despite himself, Tim is listening.

Raven, Charlie reads. Your soul is bound to the third totem, Grandfather Thunder. Grandfather Thunder appears as a flock of ravens. He embodies reverence, leadership, honour, and inspiration. He is associated with the season of winter and the element of water. His downfall is ego. You are most compatible with Wolves and Owls. Hey! I'm an Owl! Charlie kicks up her heels, spins in her chair. Whoo! Whoo!

Tim runs over there, grabs the arms of the chair in mid-whirl. Shut up, he says, leaning into her. They stare at each other. Charlie's smile slides into confusion. *She's gonna cry*, Tim thinks. He moves away, back to the window. Starts climbing out.

Hey, Charlie whispers. Wait for me.

The way down looks steep. It is steep. But Charlie's built a kind of path for herself. Footholds and handholds. Momentary plateaus where she can catch her breath and ease the burning as her muscled thighs slow her descent. Zigzag switchbacks that finally spill her out into the bottom woods, her breath coming fast from exertion and excitement.

Charlie puts a hand on her chest. She feels her heart against her thin nightdress. She's been having nightmares about the woods.

Ever since that night in the lodge when Tim and her—she shouldn't have brought him there. The sweat lodge is a *Sacred Place*. It's where the Natives did their rituals and talked to their gods.

So dark down here.

She stops suddenly, realizes that she doesn't know where Tim is. She listens for his footsteps. All she hears is the mute hum of the live woods. Then a voice:

Chaaaaaarrrrr-leeee…

It's Tim fooling with her. He's hiding behind a tree, trying to scare her. She looks around. Where is he? The Natives tell stories about things like this: ravens and foxes, tricksters who pretend to be your friend but really aren't.

Chaaaaaa-rrrrr-leeee…

Quit it!

Chaaaaaarrrrr-leeee…

Shut up!

In her nightmares, someone chases her. Watches her. She feels eyes on her now.

Chaaaaaa-rrrrr-leeee…

Stop it or I'm leaving!

She isn't scared. It's just—if they find out, she'll be grounded for life. Or worse. The last time, when she woke up in the lodge, she didn't get home till almost eleven. Her parents were on the verge of calling the police when her trembling fingers finally managed to fit key into lock. Unable to come up with a plausible lie, she told them a version of the truth. She went for a walk along the river.

In the woods? her father immediately interjected.

She got tired, and she sat down for a minute.

In the woods?

And then, she told them, I fell asleep.

In the *woods?*

The next thing I knew it was dark, she remembers saying in a piteous voice she thought she was putting on.

But the next thing *she* knew she was crying. Her father's baleful gaze. She rushed into her mother's arms.

Her parents run affiliated medical practices catering mainly to the needs of the region's ever-expanding Southeast Asian suburban population, well-to-do immigrants and their first generation offspring; parents who keep a tight reign on the activities of their children, children who awkwardly carry the facade of immigrant pride and old-world values even as a new-world of pubescent stirrings and suburban plenty beckon them to a future of chat-apps and supermalls and casual partying their parents can't even imagine.

Is it so surprising that Charlie's mom and dad will fail to identify the sweet tang of smoke clinging to the walls of their daughter's room? Their little Charulekha Nath, benefiting both from the strict no-nonsense Indian way and all the opportunities of a bountiful West where a man and woman can work side by side at twin medical practices—he's ear, nose, throat; she's neurology. Together they have accumulated enough money to pay the dowry for a hundred daughters. Though here in the West, you have just one or two, even though their giant house on the ridge overlooking the valley sometimes feels ridiculously empty compared to even their admittedly middle class Delhi villa where it was still two to a small dusty room with a window carrying the smells of sewage and sizzling masala spices.

They grounded her.

Chaaaaaa-rrrrr-leeee.

Her name. Elongated, extended, whispered in a chant, lingered on before being exhaled and allowed to dissipate like the smoke from some ancient ceremonial pipe. Will he *stop* that?

Her head pounding. Her mouth dry sour sweet.

Chaaaaaa-rrrrr-leeee.

She pulls her nightshirt against her. She's shivering now. A sudden chill.

Chaaaaaa-rrrrr-leeee.

Shut up! she yells.

Wheeeeeere are you Chaaaar-leee?

You better shut up!

Where is she? She doesn't know. She thought she was following Tim. But he's—

She looks behind her. Shiny sheen of a thousand new leaves in a wood she's seen a thousand times. It's different in the dark though. These are hunting grounds. At night, Charlie read, the fleet-footed braves could creep up silently on sleeping deer startled into slumbered slaughter. The faster she walks the more she's sure of it. She's being watched. Followed. Silly girl, her father remonstrates. Why would you go all alone in the woods? Something most bad could happen to you, you could get—

Charlie freezes. The night forest, full of pitfall dips and root trip-ups, seems to be closing in around her. *I'm sorry. I didn't mean to—*

She'll go back to the lodge, light candles. Down on her knees in the ancient chamber she'll—

pray.

A sharp crack behind her. Animal? Moccasin foot snapping a twig? In such moments does a hunt turn? Tomorrow, after school, she'll go back to the lodge, make amends, ask forgiveness from her parents, from ghosts, from ancient totems sitting inert in the ashy dirt. She hears panting. Breathing. Hers? And something else. Hot shadow echo. Tears streaming down her cheeks. She can hear the river in front of her. Terrified, she spins around and around. She pants heavy hot child breaths. She cries with her eyes closed. She feels it now. Approaching footfalls.

Leave me alone! she screams.

Then everything quiets.

The sound of the river. Inevitable. A spirit world's retribution.

Tim walks through the gaps in the dark, just one of those invisible night creatures awake, alone. His habitat: suburban streets without sidewalks bordering endless squares of self-same lawn. In such an environment, it's better to be nocturnal. By day you're exposed. Nowhere to hide. At night, you're invisible. You practically don't exist.

He walks, knowing where he's going, not entirely sure when and how he set off on this particular part of his journey. It's the China, he rationalizes. The China is good. The China makes you feel like your feet don't touch the ground while the minutes dance into hours and everything changes without you ever taking a single step. Plus he took one of the pills. Two. He took two. He remembers watching the kid, following the kid, hiding from the kid. Why was he doing that? She was crying, he could hear her, gulping and crying and trying to get her breath. Tim couldn't help her. He wanted to, but somehow he just couldn't. He trailed her, his feet barely touching the ground. He'd gone invisible; he'd disappeared. He was a ghost now, he told himself, like his mother. Charlie broke into a shuffling stumbling jog. Go home, kid, he thought. And she did. He watched her shimmy up the tree and drop through the open window. He watched her from down below, hidden in the dark, in the bush. A light turned on briefly—her bedside lamp—and then the light extinguished. Still, Tim remembers, he waited, arms folded over his chest, paying some sort of silent vigil. He was sorry. He hadn't meant to—but now—

Whatever she was supposed to do, whatever she was sent to tell him, he was done with her now.

Just a stupid kid, Tim thinks, moving down the sidewalk, feeling himself, half walking half gliding, floating fast now that he's out of the forest. *Just a kid.* The thought fills him with inchoate sadness. He was just a kid too, when he started on this journey. *And now I'm a—*

ghost, he reminds himself. *Like my—*

Never mind that. He's done with all that. He's going to—and then—it'll be—

over.

He takes a few more steps and finds himself rounding the corner. This is it. Lower Grove. The street where he grew up.

Carly. This is—

His mind feels clearer now. Tim dries his sweaty face on the filthy sleeve of his jacket.

He'll do what he needs to do. Then he'll call her. Tell her where he is, what he's doing.

Tim watches his hands fumble with the latch of the gate. How many times has he stood in this spot, tinkered with this same recalcitrant clasp? Past and present merging like city and country. Last year's cornfield sits next to a sign promising a new Costco and next year's hottest housing development. The gate into the back was his preferred entrance to the darkened chilly house when he was a teenager. Through the gate and in past the sliding glass door that opened into the living room with a near silent swish. Not that there was anybody who cared. Most of the time, his dad wasn't even around.

But sneaking in high and drunk at 3 am made it seem like his life was somehow—

normal.

What would that boy, spotty adolescent Timmy, make of this? Boy Timmy in his tree, watching the backyard and house, the scene set in perpetual gloom, a late-night TV test pattern. *Tree-vee,* Tim thinks. God he was fucked up back then. Sitting in that tree puffing on a pilfered cigarette, *smoke 'em if you got 'em,* another one of his father's brilliant sayings. Drinking whatever he could find, he slowly drained an extensive collection of high-end liquors, diluting the bottles with water. Why did he bother with the water? His dad didn't care or notice. Beige see-through Scotch wouldn't fool anyone anyway. Eventually Timmy drank that too. Boozy bilge water. He left the empty bottles to gather dust in the forest.

Tim pushes at the gate. Is it locked? No it's the same old latch. It always used to stick. Just gotta…lift the door up a bit.

Ah. There.

The gate opens with a rusty yawn. Tim takes a few steps into the backyard. He stops in the silence, listening as if remembering through the shrinking echo of past arrival: the gate's dragging stutter, his grass-cushioned footsteps, the reverberations of his own ever-present breathing. By comparison the house seems silent. No sounds of digging or other indications of life, like TV dialogue or the quiet murmur of a couple going about their domestic evening routine. *They're asleep,* Tim thinks. He has no idea what time it is. *It feels late.* He stands, facing the looming house. His father is dying.

Tim pulls the ancient twisted pipe out of his pocket. After they got high, he took it from Charlie's smoke lodge hideout. He holds it in his fist, this magic talisman, protection. He's escaped. Or he hasn't. He can't forget that summer, their shared vigil, the way he watched for his mother's return and saw only his father; his father restlessly prowling the circumference of that perfect patch of new grass. Tim was afraid, back then, afraid his father would burst into his room in the middle of the night, drag him out into the backyard and make him disappear too. Afraid, though part of him wanted it to happen. It would have been a relief. It never happened. Instead, it was just his dad, mostly absent, then suddenly up in Tim's face, trying too hard. Hey there ya are, Timmy bud! I ordered some pizza. There's a ball game on! How's school? C'mere ya little—don't be such a stranger! Tim stares at the beckoning grey glint of that sliding glass door. He won't go in. He doesn't have to go in. *Turn around,* he thinks to himself. *Do it.*

Behind him, the sloping backyard edges to a crumbling drop of tangled roots and protruding rocks. Behind him, the tree, his tree, sticks up out of the dark gap gorge, Tim's forest gully home.

A car passes on the street. It seems to slow. Then it drives on. Tim's heart beats in his eardrums. He's frozen again, trapped in memory's scrutiny. The tree and the boy up in that tree peering down at him. Watching him. The house, too, is watching, dark glass of the back door unblinking, implacable.

Finally, slowly, he turns.

His hidden vantage point emerges above, looks naked and exposed. When you're up there, you think you're invisible. A murky chill breezes up from the gully. When Tim was a boy that cold air was everywhere, wending its way up through the backyard, up the stairs, under Tim's closed bedroom door and right through him, no matter how many covers and blankets he layered on himself.

That cold wind in his chest, a hollow he'll never fill; a nebulous swirl of smoke coughed out and left behind. He stands in the backyard. This is where it happened. A blow to the back of the head. A lipstick smile flattening. A woman's body slumping to stunned nothingness. The forest sways, beckons. He'll bring her bones back to the ghost pines and the absent river hush and bury her in a wetland of unacknowledged pasts. He'll dump her skull on the couch his father stole from their family home and watch the old man's face crumble into nothing. The wind comes in gusts, branches creak overhead. Tim's thighs quiver. What are you waiting for? He steps toward the tarp-covered hole.

JUNE

Thursday, April 17—Friday, April 18

JUNE PRETENDED TO TAKE A SLEEPING PILL. It didn't work. Norm gave it to her. Of course it didn't work. She didn't take it. She can't. She might be—

She should tell him. She should do what normal couples do. Wake him up, pee on a stick, hold his hand while they wait. *It's too early*, she thinks, words zapping through her mind as she lies in bed next to her snoring husband. *Lie, lies, lying. He knows. What does he know?* After June came in from the backyard, staying out there just long enough to confirm that nobody had—that *he* was still—Norm had sat her down and very sternly asked her if she was alright. He'd asked her if she'd been having trouble sleeping. June said yes. He asked her why, what was bothering her? June looked at her hands. Norm sighed heavily. You don't really think, June had finally said, that they'll build that road? Norm didn't answer, just squinted at her as if trying to see her better. He'd looked old, then, his face pulled in by worry and confusion.

He gave her the pill. Kissed her forehead. Then, muttering something about goddamn bureaucrats, clearly still agitated from the meeting, he took one himself.

Now he snores sonorously, sternly. June slips out of the covers. *This is the last night,* she promises herself. *Then I'll—*

tell him.

She pulls on her jeans, her mud-smeared sweatshirt. She pads down the stairs and into the dark kitchen. She feels—strangely—unobserved. The feeling of someone—some other self—is absent. Her muscles ache slackly, devoid of pulsing electric tension, striated need. She doesn't feel—*him.* Tonight she's tired. She wants to sleep. She wants to be in the big warm bed, curled up under the down-filled duvet, her head on her husband's shoulder.

But she's not done. *Why not?* she asks herself, feeling suddenly giddy with the idea. Reverse the process. Cover it all up. Instead of going straight out to the site, she lingers at the back sliding door, staring through the glass into the yard masked in moonlit cloud. Norm keeps asking her what she's doing back there. He asked her again tonight, when she returned from the backyard to face his gentle inquisition. He's not an idiot. *He knows it's not—*June hasn't been eating. *Or sleeping,* June thinks. *Or cooking or shopping or doing the laundry or any of that shit. So no wonder he's—*

He's just trying to help. And suddenly she wants him to. Help her. Hold her. She thinks of smiley boy reporter, the community meeting, not even six hours ago but already a world away, red-haired lady and her piercing monotone—I'm Very Disturbed. The way the professor traced her palm with his stubby finger. The way Rose stared through her and into her. *They know. They all know.* Of course they don't. Not really. They can't. But—

If she covers it up. Then they won't—

They'll come for him, June thinks. She can't let that happen. She won't let that happen. June puts her hands on the glass, feels the cold against her palms. The backyard looks barren. Where is he? Where did he go? She doesn't want this to be about her. *Am I really so—*

Jesus. Jesus June. So she's lonely? So Wississauga is just a big sprawling nothing? So what?

And if there's life growing inside her? It doesn't seem real. One long waking dream. The big trees sway. What goes on above? What goes on underneath? Invisible demarcations, ageless patterned movements marking the microscopic shifts from life to death and back again. June closes her eyes. She's tired, that's all. The window glass feels cold on her palms. She's so tired. She curls her hands into fists, raps them gently, rhythmically, against the glass door. It's a beat deep inside her, primal and unconscious. She realizes it's the same sound she's been hearing in her head, the same rhythm she's been reflexively moving to while working in the hole. The glass trembles. She hits harder. For a moment she thinks she'll smash right through. That'll wake Norm up. He already thinks she's losing it. She just wanted him to—

Jesus June. You're pathetic.

The only problem is that everyone believes it. *You believe it, don't you?* And Rose, and Professor Nordstrom, and that horrible reporter, and buckskin lady. They all believe it. They all want to believe it. Why shouldn't they? Isn't it true? Tonight, June isn't sure. A cold hole in the ground. No one there. No one watching her. June leans her forehead against the window, feels the shudder as she bangs the glass gently, persistently, following a song lost in the pulse of her heart.

When she opens her eyes again, there's a shadow over her view. June freezes, her fists distending against the glass. A man is staring in. June gasps. But he doesn't seem to see her. He gazes through and past, like she's not even there. He's scraggly, his pale face dotted with patches of wispy beard. Young guy, June registers, he can't even grow a beard. He's wearing an army surplus jacket. The jacket's too big for him. It hangs off his skinny frame, a tattered shirt handed down to a scarecrow. June breathes again. He isn't particularly intimidating. *Why doesn't he see me?*

Get out of here, June thinks. *Go.* She feels the blood rushing, her cheeks wet with rage. The hole, the bones, the wet messy truth beneath the earth. After what seems like an eternity, the man-boy finally turns away to face the sloping spread of the backyard. *Don't you dare.* She should call Norm, call the police. She unlocks the door and gently slides the glass open. Man-boy stands at the edge, peering down at the plastic tarp cover. June steps up behind him. She wishes she had something—a rock, a club, a spear to press into his knobby back. Her hands are empty. He's lanky, tall, has a couple of feet on her. He stinks of sweat and smoke and something else, some underground odour June can't place but immediately feels overcome by. She gasps, suddenly short of air. The stranger turns slowly, as if only slightly curious about who or what is behind him. He stares at her with hazy bloodshot eyes. *He's high,* June thinks.

My husband's upstairs, June says firmly. She isn't afraid of him. Slowly, deliberately, never taking her eyes off him, she bends her knees and gropes for the handle of the heavy shovel. Tim blinks flatly, doesn't seem to notice.

It's cool, he whispers hoarsely. Everything's cool.

Get out of my backyard, June says.

Yeah, the man-boy says. Cool. No problem. Just…just give her to me. And everything will be…cool.

Some kind of junkie, June thinks. I don't know what you're talking about, she states flatly.

I saw you, man-boy says, clearly agitated. I saw you. I was…I've been…up there. He motions to the trees jutting out of the gorge.

You didn't see anything, June says. But her gaze wavers to the dark branches overhead.

Yeah I saw it! I saw everything! Man-boy shakes and spits a little as his voice rises. She's—I'm supposed to—they're mine! I have to—she's mine!

June brandishes the shovel. You get out of here right now, she says evenly. Walk away right now or so help me god I'll…

Man-boy's head lolls pathetically, his eyes bulge, confused. I grew up here, he mutters.

June steps forward suddenly. He stumbles back, loose earth sliding down the walls of the hole.

Just—he's begging now. I know you have her. I *saw* you.

He's been watching her. Then maybe there never was—

You're a liar, June says. Who sent you?

His bloodshot pupils, unfocussed, roll in the whites of his eyes. He turns quickly and grabs a handful of tarp.

Don't touch that!

He snatches it across, exposing the hole. The clouds part, silver light sticking. The hole glows. Man-boy groans.

You're a liar! June screams. She swings the shovel, connects with his spiny back. He teeters on the edge, then plunges in.

HAL
Thursday, April 17—Friday, April 18

PIZZA AND COKE ZERO, the TV turned to Scott's favourite hip-hop video hour, thugs pimped out for primetime. Just another Thursday night. Hal, back from changing out of his chinos and oxford, surveys the scene, watches Scott chew on a slice.

So, how was that road meeting thingy? Sit down, have some pizza. Scott, who'd gotten into the habit of coming over after work and letting himself in, pats the spot on the couch beside him.

Hal stands there. How was the meeting? His mind is over-full, there's too much to think about. Replays from the last few days, slo-mo and fast-forward, he keeps stringing them together like a trailer for a movie—*a thriller*, Hal thinks, *complete with conspiracy, cover-ups, and all the mad truth anyone could hope for.* The Wississauga politicos, the angry crowd, the shouts and questions. And then, out of nowhere, that protestor, whoever she was. And the woman, June, Rose's pal, she was there too, though she didn't look very happy about it.

Hello? Earth to Hal? Earth to Wississauga's favourite kid reporter?

Scott's grinning at him, his big brown eyes laughing.

Sorry, he mutters. I'm—and then, before he can stop himself: I'm on to something. Something big. He says it loudly, defiantly. It's true, isn't it?

You are?

You can't tell anyone.

I won't. I won't. Who'm I gonna tell?

It's about the road.

The road?

The expressway, Hal says, suppressing his impatience. The one they want to build along the river.

Oh, oh yeah. Scott's eyes wander back to the TV, but Hal plunges on.

It's this woman I talked to the other day. I went over to her house. I'm pretty sure she's discovered some kind of...site. You can't tell anyone. It's in her backyard, for Christ sakes. Some kind of... Native site.

Like Indians?

She's hiding it. That's why it's so weird. She lives right beside the river. They're going to run the new road behind her house. And she's got this ancient grave there. She could have a whole village buried back there. Who knows?

Wow. Did you see it?

No. She's wouldn't let me see it. She's hiding the whole thing under a tarp in her backyard. But get this: the professor who I sometimes interview when there's an archaeology angle on local stories or whatever, I called him up and he's met her! He said she came to see him. She was asking all kinds of weird questions about who lived here thousands of years ago and stuff like that. And he told me that they find ancient burial grounds and that kind of thing all the time in Wississauga. He says they're going to pave over stuff that could be a thousand years old.

Scott munches on pizza, his eyes moving between Hal and the preening bodies bouncing inside Hal's hazy TV.

And then, at the meeting tonight, there was this…woman. Some kind of activist…

Hal trails off. How does she fit into this? What does she know? It's like he's got the puzzle all figured out, but the last piece doesn't fit.

Dude, Scott says enthusiastically, this sounds awesome!

Yeah. Hal can't help but smile. Awesome. It could be. But I'm just…I'm not sure, you know? What if I'm wrong?

Scott takes a swallow of beer. You're not wrong, he says, smiling brightly at Hal.

I'm not wrong, Hal says, mostly to himself. It all makes sense. He can feel it. Out with the old, in with the new. But it's not that easy, right? Everything has consequences. That's where he comes in. His job is to let people know what's really happening. There's no wrong or right. Not really. That's not what this is about. Scott gobbling pizza, slice after slice, not an inch of fat on him. You take what you can get. Make your own rules.

Will you go over there with me? Hal blurts.

Like…tonight? Scott's finally paying attention to Hal, not the TV.

Yeah, Hal mutters. Maybe. Maybe it's a bad idea. What if we get caught?

What if we get caught? Scott smiles mischievously. We won't get caught. I mean, it's just a backyard, right? They'll be asleep and we just sneak in. It's barely even illegal. When I was a kid we used to sneak into people's backyards all the time. We'd even swim in their pools and stuff.

Hal and Scott both grew up in what were then the suburbs of the city. Hal's parents still live there, halfway between downtown and Wississauga. More city than suburb now, there are high-rises and a subway station. Hal drives over to see them every second Sunday. They eat lunch and smile tightly at each other, and then Hal leaves feeling frustrated and refusing to acknowledge exactly why.

I just…Hal says. His face feels hot, strangled, like his tie is way too tight. He isn't wearing a tie. There's something about that place, the backyard, the house…It's a feeling he hasn't been able to shake, it's been sitting with him, in him, even since before he visited the woman, maybe ever since Rose started going on about ghosts and Indians. It's not a pleasant feeling—like someone's been following him, getting close, breathing on the back of his neck, but when he turns around, there's no one there. He pictures June's empty, creepy backyard. So he's creeped out. Big deal. Grow up. This is it. This is *the* story. But you have to know for sure. Reporters do that kind of stuff. Sneak around. Deep Throat and all that. He wipes sweat off his forehead with the rough cotton shoulder of his t-shirt.

We're going over there, Scott says, grabbing the remote and turning the channel to the network news.

Yeah…okay…Hal locks eyes on the stern-faced man staring out of the TV screen. They gaze at each other through the endless movement of bright light particulate, the new matter assembling its churning worlds.

Scott's silver SUV cruises through the empty streets. Digital numbers on the dashboard glow 2:43 am.

It's really quiet, Scott says. He yawns loudly. Like Hal, he's not much of a late-night guy. They're usually asleep by 11. Scott has 7 and 8 am appointments with the before-work go-getter types.

It's almost three, Hal snaps. He cringes at the tight sound of his voice. Scott didn't mean anything by it. He never means anything by it. Hal closes his eyes. Gotta relax. He tries to fall back into the leather bucket seat. The air in the car is settled, ordered, manufactured. New car smell. *Let's just drive*, he thinks. *Let's just not have to go anywhere in particular.*

Turn here? Scott asks.

Hal pops his eyes open. A street sign lit up by the glare of a lone halogen.

Yeah, he says. This is the street. Grove. Make a left.

Here we go, Scott says, giving the SUV just a bit too much gas. The tires squeal as they take the corner.

Scott!

Sorry.

Scott slows down. The street is long, straight, gradually sloping up as it follows the river.

Is that the place? Scott wants to know.

Yeah, Hal whispers.

Hal ponders the hulking house, a typical faux colonial replete with columns framing the big double doors of the front entrance. The place feels vacant. All the houses around here do. But who knows? Who really knows who might be looking at who through dark blank windows? Hal represses a shiver, feels it inside, surging through him.

Scott opens his door and jumps out of the truck. Hal watches from the window as he moves quickly to the back gate with long fluid strides. The gate is half open and Scott looks back at Hal with a kind of told-you-so expression, the unlocked gate an invitation, a gift handed to them on a silver platter. Hal feels his face flush. He takes a deep breath and opens his door.

Scott steps into the backyard.

Wait up, Hal hisses. He creeps through after him.

It's darker in the backyard, away from the streetlights hanging over the long straight road. The night is a grainy black. Clouds spill over the stars and the full moon is just a glow lost in the inky spread of the sky. Hal can't see. He blinks, waits for his eyes to adjust. Then he steps forward, bumps into something, startles—

Fuck, *Scott.*

Scott giggles.

Quiet, Hal hisses.

They stand there. Gradually Hal's pupils widen and he becomes aware of his surroundings. Behind him is the house, all closed windows and bricked-in bedrooms. In front, a dark tree emerges from the gorge, empty branches communing with the wind. And the pit, a spreading gash. Hal steps forward. He sees the pit now. It's uncovered, the tarp thrown to the side revealing a misshapen hole, funnelling deep. Weirdly, Hal sees a gentle flickering light emanating from its depths. The wind gusts through branches groaning awake from winter. Clouds obscure a fragment moon, and the pale light from the hole intensifies. Hal grabs Scott's thick arm, pulling him back.

Come on, Scott whispers. He moves near to the edge, dragging Hal along.

At the crumbling verge, the shaky light caresses their faces, a heat coming up out of the earth. Hal feels the hot on his cheeks. Then the wind dies and the world goes quiet. And Hal hears a scrabbling sound, fingers in dirt. And a murmuring, strangely atonal, a plaintive chant.

They look at each other. Scott grins weirdly, like a grave robbing ghoul coming across a freshly dug hole. Hal surprises himself, pulling out of Scott's grasp and falling to his knees. He thrusts his head in and down.

The clouds part. The air fills with phosphorescent moonlight. Hal's eyes, blazed open.

He sees him—it—then. Lying at the bottom. Ghost creature droning his tuneless lament and clawing at the silvery soil.

ROSE
Friday, April 18

ROSE DUNKS A SLICE OF WHITE BREAD, the tea's stain a slow spread. She gums the spongy copper dough. The television murmurs a traffic update. Rose listens to the fate of intersections. The highways, discussed on television in a series of codename monikers—404, QEW, DVP—simply serve as indisputable evidence of steady decades of expansion that stand in contrast to Rose's slow shrinking presence; dwarfing vast wastelands of concrete entirely occupied by alien tank-like vehicles, SUVs they call them on the TV.

Rose dunks a cookie.

Oatmeal raisin, Rose is pretty sure. She's not sure. She doesn't taste as much as she used to. Her tongue is rusted dry, no longer at full capability, like a country that hasn't fought a war in decades, its tanks and planes left to slowly decay.

Rose's Morton fought in World War II, god rest his soul. How alone she felt when he left, how afraid she was and how determined she was not to show it. He did what he had to do. And Rose did likewise, though letters couldn't keep her warm at night and it was cold that winter, that unbearably long winter of months and years when Morton fought the Japs in a Pacific that Rose imagined teeming with clever oriental pratfalls her Morton was smart enough to avoid, of course. Built of solid Scottish stock, he came back to her in one piece so he could work at Great Lakes Starch and provide his family with a good enough living and die early of a heart attack at 63, leaving Rose alone again, her children having long since scattered.

Her children. They rarely visit now. And when they do, they're distracted, rude, anxious to be off again. How did her offspring get so weak willed and ill mannered? *They let themselves go*, Rose thinks. Her Morton was a wiry man with a bristly moustache, soft spoken and polite in that brusque way of his. He always behaved like a gentleman even under the influence of one or two, which Rose disapproved of but permitted, men being men, after all. But those lumpy children, where do they come from? With their impatient sighs and their constant interruptions—beepers and buzzers set to ring every time Rose opens her mouth to say any little thing. Always fidgeting and moaning and making all kinds of promises to do this or that before rushing off. Promises. A promise not kept is a lie, as far as Rose is concerned.

Local news comes on. Rose swallows wet cookie, cocks her head toward the television. It's her reporter, young Hal Talbot. He looks tired, Rose thinks. He's talking faster than usual. Rose's hearing isn't what it used to be. She struggles to string words together out of the rush of sentences.

Wississauga's living legacy, Hal says on screen before cutting to Rose smothered in blush and lipstick, wispy hair brushed to one side, barely covering her spotted scalp. *Bones*, she croaks portentously. *Indian bones.* Rose pauses to purse her pruned lips. She blinks defiantly at the camera. *No good will come...Cursed...Bones.*

And Hal in front of a placid suburban home. *Here in the heart of old Wississauga, an incredible discovery. Even as the city plans a future based on a massive new road behind houses just like this one, the buried* past is being discovered. *Has the area's true history been unearthed? And will it haunt our community's future?*

Hal Talbot, kid reporter, fumbling with a gate. June appears, startled, white faced except her cheeks, a blotched blushing red. The incriminating blue tarp sits stark behind her. Hal introduces himself and June blocks the way, blocks the camera's view of the backyard.

Cut back to Rose: *Bad luck*, the old lady intones. *No good can come of this.*

It would be a very significant find, proclaims local archaeologist Professor Sven Nordstrom.

Is there an ancient Native burial site in the backyard of this Wississauga household on the edge of the proposed site of the new parkway? This is Hal Talbot reporting live for Wississauga Cable Community News.

The TV goes to commercial: *The Middle Mall: Where Wississauga IS Shopping!* Indian bones. Cursed of course. Well she warned them. Nice girl, weak willed, hysterical, but still Rose tried to help her. She hasn't seen her since. The young reporter missed his visit too. She's alone again. Isn't that just typical? Put the bones back where you found them and have done with it. Cursed, everybody knows that. Rose shudders. She's chilled. They're skimping on the heat. It was warm but now it's cold. A spring freeze, the worst kind of weather. Kill the blossoms on the fruit trees. *Now we'll all pay the price*, Rose thinks. The thrum of passing traffic blowing like a wind through the window. Rose pulls her sweater tighter. She sits huddled in her frayed cardigan. In her day, the trees kept the wind from sweeping willy-nilly and freezing all the old people right to death. In her day. Rose closes her eyes. Shivers again, trembling into slumber.

She dreams of walking down great big Hurontarion. The traffic is stopped, everyone sits in their cars, frozen. She's not young, exactly, but spry, walking fast. She goes into the Wallet Valley General Store. They used to send a boy on a bicycle to deliver free of charge and give you credit to boot, not that Rose ever needed much credit, just a bit to tide the family over at the end of the month, and not every month either. She's always been frugal, paid her debts, tipped the boy a nickel, did what was right no matter what. Rose goes into the store. She remembers it as one big room lined with barrels of dried goods and sacks of flour and tea. But now the store looms, expands, twists and turns. Shelves cover the walls, reaching high up beyond what Rose can see. Walls of narrow aisles lined with flashing computer screens, flickering televisions, blaring stereos.

Rose keeps walking. The shelves teeter and lean in precariously. They're going to fall, Rose thinks. She's relieved when she turns a corner into furnishings. She emerges into a long row of mattresses. A salesman appears, that young man, reporter Hal Talbot. Try a mattress, he says. Lie back! Relax! Put your feet up! Just as if you were sleeping at home! Don't worry about your dirty shoes! It's the floor model!

Rose lies down. There's something under her. Something clammy, breathing on her neck. She wants to get up, but suddenly she's exhausted. She struggles against wet hands over her mouth. She's dying. She'll die soon.

How d'ya like it? Hal the salesman asks cheerfully. Soft enough for you? A breeze sweeps colourful brochures out of his hands. Rose feels the pamphlets cover her face as she struggles to break free.

Sorry about that, Hal the salesman says, stooping to clean up. In the mall. What breeze?

Rose jolts from her half slumber. Pain in her hips, her knees, her swollen ankles, her brittle knuckles. Cold air seeping in, spreading the tuneless rumble of rush hour traffic and the grey atonal odour of exhaust. Look at that. The window is wide open. Someone must have come in while she was sleeping and opened it. Why would they do that? Rose won't have it. She won't have open windows, the draft going through her, right into her.

Rose grips the armrests with skeletal fingers and takes aim at the walker positioned so that it's no more than a single arthritic stumble away. Her muscles, still aching from her last failed foray, creak into rusty gear. Rose pants through her wet mouth.

Something falls in the kitchenette, a pot or a cup, smashing bits scattering.

Oh!

Rose misses the handles of the walker.

Cupboards bang against each other.

Knickknacks fly off the corner credenza.

Rose falls forward.

A girl in pink holding a yellow bouquet slams into the wall.

Ah!

Rose hits the carpet with a slow motion thud. The girl's blonde head, decapitated, rolls against her cheek.

She comes to. Rose hears sighs, murmurs. Burglars? One of those horrible home invasions she hears about on the television? She lies still, listening, as the sounds move around her small rooms. Gradually she detects a rhythm, a hum almost like a chant, the almost song going louder and quieter as it swirls around her. And it's cold, Rose realizes. She tries to raise her head from the floor, but she doesn't have the strength. Not burglars, she knows. The primeval freeze moves through her, comes to rest in her rattling chest. This is something else. An uninvited guest. Evil wedging its way in. Rose feels frigid, impotent anger, her rage constricted by weakness and infirmity. They all want something. Something from Rose. She's just an old lady. What can she do for them? She just wants to be left alone to rest. But they come, they keep coming. They open the door. They bring it with them.

Then footsteps behind her. The swish of cold evening air, like a knife cutting. Rose draws a deep breath and tries to yell. Nothing comes out but a rasping exhale of spit and raisin oatmeal pap. The window slams shut and locks.

PART FIVE

JUNE
Saturday, April 19

THE DOORBELL RINGS. It's 7:30 in the morning. June shifts into Norm and sighs. Her head is on his shoulder. Her legs are wrapped around his. It's her second true sleep in weeks.

A fist pounds against the door. Then the doorbell, ringing again.

June stirs. Norm?

A muffled yell—Open up! OPP!

Norm?

Huh—wha—?

The doorbell—ringing.

Norm wakes. He was dreaming. June with blue hands, skeleton hands, walking through the felled forest in a white nightie. June straddling a stump, lace flowing around a big round belly protruding.

Norm, there's someone—

Police! Open up!

What the hell? Norm throws on his robe. Where are my—

Police!

—slippers?

Norm! June cries.

Stay here, he barks. He hurries down the stairs, bare feet slapping hard wood.

Police! Open up!

Yes, okay, I'm coming!

June stands at the top of the stairs, her naked arms covered with goose bumps. She folds her arms into her body. She's freezing.

I'm coming! Norm yells again, fumbling with the alarm code, the locks. He finally gets the door open. Two men in faded sports coats lean eagerly into Norm's face. Behind them stand two uniformed officers.

Ontario Provincial Police, one of the men in suits says flashing a badge.

Police? Norm repeats dubiously.

Police. Mind if we come in? They push past Norm into the house.

Norm? June calls from the top of the stairs. The two look up at her.

Go back to the bedroom, Norm snaps.

Can you come down here please Miss?

June! Go back to the bedroom!

Miss—

June hesitates.

June! Norm barks. She's never heard him raise his voice before. She flees.

The two detectives, portly, in their fifties, peer suspiciously around the brightly lit foyer. Melting morning light seeps into the hall through the open front door.

I'm Inspector McLintock and this is—

But what is this about? Norm blurts.

The two inspectors glance at each other.

We're investigating reports of a find of Native remains at these premises.

What?

Sir we have reason to believe that there was an excavation of archaeological significance on these premises.

This is private property. Norm speaks clearly, loudly, breathing between words. He's aware of his wife, upstairs, hiding in the bedroom, listening. I want you to leave.

Sir we'd like to—

I want you to—

If we could just take a look around the premises?

There's nothing here for you to see.

Sir it's illegal to excavate or otherwise disturb or distribute Native remains.

I don't know anything about that.

Sir. We received a complaint. I'm afraid that we have no choice but to act.

We could get a warrant to search the premises, the other, previously silent, officer intones. He steps forward, puts his fleshy face right up to Norm's. That would involve public proceedings, he says, pronouncing every word as if spitting. Very public proceedings.

You don't have a warrant?

No sir. But we would like to speak with your—

Then you have no right to be here. I'm going to ask you both to leave.

The inspectors glare at each other.

Sir, I would advise you to—

Good day, Norm says, slamming the door. He locks it and executes the security code. The red alarm light blinks on. Norm stands in the hazy hallway, lost in the interior air drifting disturbed around him, that world of billions of inexplicable particles. His feet are bare and cold. A dizzy spell takes him and he puts a hand on the wall.

Norm?

June stands at the stop of the stairs. Cheeks puffy, she resembles a teenager shaken from a weekend sleep-in.

Norm?

They're gone, he says.

Norm—I—

Norm looks up the stairs at his wife.

It'll be okay, he adds quickly.

No. Norm. It's not okay. June walks slowly down the stairs. She takes his hand, pulls him out into the backyard. They step out into the cold day just beginning. June marches Norm to the edge of the pit. Look in, she says to him. Do it.

Norm kneels, the knees of his pajamas going wet and muddy. June?

Don't you see them?

See what, June? Norm gets lower, squints desperately into the muddy hole.

The bones Norm! The bones!

June? What bones?

June sits in the kitchen staring at the steam rising from her mug of coffee.

Norm's in his study, making calls. June gave him the card of that lawyer, her old college friend Chris.

Norm's dressed now. Blue button-down shirt, red striped tie, like he's heading into the office. He's calling her now, Christine —Chris—the two of them calmly discussing—

Jesus Christ. What is he telling her?

The coffee in her mug trembles, liquid syncopating.

Morning has broken into day, overcast and granulated. She won't go out there. She'll keep the blinds closed. Norm says everything will be okay. She believes him. When the police came, at first she thought it was about what happened—

the other night—in the backyard.

She...with the—shovel.

Where did the bones go? She didn't tell Norm about him, the ragged man-boy with the wild eyes. What could she say? I hit a man with a shovel and then went to bed and had the best sleep in a month? I'm homicidal and crazy and maybe I'm—?

No, June, you're not—

He took the bones. She hit him with the shovel and he took the bones.

Norm didn't ask her anything. He just held her, there, in front of it, in front of the empty hole.

He took them, she finally says out loud. The words ring through the kitchen then disappear.

June blows steam off the liquid in her mug. In the backyard, Norm had seemed unfazed, as if he'd been expecting something like this all along. It's okay, he said. He held her close and stroked her hair. We'll be okay, he said. Weirdly, she believes him. She's the teenager who borrowed Daddy's car for a spin and crashed into the neighbour's mailbox. She's waiting in the kitchen while her parents confer with the lawyers, the neighbours, the police, alleviating the damage, patching things up before bringing the full force of their disapproval down upon her. Whatever happens, Daddy's going to take care of it. Whatever it takes, he's going to make it all go away.

Embarrassed, June inspects her fingers. Ravaged skin, thin veneer wrapped around bright white bone. Her nails are ruined. She runs a fingertip across the underside of her wrist. The jagged line leaves a faint red scratch. June swallows, tastes coffee and spit. *There were bones.* A man came, a man-boy with red in the whites of his eyes and flailing arms. He said—*They're mine. And I*—she picked up the shovel and now…June puts her head down on the table. Now there's just an empty hole. June closes her eyes.

Dreaming. People. Yelling.

People.

Chanting—

Give back the bones! Give back the bones! Give back the—

June picks her face up off the kitchen table. She hears the cracking beat of a megaphone chant.

I'm—*dreaming.*

Give back the bones! Give back the—

Is she still asleep? No—she's—

Give back the—

Norm? Uh, *Norm?*

—hearing things?

Norm!

He comes hurrying into the kitchen.

Norm?

He takes her hand. It's okay. They're just—it's a—

He leads her into the front sitting room, the piano room, Norm calls it, imagining that at some point his offspring will patiently play the grand notes of one of Bach's simpler sonatas.

June pulls at a corner of the curtain covering the big bay window. They peek outside.

Give back the bones!

Oh my god, she mutters.

It's her, the woman from the community centre. The red-haired freak who kept yelling—what was it?—I'm very disturbed! I'm very disturbed! Here the chant is different, but the ardent high-pitched cadent rhythms are the same:

Give! Back! The! Bones!

Jesus Christ, June mutters.

She dares to take a second look. I'm-Very-Disturbed is resplendent. Pale strawberry hair with a single dark feather sticking out. Around her neck a long thin scarf like the kind you see those protestor types wearing to cover their faces. She's also sporting a pair of beaded buckskin-looking pants straight out of Tonto's closet. And, on her feet, a menacing set of military issue black boots.

June doesn't know what to make of it. She represses a sudden, insecure giggle.

Give back the bones!

It's not funny.

I'm-Very-Disturbed is pacing up and down the sidewalk yelling hoarsely into the megaphone. She's got a small group with her. Five acolyte braves in dirty hoodies and ragged jeans, a mini-tribe all brandishing the same sign: *Wississauga for the Wississaugans.*

There are...*Wississaugans?*

Give back—

Uh, Norm?

They're crazy, Norm mutters.

Then June does laugh. She buries her face in Norm's shoulder and laughs till she's soaked through the fabric of his shirt.

It isn't funny, she gasps. It isn't funny.

Norm smoothes her hair. They watch the protest through the window. June wipes her face on his shoulder.

News is here, Norm points out.

June looks up in time to see the Wississauga Cable Community News van park across the street. No sign of that kid, the reporter. The chant gets louder, red-haired leader screeching with renewed intensity.

Give! Back! The!—

She's going to lose her voice, June thinks.

The phone rings. It rings four times, stops, then starts again. June holds on to Norm.

What should we do?

I called your lawyer friend, Norm says. She's on her way.

She's on her way?

Yes.

Why? Are they going to arrest me?

No, sweetie.

Norm?

I don't know.

June peeks through. June watches as Hal Talbot hops out of the van and hurriedly starts setting up a tripod. He looks flustered, his suit rumpled, his hair mussed. With the news here to make it official, a small crowd of spectators gathers. Ladies with strollers, an old retired couple, a gaggle of renovators, lawn care professionals, and cable company installers. Suburbia's daytime detritus. June's never seen so many people on her street. A cop car pulls up behind the news van, its officers not even deigning to leave the comfort of their vehicle.

Give them back! Give them back!

Chant's changed, June notes.

Uh huh.

Would you like a cup of coffee, Norm?

That would be…nice.

They retire to the kitchen. Thinking of Christine and the reporters and the police and the protestors but feeling unexpectedly relieved, June brews a fresh pot.

Finally, the doorbell dings again. They stare at each other. June has the sudden urge to burst into laughter. The doorbell goes a second time. Ding-dong. Norm takes a sip from his cup and returns it to the saucer. The sounds calm June. Normal noises: Norm's pursed lips slurping coffee, the phone ringing, the doorbell dinging. Amidst all that noise, she feels somehow relieved. Give back the bones? No. Sorry. Don't have them. *He's*—they're—gone.

The bell rings again. They're still just looking at each other. Norm sighs, gets up.

It's probably your—lawyer friend.

June stays where she is. She feels her limbs, a heaviness in her arms and legs. She wants to go upstairs and climb into bed. She's tired. Exhausted.

Angry shouts coming from outside.

The protestors: Give back the—

And the reporters: two or three of them now shouting through the wedge of half-opened doorway: Are the remains on the premises? Would you like to comment on the protest? Can we see them? On the allegations?

And Christine—Chris, June reminds herself—crisply responding: The family has no comment at this time. Please step back to the sidewalk. This is private property. We'll be making a statement at an appropriate interval. Please step back. This is private property.

June hears the door open then shut and lock. She hears the click of Chris's heels on the hallway's tiles. She imagines her perfect in a pantsuit, glaring over the reporters.

June? Norm says tentatively.

June picks her head off the kitchen table.

Your lawyer...friend is here.

Christine moves to her, crouches down, gives her an awkward hug.

Hi June, she says. Don't worry. Everything's going to be okay. You just let us take care of everything.

A flash in the ceiling. Another one of the recessed bulbs burning out.

Oh! June startles.

The phone rings. The protesters chant and wave their placards with a fervent enthusiasm that's entirely alien to the placid surroundings of Lower Grove Drive. *Don't they have jobs?* June goes back to the kitchen. She fills her coffee mug. Norm and Chris remain in the front sitting room, holding a hushed conference, tones just above a whisper. June sits down at the table. She wraps her hands around the warm porcelain. She stares into the depths of the slow swirl, top layer slightly greasy with melted milk congeal. She doesn't look up to see the duo's tentative arrival.

Ah, June, Norm says. We think it's best if you talk to Chris in here—

Alone, Chris says.

Yes, Norm agrees.

No. June shakes her head without looking up. Norm should stay. I want him to.

Chris crouches down again. June honey, she soothes, it's better if Norm doesn't stay. What you say to me will be entirely confidential. Lawyer client privilege.

June looks down, contemplates her hands. She can smell Chris's perfume. Her hands are worn and grainy against the glossy sheen of the glazed wood table. When was the last time she put on perfume?

Go ahead sweetheart. I'm going to replace this light. Norm's looking up at the ceiling. Third one this month, he says, genuinely puzzled.

June feels a sudden surge of affection for him.

We'll use your study? Chris asks Norm as she gently tugs on June's arm, encouraging her out of her slump.

June finds herself being led up the stairs. She wants to say something. Something normal.

How's, uh, Marcus? she asks, her supermarket voice loud and startling. Where did that come from? Chris's boyfriend, right? She mentioned a boyfriend when they met in the Save-A-Centre, didn't she? June just imagined him as a Marcus. Dark-haired, tall, work-out-four-times-a-week, little-Italy-condo-Mercedes-convertible Marcus.

We broke up.

Oh. I'm sorry.

In here?

Yes.

There we go, let me get the light. You just sit down. Chris leads her to the leather love seat in the corner of the room. June wants to complain. She doesn't need to be led. *They broke up*, she thinks. She lets Chris guide her, help her sit down. Chris turns on the lights, soft overheads that banish the backyard. June peeks out the window, sees a blur of blue—the tangled tarp. Quickly, she turns away.

June, Chris says, sitting next to her on the love seat. Their hips touch. *They broke up*, June thinks. Chris is in a cream shirt and blazer number. Nylons. She really is a good-looking woman. Are you alright, June? Chris asks.

June nods. She can't seem to speak. She doesn't want to cry.

June, I need to ask you some questions, okay? I know you're upset, but if I'm going to help you I need to know exactly what the circumstances are here. Okay?

June looks at her hands.

June?

Tangled up in blue, she thinks. Bob Dylan. The tarp and the river and the sky. She used to have that disc. Still does, somewhere, in the basement, boxes of CDs she never unpacked. When was the last time she listened to—

June?

Can you close the curtain please?

Chris springs up and shuts out the view. Now June, I know you're going through a hard time. But I need you to try and relax.

She tries to keep her face neutral. She feels like she might cry again. She puts her hands on her cheeks, feels the rough grain of her palms on her hot soft lips.

June? You might feel better if you take—Chris fumbles in her purse. Here. Take two of these. You just put them under your tongue and they dissolve. You don't swallow them. Okay? Here. Chris pries a hand down and drops two tiny blue tablets in June's palm. She guides June's hand to her mouth.

June snaps her hand into a fist. No!

June, it's not—it's just to—

No! I can't!

June. It's just something to calm you—

I can't!

What? What is it? You can tell me.

I'm—

June?

I think I'm—pregnant.

Chris's cheeks colour. Then fade to white. Flash of—

anger, June thinks. Annoyance. No. Jealousy.

June, you're pregnant?

June half nods. No. I mean, it was only just, last week. When Norm and I—but still. I *think* I am. I feel…different.

Are you sure?

Could Chris really be jealous *of her?* The idea fills her with unexpected confidence. Chris is gorgeous, has an important job, lives in a fancy condo downtown. But…she broke up with her boyfriend.

She's lonely, June thinks.

Have you said anything to Norm yet?

June shakes her head. Don't, she says. Don't say anything.

Okay. But…you should take a test. They have these new ones. You only have to be…a week. I…saw an ad for them. In a magazine.

June doesn't answer.

Anyway, you better not…Chris plucks the pills from June's hand, slips them back in the vial. She seems shaken.

What are those? June asks.

The pills? Nothing. They just…calm you down.

Do *you* take them?

I—they're for clients, comes in handy. I mean, sometimes I… Chris laughs uncomfortably. I mean, you wouldn't believe the stress I'm under.…

June nods. You and Marcus?

He broke up with me.

What happened?

Oh, what happened? Chris laughs dryly. We were both…
always…working. It just wasn't meant to be, I guess.

You're beautiful. You'll find someone.

I guess.

They sit together on the love seat. Their legs touching. Nylon
to sweatpant. Outside in the backyard and beyond, birds call each
other, the wind rustles new leaves.

It's so quiet here, Chris says.

Usually, June says. They both laugh.

It'll be a great place for…kids.

June nods.

They sit. The phone rings. Then Chris's cell, oddly in beat with
the faint background hum of chanting protestors: Not your bones.
Not your bones. Not your…

So, Chris says, deftly extracting her phone and turning it off.
You want to tell me what's going on?

June nods.

TIM AND CHARLIE
Saturday April 19

TIM LURKS IN THE SHADOW cast by the Colonnades apartments. It's late afternoon and the tall building blocks the sun, cutting shade into the parking lot. He's stalling. *Just get it over with.* He swore he'd never come back. But he needs money. He needs to put gas in the car. He can't go home without—

gas in the car. 50 bucks. Or, maybe, like—a couple a hundred. He has debts. The China. He was supposed to sell it. Instead he— *Maybe five. Five grand would—*

He's never gotten a penny from anyone his whole life. That cheque his dad sent him. Burned it right up, Tim thinks with satisfaction. But now. Now he's—

A buff guy in a tracksuit springs through the doors, car keys jangling. Tim slips inside. He is confronted by the same weirdly green stolid plants standing dutifully in the dusty otherwise lifeless lobby. No spring here. No summer either. The perpetual fall twilight reminds Tim of the lower depths of the woods, weird Charlie's Indian crypt, and then, after that—

the hole, Tim thinks.

The dank porous dark at the bottom of the hole where he—

I couldn't see—and—

She hit me. She fucking—

She hit him and he fell, skin against wet mud, and there was—

There was—

She was—

Only, he couldn't—he couldn't stay awake.

And she—

When he woke up, he was alone. Alone at the bottom of an empty hole.

After that, he's not sure. He wasn't even sure what day it was. His whole body ached. There was dirt everywhere, under his fingernails, ground into his clothes, in his hair, in his ears. He remembers waking up at the bottom of the hole. He remembers—digging—with his hands, on his knees—also, he took some pills. At some point. A few more of the pills. *Had to,* Tim thinks. There was this beat in his head, not drums, more like a chant, a murmured reverb getting louder and louder, settling deeper and deeper. He scraped and clawed to that horrible insistent rhythm. Rhythm.

Digging and digging and digging through rock and clay and loam, each layer colder and harder than the next.

And then?

Tim shakes his head in frustration, pain pounding the sides of his skull. *And then back in the woods, somehow.* Waking up under the tree, next to the fire pit, back to Timmy's old spot.

Only, the chanting was gone. And everything seemed— different.

The sun had been strong. The gulley all lit up, impossibly bright, irrevocably alive. Tim had fallen back against hard cold dirt, everything spinning. But he'd resisted the demand to close his eyes, to cover the bright air with his dirty dark fists.

Good fucking Jesus, his head!

Despite the headache and the way every muscle in his body felt like it had been pounded into submission, Tim forced himself to stare up into the nascent light green of the great tree's unfurling leaves, foreground offset by the stunning blue of a painted blue sky. He'd laid there until the spin settled and he'd managed to understand what he was really feeling underneath the relenting pain. Relief, he thought now, steadying himself against the lobby wall. Why? What had he done? The bottom of the pit—digging—so where were the—

Tim closes his eyes.

Carly's voice: *Don't think about it. It'll come.*

He's all messed up. His head feels like it's splitting in half. He's out of gas. He's out of the China. He wants to go home, but he doesn't have any—

money.

So back here, back to the good old Colonnades. He's not angry anymore, he tells himself. It's just what he's owed. That's all he wants. Just a little bit of what he sure as shit deserves.

The next thing is the elevator, the way its soft gliding stop seems to take two times forever. The door opens with a jerk and Tim lurches himself forward and on down the hall, a simulacrum of a man in a hurry. At his dad's door, Tim doesn't hesitate. He grabs the doorknob and pushes. It's locked. Tim yanks at the knob, rattles it. Nothing. No response. He waits a few seconds then starts slapping at the door with the flat of his hand. Dad? Hey Dad? C'mon Dad, he thinks, or maybe says, picking up the pace of his percussion. *Wakey wakey. Wakey wakey, old man. Don't do this to me. Don't fucking do this to me.*

He's going hard now, really slamming at the door—

Wakey wakey, Daddy, wake the fuck up. Don't you do this to me, ya goddam—

he's kinda—

yelling—

freaking out here—

Abruptly, Tim kicks the door. Starts punching it.

Fuck! Fuck! Open up you fucking asshole! Open the fuck up!

He's screaming now, the veins on his forehead bulging. There's no beat, no rhythm, just the rage in waves, a great dam abruptly unimpeded, a river running over and through.

Fuck! Fuck!

Tim doesn't even notice the woman standing near him.

Excuse me, she calls. Excuse me. Young man?

Finally, she steps forward and tries to grab one of his flailing arms.

Huh—wha?—

Young man, she snaps nasally!

Tim turns, the woman steps quickly away from him.

Can I help you? she asks.

Can I help *you?* he snarls.

Now she's standing in front of the open door of her across-the-hall apartment. *Woke her up,* Tim thinks. He scrutinizes her, a lady in her sixties, dishevelled in a bathrobe and fuzzy slippers. *Flu. Home sick from work.*

I live here, she proclaims. She looks at him with bleary discomfort.

Good for you. You want an award? Tim is breathing heavily. His face is blotchy from exposure and effort, his army surplus outfit liberally blotched with mud and dusty sap stains. The reek of sweat and pot and vomit fills the hallway. Tim smells himself in the closed confines.

Listen, he says. I—it's cool. I'm just trying to—

Who are you looking for? she asks.

The...the old guy. Who lives here.

Oh. She frowns. Her red nose crinkling. I'm afraid he...are you...?

Tim looks down at his boots. His feet in there, the bog soak of moist sock rot. He can feel his peeling red toes. Tell her. Why not? His mom would be her age.

I'm his son.

Oh. Oh dear. The woman digs into her housecoat pocket and pulls out a wad of tissue. She blows her nose. He...I'm sorry to say that he's—

Dead, right?

She nods. I'm terribly sorry.

Figures. I mean, I figured. Okay. Okay then. Tim jams his fists into his pants pockets. He moves down the dingy carpet toward the elevator. He can't feel his legs under him. The hallway is dark and narrow, closing in.

Wait, she calls after him. Are you...okay?

He stops, half turns. *Keep walking. There's nothing here anymore. Just some lady. Somebody's mother. Somebody's freaking math teacher or something.* Once, once upon a time, his mom helped him with his math homework. Addition. Multiplication. Subtraction.

Are you sure you're okay, young man? Maybe you should—

Did you know him?

The woman shakes her head. Not really. He was quite...private.

He was an asshole.

The woman winces. Well I wouldn't speak that way about...

So when did he croak?

He passed two nights ago.

Two nights ago? Are you sure? What time? Do you know what time?

Sick-lady math teacher takes another step back toward the sanctuary of her own apartment.

I'm sorry, she says. All I know is what the super told me. Maybe I should get the super?

She stares down at her fuzzy slippers.

Looks up.

The hallway is empty.

Tim checks himself out in the rear-view mirror of the inert Pontiac. His face, smeared with streaks of drying dirt, is pale and drawn. His hair has gone flat and stringy. His eyes bulge out of their sockets. Skin peels and flakes off the sides of his nose. *Nice look*, he thinks. *So what? At least I'm still—*

Last man standing. It's official. His dad is dead. Maybe that explains why—at the bottom—he woke up; it was warm, almost hot. And the bones were—it was so quiet. Then the sound, the song—not a song, the chant—that wordless, soundless prayer. Tim remembers lying there, just lying there and letting the pulsing heat seep into him. And then he was crying, tears running down his cheeks. Only, he hadn't felt sad, not really, just—

alive.

And he woke up. And there was nothing. His hurting head, empty. And he knew, then, that his mother was gone. That his father was—

Yeah, so, what's the problem? Time to celebrate, right? Get yourself a big steak. Ha yeah. Celebrate. A nice big juicy bloody steak.

Tim yanks open the car door and retches. Nothing comes out. He dangles his weightless head, spitting bile. Finally, he slumps back against the car's padded seat. Through the filthy window he surveys the dead dump clearing, portal to the woods, his home away from home, home on the range, home is where your heart is, home is where you hang your hat, home. *Ha. I'm an orphan. Hey Carly, guess what? I'm a—*

His mind races and his heart jumps up and down like a jack-in-the-box trapped in a hollow chest.

He doesn't know what he is.

He tried, right? *At least I tried.*

What did he expect? That after all these years he could come back, snap his fingers and make everything better? *Same shit, different day—right Dad?* Only, for a second, Carly, she was *there*. He feels his neck, the skin tight against the hard press of his throat. He imagines that he still smells it, the faint rosy waft of her perfume. Maybe he does. *She came to say goodbye,* Tim reasons. And now it's time for him to do the same.

From his pocket, Tim extracts a plastic baggie full of dirt and grey stone. The remains of the old pipe. The pipe was smashed to bits when that crazy lady hit him and he fell into the—into his mother's—but he saved what he could, hurriedly scooped dirt and shattered stone into empty plastic. *Sorry Charlie.* Tim shrugs. He carefully pours what he managed to salvage into the creased grimy paper of his father's letter, folded in half. He stuffs the makeshift envelope back into the filthy baggie. One last time, he thinks, stepping out of the car. His legs are dizzy under him. He holds onto the roof until his muscles stop shaking and he can stand without falling.

Tim sits cross-legged in the dirt under the giant tree. The sun is in decline. It's almost dusk and the air is getting brisk. He's made a fire in the pit. Real cozy like. Lazy breeze swirling ash. Pull up a stump. Make yourself at home. Smoke drifts up in naked boughs, dulls sparkling rays of the late setting sun. The giant tree towers over him. The old boulder, his sore back against it. Solid, immutable objects. Some things are for sure. Knowable. Forever. The hard rock against his stiff neck. The old tree groaning in the gloaming. The breeze shifts smoke and river air in his face. Tim coughs, his whole empty body creaking forward like a hollow tin can caught in a gust of wind.

This is like dying, he thinks. Distant decomposing breezes and smoky moments of fleeting sharp awareness. He's not dying. *Naw.* He's just going to—

close my eyes. For a bit. Get some rest.

He wakes up. The fire is blazing. The heat feels good on his face. Through closed eyes he can see flames.

Big brown pupils float over him.

Hey, he hears.

Hey yourself, he says through cracked lips.

Charlie giggles nervously.

Did you—? He gestures weakly at the fire.

She nods.

Thanks.

Here, she says, drinks this.

He reaches for it, the jar of tea. His hands shake, spilling. She covers his hands with hers. Her skin is cool and soft. Charlie helps him bring the glass to his lips. He drinks. Again. Then again. He empties the jar.

Charlie sits down next to him. *What does she want?* he wonders. Why does she keep showing up? The fire cracks. A chipmunk scampers. Tim feels himself drifting, his muscles unclenching. There's something about the way the girl just sits there looking at him, the way she just *is*. *It's like*, he thinks, *she doesn't fully exist*. He shifts, feels her camouflage jean leg against his twig thigh. He smells her scent, sweat and hints of spice and perfume. But that doesn't mean anything. Of course she's real. But real how? *She was sent here*, Tim thinks. *She was sent to me*. This realization calms him. His mother—appearing and disappearing. The bones—there, then gone. His father—alive, then dead. And Charlie—disappearing, reappearing. Sent to him. Sent to help him.

A light warm breeze blows through the river gulley. Tim looks up at the giant tree spread out above them. Wordlessly, he hands Charlie the shattered pipe bundle he's been holding on his lap. Charlie unwraps it and carefully peers in, squinting down through the thickening twilight.

It's all broken. Charlie's voice quavers.

Sorry, Tim mutters. I...

Sorry?

Yeah. I was—it's—

Charlie stares fiercely at the crushed remains. It's not good, she says. That was, like, really really old.

I know, Tim sighs. The girl looks like she's going to cry. We'll bury it, Tim says quickly. What if we bury it?

The Natives used to bury the bones of the animals they ate, Charlie says sombrely. Then they would say a prayer for them. It was so the animals could be reborn and stuff.

Reborn?

Yeah, like, so they're not all used up and stuff.

Huh.

They sit in silence. The big tree stirs, its limbs weary.

So—Tim says. Do you want to?

I…I don't know.

Why not?

I don't know. Charlie frowns, her forehead wrinkling.

Why not? Tim is insistent. He needs this. She was sent to him. Tim's never been to a—

funeral.

Why not?

Charlie's standing now. She's staring through the smoke at the running river. We can't just bury it, she says quietly. We have to… show that we're sorry.

Sorry?

It needs to be an offering, Charlie says definitively.

An offering? He'd been thinking burial. Dig a hole and drop the past in. Cover it up. Make it disappear.

Maybe…Charlie says…we should throw it in the river.

In the river?

That's what *we* do. We make an offering. We're Hindu.

Yeah? Tim's listening.

Yeah, says Charlie, getting excited. When we moved into our house we put a bunch of money in a plastic bag and we drove over to the park part of the river and I threw it in.

You threw money in? Like…how much.

Charlie shrugs. I dunno. Hundreds. For luck and stuff.

Hundreds? Tim remembers burning that cheque his father sent him, how good it felt.

And when my *daadeemaa* died my pappa flew to India and threw her ashes in the river.

Uh…Who died?

My grandmother.

Huh. So it was, like, a funeral?

Yeah. I guess. It's part of our religion.

Huh.

So are we going to do it? Charlie's enlivened. She wants to do this. They'll throw the pipe in, say a prayer. They won't be angry anymore. They'll know she's sorry. They'll understand that she didn't mean to—

Yeah, we'll do it. But first we should—Tim fumbles for it, the very last of his supply. A tightly rolled joint.

Charlie looks at it, eyes narrowed.

This is my last one, Tim snaps. He proffers the Che lighter. You wanna do the honours?

No, Charlie says. I don't know. It makes me feel all weird. Like someone's watching me.

Yeah, Tim agrees.

Charlie stares at Tim as he uses one hand to hold the other hand steady and finally manages to get his shaking fingers to wedge the joint between his brittle lips.

No, Charlie says, shaking her head. We shouldn't.

Tim ignores her. Slowly he brings the lighter toward the smoke. The flame flickers, licks at the paper. Abruptly, Charlie reaches over and grabs the lighter from his hand.

Hey? What the fuck?

The joint falls out of his lips and onto the forest floor.

We can't!

Tim closes his eyes. His body, so tight on him, like a clenched fist. He can already feel it coursing through him. The sweet smoke. God in heaven, he really needs it. He forces himself to open his eyes. The girl, Charlie, tracking his tiniest movement. She was sent to him. Give something up. Start again. Become new. *Sacrifice.*

Charlie bends down, picks up the joint and drops it in the plastic baggie.

Ah fuck, Tim groans.

Let's do it there. Tim points to a spot.

Okay.

C'mon.

They fight through the underbrush bordering the river. Charlie's in her parka again. She saw the weather report before going out. The pretty girl on Wississauga Community Cable said there was going to be a major temperature drop. She said it seriously, but she was smiling, too, like she thought it was actually kind of funny. Winter's back! Anyway, it does seem to be getting colder. There's a sharpness in the air, night falling in tiny frozen crystals.

So do we just…throw it in?

Charlie shrugs. I don't know. I think there's, like, prayers and stuff. Don't you know?

Not really. We're not religious.

Huh.

Together, they stare at the dark water's restless flow.

It doesn't matter, Tim finally says. They'll…know.

I guess, Charlie says, her voice small, unconvinced.

Some stupid prayer. Tim says again. It doesn't matter.

Charlie stares at her feet. Grey grass with just a hint of light green tramped down under her dirty sneakers. *They know*, she thinks. *Whatever we do, they'll still know.*

Do it, Tim says urgently. Do it.

Charlie holds the bulging baggie by a corner, dangling it near the river. The bank is steep and they are as close as they can get without falling in.

I can't get it far enough.

Tim thinks about this. Lean out and just drop it, he says. I'll hold onto you.

Charlie edges over to the point where bank crumbles into the river. The water lurches by, green on top, brown and brackish on the bottom. Tim takes Charlie's hand, hot and full in his dry cracked palm. Tim remembers what Charlie said about the rocks leading to the sweat lodge hut. Thousands and thousands of years old. Can a river be old? Water? How old is dirt? What about the air? Is that old?

Hold on tight, Charlie says.

Wait! Tim exclaims. In one motion he reels her back in and grabs the baggie from her.

No! Charlie screams. Stop! She tries to grab the baggie back. Tim fends her off. He digs into his pocket, brings his father's ring out onto the palm of his hand. He shows it to Charlie. The tarnished metal sits cold and heavy on his palm.

It's gold, Tim says. Charlie takes the baggie and opens it. *She was sent to me,* Tim tells himself. He lets the ring slide off his palm into the bag. Now throw it in, Tim says.

Charlie stares at him.

It's okay. I got you.

Don't let go.

I won't.

Charlie leans over the current. Tim feels himself shifting, pulled toward the bank by her weight. He pants cold evening air. Night coming. He can see his breath.

Hold on! Charlie squeals.

Do it. Tim has no strength. He feels her slipping away. C'mon!

Charlie swings her arm, launches the baggie into the middle of the current. Tim slides backward.

Oh! Charlie cries. The river leaps up, splashes her, swirls murkily, uncertainly. Tim digs his heels in, leans against her sliding weight.

Suddenly, Tim falls back, taking the girl with him. Her slick red parka rubs against his sharp stubble. Charlie scrambles to her feet, runs to the river's edge.

It's gone, she says miserably.

Tim surveys the river for signs of the bag. Birds flutter for night home nests. The wind picks up again, rustling the embers of the forest. Tim looks over at Charlie. Her hands cover her face. She's sobbing.

Hey…Tim says lamely. He struggles over, puts an arm around the girl. Charlie cries against him. Tim feels relieved. Her tears wet the front of his thin jacket.

It's okay, he says. It's over now.

No, Charlie says. No…

My father died, Tim says. He says it quietly. Maybe he doesn't say it?

After a while, Charlie stops crying. I have to go, she says. She stays though, her face pressed against his bony chest.

HAL
Monday, April 21

IT WAS A MINUTE-AND-A-HALF of sophistry, intimation, and implication. The perfect news bit, a scoop even. At first, everyone congratulated Hal, shook his hand. Even Mitch: Great stuff, he sniffed. But then the protest started and the police announced an investigation. The Boss had pulled Hal into her office. You better be right about this, she said calmly, looking him straight in the eye.

Right, wrong, does it really matter? How many people even saw his "exclusive"? Hundreds. Maybe a few thousand. More? Not more. In the big city the dumbest human interest puppy dog saved from a burning balcony segment reaches half a million. Hal's sick of regional planning committee bullshit. He's sick of old ladies and the soccer mom mayor and the pathetic pseudo-punks loitering on the back of the third level of the mall pretending they're some kind of gangland crime-wave. That was awesome, Sarah breathed. She looked at him, wide-eyed—admiration? Pity?

Meanwhile, Scott's not answering his cell.

Scott said there was nothing in the hole. He kept repeating it—I didn't see. I didn't see it. Finally, Hal stopped arguing with him. Just after sunrise, Scott left for work pale and dishevelled in a way Hal had never imagined was possible. Hal, left alone, slumped on the second-hand couch, replayed it all over and over again: swaying trees, a weird moon, the sound of the river. And then? Maybe Scott was right? *No. Fuck that.* There was—

something.

Bones, at least. Hal's sure he saw.

And the rest of it? Glowing ghost figment, *right out of Rose's playbook,* Hal thinks. Trick of the light or—

something.

Hal checks the knot in his tie, surveys the scene. Twenty or so protestors are taking a lunch break. They squat and sprawl on the lawn across the street, scratch their heads, pull at their beards, look around nervously. For three days now, he's been watching them, waiting for them to do something interesting. They scratch themselves; they cup soft fruits in their hands and eat like apes. Hal turns to the cloistered house, home to the now infamous June Littlewell. Dark and quiet, the house also squats in the faint spring sunshine. The windows are covered, curtains tightly pulled, no sign of life behind them. Everyone's waiting and nothing's happening. At least nothing that Hal can put on TV. He rubs the blond scruff on his chin. He's been shaving with an electric razor in the back of the news van. He's barely been home since the protest started. Scott gave him the razor for his birthday, top of the line complete with a digital sensor. Hal likes using it, likes the sense of being on the frontlines, too busy for even a proper shave. This is the big time *boy-o.* This is what you wanted.

But things aren't going as planned. The hippie protestors are skewing the equation, because in Hal's mind he had it all added up. It was: evil developers plus government cover-up plus half-crazed housewife patsy equals community outrage and acclaim for muck-raking junior reporter.

But now the boss is on his ass. She's heard from her boss. The corporate higher-ups who barely fund community cable in exchange for the exclusive government-mandated right to make millions selling imported pap to the masses don't like annoying elected officials, no matter how far down the totem pole. Cable community programming is supposed to be about new malls, weather-related school closures, the oldest lady in Wississauga toothlessly mashing through a piece of birthday cake while the mayor looks on, smiling. The mayor's not smiling. She's expressed her unhappiness in a series of terse "no comments." The Walletville regional planning commission has sent an official letter denying any wrongdoing or complicity and suggesting as yet undetermined legal action, should the issue fail to be properly and promptly rectified. Whatever that means. Hal knows what that means. It means no one returns his calls, no one wants to comment. He's cut off, banned from his own story. And what a story it was. Hal worked on it feverishly, slyly combining innuendo and pseudo-fact, images of powerful 18-wheelers spewing smoke, the river flowing past banks of fluttering flowers, a shallow gravesite, a bucolic backyard, all set to portentous pronouncements.

The piece danced. It suggested. It promised. It made no accusations and provided no evidence. It was perfect. It burned the house down.

Hal surveys the scene again. Every day the protest grows by a straggler or two. When he first heard about it he gave it a few hours at most. But the patchwork band seems to be settling in. *Nothing else to do*, Hal thinks. They've put up some old canvas tents. Apparently Proudfeather's actually living in the house, has the permission and sympathy of an absentee neighbour rumoured to be everything from an eco-terrorist doing time in the States to a retired middle-school principal recently divorced and gone to seed. Hal watches the red-haired protest leader bounce around, pausing here and there to encourage her scraggly band. She calls herself Susan Proudfeather. Who's she kidding? She's as white as the rest of us. Proudfeather puts an arm around one of her brood, pats another on the shoulder, flashes another a big thumbs-up grin. With the exception of a two-minute interview when the protestors first arrived, she's been dodging Hal all week, though she's found the time to create a website exhorting people from all over the country, the continent, and the world to join the protest online at Powwowforpeaceandredemption. com. Hal feels an irrational anger toward her, a bile rising from his stomach into his mouth. He wants to spit. Tastes it. He can't spit; he can't get angry. Standing there in front of the cable community news van wearing his blue sports jacket and red-yellow stripped tie, he's a target; people are keeping an eye on him as much as he's keeping an eye on them. Hal crosses his arms, suppresses a shiver. On top of everything else, Mitch and Sarah were right about the weather: it's getting cold again.

The protestors have a drum fire going. They're gathered around it, having their lunch. Hal has no appetite, not that they're offering. Some kind of bean-looking concoction boiled up on an outdoor propane range and spooned into throwaway plastic bowls. *So much for the environment*, Hal thinks. Proud-whatever-the-hell-her-name-is doesn't eat, just prances around talking to people, working her small audience. *She's loving this.* She isn't from around here. He doubts any of them are. Hal checks the cracked screen of his iPhone. It's going on 2. After lunch, she's finally committed to giving him the one-on-one interview she's been promising all week. The last thing

Hal wants to do is give an obvious flake more attention, but he can't spin his follow-up without her, and if he doesn't start spinning, he's going to lose the story and probably his job. She's a nut-bar of the first order, with her army boots, buckskin trousers and single black raven feather flapping out of her curly carrot hair. She's no more than a clown, a caricature. That's what gives her power, Hal figures. She's got nothing to lose, doesn't care how she comes across, and ends up seeming somehow authentic in her fakery. As a result, she makes them all look stupid, makes Wississauga look like the kind of place where hicks hide in their shacks, hoarding Indian skulls and clear-cutting ancient riverside forests. This was supposed to be about the little guy, evil companies and complicit governments conspiring to suppress the truth. But Susan Proudfeather and her freaking Powwow.com are making it about something else entirely, something intangible and impossible to report—race, Indians, history; it's lose-lose, nothing sticks, nobody wants to hear about it, and Hal's getting screwed for even bringing it up in the first place.

Never mind that there aren't any Indians at the protest. In fact, there is no official Native presence in Wississauga or the entire Walletville region. Hal looked it up. The last band or tribe or whatever was moved up river in the 1930s. Way up river, to a reservation three-and-a-half hours north. All that was a long time ago. There's a completely different story to tell now, a story about a sleepy bedroom community becoming a hotbed of possibility, skyrocketing property values versus economic efficiencies, the present versus the future. The bones were just a gimmick, a way to get attention. But Hal miscalculated: the past is pulling them all in, some kind of ethereal quicksand, everywhere and nowhere. The protestors wave their banners and chant their slogans and for some reason it's Hal's fault. Now the city planners and politicos aren't talking to him, the police are investigating, the lawyers are litigating, the Littlewells are in hiding, and Hal's got nothing to work with, fuck all, zero, dick—not even dick. Scott's officially avoiding him. Hal doesn't blame him. It was a bad night, a bad idea. Jesus, maybe that old bat was right after all. The whole thing starting to seem—

cursed.

She's ready for you.

Black-haired kid, maybe five years Hal's junior, his neck draped with a keffiyeh, his skinny body entombed in a ragged lumberjack coat unzipped over a store-aged Levis jean jacket. His tone is contemptuous, dismissive. He turns around and starts walking back across the street without waiting for any kind of reply. The first time Hal asked for an interview this same kid said: We don't deal with the corporate media. The corporate media? They've got to be kidding. In fact, *Proudfeather* did, indeed, talk to the news—*the frigging national news*—their camera practically kissing her ass. That night, Hal, sitting all alone on his suddenly expansive couch, forced himself to watch as Proudfeather and her followers beat on a bunch of oversized beaded tambourines and the camera panned from the earnest protestors to town officials smiling guilty reassurances.

Abruptly, Hal grabs his digi-cam and follows the kid over to the protest epicentre. Two bored members of Wississauga's finest track his progress from the front seat of their squad car. The kid gives him a cursory nod and leads him around the house through the open gate and into the backyard.

It's weirdly tranquil behind the house. Fenced-in backyards face each other. Susan Proudfeather sits alone, cross-legged on the yellow-green grass. Proudfeather seems to be meditating or something.

She's got her eyes closed. A black bird flies overhead, heading for the river across the street and down below. Not exactly sure what to do, Hal stands there, fingering the record button on his camera. Finally, he steps closer and points his camera at the seated woman.

I'm here with Susan Proudfeather, he announces, leader of the Lower Grove Street protest. His voice comes out surprisingly loud in the hush of the backyard. Miss Proudfeather, first of all, thank you for taking the time this afternoon to speak with Wississauga Cable Community News.

It's my pleasure, Susan Proudfeather says gently, opening her eyes as if she'd been waiting all along for the interview to commence. Her voice is husky and muted. She stares up and into the camera as she carefully picks her words. I just want your viewers to know that I'm not the leader, or anything like that. The group has elected me their spokeswoman. But we're a non-hierarchical entity, a community coming together to fight injustice, celebrate the earth, and bring attention to the ongoing legacy of the Wississaugan people.

But as spokesperson, Hal says evenly, I think people would be interested in hearing about your own personal background and philosophy. Your name, for instance, is very unusual. Can you tell us about it?

Susan Proudfeather slowly rises from the lotus position to stand facing him.

Proudfeather is an ancient name. It was given to me by the Squamish peoples in a traditional naming ceremony. This happened last year, when I turned thirty. Dancing arm in arm with the first peoples, I realized how far I'd come from the sanctity of nature, from being able to commune with the spirit of the earth mother. The Indigenous peoples have been here for thousands of years. We've just arrived. We need to respect and learn from their ways. I reject my white name, my settler name, and I now recognize that I am a guest on this land.

Hal takes a step back, makes sure the camera gets the entire getup, from boots to beads to feather.

So is that why you became involved with protests for Native rights?

This isn't *just* a protest, Hal. Proudfeather smiles at him reassuringly. This is a celebration, a gathering celebrating the earth and the legacy and enduring spirit of the Indigenous peoples. Of course, we have to protest, but we also have to celebrate and learn together.

But would you say you've primarily been an…activist, over the last years?

Susan Proudfeather smiles gently into the camera. You know Hal, she says softly. We're just visitors here. We're just passing through. These giant elms and maples threatened for execution are the sacred tribal lands of the Wississaugan people. And they are slated to be paved over. We all have to speak out against what's happening here. We're all pulled to this place because of its beauty and its power.

There aren't, actually, any Native people currently taking part in the protest, are there?

The Wississaugan people have been driven off their land, and now this colonial government wants to remove all traces of their culture, their way of life, by uprooting their ancestors and paving over their holiest ceremonial lands.

Are there any actual members of the Wississauga nation with you today?

They support our protest. They hear our prayers and know we are allies in their struggle for justice.

But they're not actually here?

For years the Indigenous people have been betrayed. The white man has stolen their lands, committed acts of genocide, desecrated their ancient spiritual sites, but now the tide is turning, and the truth is being heard. We believe this is just the beginning. Soon hundreds of people will come here, to this site, and join our movement for truth and redemption.

Hundreds of people? There are only about twenty right now.

Every day the protest grows. People are being drawn to the power of the ancient spirits, to the sanctity of the old growth forest that has existed beside the mighty Wississauga River from time immemorial. They feel the presence here. Susan puts a hand on her heart as she speaks. Hal zooms in.

What do you mean, the presence?

You just feel it. Everyone can feel it. The whole community knows that an injustice is in progress and that we all have to come together to stop it.

What do you mean you can feel their presence?

The Indigenous people believe that the spirits of their ancestors continue to live on in sacred grounds, providing guidance and assistance to the next generations. It is possible to feel their presence. That's why it's so important not to disturb these sacred graves. We demand the bones be repatriated to the Wississauga nation and that all plans for construction of a new road be immediately halted.

Have you actually seen any of these…spirits?

Can't you feel it, Hal? I've been down to the sacred sites. The presence there is so powerful. Hal, I think you should join me there. Come with me. You'll feel it. I know you will.

The car is ready, announces Proudfeather's young subordinate.

Hal startles, the camera jerks. He'd been in a kind of reverie with Proudfeather. On automatic pilot. He was doing the interview, asking the questions, but now he isn't even sure what they talked about. The sun makes a brief appearance through a thin layer of spring cloud. Hal shivers.

Coming with us, Hal? Proudfeather smiles enigmatically.

What, now?

SUSAN
Monday, April 21

THEY PILE INTO THE RUSTED Ford station wagon belching smoke and burning oil. Jared drives and Susan sits beside him, deliberately not speaking. She wants Hal to feel it. She wants him to feel the way the air and the sky get brighter, more intense, the closer you are to the river valley. There's something about the young reporter. Despite his typical J-school pseudo-objectivity—in service, of course, of bludgeoning away at any idea not endorsed by the capitalist industrial complex—she senses something in him. A hesitation. Or more than that. *A desire*, Susan thinks.

They drive along Hurontarion past the Middle Mall, past the Hero Burger, the Starbucks, the Walmart, and the gas station. They pull off into one of the back roads, end up on a delivery alley behind the Save-A-Centre. It looks like a dead end.

So, uh, where are we going exactly? Hal says. His voice is higher than when he's talking on TV. Susan doesn't turn around. She touches a finger to her lips, a signal to Jared to keep silent. She likes the idea of Hal nervously pointing his camera through the dirty windshield, wondering what's coming next. Uh—are we—going the right way?

Right before the dead end, the car makes a fast turn into the scraggly bushes. It's like they're driving into a marshy wood, but they come out onto a narrow track. The car jerks along, then finally lurches to a sudden stop in a little clearing overhung with pressing brush. The small space is littered with beer cans and chip bags and Big Mac containers.

Desecrated, Susan announces, lithely springing from the front seat. Go ahead, Susan says, waving her arms theatrically. Film it. Show everyone the way these Indigenous lands are being treated.

Hal gives her a look, like he wants to say something. But instead he hoists the camera to his shoulder. Susan considers him, taking in the way the reporter's whole body is hunched into itself. *What are you worried about, Hal Talbot? What are you hiding from?* She's sure of it now. The reporter does feel it; something about to reveal itself, something he dreads and desperately wants to see.

Hal Talbot films the filthy clearing. It's getting on 3:30. Mixed sun and cloud, temperature dropping quickly. Susan sees her breath in the air.

Is it really your belief, Hal finally says, pointing his camera at her, that the spirits of Native people…continue to…occupy this area?

People have been drawn here for thousands of years, pulled by the spirit of their ancient ancestors.

Yes, but what I think our viewers would like to know is—

Susan impatiently turns away from him. Wait here, she mouths at Jared. She parts a tangle of tawny vines hanging off a desiccated bush and reveals a rough path down a steep incline splattered with shopping strip detritus. Without saying a word, Susan steps through, her feet pressing a ketchup-smeared white napkin into leaves and humus. Her boots tromp the moist ground, leave heavy impressions on the muddy partial path. The clouds part for an instant, the sun catching clotted grey earth and broken scattered glass. She hears Hal hesitate, and then the slap of loafers in mud as he reluctantly follows.

Susan marches with her head up, her long legs stepping smartly. She knows Hal has to hurry to keep up, his occasional slip and muttered swear a constant reminder that he's struggling to match her pace. But she doesn't break her gait or look back. Out west, Shane led her on regular treks, and her body still remembers the imprint of those walks, the ambulatory physicality that, Susan knows, people like Hal aren't used to anymore, no matter how much time they spend on treadmills and ellipticals.

Gradually, it goes darker. The cliff grows higher over them. Now the trees are taller, wider, thicker. The wind far above blows hard enough to shiver bony branches. Hal pants ragged breaths. *Not yet*, Susan thinks. She's waiting for him to realize, to come to sudden awareness that the constant thrum he thought was Hurontarion traffic is actually the river. The great Wississauga River. Has he ever seen it before? She somehow doubts it. Up above, they picture it as a trickle, its path impeded by old socks, discarded lawn chairs, and toilet paper lily pads. But down below, it's different. The river pulls at you, makes you want to see it, makes you want to stand on its bank and lean in and let the cool flowing water rush through your fingers.

Then it happens:

The river, Hal says out loud.

Susan stops. You can feel it, can't you? She smiles back at Hal. Abruptly, she starts moving again, even faster now, her heart jarring against her chest.

They stop where the river, bending, leans into the cliff side, flows past the gorge and feeds the handful of giant trees that crest the cliff and reach toward the houses above. Do you see that house up there? Susan says. Hal hits record and Susan waits while he films her with her big pale palm on the biggest of the trees, the one defaced by the crude steps nailed into its trunk. She repeats herself then, complete with a slow-motion pointing gesture. Do you see that house? It's the house belonging to June Littlewell. She pauses dramatically to make sure that sinks in. That's the house where the ancient remains have been found. And right here, right beneath, is where the city is planning to build its road. They want to cut down not just the forest, but the *trees*. *This* tree, which has been alive for hundreds of years. Susan pats the trunk affectionately. This is a tree of life. All around us are the remains of the Wississaugan people. Is it not enough that the Indigenous peoples have been driven off their land? Must we also destroy their sacred sites? We invite you to join us in the days to come. Join our prayer vigil, our powwow for peace, add your voice to ours, and together we can speak as one and be heard.

Susan keeps her hand on the tree, caresses the trunk. Hal zooms in. She feels the power of her words, the way they're pulling at Hal. He's the portal. *Let the light in*, she thinks. *All it takes is one magical moment. Put it on* TV. *And they'll see*. She watches as he shuffles around. He's lost now, out of his element, pointing his camera at the river flowing past with an urgency he could never have imagined; at the great trees so much bigger than they look from up above; at Susan, implacable, patient, willing to wait for as long as it takes. What is he seeing? What is he thinking as the chill seeps in and the sweat dries on his skin? *What if I'm right, Hal Talbot? What if this really is a sacred place?* Up above them, a black bird circles, circles, caws. Raven? Crow? Hal, hiding behind the camera. What to point at? Nothing to see, Hal Talbot. You just have to...feel.

Hey! Hal exclaims. His excited call echoes up the cliffside and over. Someone's living here or something!

Susan drops her hand from the tree. She opens her mouth to speak, but Hal's already stepping around the tree, camera cocked. He films a small fire pit and a threadbare army rucksack slumped against a big rock.

Quiet, Susan hisses. She makes a sign toward the bushes. The wind blows and the scraggly range of bush rustles. Hal aims the camera at the crisscrossing web of grey-brown branches dotted with budding leaves.

A girl pops out of the thicket, doubled over. She stumbles awkwardly as she straightens. She's wearing a zipped-up bright red parka, the jacket dotted with bits of bark and branch.

Oh! she says. She takes a step back even as Susan moves eagerly forward. Sorry. I…thought you were…She stands there, watching them with brown baleful eyes.

Who did you think we were? Susan asks gently, her voice imbued with meaning, as in: *You see, Hal, the way people are drawn here.*

The girl looks from Susan to the camera and back again. Are you guys making a movie or something?

Kinda, Hal says. Shouldn't you be in school?

The girl stares at them fiercely.

Do you come here sometimes? Susan asks understandingly. The girl licks her lips, her eyes darting from them to the fire and the slumping rucksack.

Maybe, she says.

Who do you meet here? Hal asks.

Nobody, the girl says quietly.

I used to come down here when I was a kid, Susan says, to Hal, to herself. And then, louder: What's your name?

Charlie, the girl whispers uncertainly.

Charlie, Susan says, trying to conjure up an inviting smile. Would you like to sit down with us? We were just going to…

I've gotta go home, she says. She turns and quickly burrows back into the bramble bush.

Hal catches her retreat in the viewfinder, the back of her legs, a flash of white and blue combat-patterned khaki.

Wait! Susan calls weakly. The forest goes quiet. The river pushes past, buoying up an empty milk jug.

Well that was weird, Hal says.

Susan tries to smile. Something drew her here, she hears herself intone. Something brought her to this place just as we've all been drawn to this spot for thousands of years.

She's probably meeting some boyfriend or something. His camera, pointed down at the ground, is no longer recording. I need to get back, Hal says.

JUNE
Monday, April 21—Tuesday, April 22

LYING IN BED.

Lying.

June can't sleep. Norm slumbers, a heavy arm thrown over her. June doesn't squirm away. Let him. Let him hold her. He keeps telling her, promising her, that everything's going to be fine, everything will be okay. Will everything be okay? *Sure*, June thinks dreamily—

the bones are
there weren't any

—gone.

Outside the mock Wississaugans dance in feathers and jeans around their steel drum fire. The chanting is rhythmic, calming. It reminds June of the days she spent in the backyard, at the bottom. The beat in her head, totem soundtrack to a dream. For a moment, June wishes she were with them. Dancing. Chanting. Believing. But it all seems so long ago now.

Norm? June says, pressing into his heat. Are you asleep?

Huh?

What if they—find something?

Huh?

Tomorrow? When they search the backyard? What if they—? Chris says they think I'm…June can't finish the sentence. What do they think she is? A liar? A mental case? A grave robber? All of the above, really.

It's okay, baby, he mutters. It's all gonna…

Norm?

Go back to sleep.

June closes her eyes. *It's all gonna blow over.* She believes it, too. Feels it, a wind sweeping up from the great lake blowing the spring reek from the river valley up up and away. Already it feels like a dream she had—a diminishing dizzy night sweat vision.

Norm?

His legs are pink and hairy. He loves to floss and has a tendency to rearrange the shoes on her shoe rack, organizing them in categories: casual, business, cocktail.

Uh huh?

What are you…hoping for?

What am I…*hoping* for?

June holds her breath. Waits. She can wait. That's what she's been doing, isn't it? You know, she whispers. A boy? Or a…girl?

Norm turns to face her.

June, are you saying you're…?

It's early yet. I mean, we should…do a test and—but I think I might be…

They come in the morning. Inspector McLintock haltingly, formally, introduces everyone in turn. There's Chris, of course, and a lawyer from the provincial department of something-something-somewhere. The official court-ordered delegation is trailed by two pasty looking ladies in white lab coats, each one flanked by a young male police officer carrying an oversized black case.

For the evidence, June thinks. Norm shifts protectively closer to her. June's gaze roves from one face to another. Christine had told her that the official group might include a Native Elder to oversee proper handling of any remains that might be found. June felt weirdly drawn to the prospect of meeting him—an Indian—a Native. She pictured someone impassively handsome despite his obviously advanced age, a man who, with his tousled shock of white hair and weathered face set off by a faded red button-down open at the throat, wouldn't look out of place at the Wississauga Country Club buffet. The group moves past her into the living room and through the sliding doors into the back. There is no Elder. There's nobody to demonstrate her tolerance to with a simple sympathetic nod: sorry to say that there's nothing here for you, nothing to find, or see, or bury or…whatever. But she's sorry anyway. *For what? I didn't*—

Norm and Chris trail along, leaving June alone in the foyer. June doesn't follow them. Instead she moves into the front room. She peeks through the bay window. A squad of police are rousting the powwowers. The request for an injunction Christine submitted must have been approved. June watches the head cop blurt commands through a megaphone. Disperse. If you do not disperse…

Red-haired lady—*Proudfeather*—and several of her ardent cohorts are not dispersing. They seem to be chaining themselves to a recently constructed teepee. Even through the window and under the harsh bleat of the megaphone, June can just catch the waft of their chanting: *Give back the bones…Give back the bones…* The plaintive bleat of their voices makes June feel a sense of—not guilt, exactly, more like remorse, a complicity in acts nevertheless beyond her control. Surrounding the ardent few chained to their teepee are the rest of the protestors, who lie on the front lawn and wait their turn to be dragged to the idling paddy wagon, their bodies limply resisting, scrawny white limbs drooping as they're lifted. June can't but feel sorry for them; they seem so…pointless.

She stands there, watching, hands folded over her stomach. Though separated by the curtained window from her fellow friendly neighbourhood gawkers—octogenarians, couriers, pest management professionals, and ethnic nanny ladies with their twin and triplet monster strollers—she feels one with them, alone in the crowd, just another gawker. The police use bolt cutters to free I'm-Very-Disturbed, who tosses her ringed red hair like a wild animal as they cuff her and stuff her in a squad car. June slides her palms under her sweatshirt and over the naked swell of her still-flat belly. The police drive off, the onlookers proceed with their day, and suddenly June is staring at an empty scuffed patch of across-the-street lawn.

June climbs the stairs. She stops at the second floor landing. She considers getting back to the project of cleaning out the spare room—the baby's room—a room she previously had to force herself to go into, but now frequently finds herself just standing in, looking around moonily, pretending to herself that she's contemplating soothing colour combinations though she knows she's really just—

what?

Dreaming.

Instead, June finds herself slipping into Norm's study. She grabs the drapes to pull them aside, but doesn't. June's hand on the curtain. Fingers clutching fabric. Phalanges, metacarpals, carpals. There are bones everywhere, hard foundations under every flimsy surface.

Where is he? Where did he go? June feels the numbness she's been harbouring over the last few days leaking out of her, replaced by a great sinking misery. She thinks she might cry, but pushes the feeling back, a swallowed lump. Defiantly, she rips open the curtain.

The science ladies are on the grass beside the pit. They appear to be sifting dirt. They've spread a white tarp. June squints, sees that they've lined up bits and pieces on the white plastic. Small grey objects resembling fragments of rock. Christine and the government lawyer crane their necks like greyhounds eagerly awaiting an opportunity to chase the rabbit. They stand as near as the young cops will let them while Inspector McLintock aggressively snaps photos. June blinks as if blinded by the strobe of the flash. Sunny morning. There isn't a flash. Still the scene seems over-lit, psychedelic. June imagines that if the Wississaugan Elder were here he'd be ignoring the ridiculous proceedings altogether. He'd be kneeling near the hole, his eyes closed and his lips moving silently. He'd gently wave something above his head—wad of burning green sweetgrass, smoke rising up to the sky in languid curls, thick haze blowing in June's face, her eyes tearing, vision clouding—

Doesn't realize she's—where she's going until—

Miss! You can't! Miss!

June shoves someone—a policeman—aside as she hurtles out into the backyard. She pauses, blinking through sunlight at the startled group.

Then she runs for the pit. The crumbling edge. Earth spilling. June stumbles, lets herself fall.

At the bottom: the familiar loud hush, earth in measured tectonic shifts, in waves and tides, in slow silent perpetual decay. Dank moist dark dirt baffling—defying—time. June scoops handfuls. She digs with her fingers, her nails snapping.

I'm sorry, she whispers.

He wanted—he deserved—

Young cops jumping in after her. Lady scientists hurriedly encasing objects in plastic baggies.

Norm: Don't hurt her. She's pregnant! She's pregnant!

And that old man, his eyes closed, his face, his world, tired. Words through weathered wrinkled lips, whispered incantations between him and the wind, a spreading warm breeze that carries the scent of rot renewal up from the running river.

TIM
Tuesday, April 22

TIM DRIVES. The little red E on the dashboard flashes. His old neigh-bourhood shimmers and shines around him, spreading squares of grassy front yard waking up to the sun's truth-telling promise: spring brings summer, weather is inevitable. *It doesn't lie*, Tim thinks, *not like—*

people.

Tim's ribs ache, his mouth tastes sour and hot like a popped blister, his head feels full of burbling water coming to a slow boil. He's out of smokes, he's out of money, out of—

everything is—

too bright.

Tim squints to shut out the shimmer, weaves, jerks the car back as a front tire veers into the curb. The gas gauge flickers empty, goes dark, then comes back on. Tim's flickering too, in and out of days, remembering bits and moments, losing and then suddenly regaining the big picture.

He vaguely remembers climbing into the driver's seat of the Pontiac and popping open the glovebox. Out rolled that vial of pills provided free of charge by his good pal Clay.

He opened the pill bottle and shook its contents onto his trem-bling filthy palm.

One, two, three.

That's it?

He'd given the bottle a shake.

Four.

That was it.

He put them under his tongue, all of them, and waited for his saliva to pool at the bottom of his mouth and turn the tiny white pills into a powdery sludge. It seemed like an eternity, his heart hammering out the endless seconds as the pills ever so gradually dissolved, and then, finally, their chemical decay flowing through the wet circuitry of his mind.

He remembers closing his eyes and seeing the bundle sacrificially sinking to the murky bottom of the river.

And then?

Time passed. He lay in the spot and tongued at the sores on his inner cheeks, at times chewing, other times probing with the crusty tip of his sour tongue. He watched birds circle high above—hawks, falcons—and wondered if they were considering swooping down to snap him up for supper, but they never did. He couldn't keep track of the unfurling leaves of the giant tree, lost count, started again.

What day is it? he asked himself, over and over. *What time is it?*

He knew what he had to do. He just had to—

do it.

Carly—

Carly, I'm—

coming home.

Tim squeezes the brake as he climbs the crest. There's a cruiser in front of his old house. Why? The bright lights flash, redolent in his vision. Maybe they've found—No, it's some kind of protest.

The signs say: *Wississauga for the Wississaugans.*

Weird. More of that—Indian stuff. He squints, tries to see if Charlie is among the protestors. Naw, she'll be in school.

And the Wississaugans? Where are they? Wississauga for yuppies, for scumbag pot dealers, for husband and wife Indian doctors. Whatever, Tim doesn't give two shits, cause he's—

outta here.

Tim presses on the accelerator, shoots past with a groaning belch of exhaust. The road levels then climbs again, a slow bend following the cliff. The sun sits below the clouds, piercing Tim's indignant skull and making him sweat. He soldiers on. He knows what he has to do. Only, he has no idea. The knowledge of his not knowing branded permanently into his brain, a tattoo of a memory—a rectangle of soft baby grass growing gently in the sun. Carly's got a tattoo, a yin yang on her back above the gentle protrusion of her ass—What goes around comes around, she says, lifting up her shirt and twirling. Tim's thought of getting one too. But of what? It doesn't matter anymore. In the bright luminousness of a Wississauga spring afternoon it's easy to see: he's already marked.

He drives past the rising bluff dwellings. He's on *Upper* Grove now; bigger houses here, mini-mansions with circular driveways sculpting front yards, framing columned fronts. Tim slows again, red E sputtering back on. At the top, the houses are spread further and further apart. They sit on the bluff and look down like generals surveying a battle they know they're going to win. There are no other cars on the road. The upscale manses feel abandoned in the late morning. Tim turns, parks in a driveway in front of a three-car garage.

You have to do what you have to do, he thinks.

His father: dead.

He pictures hundred dollar bills sailing down the river like swans.

Sacrifice.

Sacri-fucking-fice.

He needs—

money.

He struggles out of the car. *Keep moving*, he tells himself. *Whatever you do, don't stop.* He scurries toward a wrought-iron gate leading to a backyard. He fumbles with the latch of the gate. It swings open. In Tim's downtown neighbourhood everything is sealed up tight—barred, shut, bolted. You know where you stand. Outside looking in. They think they're safe here. Sure, they're safe here. Tim stands in an open expanse of backyard. The spreading lawn compounds his headache, makes him want to dig under, bury his head in the dark dirt.

Tim moves to the base of the tree, Charlie's escape route. He looks up. The tree swaying in some invisible gale. Already dizzy, Tim reaches for a lower branch. He starts to climb.

Three quarters of the way up, he edges out onto a thick limb running parallel to a window. He squints into a frilly room glowing pink in the sun. Charlie's room. Tim slides the window open. The screen is back in. Charlie must take it out and put it back in when her parents are around. He pushes at the mesh, feels the wire fabric push back. *Fuck it*, he thinks. He jumps awkwardly, shoulder first. Tim flies through, lands on the carpet and rolls like he's some kind of action movie hero. He lies still on the soft shag, breathing. He can feel a cut on his temple where the ripped wire dug a groove. He doesn't so much feel it as sense it through the headache haze, the boil of his brain stewing in its own trapped juices. *Don't stop. Keep going.* Tim gets it now, seeing red, everything tinged with scarlet.

He stands, pondering the spots of blood and bits of wire on Charlie's carpet. He shrugs, turns to her dresser. A piggy bank sits on the white wood chest of drawers, ceramic oinker wearing a banker's bow tie. He works the cork plug out of its backside. Coins spill. Tim was hoping for bills. He yanks at the drawers, dumps sweatshirts, jeans, underwear. He comes up with a jewellery box. He opens it. Hands shaking, he gropes a diamond necklace, gold bangle bracelet, jewels in shifts of liquid coal. *That's more like it.*

Down the hall, he tumbles into the master bedroom. The curtains are drawn. The room feels thick, veiled in rich fabrics. Tim sinks, slogging through viscous broadloom. In front of him, the parental bed, curiously dishevelled in a scatter of pillows and lumped blankets.

Charlie's head emerges from under the covers.

Hey! she squeals.

Tim lurches back.

I'm sick, Charlie announces, sitting up in bed and focussing her baleful brown eyes on him. My mom says I have a fever.

You're sick?

What are you doing here?

Tim's eyes rove, as if searching for an exit.

Why do you have my necklace?

He looks down at his hand. Gold diamond fistful. Tim staggers into the en suite bathroom, closes the door behind him. He hears his breathing in the dark room. Then someone turns on the lights. Bright bulbs arrayed around in the gold gilt frame of an ornamental mirror. Tim blinks furiously, trying to see.

What are you doing? Charlie asks. She stands in the doorway. Her hair is matted in the back, sticks up in the front. She's wearing flannel Snoopy pyjamas.

Tim opens the medicine cabinet. He fumbles with the lotions and shaving creams and toothpastes. A delicate little glass bottle of perfume falls into the sink, smashing. Tim digs for prescription plastic. Scent rising. He brings the plastic bottles to his face, scans for words: *Take 2 before—for the relief of—may cause—if symptoms—*

What are you doing? You broke my mother's perfume. Charlie's voice is calm, as if she expected something like this all along.

Perfume. When he was a kid, his mother would sit at her makeup table in a sheer white slip, put on her face while he watched wide-eyed. How beautiful she was, puckering her lips, delicately gliding a stick of dark red over them, turning to him and blowing a slow glistening kiss. What do you think, little munchkin, does Mommy look pretty? Yes, yes, she looks pretty, more than that, she looks perfect, a flitting holograph burned in his mind, forever bending down in front of him and spraying the lightest waft of scent onto her finger, tickling him ever so gently under the chin, little Timmy giggling. There, sweetie, so you won't forget me while I'm gone...

Lavender and rose and the sharp seductive tang of alcohol.

Finger under his chin, tickling.

Tim drops pill bottles, plastic bouncing on tile.

He loved her. He loved everything about her.

He reaches in, digs around, finds another smooth plastic receptacle. He holds it up to his squinted gaze. *For the relief of.* He smashes it against the ceramic sink.

Stop it? Hey! What are you *doing?*

The bottle shatters, ragged plastic spears his hand.

Stop that!

He picks pills out of the sink, dry swallows, 2, 3, 4, 5, he counts as they wend their way down his ragged throat, counts to make it quicker, to make it last longer. Eyes closed, nose buried in his reeking jacket, but still the smell over him, on him. That smell.

Are you okay?

Tim forces himself to open up. Charlie is a silver smudge of girl. Her eyes, once so deep brown, have now gone a strange matte grey. Tim tries to smile. He feels his cheeks sliding into place.

I'm…okay.

You broke my mom's special perfume, Charlie says gravely.

Oh…yeah…I…Smashed glass and plastic underfoot, Tim pushes past Charlie and crunches his return to the bedroom. The bright soft curtains cast clouds of sunny mercury for Tim to wade through, water-bug beads scattering as he moves.

Back into the hall, he's gliding now, floating just above the rich carpets. He drifts down the stairs to the main floor, follows his legs into the kitchen.

Tim stands in swaying stillness contemplating the room's multitude of shiny surfaces: black stovetop, long empty marble counter, gleaming slate butcher-block island.

Now what are you doing? Charlie says. She's following him.

Tim contemplates the cupboards.

Charlie moves in front of him, stands between him and the kitchen counter. What are you doing? she says again. Her voice quivers the air and swirls microscopic silver darts of dust into Tim's face.

Charlie…Tim says. He sounds calm, reasonable, a million miles away. You're my friend, right?

Charlie nods slowly.

Charlie, the thing is…I need some…money. I…I'm—I'm trying to…

Charlie nods again, a serious look on her face. Okay, she says. Just don't….wreck anything. Nimbly, she climbs up on the kitchen counter. She stands, teeters, gets her balance. She pushes around jars of grains and beans and weird pickled bits of organ-looking preserves. She reaches into the back and pulls out an old tea tin. Carefully she climbs down from the counter. Her face is pale. She proffers the tin to Tim.

My mom says you always need to have emergency money at home because you never know, she says.

In Tim's hands, the tin feels light and full. He digs at the lid with long dirty nails, finally gets it open.

Charlie—Tim says, staring at the money in the tin, tight pack of bills in an elastic bundle.

Just go, she says.

He moves quickly through the front hall. Charlie follows along behind him, but he doesn't look back. He unlocks the big front door and steps outside. He stands in the quiet suburb with the tea tin under his arm, Charlie's diamond necklace dangling from his wrist. He hears a car, DJ chatter booming out of deep bass woofers, some passing Porsche convertible, *rich asswipe*, doesn't matter. The front door slams behind him. Tim's legs suddenly go weak. The Pontiac is a black hole under a murky mid-day sun. He staggers toward it, puts his hands on the car's roof to steady himself.

Tim coughs, grabs to hold his sharpening insides. He's going home. Home for a shower, a sleep, a meal; but first he wants a beer. Jesus, his mouth is dry. He can already feel it, cold burbling bubbles, taste of metal and glass tickling his tongue. Just one and then—

So let's go already. Let's—

get out of here.

He doesn't move. It's like he's stuck in quicksand, his burbling mind slowly pulling him under. His eyes are heavy. But his mind— racing, roiling. His father: dead. His mother: dead. A ghost? He doesn't know. There were—bones. Where are the—? He coughs again, fluid pooling in his throat. He turns to his side, gags something pink and yellow. He pictures Charlie, back in her parents' big bed, the covers pulled over her head.

Sacrifice, he thinks sadly.

He didn't mean to—

He won't see her again. His mother—

she's gone too.

But she came and she touched him under the chin and let him smell her vanilla hot skin. She came and he wanted to hold her, reach out to her, but he didn't, he couldn't, and now, now it's—

too late.

The sun hangs overhead. High noon. A flatbed landscaping truck creeps past, thin toddler trees in teetering rows.

Finally, Tim opens the door and carefully bends his lanky frame into the driver's seat. He turns the key and the car engine makes a weak whine. He tries again, his heart bouncing in his throat. Piece of shit. He'll buy her a new one. He'll pay off Clay, start again, forget dealing, bad idea. Carly's right, work hard, nose to the grindstone, *hi ho, hi ho, it's off to work you go.* How much is in the tea tin? The Pontiac jerks, groans, and when Tim gives it a pump of gas it staggers to life. *What's a grand to a coupla Indian doctors?* In a week they'll make it back. They're rich, they'll get her another necklace. A prettier, bigger necklace. The front yard churns, grass roiling. *Easy there. You're okay.* Things are hazy, the high sun leaving streaks on his eyeballs. Tim digs a shaking hand into his pocket, pops two more of the blue jobbies from Charlie's parents' bathroom. Then two more. Then one for good luck. He rubs his eyes with a fist to make the lights go away. Okay. Now it's time to—

go.

He blinks. *A rolling stone gathers no moss.* Right dad? His mouth, all cottony floral, like he ate a scented tissue. He's dying for a drink. A cold beer. Sour sweet with that carbonated tangy alcohol ache bursting over the back of your throat. Cold. Just cold. Driving now, Tim wavers down the road. He ponders the vast sky. Intersecting lines of smearing light. Geometric studies of parallel paths: alternative future possibilities. Tim sees lines of blood. Endless perpendicular distances, astral projections of pure life essence slipping through the either-or of never-never land. He's gotta go. Tim's a tiny piece of a bigger puzzle, a graphed chart delineating the slow shrink of the land parcelled into smaller and smaller squares. He never finished high school. He never learned about angles, graphs, the way the infinite can be encased, reduced to a manageable series of equations. It doesn't matter. The road is a straight-line vein. He closes his eyes. Lines and more lines. Bright lines flaring on his brain.

PART SIX

JUNE
Thursday, June 26

BUT I SAW...

Doctor Solomon clasps his hands together as if in solidarity and prayer.

The mind plays tricks, June. We have to accept that. Your mind is tricking you. Showing you things that aren't there. Accepting that is part of your healing.

June looks at the photograph on the wall over the doctor's head. They're in his office. Apparently she'll be seeing him three times a week now, part of some kind of agreement worked out between Norm, Christine, and whoever else cared to witness her *scene*, as they are collectively calling it, in the backyard. And Norm's hired her a chaperone, the housekeeper, he's calling her, a Filipino woman named Mary-Beth. She's in her late twenties, just a few years younger than June, and according to Norm her job is to keep June from getting tired out. Mary-Beth's to do the cooking and cleaning. But June knows that her main role is to keep an eye on her.

Do you need anything miss? Mary-Beth keeps asking.

No thank you, Mary-Beth.

What does she need? Under Mary-Beth, the house has reverted to its normal state of cloaked quiet. He's gone, June knows. If he was ever—

He was. She's not supposed to say it. But he was, no matter what else happened.

Now that she's barely leaving the house, June is actually missing the protestors. She found their constant chanting somehow calming. They reminded her of—

In college her roommate used to play a tape of ocean waves hitting the surf. June would close her eyes, lie back in her bed and contemplate the waves. June lets her eyes close and her head drop. Just for a minute. June feels herself detaching; she drifts away from herself, from her past and future, from what she did and didn't do.

June? Ah, June?

She startles. Doctor Solomon sits in his leather chair, pondering June's spaced-out hunch.

So June, he says, a hint of a smile peering through his bushy brown-flecked-with-grey beard. When they searched the backyard, how did that make you feel?

Doctor Solomon's voice is low, a cross between the famous mellow baritone of James Earl Jones and, June imagines, the Hebrew magic of some ancient rabbinical coven. He's a skinny Jew who grew up in the city, wears tan slacks and polo shirts. June doesn't know many Jewish people, has always imagined them as mysterious, attuned to spiritual forces only they can communicate with. June prefers to close her eyes when she talks with Doctor Solomon. Which Doctor Solomon says isn't such a hot idea. He says she needs to focus, needs to stay in touch with the real world.

They didn't have any right to—but we couldn't stop them. They had a search warrant. Chris said it was better to—

Yes, but how did you *feel* about the search?

The doctor pushes horn-rimmed glasses up his nose.

I...I felt bad for poor Norm. He doesn't need all this.

Yes. Go on. Doctor Solomon runs a hand through close-cropped greying hair, a gesture of patient impatience, a character actor performing constancy of wisdom.

It's like...it's crazy. Like maybe I really did...I mean they're taking it so seriously, when all I did was...

Was what?

Dig a hole.

Is that *all* you did, June?

I—well, no...I mean, *no*. Obviously I...June sighs. I, uh, enabled my depressive sense of alienation, which lead to, uh, delusions that fostered further, uh, isolation and depression. She shrugs. Those are the doctor's words. June looks at him for approval.

He stares back at her: *And?*

June looks down at her knees. What she needs is a cup of good strong coffee. There's no coffee in the house anymore. Bad for the baby. Norm's doing the shopping now, loading up the cart with natural sundries—herbal teas that promise easy pregnancies and above average toddlers with bright eyes and pleasant dispositions.

And...anyway, June finally mutters under the doctor's gaze. They didn't find anything.

Of course they didn't find anything, the doctor assents comfortingly.

Norm's been taking time off work, June says. He gets nervous if I go outside. He said maybe we should move. But I said I think we should—stay.

The doctor nods approvingly. He's a specialist in depressives.

That's what I am, June thinks. *That's what he said I am.* It's better to stay, right?

Why do you say that?

It's an…opportunity to face my…my…June's stomach gurgles organically, herbally, uncertainly.

You're right June. You need to confront the source of your feelings of unhappiness and low self worth. June, I want you to focus on the real. I want you to ask yourself why you were digging the pit, what story you were trying to tell yourself and the people around you. I want you to keep focused, June. Stay focused on the person you were in that time, and how you are different, how you are *becoming* different now. Will you do that, June?

June nods blearily. Doctor Solomon, she senses, is not convinced.

June, I want you to get better. But to do that, you need to help yourself. You need to accept that your perception of events is just that, June: a perception. You had a belief. You invested in that belief. You felt like that belief would make everything else matter, would infuse your nascent depression with meaning. You constructed a belief, June. You had to believe in it—even if it wasn't true.

The picture over the doctor's head: three brown women in brightly coloured wraps strolling along a lush tropical river balancing loads of provisions on their heads.

But, June protests, it wasn't just a…I mean, I *saw* them.

You believed you saw bones. You believed what you saw.

But—

There were no charges. Isn't that correct June?

Yes.

And that's because they didn't find any bones, did they June?

But they found—

The forensic unit concluded that what they found in backyard were just bits of old stone, not bones at all. Isn't that the truth, June?

But the stone was…the report said it wasn't just…stone. It was fragments of some kind of ancient pottery. There was even a pattern.

June.

Doctor?

June. *Is* what I'm saying true? You *did* see the report. There were *no bones.* Do you accept what you read in the report?

Yes. I saw the report. Norm and Chris showed it to me.

And you believe what the report says? Think carefully now. Are there any doubts about the report?

I just—

Yes? Or no?

—

June?

The women smile, their bundled burdens balanced so perfectly and precariously.

Doctor Solomon gets to his feet. I'll see you again on Wednesday and we'll continue this discussion.

Doctor? Can I just ask you—before you go—

Yes, June?

That's one thing she likes about Doctor Solomon. He sticks to his timetable, but with the languid fluidity of a tropical citizen; he doesn't give the impression of always hurrying off.

When did you move here? To Wississauga?

Oh, let's see now…Let me see…I lived in the city when I started my practice, and moved out here about—the Doctor chuckles his appreciation of time's speed—well almost fifteen years ago now.

But why move here? I mean, aren't there more…more of your… patients—in the city?

Oh, you'd be surprised, June. Doctor Solomon smiles convincingly. You'd be surprised how many there are around these parts. The doctor stands, looks down at June. You take it easy now, and get plenty of rest.

They move into the small waiting room area, Mary-Beth jumping up perkily, ready to drive her home.

In the elevator, June leans against the mirrored wall and closes her eyes. A brief burst of chanting—aye ya ya ya ya—surfs through her mind, and then the doors are opened into the lobby and Mary-Beth is leading her out.

Mary-Beth drives attentively. June lowers the passenger window open, lets spring air blow her bangs off her forehead. She needs a haircut. She needs to start taking care of herself. All of this, it must be bad for the—

The doctor says she needs to accept what happened. She needs to come to terms with her actions.

But June doesn't accept. She doesn't believe that believing is all the doctor says it is, the flick-of-a-switch it's-all-in-your-head solution to explain how you can go from being nearly handcuffed and hauled off to jail and then you're just—What? Exonerated? Free? You can go now, June. You don't need to worry anymore, June. But it's hard to believe—there's that word again—that what she saw and felt and knew was just some kind of…delusion. The old Indian, the Elder, silently mouthing prayers. She saw his face: stoic, but behind his eyes a still, deep pool of knowing. He *knew*; he believed. Okay he wasn't there. Not really. She made him up. June can accept that. They carried her into the house. Doctor Solomon appeared out of nowhere, gave her a shot *to calm her down*. June remembers thinking about the baby, not wanting the shot, trying to pull away. It's okay, Norm said, holding her hand. She fell asleep.

Is belief really so powerful? Can it really make the world change and change again?

The *whole* world?

Her world, at least. Sunny breeze on her face. It feels good.

Turn here, Mary-Beth.

Miss?

Make a right here.

But Miss? I take—home. Is no good way, turn.

It's okay Mary-Beth. I just want to...drop in on a—friend. An old friend.

Mary-Beth bites her lower lip. Doctor Norman says to take you to home, Miss.

He's not a doctor Mary-Beth.

Yes Miss. But he says—

He's a dentist, Mary-Beth. And we will go straight home. I promise. Right after. There, yes, turn here.

You won't be long?

No Mary-Beth. I promise. I won't be long.

Gnawing her lower lip, Mary-Beth makes the turn.

Now a left onto the Parkway, June says encouragingly. Then you're going to make a left turn at the second light there. You see that little road there, Mary-Beth? The one in between the two malls?

Yes Miss.

That's where we're going.

Okay Miss.

Just a quick visit, Mary-Beth.

June ascends to her assigned floor, breathes deeply, walks quickly down the hall hoping the ladies at the nurses' station playing cards won't notice her, won't ask her where she's been.

She's gone to the hospital, one of the nurses calls after her.

What? June turns around to face them.

Your *friend*. Rose. She's in the hospital.

They stare at her malevolently.

When?

Where have you been anyway? The old folks have been asking about you.

Is Rose okay?

They shrug.

Now home miss, Mary-Beth says hopefully, putting the car in gear and preparing to pilot through the thickening shopping traffic.

No, Mary-Beth. One more stop. We have to go to the hospital.

Miss, why? Miss are you sick? I will call—

June deftly snatches the cell from Mary-Beth's lap.

Miss!

Mary-Beth, I'm not sick. It's my friend. She's sick. In the hospital. We have to go there. We won't call anyone.

Miss. No! It's not good for you, you can get sick at the hospital, so much sick—it's bad for you and the baby, Miss. We go home. Doctor Norman—he says, I take you home.

Mary-Beth, I have to go. Just for a quick visit.

No Miss, please! Let me—call.

Mary-Beth reaches for the cell. The car swerves.

June dangles the cell out of the passenger window.

Mary-Beth, she says calmly. Take me to the hospital or else I'll drop the phone out the window and you'll be fired.

Belief is having a purpose. It's doing something and knowing you are doing it for a reason. Because you believe. June doesn't know how or why she believed what she believed. It seems so…ridiculous. Ancient Native explorers, first man to stumble into the lush abundance of the Wallet River Valley. And he led them: and it was good. A proud, strong man glowing like the summer sun, infused by the power of the tribe, of his doomed vision for the future—today, tomorrow. So who killed him? Who snuck behind him, crashed in his skull? And what belief did they have, what story did they tell themselves before and after doing what they did? Is everything just…stories?

No. Not everything.

A man standing on a ridge overlooking a river gully. A man surveying a territory resplendent with life's eternal possibility, a human being so free and unencumbered, a first man with all the possibilities of becoming still ahead of him—in this June believes. She's seen it. Nothing can change that. Even if it's crazy.

She turns, takes the elevator, turns. Mary-Beth trails behind her, scowling. June enters ward 9B. The ward smells like Rose's room—Meals on Wheels, flesh gone slack. June expected something more antiseptic, something clean and astringent. But the smell is old and dirty.

Behind the nurses' station three ladies loll with a familiar air of disaffected nonchalance.

May I help you? comes the predictable, eventual, opening.

Yes, I'm here to see Rose McCallion.

McCallion…McCallion. The nurse checks a list. Oh. Right. She's in the ICU. You can only stay fifteen minutes. Are you family? You have to be family.

I'm her niece, June says.

The nurse points to an adjacent room laid bare by a long window. Through the window: huddled forms encumbered by sheets, snaked by tubes.

Please wait here, Mary-Beth, June says crisply before walking into the room, her boot heels clicking. *This is where it ends*, she thinks. Even for Rose. Dread is a sinking pit of imagined bones, the taste down there, the air in your lungs. June thinks of the Elder praying in her backyard: a crumpled wizened warrior permanently clinging to a world that doesn't want him. *He wasn't really there.*

Rose is alone. Lying inert on the big hospital bed she looks more like a dried frog than a human being. Her machines are myriad, cables and connectors leading to and fro in cyborg-like array. June drags the curtain closed around the bed. At least give her some privacy. Jesus. She's a hundred years old. Give her some dignity. The curtain does nothing to close out the coughs, groans, and mutters emitting from the other seven beds in the ICU. Stepping toward the head of Rose's hospital bed, June hears the murmurs of anxious bedside relatives, barely uttered words she can't quite make out.

Rose? she says quietly, mimicking the hushed cadence of the swirled sounds all around them. Can you hear me, Rose?

The old lady doesn't stir.

What's wrong with her? June can't tell. Rose? June leans right over face to face. Is she—? Should she call the nurse? Rose?

The old lady's eyes flip open. They widen and dart. Rose blinks.

It's okay, June half whispers. You're in the hospital. She squeezes then quickly releases the old lady's hand. It's like holding tissue paper. IV into a decrepit, hollowed-out blue vein. It's June, Rose. June from—

Rose's eyes narrow.

How are you feeling, Rose?

Stupid question. She can see it in the old lady's face. How is it, dying? How is it wasting away all alone in a room full of sick strangers?

Well it's what people say, isn't it? At least she's here. June takes a deep breath and flips down onto the uncomfortable orange chair wedged in beside Rose's various machines and the side of the bed. *What else can I say?* Mary-Beth is probably freaking out. What if she calls Norm? June's put him through enough. She'll just stay a few more minutes. Poor Rose, all alone. It's sad and all. But really, how else could it have ended?

Then, Rose's lips start moving, the crusts of spit in the corners of her mouth cracking.

Rose, June says. Don't try to talk. You need to rest. It's alright Rose.

Rose shudders, seems to be struggling to speak. Of course it isn't alright. Rose is dying. Anyone can see that. The old lady is dying all alone, with no family, with nobody to be with her. But that's not June's fault. She has her own responsibilities. A husband. A—June folds her hands over her belly.

It's...Rose suddenly croaks, her hawk eyes sharpening to focus.

Yes? Rose? I'm here. It's what? June leans in. She can feel Rose's ragged exhalation on her ear, her cheek. *After this, I'll go.*

It's...

Yes, Rose?

...not...your...fault...dear.

Not my fault. Of course it's not my fault.

I don't understand, June says reluctantly. What's not my fault? Rose blinks, tosses her shrunken head.

He came...Rose whispers, brown bubbles popping in the dark gap between her lips.

Who came?

Not...your...fault...

Rose? Who came?

Your...Rose closes her eyes. Machines beep in staccato imitation.

Who came Rose?

The old woman's eyes flutter open again, cloudy blue staring straight through. June can't look away, as much as she wants to.

What is it Rose? Who came? She hears her own voice, a panicked breaking whisper.

...ghost.

What we believe, what we don't believe. June forces herself to arrange her face and smile comfortingly down at Rose.

I'm sorry, Rose. But I really have to go.

TIM
Thursday, June 26

WHERE?

Dizzy.

Gotta—

Tim grips the metal railings of the bed. He manages to pull himself up into a sitting slump. His head lolls, thin neck useless. Tim contemplates the whites of his pallid thighs. A swathe of black stitches holds together a vertical gash. He falls back, exhausted. *No. I gotta—*

Tim takes a deep painful breath and tries again. He slumps forward, his face in the crotch of his hospital nightgown. He hears footsteps, the swirl of a curtain, someone coming.

And just where do you think you're going, mister? The tone is jokingly annoyed. Hands push him back. A face lowers. It's a nurse scowling distastefully, permanently, her coffee yellow teeth showing.

There, that's better. Can you hear me?

Tim breathes, nods. It hurts. To breathe. To nod.

Where? Comes out: Whuuu…?

You're in the hospital.

Whuuu? Wuur?

You're in the Hospital. Wississauga General Hospital.

…nuuuuuu…Tim grabs the rails, tries to hoist himself up over the side.

Calm down now, we're going to take good care of you. You just need to calm down.

Tim hits the bars of the bed with fists. The rails reverberate.

Just relax now, you're okay. I'm just going to—

No no no no no no no—

We better—

More footsteps.

—2 ccs—Ativan—

Footsteps receding.

Tim closes his eyes, sees black.

Is there someone we can call? Family? Friends?

Tim blinks, considers the doctor high above him. A trick question? He was driving away from Charlie's. And then—what happened then?

—Carly—

When can I go? he rasps. His throat is sore, dry. He reaches a shaking hand for the water on his bedside tray.

Here, let me help you. The doctor holds the cup as Tim bobs for the bendy straw and sucks.

There, how's that?

Tim nods. Thanks.

The doctor looks down at him.

You're a lucky young man, you know that? When they found you you'd already lost a lot of blood. Multiple contusions. A concussion. Bruised ribs. We put twelve stitches in your scalp. And of course, the coma.

Tim can feel the stitches in his head, a tightening bald patch.

...extreme toxification of the system. High doses of narcotics in your blood. Weakened heart rate and pulse as a result of the system being drugged to the point of shut down. Plus dehydration and malnutrition. You could have had a heart attack and dropped dead, son.

Son? I'm not your—

How luung?

What's that? The doctor leans close, stethoscope dangling.

How long? Tim manages.

How long? You've been in and out of consciousness for, let's see, the doctor consults the chart in his hand. Almost two months. We thought we were going to lose you.

Prescription, Tim mutters, staring at the blue curtain the doctor's pulled around the bed. Took, a few, too many...

You don't need to explain anything to me, son. You're going through a hard time. I get that. I'm just saying—look, if you had collapsed on your couch watching TV at home alone, you'd be dead now. Do you understand me? Consider yourself lucky that someone saw you on the side of the road. Think of this as a second chance.

Tim shrugs.

You need to rest. And you need to get plenty to eat and drink. We'll move you out of the ICU tomorrow as soon as there's a bed empty upstairs. In the meantime, I'd like you to talk to someone. She's a...doctor on our staff. A psychiatrist. She can help you with the memory loss, okay? Help you figure out who you are.

Tim shrugs.

The doctor stares down at Tim, who turns his head to the curtain isolating his bed.

Blue, Tim thinks. Blue like the shimmering sky. And behind it? Bodies. Empty. Empty bodies.

He wakes up slowly. His head is fuzzy, the blood pounding against his skull when he tries to think.

I'm better. Time to—

Time is money, Timmy boy!

Thanks Dad. Thanks a bundle. And good luck down there, by the way, good fucking luck.

Carly says there's no such thing as luck. Carly says everything is connected, everything happens for a reason.

—Carly—

To his left, the curtain is peeled back, revealing a withered shape draped in sheet. Tim sees a shrunken crab-apple crone's head. To his right, a machine man, inert chest getting air in processed pumps. Where is he, really? What weird hell? Dreaming. He dozed off. He's still dreaming. No. Awake now, he can feel the pinch of his stitched scalp, the pressure in his chest when he breathes too deep. The ancient specimen next door twitches, mutters, falls still.

Everything around him humming in place, in still repetition. Tim has the sensation of night, greyish suburban gloom. Suddenly he longs for the forest gully. The crackling bonfire, the feel of the cold earth against his back. The metallic taste of the air, trees swaying in a cold spring breeze while the river runs its endless marathon.

Nurse! Nurse! Nurse! Nurse! He stabs the red button.

What can I do for you? She glares down at him.

It really hurts. My…head. *It's true*, Tim thinks. *It really does hurt.* Can you give me something to—?

Let me see, the nurse says, scowling at a point over him. I'll be back. She turns to go, the soles of her white sneakers squeaking.

And nurse?

Yes? Sighing.

Can you—when they...brought me in—did I...have anything?

You want your personal effects?

Yeah—I—

I'll be back.

Tim waits. He has to fight off the urge to close his eyes and drift into sleep. Stay awake. No sleeping. Not here. Zombieland. *You snooze you lose.* He turns again to ponder the withered golem with yellow crust in the curves and cracks of her shrunken lips. Her breathing comes in a series of sporadic fits and starts. She twitches, arms and legs twisted and gnarled like old tree branches. Then her chest trembles still. Tim stops breathing too. Waits. Waits. Finally she inhales with a weak sigh. Tim exhales, slumps back against the bed.

Then he does close his eyes. *Just for a minute. While I'm waiting.* What is he waiting for? He's waiting for the nurse, for the old crone in the next bed over to die and hover over him, invite him to join her as she floats on up to that perfect patch of grass in the sky. Why not? Where else do you have to go? No. That's not what he wants. He wants something else.

He has to—

He needs to—

—*Carly.*

The nurse returns with a plastic shopping bag and a small plastic cup.

She hands the little cup to Tim, saying, Here, the doctor says to take these.

Two green pills. Tim doesn't ask what they are. He swallows them with water, but even so, feels them sticking to the inside of his dry throat.

Thanks, he says, not sure if he's being sarcastic or not. The nurse nods. She stands at the foot of his bed swinging the bag.

Is that my—?

This is everything you were brought in with, she says, frowning at him as if daring him to contradict her.

Okay, Tim says.

He reaches out for it.

The nurse drops the crumpled plastic bag on his bony chest.

Thanks.

She stands there, looking down at him.

Thanks, Tim says again.

Nurse spins on her heels, rubber squeaking as she leaves. Tim feels the bag light on his ribs. He dumps the contents out on his lap. He smells his clothes right away. Rough dirty fabrics reeking of mud and blood and smoke. He can practically taste it. The forest river crevice.

Tim pulls the cargo pants up to his face. One leg torn and bloodied. He slips a hand into a pocket. Nothing. And the other. Empty. Tim does the same for the back pockets. First one: empty. Second one: Hello, what's this? He pulls out a single thin bent joint. Well then. How's that for luck, Carly?

He puts the joint on the tray next to his bed. He rifles the hip side pockets. He feels a hard rectangle. Pulls it out. Perfect. Just perfect. Che Guevara ready to light what there is to be lit. And? He pats the pockets again. In case he missed something. No. That's it.

He drops the pants over the side. Next up is his shirt. Bloodied, cut in half. It's a total write off. Tim dangles it over the rail, lets it fall from his fingertips. His old life. So. What's left? Everything you were *brought in* with. His hands move through the folds where the sheet meets the hospital gown. He comes up with a soft brown tattered leather wallet. He digs a finger into the fold of the big pocket. Please please please. Finger slides along the interior.

Nothing. Ripped lining. No cash at all. ID gone too. No wonder they don't know who he is.

But, Tim wonders, where's the car? Fuck! The car! He'll buy her—them—a new car. He just needs—

that tea tin—

full of—

Indian doctor—

cash.

Think. Fucking hell man! *Think.*

He was driving away, away from—

singed neurons, smoky receptors.

He doesn't have a clue.

Wississauga.

Tim falls back on the bed. If he's going to make a move, the time is now. His pain has receded to a cloud on the horizon. They want him to see some—shrink. They'll lock him up. He's crazy. Of course he's crazy. He sees ghosts. He's been living in the—

freaking woods.

Carly says there's no such thing as crazy.

—Carly—

I'm—

He has to get out of here. Now. Right now. Find the car, wherever it is. He doesn't remember, only: the tea tin roll of cash wedged under the passenger seat. *It could still be there.* He wrestles the rail down and swings his bare feet on to the cold industrial tiles. The hospital gown tickles his knees. Tim yanks the drip out of his arm. He bends down, grabs his pants and pulls them on. Got everything? Anything? He fumbles around the bed for the joint and the lighter. Light spilling in from the nurses' station just outside the door. Any second they could come in and—

Don't think. Act. Escape. Escape from Wississauga.

A few steps and he's at the golem's bed. For a moment, he considers pinching her nose, smothering her rubbery mouth with his big rough palm.

He'd be doing her a favour.

Her limbs twitch in faint protest. Her heart monitor beeps, slower then faster.

He's not a killer. *Sorry old lady. You're on your own.*

Tim pulls the plug on the heart monitor. An alarm sounds. Tim slinks across and stands in the corner. That evil-looking nurse rushes in, followed by another. Tim slips out past the empty station, and on into the elevator, which just happens to be waiting for him.

Outside Tim breathes big. The air hurts his ribs, his bruised heart, his stitched-up head. The cool spring night slips up his gown, tickling his gaunt chest. His bare feet grip the sidewalk. His soles, his skin, everything tingling, trembling, hyper-alive. Tim feels the rush of it, adrenal possibility, escape. *Yeah, right, how far am I going to get? I don't even have my boots.*

No boots. No cash. No luck, Carly.

He peers into the hospital parking lot. The rows of cars remind him of the trees of the forest gully. They're a place to disappear into. Tim breathes the taste of metal and exhaust and the faint promise of fresh air. He takes a few tentative tottering steps forward. He wants to run, he wants to spring into the anonymous night of parked cars lining dimly illuminated streets. He teeters forward. The bright hospital lobby lights fade. Tim penetrates the parking lot's pallor. Grey air pushes through him. The hospital gown flutters around his knees.

Tim digs into his pants and pulls out the joint.

Steadied now, Tim wends through the parking lot, makes for the lone phone booth on the opposite curb. He likes the way his long bare feet slap asphalt. He imagines himself as some kind of suburban mutant primate, man-racoon-skunk-squirrel, as at home trolling the parking lots and backyards and dumpsters as he is in a forest river gully. The hospital gown flutters around him, and Tim thinks of Halloween ghosts in billowing white sheets. Did he ever—yeah, sure, when his mother was—when they were still a—

He looks down. He can't see his feet. He's floating now. It's a strange familiar high he's on, a nice combo, one last twist of the China pot and whatever pain pills the nurse kindly provided.

Tim stabs zero with a still-jagged nail and waits for the machine-operator.

For what city, please?

Collect call from—

Will you accept the—

Carly? Carly? Carly! It's—

Will you accept a call from—

Then her voice: Yes. Okay. I'll take the call.

These charges have been accepted. You may proceed now. Thank you for choosing—

Carly!

Tim?

Carly!

Yes. Yes, it's me. Where *are you*, Tim?

I—ah—just got out of the hospital.

The hospital? Are you okay? What happened?

I'm okay. I'm—

What hospital?

Huh?

What hospital were you in?

Wississauga General.

Wississauga?

Yeah—I—I was looking for my—

Tim hears noises behind him. Figures stomping through the parking lot, shouting to each other. He wants to say he's sorry. He wants to say she was right all along, always has been. He presses the phone hard against his face, feels the stitches in his scalp bulge.

Listen, Carly, I'm in a—his voice cool, easy. I'll tell ya all about it later but I'm in a bit of a—I got in an—ah—our—car. But it's cool, there's—I mean, I can—only I need…could you, maybe, uh, come and get me?

Tim. Carly's voice in the night through the phone and across buildings and houses and schools and malls and empty lots and highways and factories and boulevards and discount outlets and box stores and backyards and small patches of forest adorned with sluggish rivers, dry ponds, and oily swamps. Tim. Are you *high?*

No…I'm, hey, I'm—

How could you just *leave?* I didn't know where you were! What was I supposed to do? You just disappear? You just take off? *Jesus,* Tim. You stole my car? You stole my car! And there's people looking for you. That creepy Clay guy came by. Are you *dealing* for him now? And a lawyer called. Some woman. Your father died, Tim. Do you *even* know that? *Fuck*, Tim! I can't do this anymore. Do you get that? Don't call me! Don't call me ever again.

He stands, listening to the long-distance hum of empty space. He feels the cold plastic pressed against his ear. Behind him: shouts and footsteps, getting louder. Tim holds the phone to his ear just a little longer. Then he drops the receiver. Eyes closed, there's only the permeable darkness, the streaks of light on the insides of his head. He feels himself floating. Away, or back, it doesn't matter. He doesn't fight it. He falls into it.

HAL
Thursday, June 26

THE MAYOR'S LOOKING GOOD, Hal thinks. She's in a summer char-treuse pantsuit, augmented by a simple but elegant strand of pearls. She smiles radiantly, addressing the modest crowd of thirty or so geriatrics bussed in from the senior centre for the photo op. The air is bright, the sun shines, a gentle breeze blows off the river. There could hardly be a nicer day in the Cartwright Falls Riverfront Park: green grass, maple trees, and picnic tables framing the river right before it drops off into the gully. Here in the northernmost boundary of Wississauga, the mayor unveils a plaque dedicated to Rose McCallion.

She was one of Wississauga's great founding matrons, the mayor intones dryly, a woman of courage, wisdom, and what they called, back in Rose's day, *pluck*.

The gathering chuckles. Hal doesn't join in the subdued laugh-ter. After all, he isn't a participant in the ceremony. The Boss made that very clear. He's not to get "personally involved" she said. *Of course not*, Hal thinks. *I'm just a mouthpiece. I'm just supposed to tell it like it is.* How is it? He knew Rose better than anyone here. The racist, misanthropic old lady hated the mayor, couldn't stand the city bureaucrats, and considered present-day Wississauga a concrete

Sodom and Gomorrah of shopping centres run by dusky shysters hell-bent on tricking old ladies out of hearth and home.

But Hal's just a reporter. He doesn't have opinions. He doesn't want to have an opinion. At least he still has a job. He stands to the side and surveys the scene through the viewfinder of the Cable Community News camera. The mayor utters one last platitude. There is a smattering of scattered applause. A velvet cover is pulled back to reveal the plaque. It's an antique-looking copper signpost with gold raised letters saying simply, In memory of Rose McCallion. Accompanied by the chronology of her birth and death, the memorial already looks suitably old, already conveys the authority of authenticity that all good plaques should exude.

The plaque unveiled, everyone claps again. *Instant history*, Hal thinks. Cake and coffee are served on an already erected folding table. After an appropriate interval, Hal approaches the mayor. He's a bit tentative. He hasn't spoken with her since the protest. But she greets him warmly, grasps his hand in both of hers and effusively thanks him for coming. Hal plays along, lobs a few softball questions for the nightly news. Rose deserves better, but his heart isn't in it. He's Hal Talbot, community news reporter, in charge of ribbon cuttings and plaque unveilings. He thought he'd be fired, reprimanded, promoted…something. But nothing happened, no grand inquisition, no major debriefing, no nomination for journalist of the year or unexpected job offer from the City. Just…nothing. Did they find bones? They claimed they didn't. Hal's not sure. Nobody's talking about it. A report was released. Apparently they found *something*, stone fragments, maybe old, maybe not that old. That archaeologist at the university is studying them, taking his time. The road's going full speed ahead, in the meantime. *Mean time*, Hal thinks, politely thanking the mayor. They shake hands again. Any time,

Mr. Talbot, the mayor says merrily. She looks him in the eye and he looks away. Poor Rose. He did what he could, didn't he? If it wasn't for Cable Community News, who would have known the old bird even existed?

The ceremony is already breaking up. The seniors are being herded back to their bus, and the mayor is glad-handing her way over to a waiting town car. Hal trudges back to the news van, starts packing up the equipment.

Need some help there?

He looks up, sees Scott standing over him.

Hey! Hal can't help but smile. What are you doing here?

My last appointment cancelled. Scott's also smiling, his big white teeth flashing in the sun. And I remembered you said you'd be out here. So I thought I'd see if I could find you. It's such a... beautiful day.

Great, Hal says.

Two weeks ago they started talking again. It was no big deal. Hal's phone chirped. A text from Scott: Hey. Whassup? Later on that night, they talked on their cells. The conversation was light, upbeat. There were none of the awkward pauses that had come to dominate their once easy-going relationship. They didn't discuss it. They didn't even mention it. The Incident. That's what Hal has started calling it. The night sky roiling. Mournful ghost creature in the pit, the way he looked at them and through them. The way the air all at once filled with the scent of rotted spring nectar as if the coming season, and Hal, and Scott, and the pit, and whatever it was that lingered—that lived—down there, had suddenly been trapped under glass, left to slowly rot then dry out and die in some stifling specimen jar. Hal hadn't forgotten what he'd seen. But The Incident went grainier and grainier every time it replayed in his mind. Now when he watches the scene, images shoot by in a whirlwind of accidental angles and sightline shadows. It's over in a matter of seconds like a camera dropped then hurriedly picked up again, still filming. It's not that he's avoiding anything. It's more like—

what's the point?

So, uh, Scott says, you wanna go for a walk?

Hal takes a quick look around. The mayor is being helped into her car by her driver, seniors are loading into their bus, various city employees, bureaucrats, and low level politicians are idly chatting near their vehicles, finishing their coffees, taking final drags on their cigarettes, sending texts.

Uh…yeah, sure. He folds the tripod away, closes up the van. They stroll leisurely down the paved path toward the river. Hal resists the urge to look behind him—the mayor and her functionaries staring, noting, revising. In the distance, you can just hear the faint sound of trucks—*men at work*, Hal thinks. It's the new road, already under construction. The road will peel away from the river right before the falls, emerge from the gorge and head north and west to connect with the highway. It won't open for another year-and-a-half, but Hal's heard that progress is good, work is on time and on schedule. Trevor's covering that beat now.

So, Scott says. How are things going?

They're walking close to each other. Hal feels Scott's presence, a reassuring undeniable bulk. Their fingers brush. As if by instinct, Hal grabs and holds onto one of Scott's huge paws.

CHARLIE
Friday, June 27

CHARLIE'S CLASS mills about the school bus. It's Keep Wississauga Clean day, the last day of school, and they've been bussed out to the riverfront park. The cool kids giggle as Ms. Kiddell passes out garbage bags. Charlie doesn't get what's so funny. She takes her bag, emblazoned with the logo of the phone company. She puts on the plastic gloves, provided courtesy of the local pizza chain. Charlie quickly separates herself from the group. She moves off toward the river where the wind blows cardboard coffee cups into the weeds that line the bank. She can feel the other kids looking at her, then turning away. Well, so what?

She doesn't care what they think.

It's been strange, this spring turning into summer observed mostly from the confines of her room. Her parents are taking turns coming home early. They watch her carefully. She can be alone, but never actually alone. Charlie's dad had a new security system installed. It sounds an alarm whenever Charlie opens her window. To keep her in, or him out? She sits in her room and stares out into the falling night. Where is he? Will they ever find him? She doubts they're even looking. She hadn't told them much. Or anything, really. She just sat there, arms crossed, watching them, silently playing the role of little girl victim. Should she look for him? She pictures him in the gully, skinny and boyish, permanently lost under the hot asphalt of the new expressway. Where would she look for him?

On Saturdays, her mother takes her to the library. She reads books about world wars, palaeontology, ontology. She borrows DVDs of old black and white movies, luminescent actors swaddled in elegance breaking into song at the slightest provocation. And so the spring is going, quickly and yet slowly, too, the season hurtling past even as the days move with near intolerable lassitude, dun sun hanging in the sky, air conditioner cycling on and off, world wars blurring into theories of being and nothingness.

Another month of school left. Actually, Charlie doesn't mind school that much anymore. The kids are just as cruel and vapid, but Charlie is no longer affected by their rolled eyes, disgusted grimaces, and abrupt silences. She's still getting used it—the feeling of not caring. They can say what they want. Charlie blinks up at the sky then looks back at the group. It's warm out and Katie Mills sports a short white skirt and tight pink T-shirt. Her bare legs are somehow already tanned golden. Charlie pulls garbage out of the weeds—cups, cans, bottles, take-out containers. Why so much garbage? The cool kids will spend their summers at camps and cottages and tours of Europe. They'll go swimming, canoeing, sailing, horseback riding, waterskiing. Charlie's not jealous. She'll do things too. Next year, she'll start high school. Only three more years until she goes to college. *In the city*, she thinks.

Lost in thought and the act of pulling a cracked Starbucks Frappuccino cup out of the thorned limbs of scraggly bush, Charlie doesn't notice him. He has his head down too, walking hunched over, assiduously filling his bag.

They bump hips.

Sorry, Charlie says quietly.

The new kid looks up at her. Actually, he joined the class in January, but everybody still calls him the new kid.

New kid's wearing dress pants that he has to keep hitching up because they're too big for him. And a dark blue turtleneck, despite the weather. And brand new shiny black running shoes lacking a swoosh or any other kind of identifiable marker.

Yes I am sorry, the boy says in response, furrowing the pale brow below his nearly shaved brown hair. His accent is thick, Russian or something like that.

It's the first time she's heard him speak. It's the first time anyone has talked to him. The new kid has cobalt blue eyes. He stares at her.

They gather garbage. They are near enough to each other to know, now, that they are working together. Charlie gets her bag caught on a branch. The new boy pulls it off for her. Charlie nods thank you, snares a mustard-encrusted napkin.

Slowly they follow a trail of detritus toward the grassy centre of the park. They ignore the background noise, the other kids long since settled into a prolonged loiter, randomly shrieking insults and, when Ms. Kiddell isn't looking, feverishly fingering their smart phones.

At the park's centre, they bump hands while both reaching for a crushed cigarette pack sitting on the base of a commemorative plaque nobody seems in a hurry to read. They look up. Shyly, they ponder each other.

What's your name? Charlie asks. Even the teacher just calls him the new kid.

New kid hitches up his smooth, tan polyester pants. My name is Roman, he says.

Oh, Charlie says. Like the ancient Romans?

The boy smiles, shrugs.

My name is Charlie.

Ah, the new kid says. Char-lee. He frowns, confused.

Charlie's a boy's name, Charlie offers.

The boy nods regretfully.

They stand there awkwardly, looking at the grass, at the sky, at their feet. Charlie scans the plaque. *In Memory of Rose McCallion.* Hey! she cries. I knew her.

You. Know. Her...? the new kid repeats slowly.

I *knew* her. She was at the rest home we visited. Remember? In the Spring? Her name was Rose and she was the oldest lady in Wississauga.

The boy carefully scans the plaque.

She died, I guess, Charlie offers.

She was one hundred years and four years old, the new kid confirms.

Yeah, Charlie agrees.

She was very wise? the new kid suggests.

I guess, Charlie says.

Roman nods thoughtfully.

Ms. Kiddell claps her hands and yells something about the bus.

Together, the two of them head over to the parking lot, bags of garbage bouncing against their knees.

JUNE AND SUSAN
Tuesday, July 22

JUNE SITS ON A PADDED CHAIR in the backyard listening to the rumbling machines. The sound is a feeling, distant and peaceful, like the gentle tremble of a car as you drift off to sleep in the back seat. It's not far, of course. Right in front of her. The river gully forest falling. Norm is livid. He keeps threatening to put the house up for sale. *While we still can,* he says portentously. June doesn't see it that way. The sky isn't falling with their property values. The baby beats inside her. June feels it: intersecting inevitabilities of past and future, nowhere to go, no space to occupy that isn't already taken over. Where else would they go? Soon it'll be like it always was. *People forget,* June thinks. What Norm believed, what she believed, what the people believed when they knew the land the way the doctor scanning an ultrasound knows the tiny forming organs of an unborn child.

June no longer goes to see Doctor Solomon. Mary-Beth lurks inside, watches her carefully but no longer follows her from room to room, place to place. She's allowed to be alone again. *Like before,* she thinks. Only: she can just make out the faint cries of the men down below. They are small figurines, toy men playing lumberjack, playing construction.

June scans the backyard. The hole is filled in and covered over. Grass has been planted and over the last few months June has watched thin, fragile stalks turn thick and aggressive, pushing out of the rich brown earth. June waters every second day. A fly lazily circles June's head then buzzes off toward the gorge. *It's almost August already*, she thinks sleepily, though it's one of the first truly warm days she can remember. Summer now. Soon they'll turn inward, live in air-conditioning behind locked doors. June luxuriates in the exhausted near silence of the afternoon heat. Her T-shirt rides up her midriff. A pair of short shorts. The air, not yet humid and stolid, caresses her thighs. June blinks, holds her face up to the sun. The backyard gets more sun now that the trees that once grew up and out of the gully are slowly being thinned. Those trees are hundreds of years old, Norm rants. June consoles him with a hug. You tried honey, she says.

June's focussing on the present. Rose is dead and the spot where her small cottage once stood is about to become a cellular phone superstore. In the present there's the sun on her face and sweat trickling gently down her arms and newly gaunt hips. She's been waking up nauseous. Despite the urgings of Mary-Beth and Norm, she isn't eating much. Most foods repel her. Her stomach, if anything, seems flatter than it's been since she was a teenager. *But my boobs…*In a few hours, she'll be comparing mutations with the group of expectant mothers she meets at the Second Cup in the mall twice a week. June will have decaf. She found a meet-up for the group online, did a search, *new moms Wississauga*. In the meantime, June has calls to return. Her mother, who wants to know how she's doing, exactly, precisely—Any weight gain, honey? Her mother keeps threatening to visit for a week, a month, a year. *So let her.* June's always gotten along with her mother, though they'd never really been close. But now, June feels, it's going to be different.

And Chris called. They've stayed in touch. They don't talk about what happened. Chris is dating an executive she met at a corporate fundraiser. He buys her expensive gifts. It isn't going well. She calls often, ostensibly to see how June is doing, though the conversations quickly veer to the inevitably much more interesting subject of Chris and her life. Dear god, she says, I'm like one of those girls in *Sex in the City*. Ugh, don't let me be the nasty one. June will call her back. Reassure her. She isn't the nasty one.

The sun feels so good on her face. She feels, overall, better outside. She sighs. Breathes. Her body taking over, imposing its own rhythm. The near imperceptible shake of the ground as the men below her go about their business.

The gate screeches, rusty hinges protesting.

Susan Proudfeather strides boldly into the backyard. Oh! June jumps up, knocking the lawn chair backwards. Proudfeather freezes. They stare at each other.

Her father, giving her a curt hug and a handful of hundreds. To help you get back on your feet, he'd muttered. She'd let him down. That's the way he saw it. They'd barely talked since he'd come home and learned of everything that had happened while he'd been off exploring ancient ruins.

So…her father had said, disengaging, looking at anything but Susan. Taxi will be here in just a minute.

That's what hurt the most. He'd called her a cab.

Dad, she'd said, holding the money, not sure what to do with it. She didn't want it. But she needed it. You don't have to…I didn't mean to…she trailed off. She'd seen that look before—on her mother's face. Blank and closed down.

In the taxi, the left turn signal, ding ding ding ding, waiting to swing out onto Hurontarion. Ding ding ding ding. The driver, edging forward, forward, waiting for that elusive break in traffic.

Excuse me, Susan says. I…I've forgotten something. Can you please turn around?

The toll, already north of twenty bucks.

Sure, Miss, no problem.

What are you doing Susan?

This is a bad idea, Susan.

She hadn't been back since she'd gotten out of jail. Part of the bail agreement. She'd spent her last two thousand dollars on bail and legal fees for her and Jared. The cab turns right then left and they accelerate gently onto Lower Grove.

This is a VERY *bad idea, Susan.*

Actually, can you just—stop here please?

The cab glides to a halt. When she moves to open the door, she realizes she's still holding the money her dad gave her in a tight fist. *Goddamn money.* Getting out, she jams the bills into a pocket. She stands, leaning against the hot door of the taxi, staring at the big house. Is this what you want to see? she asks herself. The house, like all the others, looks only vaguely occupied. As if, Susan imagines, it's occasionally used as a set for a television series about a happy family ripped apart by tragedy. Cancer, car accident, dropout daughter on drugs. The shades are pulled and the windows are closed. Don't even think about, she hears herself mutter. *Is that who you are now? A mutterer?* It's impossible to tell if anyone is home. *No one will be home.* She's probably out shopping or something.

Susan. No. Don't even—

Can you wait here please? The driver looks at her, bemused and disinterested.

The meter ticks upwards.

And just like that she's opening the gate and slipping into the backyard.

Proudfeather wears jeans and a faded aquamarine T-shirt advocating the saving of whales. Only her black combat boots remind June of the crazy person who chained herself to a makeshift teepee, who pounded relentlessly on a drum and led the chanting that spread across the neighbourhood in waves of hypnotic reverberation. *I'm-Very-Disturbed*, June thinks inanely.

Oh! Sorry! I—Susan blurts, clearly surprised to see June—to see anyone—in the backyard. She abruptly turns to go.

No, wait, June calls. Hold on.

Susan freezes.

I thought you weren't allowed to be here.

I'm...not. Susan Proudfeather turns and stares defiantly at June.

June tries to glare back, but feels her expression softening. It doesn't matter. It's all in the past. Even yesterday feels like a long time ago. Babies are made, forests are cut down, lives are altered in the space between seconds, minutes, hours. It's the present that unfolds, that actually happens.

I'm on my way out of town, Susan says, her own tone softer now. And I just wanted to—anyway...I'll go.

June shrugs uncomfortably, looks away, look down at her emerald patch of new grass.

So that's where...?

June reverts back to Susan, half-surprised to see her still standing there, now also staring at the growing square shining in the sun.

Is it okay if I—?

Without waiting for an answer, Susan strides into the centre.
She stands there, not moving. The river gurgles distantly. There's
the beep-beep-beep of a truck backing up. The muted shouts of
men at work. The squawk of birds, the close-up buzz of a dragonfly.

Abruptly Susan falls to her knees. This is where he was,
Susan says.

June feels the sweat on her.

Susan puts her ear to the dirt. She stays that way, prostrate.
June watches, resisting her urge to jump up and go inside, lock the
door behind her. Stay. Stay and watch. Whatever happens, whatever
happened, June has to accept it. She wants to somehow convey that
to the woman, Susan Proudfeather, her pale face gone so pinched
and sad. It's too late. There's a before and an after. Things happen.
Life goes on. We forget because if we don't, we go crazy. You can't
keep going back to it, looking for the truth, moment by moment,
frame by frame, like a detective searching security camera footage
for clues.

After a time, Susan gets to her feet. I'm going now. You'll never
see me again. She looks at June, apparently waiting for a response.

With her pale blue eyes and white scrawny limbs June imagines
Susan as something from another planet. *But she's my age*, June
thinks, almost incredulous. Before, she'd thought of Susan as much
younger, a recent graduate, a girl who didn't know any better. But
now, face-to-face, June sees that's not the case at all. There's an aura
of time-worn experience around Susan, a kind of toughened will-
ingness. When the protests first started, June had hated her, made
jokes about her, wished her gone, even dead. But after a while, she

found the presence of Proudfeather and her merry band weirdly... soothing. And now, June is suddenly confronted with a new feeling: possessiveness toward the woman in her backyard. She knows, June thinks. She knows he was...

Where? June says, her voice coming out urgent. Where are you going?

I'm going to Toronto. Susan scrunches up her pale pink mouth as if she's tasted something sour.

What will you do there? June tenses for resistance to this line of inquiry—what business is it of yours?

But Susan answers eagerly, almost hungrily. I need to get a job. I'm broke. My friend works at a shelter for women leaving abusive relationships. She says there's an opening there, admin, mostly, and fundraising. Susan says the last word like it's a question. Fundraising? She scrapes at the new grass under her feet with the fat heel of her boot.

June winces at the emerging divot. Where will you stay? she says quickly.

My friend is going to let me crash at her place.

A car horn blares—one loud, prolonged bleat.

Oh! June yells, jerking back, almost tripping over herself.

My cab, Susan says apologetically. Then, yelling: Yeah, yeah, I'm coming!

Shit, June says, righting herself and delivering an embarrassed smile. That scared me.

Are you okay? Susan scrutinizes June with new interest. Why should June care where she's going? Who she's going to stay with?

June self-consciously brushes damp hair from her forehead while Susan looks her up and down.

You're pregnant, Susan finally says.

How did you—?

I...I can see things like that. In people.

Susan turns to the river gulley. She surveys the missing trees, the movements below. They didn't waste any time, did they?

June steps over to Susan's vantage point. They stand side by side watching the goings on laid bare by the breaks in the cover where trees used to be.

Pregnant...Susan says ambiguously. So I guess you won, right?

Won? What did I win?

Susan laughs mockingly, sadly. You know. She waves her arm, her motion encompassing everything: the house, the back-yard, the slowly emerging four-lane parkway beside the sluggish river. But mostly, the gesture seems to be referring to June herself—thirty-something homemaker living in one of Wississauga's toniest neighbourhoods awaiting the birth of baby #1 and the return home of doting dentist daddy-to-be.

It isn't my fault, June blurts defensively.

But there *were* bones.

June looks down. Susan's boot heel still pawing the soft grass and softer earth underneath.

Yes, she says.

Where did they go?

I don't know.

You don't know?

They were here. Then they were...gone.

That's what happened? Simple as that, huh?

June shoves her hands in the pockets of her shorts.

Susan rolls her eyes.

I think you should leave now, June says softly, as if it's a suggestion.

I'll leave. I'm leaving. So why don't you tell me the truth?

I did.

Susan seems to consider this.

I *did*. June wants to shout in the face of this maddening woman. I fucking did!

Who do you think took the bones?

How would I know?

Don't you get it? It's a cover-up. It's all about...she points to the work below, her long skeletal finger quivering. And you, bringing a child into this world, after...after you let them—

After I let them *what?* June makes fists in her pockets. But she speaks calmly. You can't change things. You tried. And look what happened.

You know what? That's what *they* always say. But it's not true. You *can* change things.

Susan's cold, visceral stare reminds June of Rose. The way she seemed to be able to cut right through her.

I changed you, didn't I?

You should probably go now, June suggests again, softly, desperately. She tugs down on her short tee. I'm sorry you went to jail, she says. But it wasn't my fault.

Susan Proudfeather's mouth twists. *She's going to say something horrible*, June thinks. But instead, Susan pivots in her heavy boots and is gone.

June breathes, feels her body go limp as the dread drains out of her. She listens for the sound of the cab driving away. Then, slowly, carefully, she crouches down to inspect the damage.

Acknowledgements

I'm grateful to everyone at ARP, particularly editors Josina Robb and Kathleen Olmstead for their editing acumen and dedication to this book. Thank you, also, to Anne Collins for early commentary, and especially to Lauren Kirshner, whose insights were invaluable. For joining in on the crazy idea of serializing the novel online, thanks to my pals at *Geist*, *SubTerrain*, *The New Quarterly*, and *Taddle Creek* (Conan!) with a special shout-out to my friends and colleagues at *Broken Pencil*—Tara, Alison, and JV—for their help and support. Thanks to my parents, Sam and Nina Niedzviecki, for babysitting, crowd wrangling, and fancy socks! Finally, I am, as always, indebted to Rachel Greenbaum, for sticking with me through the long process of bringing another book into the world; I couldn't have done it without her and I wouldn't have wanted to anyway.

HAL NIEDZVIECKI is a writer, speaker, and culture commentator whose work challenges preconceptions and confronts readers with the offenses of everyday life. He is the author of eleven works of fiction and nonfiction and the founder/publisher of *Broken Pencil*, the magazine of zine culture and the independent arts.